JUDITH STEIN—Her dreams of a Jewish homeland would be challenged by Stalin himself.

IVAN NEJ—In the deepest recesses of Lubianka prison, he lies in wait for the day when he can strike back at the beautiful woman who betrayed him.

ANNA RAGOSINA—The madonna-faced beauty with a talent for terror.

RUTH VON HASSELL—The Jewish daughter of Prince Peter, she married a man whose dark past could betray them both.

JOHN HAYMAN—Son of a Russian princess and a Red commissar, his destiny was conflict and danger.

RAGE AND DESIRE

By Leslie Arlen
from Jove

THE BORODINS

THE BORODINS
BOOK V
RAGE and DESIRE

LESLIE ARLEN

A JOVE BOOK

RAGE AND DESIRE

A Jove Book / published by arrangement with
the author

PRINTING HISTORY
Jove edition / November 1982

ISBN: 0-515-05852-1

Jove books are published by Jove Publications, Inc.,
200 Madison Avenue, New York, N. Y. 10016. The words
"A JOVE BOOK" and the "J" with sunburst are trademarks
belonging to Jove Publications, Inc.

PRINTED IN THE UNITED STATES OF AMERICA

Except where identified historically, the characters in this novel are invented, and are not intended to represent actual persons, living or dead.

Chapter 1

RED SQUARE WAS CROWDED, IN A MANNER SELDOM SEEN EVEN on May Day. Throughout the morning the crowds had been hurrying towards the center of the Soviet state, clattering over the Moskvoretsky Bridge from the university areas south of the Moscow River, swarming out of the city proper, north of the river. Now they packed the forecourt of the Historical Museum, the façade of the state store, GUM, the steps of the Cathedral of St. Basil, above which the gilded onion domes were beginning to gleam in the midday sun. Many had been here only a week before, to celebrate the Japanese surrender that had brought a final end to the most ferocious war ever experienced by man. But that had been a sham celebration; Soviet Russia had been at war with the Japanese for only a few days. This summer morning in 1945 they honored a heroine of the Soviet Union, a woman who had fought with the partisans through four long years to bring down the might of Nazi Germany, and even more important, a woman who had been a heroine to all music lovers—and what Russian was not a music lover?—long before the gray-clad hordes had ever swept across the Polish border.

Few of the spectators were allowed into the square itself.

They were marshaled at its edges by the soldiers and policemen who stood guard. The gleaming cobbles, the parade ground of all Russia, was reserved for the nation's rulers, and for the family of the dead woman. But there was only one blood relative present, a young man obviously ill at ease in the center of so many famous and powerful personages. Gregory Nej was a big man, whose height was an obvious heritage from the Borodins, but his dark hair and eyes and his somewhat sharp features were pure Nej. He wore the deep green uniform with the crimson badges of an officer in the Red Army, although there was no comrade in even this vast crowd to recognize him and recall a shared wartime adventure. Now he stood immediately before Lenin's tomb, facing the wall and the towering buildings of the Kremlin behind, a lonely figure in a vast crowd.

On Gregory's right was Marshal Joseph Vissarionovich Stalin, the true hero of the recent war in the eyes of his people, the man who had guided them through the most traumatic four years in their history. Of no more than medium height, solidly built—even, perhaps, running a little to stomach, as was to be expected in someone his age—Stalin surveyed the scene from behind the barrier of his walrus moustache, which effectively concealed his mouth and gave his face a perpetually benevolent expression. His eyes were opaque; they guarded the immense secret plans that never ceased to roam that all-encompassing mind.

That Marshal Stalin himself should take the position of honor at the funeral of Tatiana Nej was entirely understandable. The magnificent blond aristocrat had survived the revolution and the civil war by captivating Vladimir Lenin as much as she had captivated everyone else, including her own servants— one of whom, Ivan Nej, had managed to secure her as his own as the price of saving her life. Later the self-effacing Party secretary, following Lenin's untimely death, had made use of her propaganda potential as he himself had progressed towards the ultimate dictatorship of the Soviet state. Lenin had given Tattie her dancing school because he liked to watch her perform; it was Stalin who had sent her and her troupe on the European tour that made her a world figure, and thus lifted Soviet culture into the forefront of the new art forms. And it was Stalin who had later appointed Tatiana Nej commissar for culture, despite her patrician background, despite the machinations of her exiled brother, Prince Peter, who was in constant conflict with the Soviet state, or of her American sister and her powerful in-laws. Of all the Borodins—once the premier princely family in tsarist Russia—Tatiana alone had elected to remain in her motherland, no matter what might have happened to it, or indeed to her, during the savage years.

And now she was dead, tragically struck down by an out-of-control truck, while on her way to the Moscow airport in the company of her British lover, off to begin a new life in the capitalist West, where she had always truly belonged. No doubt there were those in the crowd who were whispering superstitiously that such a catastrophic end to her dreams was no more than she deserved, that fate had certainly taken a hand. But the majority could more legitimately mourn her passing, as Marshal Stalin was obviously doing.

On Gregory Nej's left there stood his uncle, Michael Nej, a true friend to his sister-in-law Tatiana, with his wife Catherine and their daughter Nona. There could hardly be any cause for surprise in seeing, also, Vyacheslav Molotov, small and dark and intense, or Lavrenti Beria, tall and bland and balding, the sunlight glinting from his rimless spectacles. Here were the true pillars of the Soviet state, the survivors of all those who had been condemned and executed during the purges of the thirties, the men picked by Stalin himself to support him—and no doubt to succeed him, in the fullness of time.

But one such man was conspicuous by his absence, and this had the onlookers whispering. Of all the Politburo, surely Ivan Nej had the most reason to be here. Not only had he always been even closer to Stalin than his brother Michael, not only had he been the deputy commissar of the secret police, but he was also the dead woman's husband, the man who had appropriated her from out of the wreckage of the Revolution. It was true that their tumultuous quarrels had often blazed across Moscow, and perhaps she had flaunted her lover in his face too many times. Yet he should have been here.

So the rumors began to gather and spread—that Ivan Nej was disgraced and under arrest and that the cause of his fall from power was not political but criminal, that he had been unable to bear the departure from his life of the woman he had always adored, that the accident had been no accident, but an act of deliberate murder, planned and carried out with its usual ruthless precision by Ivan's own NKVD, the secret police. And that Joseph Stalin, in his anger at having his word betrayed—

he had personally granted Tatiana Nej permission to emigrate to England—had turned on his most trusted aide.

No one in the crowd would ever know the truth, of course. Even though it seemed likely they would read an announcement in *Pravda* that Ivan Nej had been executed for crimes against the state, they would never know for what crime, precisely. People never learned the truth of such matters in Soviet Russia, and most knew better than to ask. It was enough to observe that Ivan Nej was not here today to watch the ashes of his wife placed in her niche in the wall of the Kremlin, that his brother and son *were* here, and that Marshal Stalin grieved. He even appeared to wipe a tear from his eye as he threw both arms around Gregory Nej's shoulders, and hugged the boy close for a moment, before stepping back to salute the commemorative plaque.

And then Stalin hurried off towards the Kremlin, followed by his aides. For a man with the entire weight of all the Russians resting on his shoulders, even a few moments for mourning a dearly beloved friend were strictly rationed.

The ripple of pistol fire filled the huge, windowless room. Pieces of cardboard flew, and the trapped air became heavy with cordite.

Gregory Nej left the firing bays and walked forward, boot heels slapping the concrete floor. As ever, he wondered how soundproof this cellar was, how much of the noise seeped upwards to the street outside Lubianka here in the heart of Moscow, and what the good citizens who had spent so much of the past four years under fire must feel to hear crackle of gunfire beneath their feet.

As if it should matter to an officer in the NKVD what any citizen thought, and even less to an officer of the Special Section. And Gregory was not merely an officer, but an instructor.

As if anything should ever matter again. He was alone. Utterly and irrevocably.

He had, in fact, long ago accepted loneliness as a concomitant of his job, had deliberately linked himself to his father rather than his mother, knowing that he would never be able to reconcile Tattie's exuberant internationalism with the Communism in which he had been educated. Thus he had volunteered for his father's special units, determined to bury himself in the task of making Russia once again a great power. But his mother had always been there. Never had he doubted her survival, even during the war years when she had been a partisan behind the German lines. Thus he had been the more upset to learn of her decision to leave Russia and go away with her English lover, even while recognizing that such a step was entirely in keeping with her flamboyant character.

But now... the memory of that shattered body would remain with him for the rest of his life. The sight of her had been bad enough. The sudden suggestion that his father might have been responsible for her death was more than he could bear. He had not known what to do, where to turn. Certainly he could not look for aid from his Uncle Michael, who heartily disapproved of the NKVD. He had only his work, and his loneliness, to sustain him.

He reached the targets and inspected them. Any one of those bullets would have killed a man. Yet they were not perfect hits, and it was his business to deal only in perfection. He turned to face the recruits and drew a long breath. There were twelve of them, eight men and four women. They wore khaki overalls, dark with the sweat that still dribbled from their hair; immediately before coming to the range they had spent an hour jogging around and around the gymnasium—because in most cases, they would have to shoot in less than ideal circumstances, when they would be similarly exhausted, with gasping lungs and sweaty hands. Eight boys and four girls; he did not suppose the eldest of them was much over twenty-one. But then, he was only twenty-five himself. Five years ago *he* had stood over there, *his* palms sweaty on the butt of a pistol, awaiting the verdict of *his* instructor. And that had been Anna Ragosina, the most-feared of all his father's special agents, the most deadly woman in Russia, it was said. Five years of war against Nazi Germany, added to his birth and his name, had taken him to her position within the organization, but never to her reputation.

Yet he must also deal in perfection.

"Up," he said. "You must keep your shots up. Hit your enemy in the belly, and he will undoubtedly die, but slowly. He will be able to return fire, communicate with his own people, make use of himself. A bullet in the chest is quicker and more effective. It robs the enemy of the ability to think, to act, to fire."

They stood at attention as he walked past them, trying to

control their breathing, one girl blowing away a strand of wet yellow hair that had flopped across her eyes and mouth. They wished to please him, not only because he was Captain Nej, their instructor, and not even because he was the son of their erstwhile commissar, Ivan Nej, but because, he suspected, they liked him. That was a terrible admission for an instructor in the NKVD to have to make. But it was so, and they knew that he had come here straight from his mother's funeral. They were trying to convey their sympathy without daring to express it in words.

Had he ever liked Anna Ragosina? He was not sure of that. He had admired her, certainly, as he had envied her. And feared her. And once loved, or at least desired, her. He shook his head to rid himself of the unwelcome thought, placed his cap on his head, walked along the corridor to his office, opened the door, and stopped in utter surprise, because there she was, standing by the window.

He stepped inside and closed the door, uncertain of his feelings. Once again there was the fear, and once again, too, that other emotion, which too often filled his dreams. Anna had not changed. She remained the most exciting woman he had ever seen. For all her experiences, and even those he knew of must have been quite horrific, her face still suggested a madonna in its perfect pale symmetry, its calm repose, shrouded in that straight black hair he remembered so well. Like him, she wore a uniform, but it was easy to decide that her body had not changed either, was as firm-muscled and slenderly strong as it had ever been. She had yielded that body to him once. Correction. She had commanded him to use it, here in this gymnasium, because that was a part of her training method.

"Well, Comrade Nej?" she asked, smiling at him. "Comrade *captain*, I understand. Are you not pleased to see me?"

"Anna Petrovna?" He held out his arms, but she allowed him only a formally chaste kiss on each cheek. "But . . . I had heard—"

"That I was retired?" Anna sat down and crossed her knees, lit a cigarette before he could reach his own matches. "I have been on a vacation, Gregory Ivanovich. Mine was a long war."

"I know." He sat opposite her, behind the desk. "From which you have emerged a Heroine of the Soviet Union. Will you believe that I wished to join you and the partisans behind the German lines? But I was prevented."

"By your father. I remember. I can even understand why he did it. He wished to salvage something from the wreckage of his family."

Gregory leaned forward. "Tell me of my sister."

"We fought together." She shrugged. "I saw Svetlana's body after the Germans were finished with her. But I was commander of the unit in which she served, there in the Pripet. Her death is my responsibility. I would have you know that, Gregory Ivanovich."

He sighed, and leaned back. "Others died. Millions of others died. And at least you protected my mother—from the Germans, that is."

Anna Ragosina's mouth twisted. "I understand your grief. I was down there this morning, in the crowd, watching you mourn. And I mourned with you. Your mother and I were never friends, but I admired both her courage and her talent. And her beauty. Do you hate your father very much?"

Gregory flushed. "I . . . it is difficult to hate one's father, and it has not yet been proved that he is guilty." He looked up and smiled. "But you are back with us. I am so glad. You have come to command the section?"

"I have been given no assignment yet. I too had thought my career was over. But Marshal Stalin himself sent for me." She shrugged. "So I have come." She studied him for several seconds. "I am glad that you are pleased to see me, Gregory Ivanovich."

Flushing again, Gregory looked down. That she had also, in her time, been his father's mistress, his father's creature, was the most haunting memory of all.

"Why Marshal Stalin has sent for me," Anna went on, "I have no idea. Perhaps I am to be an instructor again." She smiled at the young man. "Or perhaps he wishes someone killed."

Gregory leaned forward again. "Anna—"

Anna got up, adjusted her cap, and glanced at him. "I have only been in Moscow a few days. I do not like my billet. May I come home with you?"

"With me?" Gregory also got up, his heart pounding. "If . . . if you wish."

"Until Marshal Stalin summons me," Anna said with another smile, "he can have no objection if I occupy my time. Will you not occupy my time, Gregory Ivanovich? You were happy to do so, once before. Until the marshal reveals what is in his mind."

Joseph Stalin stood at the window of his office in the Kremlin and looked out at the square, over which the crowds, no longer restrained, now wandered, pausing to gape at the new plaque, to whisper to one another, and then to look up at the citadel itself. Some of them might even know where the marshal's office was situated. But they would not be able to see him, behind the bulletproof glass.

Stalin looked somber; his shoulders were hunched. A casual observer might have supposed he was still depressed by the funeral, the last contact with a woman who had brought some gaiety and color to the Soviet monolith. But the men in the room with him knew that all memory of Tatiana Nej would have already faded from his mind, that he was entirely concerned with affairs of state, and with the momentous fact which had suddenly been brought to his attention.

He turned, and the four men seated before his desk hastily sat up straighter. Stalin returned to the desk, sat down, picked up the enlarged photograph that lay there, and studied it yet again. Then he raised his head.

"*One* bomb did this?"

Molotov and Michael Nej each looked at Beria. He was commander of the NKVD. Intelligence of what was happening in the rest of the world was his responsibility.

Beria took off his pince-nez, polished the lenses, and cleared his throat. "One bomb, Joseph Vissarionovich."

Stalin stared at him for some seconds. "One on Hiroshima. One on Nagasaki. Presumably the Americans have more of these bombs?"

"Presumably," Beria said.

Stalin turned his head slowly and looked at the fourth man in the room, the only other man wearing military uniform. "What would happen if they attacked the Soviet Union with such bombs?"

Marshal Zhukov's big features were grim. "We would be destroyed."

"Have we no planes, no antiaircraft guns?" Beria demanded.

"Certainly. We would shoot down many of their planes.

But only half a dozen need to get through."

"Only *one* airplane needs to get through," Molotov observed, "if it is carrying such a weapon."

"And there is no defense?" Stalin mused.

"Only to have an armory of such weapons ourselves," Zhukov said. "Then the Americans may be afraid to use theirs. It will be the same situation as with poison gas. The Germans were afraid to use gas in the war, because they knew they would be gassed in return."

"And we will have such bombs," Beria said eagerly. "Our scientists are working on it now."

"When will they produce one?" Stalin asked, his voice deceptively soft.

"Well, that I cannot say, Joseph Vissarionovich. It is a matter of physics—formulas and the like." He attempted a smile. "With natural phenomena as powerful as these bombs, it does not pay to make too many mistakes. One must proceed step by step."

"How long?" Stalin demanded.

"Well . . . it could be tomorrow. Or it could be well . . ." Once again Beria removed and polished his pince-nez. "Several years."

"Several *years?*"

"Several years, during which the Americans and the British will have a total monopoly of world power," Zhukov commented gloomily.

"And they hate us," Molotov muttered. "They only supported us against Hitler because they hated him even more."

Stalin chewed his lip, appearing to suck his moustache in the process, and then turned to the one man in the room who had not yet spoken. "Well, Michael Nikolaievich? These people are your friends."

Michael Nej sighed, even though he had known that such a remark was bound to come. Though his hair was almost white, Michael did not really show his sixty years; his face, which he kept clean-shaven, was as powerfully composed as ever and the features were as clearly etched as in his youth. His vigor had not diminished from the time he had commanded the Red armies that finally drove out the Whites and took Sevastopol, to the recent years when he administered the defense of Leningrad. Of them all, not excluding Stalin himself, his pedigree as a Bolshevik was the purest.

As a revolutionary soldier and as a commissar, he had stood in the forefront of Russian affairs for nearly thirty years, and he was one of the few men that Stalin trusted absolutely—nor was that trust apparently in the least affected by the sudden arrest of his brother, an affair which to him remained a mystery, even if he had long anticipated it. Yet he remained nothing more than the deputy commissar for foreign affairs. Partly it was because of his personal lack of ambition, and thus his lack of that ruthlessness so often required from a revolutionary leader. But most of all it was because of the events of his private life, the fact that he also had once been the lover of a Russian princess, Tatiana's sister Ilona, and that, even more strangely, he had then become the friend of her American millionaire husband. In a manner not achieved by any of his comrades, he had managed to bridge the gap between Communism and capitalism, at least in the mind—an ability which, he knew, made him not the less valuable to Stalin.

"The Americans will never use the bomb against us," Michael said quietly, "except in self-defense."

"Oh, yes?" Molotov inquired. "What were they defending when they dropped it on Hiroshima?"

"They sought a quick end to the war," Michael said, "a means of avoiding an invasion of the Japanese mainland, with all the bloodshed that would have entailed. The Americans have no need to wage an aggressive war now. They have everything they need, right there in America. Like us, they are interested only in their own security."

"We had all better pray that you are right," Marshal Zhukov said.

Stalin cleared his throat, and they turned to look at him. "I agree with Michael Nikolaievich," Stalin said, and smiled, a slow relaxation of the moustache. "They genuinely seem to wish to share the fruits of victory with all their allies." His smile broadened. "Even with Chiang Kai-shek."

"Are they going to share the secrets of the atomic bomb, as well?" Molotov asked.

Stalin's smile faded. "Weeping and wailing and gnashing our teeth is not going to help, Vyacheslav. We are faced with a situation, and we must make the best of it. For the moment we are hopelessly outgunned. *That* we must seek to change. But in the meantime, we must press ahead as rapidly as we can with our plans. Comrade Molotov, I put you in charge of our internal reconstruction. You can have Nikita Khrushchev as your aide, since you will have to continue with your duties in the field of foreign affairs as well. Khrushchev is the ideal man for the job, but I wish him to be answerable to you. Our people think that now the war is over, all their troubles are also over. Convince them that their troubles are only just beginning. European Russia is wrecked. I wish to see it reconstructed within twelve months."

"That is impossible," Molotov said.

"If it were simple, I would not be placing you in command of it," Stalin said. "You will *make* it possible. Do whatever you have to. But see that it is done. I want your blueprint for a new five-year plan on my desk a week from today. You understand?"

Molotov sighed, and then nodded.

"You will also have overall responsibility for eastern Europe," Stalin said. "Our troops occupy, quite legitimately, Rumania, Bulgaria, Yugoslavia, Albania, Hungary, Poland, Czechoslovakia, half of Germany, and half of Austria. It is a pity we did not manage to move into Greece before the British, but there is still hope of accomplishing something there. Now, Vyacheslav, I want the governments of those occupied countries to become our close friends and allies for the foreseeable future, before our troops come home."

"That is equally impossible," Molotov said. "Even if they all sign reciprocal defense treaties with us, who can trust them? Think of the Rumanians in 1940, or the Poles."

"It really does distress me to be surrounded by men who keep telling me things are impossible," Stalin said. "What you will have to do is see that these governments are in the hands of people we can trust. That will not be so very difficult."

"You are talking of a Communist Europe," Molotov said.

"The dream of the Party," Beria muttered, "for twenty years."

"Longer than that," Stalin reminded him. "And alas, the *total* Communization of Europe will have to wait a while. But eastern Europe, those countries nearest to us—that is not only possible, my comrades, it is essential for the good of the state."

"Such a plan is madness," Michael Nej said.

Every head turned to stare at him; no one else present would have dared say as much to Stalin.

"Why do you think that, Michael Nikolaievich?" Stalin asked softly.

"Do you suppose the Americans will stand for it, Joseph Vissarionovich? We have just agreed that we are helpless before their power, at this moment. And at this moment you would deliberately provoke them?"

"The Americans and the British agreed at Yalta that eastern Europe was ours," Stalin said. "It is all down in writing. They cannot change their minds now."

"They agreed that we should obtain our reparations from the countries that fought against us," Michael said. "And that it was our responsibility to reeducate them, away from fascism and towards democracy. Not that we should make them into puppet states, colonies."

"My dear Michael, you paint too extreme a picture. I am proposing no more than that we reeducate these people away from fascism and towards democracy. Soviet democracy."

"The Americans will object," Michael insisted. "They may love us at this moment, but soon they will be as suspicious of us as ever."

"Then we shall allay their suspicions," Stalin said. *"You* will accomplish that, Michael Nikolaievich."

"Me?"

"You. Because—thanks to George Hayman, and his wartime dispatches from Leningrad, and his empire of newspapers—you must be the best known of us all, in the west." Stalin allowed himself a smile. "Except perhaps for me. As deputy commissar for foreign affairs, you will have special responsibilities for Europe."

"But . . ." Michael looked at Molotov.

"Oh, Vyacheslav will officially command the operation. What I wish you to do, Michael Nikolaievich, is present the plan to America and Britain and France, in such a way that they cannot take exception. This latter-day League of Nations they are erecting . . ." His voice filled with contempt. "I would have you put your case there. Represent our interests." His smile widened. "It is to meet in London, in January, and then it is to have a permanent home in New York. You have always wanted to visit America. You will be able to see your son again."

"America?" Michael flushed, partly with excitement and partly with embarrassment at the mention of the son he had fathered by the Princess Ilona Borodina, before she had married George Hayman. Then the flush faded. "It will never work," he said stubbornly.

"It will work, if we all remember that it is essential for the safety of Mother Russia. I say to you what I have said to Vyacheslav. Do what you have to do. Be as ruthless as you have to be. And yes, lie if you have to. Take advantage of all the goodwill the people of Europe—the ordinary people, Michael Nikolaievich—feel towards us and towards *you,* for what you did at Leningrad. You are buying us time. Time to reeducate these people into joining forces with us forever, time to eradicate their outmoded institutions and ideas, and time to dispose of those leaders who would oppose us. And who knows, Michael? *If* we manage it right, we may even buy sufficient time to have a bomb of our own." His gaze swept them. "We have sat here long enough. You all have work to do."

The men stood up.

"You remain, Lavrenti Pavlovich," Stalin said, but he went to the door with Michael and threw his arm around his shoulders. "You have not asked about Ivan."

"I knew you would speak to me of him," Michael said, "when you chose."

"You understand that there is a strong suspicion that Tatiana was actually murdered? And poor Bullen, of course. By Ivan's orders."

"I have heard a rumor."

"Well, he will have to stand trial," Stalin said. "No man in Russia is above the law."

He paused, but Michael did not reply. He was used to Stalin's little flights of humor.

"So for the time being he is under arrest, in one of those cells where he has incarcerated so many other poor wretches," Stalin said. "He has not been ill-treated in any way. This is a civil matter, not political. If he can disprove the charge, then no one will be happier than I. You know this, Michael Nikolaievich?"

"I never doubted it, Joseph Vissarionovich," Michael agreed.

"Would you like to see him?"

Michael hesitated, and then shook his head. "Only if he asks for me. But if he did murder Tattie, I have no wish to see him."

"Yes," Stalin said. "I feel the same." He squeezed Michael's shoulders. "I am sure you will be able to make the Haymans understand that, when you see them in New York."

Stalin slowly lowered himself into his chair and gazed at the commander of the NKVD. Beria looked away uneasily.

"I know it is a sorry business, Joseph Vissarionovich," he said. "No one is more aware of that than I. But I blame Ivan Nej. Espionage was his responsibility. He was the man who created all those special units, sent them all over the world. And they reported only to him. Although I was commander of the NKVD, they reported only to him. He created a force within a force. And you supported him in that, Joseph Vissarionovich. I cannot be blamed for his mistakes."

"No one is blaming you for anything, Lavrenti Pavlovich," Stalin said. "And looking over one's shoulder is always a mistake. I know the power I gave Ivan Nej. When I did so, I needed such a man, such a force. But I also watched him growing more powerful, until he became *too* powerful, and then I swept him away." His hand moved, abruptly, across his desk.

"Only because he finally overreached himself," Beria grumbled, pursuing his point. "Had he not done that, had he not murdered his own wife—"

"Do you really think that?" Stalin asked very quietly. "Do you really think I am reduced to waiting for people to overreach themselves? And do you really think Ivan Nej ever did anything that was not dictated by me?"

Beria's head slowly came up, his jaw slipping. "But..." He licked his lips.

"This is in the strictest confidence, of course," Stalin said, "between you and me. Anyone who might ever suggest such a thing will be regarded as guilty of treason."

Beria swallowed. "She...she was your friend," he muttered. "All Russia thought—"

"That I loved Tatiana Dimitrievna as I might have loved a sister? But that is quite true, Lavrenti Pavlovich. Yet she was setting out to betray us."

"By marrying an Englishman?"

"By taking herself to the West. You knew her, Lavrenti Pavlovich. Can you imagine her giving press conferences? She had planned to give her first on the plane, as soon as it took off from Moscow. Tattie, who knew almost everything that has happened inside Russia from November 1917? Do you really suppose we could allow her to write her memoirs, as Hayman would certainly have persuaded her to do?"

"Then why did you grant her permission to emigrate at all? Surely—"

"How could I refuse Tatiana Nej, the great dancer, the immortal, and still preserve our image with the West? Her affair with Bullen was well publicized, as was the role she played with the partisans down in the Pripet. She is more famous now than ever. To have refused her permission to go off with the man she loved would have been to resurrect the image of the thirties, and that image must be buried forever, Lavrenti Pavlovich. Believe me, I grieve for what had to be done. I grieve most deeply. But it did *have* to be done."

Beria was slowly getting his breathing under control. "But Ivan Nej—"

"Will never dare make such an accusation. Not if he hopes to survive, and he does hope that. But I think it might be best if he were never to come to public trial at all. You understand me?"

"I . . ."

"I do not wish to discuss it any further. You have carte blanche. We have more important things to do, you and I. Vital things, Lavrenti Pavlovich." He leaned across the desk. "We must undo the wrong caused by Ivan Nej's mistakes."

Beria frowned at him. "You have another task for me?"

"Oh, indeed. I have the most important task in all Russia for you, Lavrenti Pavlovich. You see, I am aware that I am taking a risk in defying the Americans. It will come to that, whatever Michael Nej can accomplish, whenever they realize just what we are attempting. I regard the risk as justifiable, even necessary. But it is a risk, nevertheless. And we will not be able to sustain it for more than a few years. I give us three at the most. By the time three years are up, Lavrenti Pavlovich, we must be in a position to meet the Americans on equal ground. By that time we must have atomic bombs of our own. And I do not think we can afford to wait for our own scientists. I want those formulas, here in Russia, as soon as possible.

That is your task, Lavrenti Pavlovich. Get me those formulas."

Beria stared at him. "But how? From where, Joseph Vissarionovich?"

"From America, my friend. From America. That is where they are to be found, is it not?"

Beria scratched his bald head. "From America," he muttered.

"We have people over there?"

"A few," Beria said. "But it will take time. We have had agents in England, and France, and Germany for years. But up until 1941, America did not seem important to us. Or to you."

"Lavrenti Pavlovich," Stalin said gently, "I am not interested in 1941. I am interested in 1945. And time is the one thing we do *not* have. I thought I had made that clear. Your entire efforts must be devoted to the United States. I want a task force of agents created to cover the whole country. That should not be difficult, with refugees going back and forth. You have agents in these refugee camps already?"

"Of course," Beria said.

"Well, see that they get to the head of the lists for emigration to the United States. And do not assume that the atomic secrets are the only things we are looking for. I want your people to infiltrate and recruit in every walk of American life. I want them to use the same methods we have used in the past, in Germany and in England, and especially in France, of getting into the trade unions and causing the maximum disruption. But in America, and in our present circumstances, there must be no link with us here. Your agents must relate to a central control in the United States, and whoever *they* recruit must believe that this is genuine, homegrown, American communism. Do you understand me?"

Beria nodded, but his expression remained uncertain.

Stalin sighed. "Who is your area commander in America?"

"Dimitri Bogolzhin."

"He is a good man?"

"One of the best," Beria said.

"And how do you contact him?"

"He contacts me, by code, in ordinary letters written to an intermediate agent in England. You understand, Joseph Vissarionovich, that we have pursued no active policy towards the Americans, as yet. Bogolzhin's duties have related only to gathering information, nothing more than that."

"He does not seem to have been very successful with this atomic bomb."

"Well . . ." Beria flushed. "We have known for some time that they were working on an exceptional weapon."

"Why was I not informed?"

"Because Ivan Nej was handling the matter. I had assumed he was keeping you up to date."

Stalin gazed at him for some seconds. Then he said, "Well, you are in command now. I want you to appoint a new area commander for the United States. This person is to have complete control of the whole of North America, to be answerable only to you and to me. He, or she, will employ agents known only to himself, and will be responsible for disposing of them when they are no longer of value to us. This person will cause the maximum disruption of American industry and indeed American society. This person will be responsible for obtaining the atomic secrets."

"Such power . . ." Beria sighed. "It is a great responsibility. It will demand qualities of decisiveness and courage, since decisions will have to be taken without reference to us here. I doubt Bogolzhin is really the man for the job."

"I have no doubt that he is *not* the man for the job."

"And finding someone here to send over will not be easy. So many of our top people were killed by the Germans. Oh, it will be difficult."

"I said he, *or she,*" Stalin reminded him. "The most suitable person for the job, Lavrenti Pavlovich, the person who is best equipped in every way for the task we require, is right here in Moscow at this moment, waiting to be given an assignment."

Beria's head came up. "But she is Ivan Nej's creature," he protested.

"You gave her the task of arresting Nej, did you not?"

"On your instructions, Joseph Vissarionovich. I was unhappy about it."

"Yet she did it, and without a moment's hesitation. Believe me, I know this woman. I have studied her since the beginning. And I can tell you that she is nobody's creature. Of course it was Nej who took her out of school. He wanted a woman of his own, as he could never actually own Tatiana Dimitrievna. It was nothing more than that, then. But he trained her to be his own shadow. And now she is far superior to him at his best. And she speaks English. I want her sent to America."

"But...Joseph, Anna Ragosina is a well-publicized figure. Certainly she is known to the FBI."

"Her *name* is well known, Lavrenti. There is not a single photograph in existence of Anna Ragosina. She will go to Washington as a confidential secretary at the embassy, under an assumed name. Only our ambassador need know who she really is and what powers she really commands."

"And suppose she meets someone who can recognize her?"

"Oh, really, Lavrenti. You are becoming a pessimist. How could she do that?"

"What about John Hayman? He fought with her in the Pripet for four years. Do you not suppose *he* knows what she looks like?"

"There are a hundred and thirty million people in the United States, Lavrenti Pavlovich. The odds of her encountering John Hayman in the street are therefore one hundred and thirty million to one. And as a confidential secretary at the Soviet embassy, she is not likely to be invited to any party where the son of a millionaire like Hayman is likely to be. By all means remind her of the danger. But I do not think she will require any warning. She is capable of looking after herself." Stalin leaned across the desk. "Send Anna Ragosina to Washington, comrade. We need those atomic secrets, and she will get them for us."

Michael Nej opened the door of his apartment, slammed it shut behind him, and threw his coat and scarf on a chair. "Catherine?" he called. "Catherine?"

His wife bustled out of the little kitchen, wiping her hands on her apron. Catherine Lissitsina was in her middle forties, a compact woman whose short straight hair remained as black as the first time he had ever seen her, and whose features were a crisp reminder of her Tartar ancestry. They had been married for more than twenty years, and before their marriage she had lived with him as his mistress for several months, yet she still approached him with cautious deference, as if never sure when the illusion would end. Yet they had found contentment. They had adventured together, become parents together, had survived the horrors of the Leningrad siege, and in this three-room apartment, in a building reserved exclusively for senior commissars, she had, through him, achieved the pinnacle of social and financial success for any Russian woman.

"Catherine," he said a third time, kissing her forehead. "Where is Nona?"

"At the university. She will soon be home." Catherine frowned at him. "There is something wrong?"

Michael smiled at her. "Not for you, my love. I have splendid news for you." He held her at arm's length. "How would you like to go to London?"

"London?" She was incredulous.

"England."

"Oh, but..." Her mouth sagged open, and she half turned her head. "Comrade Petrova is here."

Michael's hands fell from her shoulders, as he turned to face the kitchen doorway, and the tall, heavy woman who stood there. "Judith?" he whispered. "Judith! My God. But... *Petrova?!*" He stook a step towards her, and halted, conscious of his wife's gaze.

Judith Stein Petrova smiled. "I have married Boris." Her shoulders rose and fell. "Well, he has been asking me for years."

"And come back to Russia? Judith!" He stepped forward to take her in his arms.

Catherine watched them, her face expressionless. She herself had been only a child during the First World War and the revolution, but she had read all about those days, as any good Russian should. Thus she knew that she was watching the past come alive before her eyes. Judith Stein had been among the most famous of the women who had taken the lead in those tumultuous events, and had become the mistress of Lenin's close friend, Michael Nej himself, before fleeing him, and Russia, after the Bolsheviks executed her parents.

To Catherine's knowledge, Judith and Michael had seen each other only once since 1920. Judith had lived in New York and in London, and later even in Germany, working for the Zionist cause—her true cause—and she had spent three years in Ravensbrück Concentration Camp as a result. Yet she had survived all that, and she was here in Moscow, a handsome woman, with her statuesque figure and her black hair streaked with gray. She wore a smart dress and high-heeled shoes, and looked far more fashionable than was possible for any Russian woman in 1945. And she held Michael once again in her arms.

He stepped back with a quick glance at his wife. "Had you and Catherine met before?"

"Yes, briefly," Judith said. "Don't you remember, in 1933?" She smiled. "But she has made me very welcome."

"And now you are here," Michael said. "After all these years." His arms moved, as if they would have embraced her again, and then fell back to his sides. "Just as we are leaving."

"Are you really going to London?"

"For a little while, at least," Michael explained. "I am to represent the Soviet at the United Nations. Who knows? We might even be going to New York, afterwards. It is to be the UN headquarters, eventually."

"But that is marvelous for you," Judith said. "You'll be able to see George and Ilona." There was no trace of jealousy in Judith's makeup. That Michael had loved Ilona Borodina before herself was no cause for regret; Ilona had been her best friend. "And John," she said, her voice at last uncertain, as she glanced at Catherine.

"Yes," Micahel said. "I am looking forward to that. Fate works in mysterious ways, doesn't it? John Hayman spent the entire war here in Russia, fighting with the partisans, and I never saw him until six months ago. Now I am to live in the same city." Again he glanced at Catherine.

She kept her face stony, because she too must never feel jealousy over this living legend. That Michael was to see his son, John, again, and his son's mother, must be viewed only as a cause for celebration, whatever reservations she had. "And Nona?" she asked. "Will Nona be able to come too?"

"I don't see why not," Michael said. He sat down and gestured for the two women to join him on the sofa. "But first, a celebration. I knew Boris was back in Russia, of course. But I did not know you were with him. We will have a supper party, eh, Catherine?"

"Of course." But as she watched Judith, and the series of shadows which flitted across that strong face, Catherine realized that *she* was the intruder here. These two old comrades had much to discuss. She got up. "I will make some more tea," she said.

Judith watched her leave the room. "I . . . I heard about Tattie," she said. "I could hardly believe it."

"None of us can believe it," Michael said. "Life can never be the same without Tattie."

"Is it . . . is it true what they are saying?"

"That Ivan was responsible? Yes. I'm afraid it may well be true. But if it is, he will suffer the full penalty. I give you my word."

Judith looked at him. They had both known Ivan for too long, and she herself had experienced his callous anger. There was nothing more to be said about him. Besides, she had other things on her mind. "Catherine is very kind," she said.

"Why yes, so she is."

"And you are happy?"

"I am very contented," Michael said carefully, "at least in my domestic life." He smiled. "Perhaps I am too old to look for happiness anymore. That kind of happiness. I *have* been happy, in the past."

She glanced at him, flushed, and got up. "Have you ever forgiven me for deserting you? . . . Or George, for helping me escape?"

"You, certainly. I knew that you could not stay here, then."

"But not George?"

"It was a long time ago, Judith, and George and I have fought shoulder to shoulder more than once since then. Now it seems we may be going to do so again. I am looking forward to that."

"But not to your mission."

Judith, Michael recalled, had always been the most embarrassingly perceptive of women.

"There are difficult times ahead," he said. "And it is my task to convince the West, and especially the Americans, that we are not all still red-handed Bolsheviks, intent only upon mass murder and world Communism."

"And is that the truth?" she asked, then bit her lip. "I'm sorry. But—"

"It is hard to forget." He sighed. "Your parents were murdered, Judith. There was no excuse for what Ivan did there. As for murdering Tattie . . . Ivan is a relic, I suppose, of all that is hideous in our past. Certainly *that* is not going to make my task any easier. But you know, many of the things he did, and the things I had to do, *were* necessary for the construction of the Soviet state. There was no other way it could have come about. And you will not pretend that you could ever consider a tsarist restoration."

"No," she said. "I could never accept that." It was her turn to sigh. "Although Peter still hopes for it. He and Ruth are living in Stockholm now. I. . . I stayed with them after I got out of prison." She looked at the floor, because while she had had to share Michael with Ilona Borodina, Michael had had to share her with Ilona's brother, the Prince of Starogan.

"Yes," he said. "Well, I do not blame Peter either. His family was murdered; his home was destroyed. I suppose he still regards Tattie as having been raped and kidnapped by Ivan."

"He does," Judith said. "And now that she has been *murdered*—"

"I told you, Ivan will be punished. But I feel sorry for people like Peter. To live on memories, to have so much hate. . . and to be unable to do anything about it."

"While you," she said, "can do so much about your memories."

"I have been fortunate."

She took a turn around the room, paused at the window, then faced him. "I too, have been fortunate. I have been condemned to death at least twice, and I am still here. But people like you and me, Michael, owe a debt to that fortune which has preserved us."

"I'm sure we do." His eyes were watchful.

"I. . . I married Boris on condition," she said.

"You do not love him?"

"I think he is the nicest man I have ever known. But perhaps, like you, I am too old to feel love anymore. As you say, I have loved, and been happy. That is sufficient for one lifetime."

He gazed at her. Does she mean me, he wondered? Or Peter Borodin? Or perhaps even George Hayman?

"So?" He forced a smile. "Yours is a platonic marriage?"

"Of course not. But I came back to Russia, not to be a housewife, but in order to continue my work. I think there is more to be done here than anywhere else in the world, at the moment."

Michael frowned at her. "For Zionism, you mean?"

She came back across the room, sat beside him, and held his hand. "There *is* going to be a Jewish state, Michael. And it will be Palestine. After two thousand *years,* my people are going home."

"I thought the Arab League had already given an opinion on that."

She tossed her head impatiently. "There will have to be negotiations. There is room for all. But it is our home. *Our* home, Michael. That means Russian Jews as well as German Jews and British Jews and American Jews. *Our* home. There are five million Jews in Russia."

"Slightly more," he said, "at the last count."

Her fingers tightened. "Will you help me?"

He hesitated, looking into her eyes. Then he shrugged, and smiled. "I'll talk to Joseph Vissarionovich. He's in an internationalist mood at the moment. We'll talk to him together, Judith."

Chapter 2

ANNA RAGOSINA SLOWLY SEEMED TO UNCOIL FROM THE RIGID attention at which she had been standing, her head drooping so that she could look down on Beria, seated at his desk.

He smiled. "You may sit down, Comrade Ragosina."

He watched her slowly sink into the chair before his desk, and leaned forward to offer her a cigarette. He wondered if he was afraid of her. Certainly he was afraid of the *thought* of her, the *idea* of her. He supposed she was about the most beautiful women he had ever seen, with her cold madonna face, which had shown no change of expression even when she was utterly surprised, as she was now; in her slender, undoubtedly hard-muscled body, which yet filled the bodice of her tunic to bursting; in the length of her booted legs. Ivan Nej's creature. But now turned loose by the collapse of her master. It was an interesting consideration that presumably she was now *his* creature. His to command. Even to his bed, if he dared. All that white flesh—he was sure she would have white flesh; he could not conceive of a woman like Anna Ragosina ever wasting the time to lie in the sun—and all that suppressed passion—he was equally sure that behind that madonna face and those icy green eyes there must lie a volcano of passion, waiting to be aroused—would be placed at his disposal if he were merely to raise his finger. Anna Ragosina always obeyed orders.

But would he have the courage to raise his finger?

"Would you like a cigarette?" he asked, pushing the box across the desk.

She shook her head, a quick, almost impatient movement. "I will have complete local control?" she asked.

Power. That was what she craved. Power. "That is what I have said."

Anna gazed at him. She found it difficult to believe what she had just been told. An independent command. It would be her second. But there could be no comparing leading a partisan group behind the German lines and leading all the Russian agents in the United States. Where John Hayman lived. She felt the heat rushing to her cheeks, and half-smiled, which encouraged Beria to do the same.

She could read his mind effortlessly. She was certain he desired her. She was also certain that he would do nothing about his desires. For all his size, and his apparent power, he was a timid, little man who would hope for some sign from her that his advances would be acceptable. So why not give him such a sign? Not that his advances *would* be acceptable. She had never found any man's advances acceptable. Sex with Ivan Nej had been like sleeping with a corpse. And Gregory was too confused, too guilt-ridden, and too anxious to prove himself. Still.

She had only *wanted* to sleep with one man: John Hayman. And when she had been given command of the Pripet Marsh partisans, where she knew that John Hayman and Tatiana Nej and the remnants of the dancing school had taken refuge along with the shattered remnants of the Ninth Army, she had been sure her dream was going to be realized. They had spent four years together in that marsh, and killed together and eaten together and bathed together—and she had kissed him, once. But he had been in love with Natasha Brusilova, and like all the others, he had hated and feared *her*, even as he had been fascinated by her. So her dream had changed. Only a little. From the romantic to the cruel. But all her dreams were cruel— because she had been able to make so many of them come true. Perhaps one day she might even be able to make her dreams about John Hayman come true. He lived in the United States.

"Your only risk will be of meeting John Hayman," he said, momentarily startling her. "There is no doubt that he would be able to recognize you."

"No doubt at all," she agreed. "So would Natasha Brusilova, his wife, and so would his mother, Ilona Hayman."

"Well, that is something to remember. But it is really a very small risk. You will be in Washington, and the Haymans live outside New York, I believe. Nor will they have anything to do with your objectives."

Anna's head came up. "On the contrary, Comrade Beria. They are my principal preliminary objectives."

Beria frowned. "Are you mad?"

Anna did not even blink. "You cannot send me to infiltrate an entire country without permitting me some picked assistants. Besides, you have given me carte blanche."

Beria's frown deepened. "Well?"

"I want Gregory Nej assigned to my mission."

"Gregory *Nej?* Now I know you are mad. There is no possible chance of *his* not being recognized. His link to the Haymans is well known."

"We *wish* him to be recognized, Comrade Beria. Listen to me. You are sending me to organize a vast network of agents, and also to obtain what must be the most closely guarded secrets in the world. I am going to need all the help I can get. *We* are going to need that. I am going to need people in places where nobody else can reach. George Hayman is America's most powerful newspaper publisher. He also happens to be Gregory's uncle."

"Oh, indeed. But he also knows Gregory to be a member of the NKVD, and a totally dedicated member of the Party."

"He knows that Gregory *was* that, Comrade," Anna said. "But a great deal has happened since they last met. Gregory's mother is dead. There are rumors that she was murdered." She held up her hand, as Beria would have spoken. "I do not know the truth of the matter, Comrade, nor do I wish to know. I merely ask you to put yourself in George Hayman's position, were he to receive a letter from his nephew, now virtually an orphan, asking if he might visit the United States. I predict George Hayman would be delighted. I am sure Ilona Hayman would be delighted, especially if she also receives a letter from Michael Nej, asking her to accept Gregory as a guest."

"Why should Michael Nej do that?"

"Because Gregory Ivanovich will ask him to. And he will be happy to oblige, since he is aware how miserable the young man has been since his mother's death."

"I still fail to see what you hope to accomplish," Beria said.

"Supposing Gregory Nej goes to the United States, obviously unhappy and confused about what has happened. And suppose he is attracted by the life over there, and decides to defect. A captain in the NKVD—it will set America on its ear. Certainly he will become of great interest to the Pentagon and the FBI. With George Hayman to vouch for him, and with the information he will be able to give the Americans, they will most certainly come to trust him. And we will have one of our people in the very heart of the American military system." She leaned back and crossed her knees. "I think that will be of great help to me."

Beria stared at her. The simplicity of her scheme was the truly amazing thing, the way she had taken an existing situation and twisted it to suit her own ends. He began to understand why Stalin had picked her for the job. "But will he do it?"

"Gregory Nej will do anything I require of him."

"I meant, will he be *able* to do it, convincingly?"

"Of course," she said. "He is a very capable boy."

Beria allowed his gaze to drift slowly up and down her body. "You are a surprising woman, Comrade Ragosina," he said. "Behind that lovely mask of a face you have the brains of a man. I wonder how many other secrets you keep locked away."

It was the nearest he would ever come to a proposition, she knew. But she had just obtained what she wanted. He deserved some reward. Besides, he was the head of the NKVD, a man possessing power of life and death over all his operatives. And she suspected he would be an easier man to manage than Ivan Nej had ever been.

She smiled at him, and allowed her right hand to drift to the top button of her tunic. "All my secrets, Comrade Beria, are now yours to command, are they not?"

"Judith Stein!" Stalin came around his desk to take her hands and kiss her on both cheeks. "I met you once, on the platform in Leningrad, when you were about to depart for the southern front with Michael Nej. Do you remember?"

"I remember, comrade," Judith said.

"And now you are back in Russia. I can hardly believe it. It is a great day for us. A great day for Communism." His smile faded. "But I am told you wish to leave us again."

Judith glanced at Michael and flushed. "I—"

"I have read your memorandum." Stalin returned behind his desk, sat down, and tapped the sheet of paper lying on the blotting pad.

"It is not for myself, comrade," Judith explained. "I would be happy to spend the rest of my days here in Russia. I only felt it would be best first of all to go to Palestine, to talk with the people, to see for myself the conditions there, the conditions our people will have to experience, the feeling of the Arabs, the—"

"It is, of course, quite impossible," Stalin said, "at the moment."

"Impossible? But . . ." Again she glanced at Michael, who waited, stony-faced.

"My dear Comrade Petrova," Stalin said, gesturing her to a chair. "Have you not looked around you? Can there be a country in the world more devastated than Russia?" He allowed himself a smile. "Unless perhaps it is Germany. But they lost the war. We *won* it. It is our task—it must be the task of every Soviet citizen—to contribute to the rebuilding of our country. And you would have me send several million of our people away?"

"Not send them, your excellency," Judith said desperately. "I do not suppose all of them will wish to go. But those who do—"

"No one can be spared." He held up his finger. "Not for the moment. In a year, perhaps two—who knows? It may be possible for me to reconsider the question."

Judith's lips tightened into a thin line.

And Stalin smiled again. "That is not a very long time, Comrade Petrova, not a very long time at all. And there is no need for you to abandon your plans. I think it would be a very good idea for you to visit Palestine. More than that: I will *send* you to Palestine as my special envoy, to investigate conditions there for our people. Would you not like that?"

"I . . . you are too generous, comrade."

Stalin got up again and came around the desk to lift her from her chair and embrace her again. His geniality seemed to fill the room. "It is my business to do the best I can for my people. For all my people. It is my responsibility to help them, providing they in turn help Mother Russia. Michael will see to your passport."

"I . . . I do not know how to thank you, comrade. But Boris—"

"I think Comrade Petrov will have to remain here and get on with his job," Stalin said. "But you will only be going for a short visit, comrade. You will soon be back with your husband. I wish you every fortune, and every happiness." He continued to smile until the door closed behind them. Then he returned to his desk and pressed the switch on the intercom. "I wish to see Comrade Beria," he said.

While he waited, he tore Judith's memorandum into strips and dropped them into the wastepaper basket.

"Tell me about Judith Stein," Stalin said.

Beria frowned. "Judith Stein? You mean Judith Petrova?"

"That is who I mean. She is back in Russia."

"Married to Petrov, yes. I referred the matter."

"Indeed you did, Lavrenti Pavlovich. Now I wish you to refresh my memory about her. Everything about her."

Beria looked at the ceiling. "Born 1888, of a well-to-do Jewish family. Moscow. Father a lawyer. Engaged with her brother Joseph in socialist activities from early age. Took part in the Moscow uprising, 1905. Arrested, but released on intercession of Prince Peter Borodin of Starogan. Again involved in socialist activities, notably with Mordka Bogrov and Michael Nej in the Stolypin assassination plot. Arrested with them and sentenced to death. Sentence commuted to life exile in Siberia by the tsar, again on a plea from Peter Borodin—"

"Her lover?" Stalin interrupted.

"I would say so, Joseph Vissarionovich. She was released in the general amnesty of 1914 to celebrate the twentieth year of the tsar's reign. Lived as a bourgeois at the beginning of the Kaiser's War. Served as a nurse. Was recruited by dissident royalist elements to take part in the Rasputin assassination plot. Believed to be present at his death, although I have no certain information on that. Happened to be nursing the tsarevnas through an attack of measles when the Romanovs fell, was exiled with them to Siberia. Found there by Michael Nej, and returned to Petrograd as his mistress. She lived with him for three years during the civil war. But then her parents were executed—they had previously conspired to aid the escape of

Peter Borodin, one of the most-wanted of all the counterrevolutionaries."

"I see. Go on."

"So she fled the country. With the aid of Hayman, the American newspaperman. She then lived in New York for several years, working for Hayman's newspapers—there is some evidence that she may have been Hayman's mistress, as well, during that time—and became involved in Zionism. She left New York for London in 1929, spent some time in Berlin, and then lived in Paris, until 1941, with Petrov. When the Germans invaded Russia, Petrov naturally lost his diplomatic immunity in France. He was sent home, but she was sent to Ravensbrück Concentration Camp. Somehow she got out of there alive, around the end of the war. I have no details on that. Then she lived briefly in Stockholm, again with Peter Borodin, and that is where she was found by Petrov, who married her."

"You mentioned a brother."

"Joseph Stein. He also fled Russia in the twenties. He was murdered by a Nazi mob in 1933."

"And a sister?"

"Rachel Stein. She became the Princess Borodina."

"Prince Borodin married a *Jew?*"

"It was at the end of the Kaiser's War. During the civil war, in fact. Things were very confused. In any event, the Princess Borodina died, also in New York. There was one child, a girl, who still lives with her father. You may remember the name—Ruth Borodina?"

Stalin nodded. "I remember Ivan Nej making an awful mess, by mistakenly arresting her in 1938. Now Petrov."

Beria shrugged. "Not a great deal. He is younger than his wife. He was prominent in the Moscow Soviet. He has always shown a talent both for languages and diplomatic work, and his father was a bourgeois businessman. So when it was necessary to have an unofficial diplomatic representative in New York, in the early twenties, Lenin chose him for the role. He had to pose as an import-export merchant, you see. He did well there, but when relations with the United States were normalized, and we could have an ambassador in Washington, he was moved to Paris. He remained there until 1941, as I have said. During the war he served in Leningrad under Michael Nej, with some distinction."

"Hm. Presumably he would have met his wife in New York," Stalin said.

"I think that is most likely," Beria agreed.

"When she was working for George Hayman, and no doubt seeing a great deal of her sister, the Princess Borodina, and the prince."

Beria nodded.

"And now she is back in Russia, agitating for would-be Jewish emigrants to be allowed to go to Palestine. I do not like it, Lavrenti Pavlovich. I cannot believe she can feel anything but hatred for us. And now...Palestine? The whole thing smacks of conspiracy. It could all be a plot to embroil us with the Arabs."

"You wish her to be arrested?"

Stalin regarded him with a pitying smile. "She is an international figure, Lavrenti Pavlovich. That would not do at all. Nor can we have another accident, so soon after the last one. No, no. I will allow her to go to Palestine, or wherever else she wishes, to investigate conditions for Jews, eh? That is what she says she wants to do, and letting her go is the best way of finding out what she is truly up to. But you will have her shadowed at all times. And Lavrenti, under no circumstance is Petrov to be allowed to leave the Soviet Union. You understand me?"

"Of course." Beria got up.

"That other matter," Stalin said, still appearing to study various memoranda on his desk. "It is in hand?"

"Of course," Beria said again. "Comrade Ragosina leaves for Washington at the end of this week, and...ah, other arrangements, which she thought necessary, are also being prepared."

"I do not wish to know the details of her operation," Stalin said. "I want results."

"And you shall have them. I must say, Joseph Vissarionovich, I take back everything I said about her. She is a remarkable woman, truly remarkable. I have the utmost confidence in the success of her mission."

Stalin raised his head to gaze at him, and Beria flushed. "I was sure you would, Lavrenti Pavlovich," Stalin said, "when you got to know her better."

* * *

Anna Ragosina lit her cigarette, inhaled deeply, and blew a thin stream of smoke towards the ceiling of the little bedroom. She rarely smoked; it was a bourgeois habit, she had been informed, but one she indulged because it was necessary to alleviate some of the seething discontent she always felt immediately after sex.

Partly it was her surroundings. The small, bare room, the narrow bed, the thin walls that brought all the other families in the apartment building into their midst—even brought the Moscow traffic, several stories beneath them, into their midst. Partly it was the inadequacy of the man.

But today the cigarette was hardly necessary. However unsatisfactory the past ten minutes, she was still elated, because she was going to America.

America! The fact was only just sinking in. Of course her response had been brilliant. Beria had been impressed, so impressed that afterwards he had been obviously infatuated with her. He had not the slightest suspicion that she might be a bubbling cauldron of uncertainty, of hope and fear and confusion, behind the mask. Neither had he suspected her distaste.

Nobody had ever suspected any of those things of Anna Ragosina. And no one ever would. Even Ivan Nej, who had created all this, had never truly known what went on behind her green eyes. And he *had* created her. She had no illusions about that. He had taken a bitter, angry schoolgirl and molded her into a female replica of himself, had taken all the simmering hatred felt by an orphan whose parents had been executed by the secret police, and convinced her that the hatred could never be used against the state, but that it might find its best use in working *for* the state, with every man and every woman her enemy, and only Ivan Nej her friend. Already he had been falling in love with the cold magnetism of her green eyes, the supple sexuality of her strong, slender body. That she might hate his caresses, that she might loathe him as a human being, had never occurred to him, just as it had never occurred to him, when it had been necessary to find a scapegoat for the botched arrest of Ilona Hayman back in 1932, and he had chosen Anna, that she would ever return to haunt him. But she had. And now *he* was in a cell, where she had put him, with every suggestion of personal humiliation that she could think of, and she was on her way to America to create a new system, to control an entire continent. And she was only thirty-five.

The future was quite dazzling—assuming she succeeded. But Anna Ragosina, having lived seven years with Ivan Nej, and five years in a labor camp, and four years in the Pripet Marsh, fighting Germans, had no room in her makeup for fear. She would succeed, or she would die. It was as simple as that.

But she *would* succeed.

Gregory moved in her arms, nuzzling the flesh of her neck with his nose. In many ways he was very like his father, but he had that streak of Borodin nobility which his father had entirely lacked.

"I am not sure I can do it," he said.

"You can do anything, if you wish." Anna stubbed out her cigarette. He was going to need even more reassuring.

"Deceive my own kinfolk? And afterwards . . . I will be known to have been a spy."

"Afterwards, you will be known as a Hero of the Soviet Union. Successful spies are always heroes."

"Will I be able to see you, Anna? From time to time? If I could see you from time to time . . ."

She looked down the length of her own white body, and then down the length of his. If she had been his father's creature, then he was hers, utterly and without reservation. She was the only rock upon which his chaotic world could seize, and grasp, sure that she would never change, and that she would never desert or abandon him—unless it be for the good of the State. But perhaps he thought she would never abandon him even then. It was a supposition to be encouraged, whatever the risk. But she had always enjoyed risks.

She put down her hand to stroke his chest, and pinch his nipples, which he seemed to like. "You will be able to see me, from time to time," she promised. "I will arrange it."

The jailer turned the key, slipped the bolt, and the door swung inwards. Lavrenti Beria stepped through; the door behind him remained open, although the jailer retired some distance.

Ivan Nej's head moved. There was an admission of defeat, Beria thought. Ivan had been in the secret police for long enough to know that the only hope anyone ever had of surviving his cell was to withdraw entirely into the privacy of the mind, to convince himself that whatever happened to the body was a passing evil, and above all, never to hope. But Ivan, he supposed, after his years of intimacy with Stalin, would find it impossible not to hope.

Just as, presumably, he would find it impossible not to hate his erstwhile master, when he learned how completely he had been abandoned. That hatred it might be possible to tap and cultivate, Beria thought. After all, Joseph Vissarionovich was sixty-six years old, and though he revealed no sign of age in his thinking, nevertheless he could not go on forever. Ivan Nej, with his penchant for intrigue, and his utter ruthlessness, might be very useful when the moment of Stalin's demise arrived, providing he was prepared to recognize where his own best interests lay.

The little man was naked, and he had been shaved—not only his head, but the moustache on which he had prided himself, and his pubic hair as well. His sharp features no less than his thin body seemed pitifully exposed, pitifully white. Anna Ragosina had done that, no doubt, because she would have been shaved in the labor camp to which this man had once sent her, and Anna Ragosina never forgot an injury. Beria could only imagine what she had said to Ivan, how she had smiled at him, as she had had him stretched on his back, entirely at her mercy. He almost shivered.

She had also taken away Ivan's spectacles, so that he could only blink at the intruder and attempt to identify him.

"Wheels turn, Ivan Nikolaievich, in a mysterious manner," Beria said.

Now Ivan looked directly at him; he had recognized the voice. "They will turn again," he said.

"Not for you, Ivan," Beria said. "Not without my help. There is to be no trial."

Ivan's head jerked.

"That is Joseph Vissarionovich's decision, Ivan," Beria said softly. "Not mine. I might even think it is a wrong decision. But he fears that you know too much."

Ivan said nothing. He could only wait to learn his fate.

"He does not wish to know of you again," Beria said, still speaking very quietly.

Ivan's body seemed to ripple, like a snake's. His head drooped.

"But I have decided to exercise my discretion, and to consider the future," Beria said.

Ivan's head lifted again.

"You will go to cell number forty-seven," Beria said.

Ivan caught his breath. He had placed many people in cell number forty-seven. It was the deepest and most remote of the cells beneath Lubianka, from which no scream could ever be heard, not even the pleas for mercy from the wretches he had allowed to be starved to death down there.

"You will remain in cell number forty-seven," Beria said, "until I see what the future may hold. You will be well fed, and I will give you books to read and clothes to wear. You have nothing to fear from me, Ivan, not if you behave yourself."

Ivan inhaled slowly.

"And when I release you, when I return you to your uniform and your power," Beria said, "if I find it convenient to do so, you will be properly grateful."

"Yes," Ivan said. "Yes, I understand that."

"You will have a great deal of time to think," Beria said, "of how you have been betrayed, and abandoned, and then rescued. You will have time to think of your betrayers."

"Yes," Ivan said.

"Of whom will you think most?" Beria asked.

"I will think of Anna Ragosina," Ivan said.

Beria raised his eyebrows.

"I will think of having her down here," Ivan said, "to do with as I please."

"That is interesting," Beria remarked. Disappointing, he thought, but definitely interesting. "Well, Ivan Nikolaievich," he said. "I will see if that can be arranged for you. When she has completed her present mission." He closed the cell door behind himself.

Chapter 3

GEORGE HAYMAN STOOD OUTSIDE HIS DAUGHTER'S BEDROOM
door, knocked, waited a moment, and then went inside. Felicity
Hayman seldom answered knocks. She had a weakness for
sitting in windows, staring out at the falling snow.

"Martini time." He held out the glass.

"Just what I was wanting." She took it and kissed him on
the cheek. Felicity was more Borodin than Hayman, George
had always thought. Her height she obtained from both sides
of the family, but the pale skin, the yellow hair, and the softly
rounded features were all inherited from Russia—just, he supposed, as her introspection was also a throwback to the steppe.
"Are the others here yet?" she asked.

"No. But they will be, any moment. And your mother and
I would like it if you'd come down, anyway." He smiled at
her. "We have news."

Her head turned sharply, and George wished he had phrased
his remark somewhat differently. News, when your fiancé has
been reported as missing, believed dead, can only have one
meaning, even four years after the event.

Sometimes, as whenever he was with this girl, George felt
very old. He was in fact sixty-eight. His shoulders were slightly

stooped, although that could have been the effect of the golf on which most of his energies were nowadays concentrated; he still topped six feet. His dark hair was streaked with gray, but he had not allowed himself to become fat, although his paunch was certainly visible. But he had too much time on his hands, lately. Time to worry about this girl. Girl? Felicity was thirty-two years old. And they were strangers.

He presumed a father is always something of a stranger to his daughter, once she ceases to be a little girl. In the case of Felicity and himself, the growing apart had been accentuated by the war. Unlike his wife Ilona, who had spent most of the past five years at home, he had spent most of them in Europe, carrying out various missions for Franklin Roosevelt, a sort of unofficial ambassadorship that was apparently not yet ended, in view of the request he had just received to pay President Truman a visit in Washington. But when he had last been continuously based in New York, in 1938, Felicity had been a laughing young woman, pursuing her riding with unflagging enthusiasm, looking forward to a life to be lived entirely in sunlight. When he had come home again, last summer, she had been an old woman of thirty-two, her fiancé a heap of bones somewhere at the bottom of Pearl Harbor, her life smothered by a gray mist of despondency and hopelessness.

Out of which she had no apparent desire to emerge. There was the real problem, and it was a problem he was willing to admit he neither understood nor sympathized with.

"It's from Russia," he explained. "You never met your cousin Gregory, did you?"

She frowned at him, trying to marshal her thoughts. "Gregory? Not Aunt Tattie's son by that monster?"

"That's right. I liked Gregory, though. And it seems he wants to come visit with us for a while. It's been several months since his mother's death, and he's apparently still quite shaken by it."

"He wants to come . . . to Cold Spring Harbor? A *Russian?*"

George escorted her through the door. Exiles, he had discovered, even those who belonged to his own family, fell into two categories: those who never forgot their antecedents, and those who never wanted to remember. And Felicity had been to Russia only once in her life, although circumstances had made it a lengthy visit. But she had been only four years old when she left. He doubted she remembered anything of it. Her distaste for things Russian had to be the result of hearsay and reading.

"Well," he said, "I think it's a good thing for the Russians to get to know us, and us them. Don't you? Especially when they happen to be related to us." He listened to the growl of a car engine.

Felicity shivered, and finished her martini as they went down the stairs together. "I have no desire ever to visit Russia again," she said.

"Well, maybe you'll be able to encourage Gregory not to go back. Not a word to a soul when we go downstairs, though. Your mother wants to surprise them." He quickened his steps as the front door opened.

"Granddad!" Diana Hayman ran across the parquet floor, to be swept into the air as they reached the foot of the stairs together. George had long ago admitted to himself that after Ilona, Diana was the most precious creature in the world, to him. It was not just that she was his first grandchild. It was not even that she represented conciliation, in that her birth had at last encouraged Ilona to accept George junior's wife, after so much initial hostility. It was mainly because, in her vivacity, the precocious strength of her character, and her utterly blooming beauty, she was the most marvelous human being he had ever encountered since that day, forty years ago, when he had ridden into the doomed city of Port Arthur, with Japanese shells already bursting about him, and come face to face with Ilona herself.

Diana was twelve, and just about to burst into triumphant womanhood. She was the strangest of contrasts, to George, for like her mother, she was hardly five feet tall, and again like her mother, her hair was the darkest of brown, through which occasional facets of red rippled like shaded lights on a moonless night. But her face was pure Borodin, except that her nose was somewhat longer than the clipped Russian variety, while her eyes, wide-set and sparkling, were quite impossible to pinpoint, from a family point of view. Neither blue nor gray, brown nor green, they added the final touch of uniqueness which would, he had no doubt at all, soon make her the belle of New York.

But for the moment she was all her grandad's, and remained in his arms as she leaned forward to kiss her Aunt Felicity.

Then George greeted George junior and Beth, the tall, fair newspaperman towering over the tiny, dark artist who was his wife.

"How're the roads?" George asked.

"Icy," Beth replied. They exchanged a quick kiss.

"I put chains on," George Junior explained. "I think it's going to get worse."

"Ilona!" Beth, followed by Diana, hurried across the hall to greet her mother-in-law, who had appeared in the lounge doorway, and George quickly turned to his son.

"Have you seen John?" he asked in a low voice.

"Yesterday. He's not interested," George junior said.

"He's coming today, so maybe we could have another chat."

George junior shook his head. "He'll never work for me, Dad, and you know that. Not after the life he's led, his background . . . Now, if *you* were to forget this retirement nonsense, and come back—"

George grinned at him. "Losing money, are we?"

"You wait until you see our profit sheets," his son said. "You'll eat your heart out with jealousy. But seriously, Dad—"

"No dice," George said. "Strictly between you and me, I've got a date at the White House next week. Looks like they may have found something for me to do. And you know what? I'm excited about it. But I'll have a talk with John." He looked through the window at the Studebaker skidding to a halt on the drive. "Here they are."

George raised his wine glass and smiled down the table at his wife. These Sunday dinners had become the most precious moments of their lives, since John had come home with his Russian wife and his baby son. Neither of them wished these gatherings ever to end. And why should they? he asked himself, and Ilona, with his smile.

Ilona was fifty-nine now, but she sat very straight, and her face carried few lines, while it was not easy to detect the streaks of silver in the waving masses of golden hair, presently coiled in a chignon on the back of her head; she had been born to the oldest princely family in all Russia, and had no intention of ever cutting a single hair, even if she had been an American citizen for thirty years. She dressed with a quiet elegance, could have stepped straight from the pages of *Vogue,* even if, owing to the war, she had recently had to buy her clothes, including the blue woolen dress she was presently wearing, from Saks instead of direct from Balenciaga in Paris.

Prosperity and elegance were not a recent experience for either of them. Ilona had been born the Princess Borodina; George had been born the heir to Hayman Newspapers Incorporated. That she had thrown away her birthright in the mad impulses of her romantic nature, while he had built and expanded the old *Boston People* into the *American People,* and his father's publishing house into a worldwide concern, was neither here nor there. He had done it for her; she had sacrificed everything for him.

And now their family had come home. Forever. Natasha sat on George's right. With her slender, hard-muscled body, her crisp, composed features, her short auburn hair, she once again looked the prima ballerina she had been before the war, with not a trace of the bitter four years she had spent as a partisan in the Pripet Marshes. Yet they had been the most profitable years of her life; they had brought her marriage to John Hayman, and thus little Alex, who sat in his highchair immediately behind his mother, turning his banana puree into a face pack.

Diana sat next to her new aunt, by whom she was obviously still fascinated, with her father on her other side, next to Ilona. Beth sat on George's left, Felicity in the middle, and John on his mother's right. The Hayman family, George thought—generations two, three, and four.

All except John, who was neither a Borodin in appearance nor a Hayman by birth. Yet he had been brought up as a Hayman, and if with the passage of time he had felt it necessary first of all to act the Borodin, and then to fight for his father's people, he had never disclaimed the prerogatives that went with the Hayman name. Until this refusal to resume working for his younger half-brother.

Presumably the war had left a great number of young men uncertain of themselves, even young men with a more positive sense of identity than the exiled scion of a Russian princely house who had discovered only in manhood that his true father was a Bolshevik commissar. Those like George junior, who had fought as hard and as successfully as anyone, and had as many decorations to prove it, but who *knew* who and what he was, and had always known he had a certain place to fill on his return to civilian life, were the exceptions.

But for John, more than most others, drifting would be a dangerous pastime. Somehow he had to contain three completely opposing philosophies, all the time battering at his consciousness, pulling him apart.

Thus John, George reflected, would probably be most affected of them all by what Ilona was about to say.

He tapped his glass with the back of his knife, and the tinkling of the crystal caused conversation to slacken, heads to turn.

"Your mother has some news for you," George said.

"Your cousin Gregory is coming to America," Ilona said, "to visit with us."

There was a moment's silence.

"Gregory?" George junior was the first to recover. "Gregory *Nej?*"

"Uncle Ivan's son?" John asked.

"The same."

"But . . . he's in the NKVD," Natasha said in her softly accented English.

"That doesn't necessarily mean he's an ogre," Ilona objected.

Natasha flushed, and looked down. Like her mother-in-law, she had also been in the Lubianka.

"You never encountered him in his professional capacity did you?" George asked, also speaking quietly.

Natasha shook her head. "He was far too young."

"But will they let him in?" George junior inquired. "What about the FBI?"

"I'm going to work on that," George said. "I'm prepared to vouch for him."

"Are you sure?" Natasha asked.

George squeezed her hand. "He can hardly discover any vital state secrets here in Cold Spring Harbor. And he seemed pleasant enough, when I met him in 1941. So he has a thug for a father. That could happen to anyone. He also had Tatiana for a mother, and Svetlana for a sister. He must be feeling pretty lonesome, and pretty mixed up, about all that has happened. I think we should reserve judgment until we get to know him. If George doesn't want to show him any newspaper files, that's quite all right with me."

"Well, I . . ." George junior flushed.

"Does he speak English, Granddad?" Diana asked.

"There's a point," her father agreed.

"He speaks English very well," Ilona said.

"Well, John?" George asked.

"I met him in Moscow," John said. "I liked him."

"Well, then—"

"But he was trained by Anna Ragosina."

The table waited. John Hayman had spent the four years in the Pripet under Anna Ragosina's command. He probably knew her better than anyone else in the world did, except for Ivan Nej.

And Gregory himself?

"I had rather formed the impression that you got to like the famous Anna Ragosina," George remarked.

"She was a brute of a woman," Natasha said. "As cold as ice. And vicious."

John gazed at his wife. "I suppose," he said at last, "it is impossible to live and work with someone for so long, and owe your life to them—all our lives, Natasha, you know that—and not have respect for them. Some of the things she did were horrible. But then, what the Nazis did to us, to Svetlana, were horrible too. It was a horrible time. People like Anna Ragosina were necessary then. Yes." He continued to look at his wife. "I did get to like her. Or at least to admire her. But she was what she was because she had been trained to it. She could never for a moment forget her training."

"Meaning Gregory won't ever be able to forget his?" George junior asked.

Again John hesitated, then he shrugged. "He's Aunt Tattie's son. I'll be glad to see him again."

"An exhibition?" Ilona asked. "Oh, my dear, how wonderful for you."

Beth Hayman sipped coffee. "Well, it's still at the talking stage. But the Streseman Gallery seems very interested."

"And will it have . . . well . . ." Ilona flushed. When she had first met her prospective daughter-in-law, she had been shocked by the nudes Beth painted, and had allowed the embarrassment to grow into a dislike, overcome only by years of patient spadework.

"I'm afraid so," Beth said. "I'm sorry, Ilona. They say I do them best."

"But there'll be none of me," George junior teased. "There's a promise."

"Well, I . . . shall certainly come to the exhibition," Ilona said.

"And buy something," her son insisted, "for an outrageous price. That will get everyone else going."

George poured brandy for the men, and walked over to hand a glass to John, who stood alone at a window.

"Still coming down," John said, watching the snow.

"So you'll spend the night," George said.

John glanced at him. "Well . . . I wouldn't say no."

"Then it's done." George sipped his brandy and watched the fading afternoon. "I hear you've had a chat with George junior."

John waited.

"So what *are* you going to do?" George asked.

"Well . . . for the time being, I'm working on those memoirs you so generously commissioned."

"And are half-finished," George said. "I may be retired, John, but I keep in touch, especially with things I've commissioned."

"Yes, well . . . I thought it best to get on while it's all so fresh in my mind," John explained.

"So you'll be finished in another couple of months," George suggested. "Then what?"

"Well . . . maybe then's the time to think of something."

"But not the paper?"

"Come on, George. You know I was never any good as a newspaperman. Even as a chess correspondent I was fairly hopeless. If . . . well . . ."

"If you were running things, it would be different?"

"I didn't mean that." John shrugged. "But of course it would be different. I'd have known, almost from birth, that I had that job to do, just as George junior has always known that."

"Do you resent the fact that you didn't?" George had always treated the various members of his family with absolute straightness.

John knew that, and he merely shook his head. "No, I don't. George is *your* eldest son. The papers are his. The entire company is his. I'm just a peculiar offshoot of Bolshevism."

"That's a profound point of view."

"It's the truth."

"Hm. You're not still corresponding with Peter?"

John flushed. "Uncle Peter has written me, yes."

"Still as rabid as ever?"

"If you're asking if he still dreams of regaining Starogan, of setting a tsar back on the throne, the answer is no," John said. "But he does still regard Communism as the worst thing that has happened to the world since the Mongols."

George frowned at him. "You don't mean he's going back to that counterrevolutionary nonsense? There's no room in the world for that sort of thing anymore, John. And in Europe, with the Reds commanding half the continent, it'd be downright dangerous. Even in Stockholm."

"He's left Stockholm. He's gone back to England."

"England? My God, the crazy fool. They have a left-wing government themselves."

John smiled. "Your Republicanism is showing, George. They have a Labor government. Not quite the same thing as a Communist one. Okay, so he's invited me to tell him what my plans are, and has suggested he might have some for me. I haven't replied yet."

"But you're going to. John, for God's sake. You'd fight against your own father?"

"I don't know. George, I have the highest respect for my father. For a lot of individual Russians." He gave a guilty smile. "Even for Anna Ragosina. Yet the fact is that they murdered my grandmother and all my aunts and uncles. And Natasha's parents as well. However patiently they may be going about it, they are hell-bent on seeing the whole world Communist. And their system throws up people like Ivan Nej and even Anna, and gives them total authority over ordinary lives."

"You don't accept that it was necessary for the revolution?" George asked. "That it may be tempered in this generation? That it may be possible to work with them as with any other foreign government?"

John stared out of the window. "No," he said at last. "I never told you this, George. I never told anyone, although I think Sasha knows. But in the Pripet, Anna took a shine to me." He blushed a little, and shrugged. "Well, I was her second-in-command, and we spent a hell of a lot of time together, especially when Sasha was pregnant."

"And?"

"It was her outlook I couldn't stand. Nothing mattered except what she wanted then. There was no moral value involved. No concept of ethics—or even love, I don't think. I was a male animal, she was a female animal. We shared the command. We fought shoulder to shoulder, and we killed shoulder to shoulder. In her eyes it was equally reasonable that we should sleep shoulder to shoulder."

"It happens, in those circumstances," George said.

"With Natasha in the next sleeping bag?"

"I see what you mean."

"To people like Anna Ragosina, nothing exists beyond the material world. Nothing else at all. Our society—Western civilization, if you like, coming out of Rome and before that Greece—is based on ethics, George. Take that away and we're just a herd of swine grubbing about for the biggest turnip in the trough. There *are* no ethics in Russia, except for the domination of the state. And the state is only a group of very human men and women, whose whole concept is that *they* should stay at least where they are. Within that framework, everything goes. True, a lot of our own politics are corrupt. But we know that, and we try to do something about it. In Russia there's no corruption at the top, because the word isn't recognized."

George nodded. "So they're different."

John finished his brandy at a gulp. "Sometimes your tolerance drives me mad. Okay, you can afford to be tolerant. You've done it all. You've survived it all. And you have enough confidence in the good old USA to believe we'll always survive it all. Well, we survived Hitler. But it cost us a few hundred thousand lives, and the world as a whole quite a few million. Stalin is a much tougher nut than Hitler."

"I hadn't realized you were quite so emotionally involved," George said.

John smiled. When he smiled, all the anger disappeared. "I'm just explaining why I can't really get onto my father's wavelength, much as I care about him."

"And you're also explaining why you'll never be exactly a bosom buddy of Gregory's."

John's smile faded. "I said I'd give him the benefit of the doubt, George. You may be right about him. I hope and pray that you are."

"But you'll always remember that he's Ivan's son."

"I'll always remember that he was trained by Anna Ragosina, George. That's what really counts."

* * *

It was best when the house was silent, especially after a day when it had been filled with conversation and laughter. Then the house itself seemed to appreciate the quiet midnight hours.

It snowed steadily, adding to the several inches already coating the lawn, replenishing what had been swept from the drives, slowly submerging the cars in the forecourt; George and Beth and little Diana had also decided to spend the night rather than undertake the long drive back to New York.

Felicity's bedroom overlooked Long Island Sound and the snow-coated beach. In summer the beach was one of her favorite haunts, but she adored it, even in winter. There were never any people when she went walking, which was early in the morning or in the evening in warm weather, and in the middle of the day in the winter months. She had not walked today because it had been necessary to sit and entertain the family, but she would certainly walk tomorrow.

Felicity was well aware that her parents—all the family, in fact—thought that she was ill. Father had once hinted in his gentle manner that if she ever felt the need, he was friendly with a very good psychiatrist who could perhaps relieve some of her anxiety and depression. Nothing had come of the idea, both because Father would never pressure her into doing anything against her will, and because Mother disapproved of the very word *psychiatrist*. Mother was old-fashioned, and people who were sick in the head were mad. There were no shades of gray.

George junior was more practical, and had told her that what she needed was to get up off her backside and find herself a job. But her brother had always had a briskly pragmatic view of life. He had even suggested that she go to work on the magazine their mother had founded, *You*. Ilona's monthly magazine, covering fashion and the arts as well as politics, had been a financial success, despite the skepticism of her husband and her son, but she had virtually retired since George had given up day to day control of the newspaper group.

Beth had been more practical yet, and had actually offered her a job as a model. But that was unthinkable. Beth had been perfectly frank about it, if a little guilty. Felicity was a true Borodin woman, tall and slender, with large breasts and powerful thighs. "You would make an almost perfect nude study," Beth had said.

But Beth hung her pictures in public galleries, and even, from time to time, sold them. Besides, she did not *have* to work, so why should she? Sitting in an office, or even on a stool in the altogether would interfere with her thoughts.

John, predictably, had said nothing at all. But that he was sharing the family concern was evident from the way he looked at her.

She wished she could reassure them, but her attempts at reassurance only made them look at her the harder. She had tried to explain that she no longer grieved for David Cassidy, not in the active, heartrending sense she had known for the first year after his death, and which they assumed she still felt. But she was still in love with him. His smile, his walk, his touch, his kiss, were all a daily recollection. They had never done more than kiss: she had always had the greatest reluctance to share her body with anyone, and certainly not with anyone who didn't have a legal right to it, because it *was* an almost perfect body, and she had the strangest feeling that once it had been possessed by another, it would never be perfect again.

The family would not understand that, either. They had wondered about her, even as a girl—why she had never had any steady boyfriends, why she had taken so long to become engaged. Saying that she had to *know* had brought mixed reactions, even from Mother, who certainly claimed to have *known* the moment she had first seen Father. But that had been a long time ago, and nowadays Mother merely smiled wisely and said, "My dear, you only get to know a man after you have married him. It is one of life's great gambles."

Which was ridiculous. Mother, for all her tangled youth, believed that you only knew a man in the first place if he was worth knowing, socially. But Felicity *had* known once, in her first term at college. The young man was Daniel Rourke. She had made the mistake of inviting him to Cold Spring Harbor for a weekend. Of course Daniel had known about her famous parents, but they spent little time talking about them, and in retrospect, she supposed that he could not have been prepared for the immense wealth and elegance the Haymans so took for granted. The family, even Mother, had been scrupulously polite, and had tried to make him feel at home, but they clearly had not approved. And Daniel had not approved of them. Well, she supposed that he *had* been "a bit of a Lefty," as George junior had put it.

More than even she had suspected, because afterwards he had placed her firmly in the class of capitalist exploiters, and had dropped her the following term. Felicity had been devastated, had supposed she would never recover, and had never forgiven her mother for being so obviously relieved that the romance was over. But she *had* recovered, and she had known again, with David Cassidy—and even she had to admit it had been such a relief to feel that this time the family was entirely behind her.

But that hadn't been allowed to work out, either. And if she was ever to marry, even if she was ever to love again, she would have to *know* again. That was what she was waiting for. It was an expectation every time she went for a walk on the beach. If she hated meeting *people* on her private excursions, she had no doubt at all that one day she would meet the man who would be able to take David's place. Repeated disappointment was not discouraging. It would happen one day, because it had already happened twice. And then she would be glad she had waited to share.

Thus if family gatherings like today, watching the happiness of John and Sasha, and George junior and Beth, left her feeling temporarily miserable, she always soon recovered, almost the moment she was again alone. Besides, the amount of time she spent by herself, with nothing to do but think, made her able to see them, to see the whole world, in its true perspective. There was certainly, and obviously, something wrong in the amount of wealth and power commanded by this little group of people, and all the other little groups of people who owned chain stores or banks or investment companies, while people like Daniel Rourke would have to struggle all their lives. There was something almost obscene in the confident happiness of the wealthy, when so much of the world was in such a disastrous state. And there was something distasteful in the way in which they, and their friends in high places, presumed to dictate policy and progress to that impoverished rest of the world, secure in the possession of the most powerful weapon the world had ever known.

The thought sometimes made her shiver with apprehension.

That her feelings were ambivalent did not trouble her. Had David Cassidy lived, had they married, she would have helped to preserve the structure, the inviolability of her caste—David's father was a banker. But she prided herself on the certainty that she would still have devoted a great deal of her time to thought. And all her solitary hours of thinking had made her absolutely certain of one thing: when she again *knew*, she was going to marry *whoever* the man was, no matter what anyone said.

The door was opened for him, and George Hayman stepped into the Oval Office. He had been here too often in the past to be overawed; he had often thought that, for a committed Republican, he had spent far too *much* time here since 1933. But certainly he had never expected to find himself here again, for he had retired from the newspaper business as well as from politics. That a task of some sort must be involved was the reason he had decided against telling Ilona anything yet.

"Mr. Hayman. Good of you to come. You've met Dean Acheson, General Marshall."

George nodded, and shook hands. Actually, he knew both the secretary of state and the General far better than the new president himself, but that was the way of American politics.

"Sit down," Harry Truman invited. "How's retirement?"

"I'm not bored yet," George said carefully.

"But you soon will be." Truman's smile was sudden and unexpected, breaking through the essential grimness of his face. "Maybe you should do some traveling."

"Like the traveling I did for President Roosevelt?"

Truman gazed at him for some seconds, then pointed. "Whatever is said here, stays here. Got that?"

George nodded.

"Well, I'll tell you," the president said. "And don't get me wrong. In my book, Franklin Roosevelt was the greatest president this country has ever had, or ever will have. And he was my friend. But he just never came to grips with this Communist business. I guess it was because he figured every nation has a right to choose its own form of government, which can't be wrong, and because he always thought the tsars were even worse than the Reds. Well, maybe he was right there too. But the tsars were England's problem, and Germany's. The Reds are ours. Now, I went along with what FDR had worked out at Potsdam. I didn't have much of a choice. But I didn't like it, and Dean didn't like it."

"But we kept our fingers crossed," Acheson added.

"And it isn't working," Truman said. "As you know, Yugoslavia has now put in a Communist government. Add that to Bulgaria and Albania. Now, you're not going to tell me any of those governments would be where they are today if there wasn't a Red army occupying their country. You with me?"

"There is also a Red army occupying Poland, Rumania, Hungary, half of Germany, and half of Austria, not to mention all of Czechoslovakia," George said.

"Right every time."

"That's all of eastern Europe," General Marshall said quietly.

"Except for Greece," Acheson said.

"And *they're* having a shooting war to decide which way it goes," Truman said. "The salient fact is, Hayman, the Russians are still fighting the war, and we've stopped. What's more, it's going to be damned difficult to persuade our people, even to persuade Congress, that we should start again. I can tell you that Churchill feels the same way I do. He can see it happening in France and Italy—maybe even in England, one of these days. He's coming over here in the spring, and I'm going to get him to address both Houses and see if he can put across to them what's happening. But before then, I want to *know* exactly what's happening."

He paused, but George preferred to wait. The president glanced at his secretary of state.

"Of course, we've got all the treaties, all signed and sealed," Acheson said. "We've got a constant two-way conversation with the Kremlin. And we've no real *proof* that they're doing anything they shouldn't be doing, that these Yugoslavs and Albanians and what-have-you don't really *want* to live under extreme socialism. The evidence is all circumstantial. And it's all so clouded in doubletalk and diplomatic terms that it's difficult to see the forest for the trees."

"We'd like talks to take place away from governments," Truman said. "A conversation about the future, between old friends. And it turns out there's an old friend of yours heading the Russian delegation to the opening session of the United Nations in London next month. If you happened to be in England at the same time, Hayman, he could hardly refuse to see you."

"What do you think Michael Nej would tell me?" George asked. "He may be a friend, but he's also high up in the Politburo. And he believes in what he's doing."

"Still, a lot more is likely to come out in a chat between

friends," the president said, "than between two ambassadors who basically distrust each other. But it's also possible that if you were to take a trip to Europe, look up other old friends in, say, Prague and Warsaw, with Nej's okay, you might be able to see things our official people can't. No one would know you're reporting back to this room."

"You don't feel I'm a little old for cloak and dagger stuff?" George asked.

Truman smiled. "How old is old? You look pretty fit to me."

"There's also the point that I've spent most of the last five years in Europe. And was there only six months ago. I'd kind of hoped to spend some time with my family."

"Take them with you," Truman suggested. "That's a good cover. You'll be on a vacation."

"And what about deceiving an old friend?"

Truman's smile faded into a frown. "I hate to sing the 'Star Spangled Banner' at you, Hayman, but this could be vital, to you as much as to the rest of us. Do you want to see your sons and your grandsons back in a shooting war?"

"Can it possibly come to that?" George asked. "We have the bomb. They don't. Can't you, at any moment you like, hold up your hand and say, that's enough?"

Truman glanced at Marshall.

"Not so simple," the general said.

"It's not damn practical at all," Truman said, "and the Reds know it. How the hell could I ever consider dropping an atomic bomb on Europe? Not unless somebody over there was threatening to drop one on us. Now that'll come. Make no mistake about that. We'll hold it back as long as we can. The security down there in New Mexico makes it as tough to get into Los Alamos without a pass as it is to get into heaven with a cloven foot. We know that if the chips were ever really to go down, the bomb is our trump card. But only at the very end. And the Russians will have a bomb, eventually. My people tell me there's no doubt about that. I'm not eager to let them have all of Europe first."

"But if you won't stop them by force," George said, "what have you got in mind?"

Truman leaned forward. "Making people aware of what's happening. Not just people here in the U.S. The people of

Europe as well. I want facts that will *prove* what the Reds are after. Facts I can make public."

"And you think I can get them for you," George said.

"If I didn't, you wouldn't be here. How about it, Hayman? For a last time? And the most important time of all."

"Franklin Roosevelt said that to me once. Not so very long ago."

"He was an optimist," Truman said. "Will you do it?"

George hesitated. "I think you should know, Mr. President, that Michael Nej's nephew, Gregory, has written to ask if he can come and visit with us. He's arriving just after Christmas."

"Hell, I'm sorry about that. But can't your son give him a whirl while you're away? It won't be for very long."

"Oh, it's a bit inconvenient, of course," George said. "But I wasn't thinking about that. Gregory Nej is a captain in the NKVD."

The president leaned back. "You *do* have some contacts."

"You mean you still want me to go?"

"More than ever."

"Well, then, maybe you'll make sure this boy has no trouble with Immigration."

"Why don't you pick him up in England and bring him back with you? I'll guarantee his entry."

"That sounds fine," George said. "Well, it'd be nice to see a Europe where there aren't actually guns going off all the time."

"Good man." Truman stood up and held out his hand. "Dean'll brief you."

George shook his hand, looking the president in the eye. "You said getting into the atomic labs is harder than getting into heaven, without the right credentials. How's security here in Washington?"

Natasha Hayman waited in the door of the little office until her husband paused in his writing to stare out the window. The apartment overlooked Central Park, and John spent a lot of time gazing at the snow-covered hills. Natasha could understand that. Remembering what had happened in the Pripet, the rain and the burning sun, the mud and the snow, the hunger and the cold, the savage fight for survival and the even more savage fight against the Germans, was not at all difficult; it came back to them both in their dreams. But putting it down for serialization in New York's biggest daily was something else again.

"Sasha?" He half turned his head. "Come on in."

"I didn't want to interrupt a train of thought."

He smiled at her. "I'm waiting in a station. What's up?"

"A man telephoned," she said. "His name is Arthur Garrison. He says he knows you."

"Arthur Garrison? Doesn't mean anything to me."

"He says he used to play chess with you, at college."

"That's going back a bit."

"Well, he wants you to call him and make a date to meet. It has to do with writing a book, I think. On Russian chess. Modern Russian chess. He says it's the best in the world. Better even than the Americans."

"He could be right. But I'm not really up to date on it."

"He said, since you'd spent four years in Russia—"

"For God's sake," John said. "Does he think we spent our time playing chess?"

"Well," Natasha said "I thought you might like to think about it, so I wrote down his telephone number. You'll be finished with these memoirs in a month or so."

She had slowly crossed the room. Now he put his arm around her waist to hug her against him. "We won't starve, if that's what's bothering you, my love. Not immediately, anyway. The old man is paying me well for this little lot. Way above the odds. But I didn't say no."

"I'm not thinking about the money—really," Natasha said. "But you'd go mad if you didn't have something to do, wouldn't you?"

"I guess I would. But chess . . . that's in the past. And that too was charity, you know, Sasha. George gave me a job as chess correspondent for the *People* because I happened to know a little about the game, and I sure as hell didn't know anything about anything else. And then, afterwards, writing about chess was a good way of getting in and out of Russia, when I was working for Uncle Peter. But I can tell you there's very little money in it. And it's not something I really want to do. I'm thirty-seven years old, Sasha. I've got to find something I can *do* with my life. Something that *means* something. Can you understand that?"

"Of course I can. I do. But I don't want you to work for

Peter Borodin again. Not ever."

"Because I'd be working against Russia? You hate the Bolsheviks far more than I do."

"Because it's too dangerous," she said. "John, you'll find what you want to do, soon enough. But until then, life has to be lived. See this man Garrison. At the least you'll be doing something you enjoy. You do *like* chess, don't you?"

He smiled. "Until you came along, my love, it was the only thing I did enjoy. Okay. I'll see Garrison. But I'm not promising anything."

John suggested the Oak Room, but Garrison preferred a little trattoria in the Village. "I'm paying," he explained on the telephone. "And my name ain't Hayman."

It made an unpromising beginning. But Garrison turned out to be a huge, friendly man with a grip like a grizzly bear's, and a smile suggestive of the cavern the bear might live in. "You won't remember me," he said, "but I sure as hell remember you, John. You played some pretty good chess back then." He had seated them in a corner, well away from the street door, and sat with his back against the wall.

"You're probably suffering from amnesia," John said. "I always played lousy chess."

Garrison did some more silent guffawing. "I've always read your column."

"Yeah? There hasn't been one in this country for years."

They ordered spaghetti and meatballs and drank beer. "I have a feeling you don't like me," Garrison remarked.

"And I have a feeling you wouldn't know a French Defense from a French letter," John said.

Garrison roared with laughter. "Well, I sure didn't ask you to lunch to find out," he admitted. He filled the cavern with spaghetti for several seconds, maintaining a constant link between plate and lips, and chewed thoughtfully. "How's your mother?"

John preferred smaller wraparounds on his fork. "She's well."

"And your famous aunt?"

"She's dead," John said. His brain was sending out warning signals, but he had been around long enough to be patient.

"It wasn't an accident, I've heard."

John merely looked at him.

"So if you don't want to talk about it, I don't blame you. But she must have had some pretty good innings. That partisan stuff, down in the Pripet . . ." Garrison did some more chewing. "That really must have been something."

"It was."

"And of course, you were fighting for Mother Russia."

"I was fighting for my life," John said. "And for the life of my fiancée. Faced with the same choice, I'd have done as much in Norway, France, or Italy."

"Sure you would," Garrison agreed, and drank some beer. "But it was Russia. Because you're Russian, by birth and parentage, and your fiancée was Russian, just like now she's your wife."

"Ten out of ten." John finished his meal, and pushed back his chair. "It was a great lunch." He got up. "Don't call me again. Or I'll have the number changed."

"Sit down," Garrison suggested. "There's ice cream to follow. Neapolitan." But suddenly all the humor had left his face. "So we've been assing around. Try that."

John looked at the piece of cardboard Garrison handed him. "Federal Bureau of Investigation? You expect me to believe that?"

Garrison shrugged. "You can call the boss, if you like. I'll wait."

John gazed at him for several seconds. Then he sat down again. "Are you investigating me?"

"Should I be?"

"I'm sure you could think of a reason. Or even plant one."

"So we sometimes get a bad press," Garrison agreed, with rancor. "I want to talk. You know, Mr. Hayman, you're a pretty confusing character. Tell me when I'm wrong. Your father is a member of the Politburo in Moscow, your mother is the wife of an American millionaire who votes Republican. Your aunt has just been assassinated, after a distinguished dancing career, and after separating from the commissar for internal security, who just happens to be your uncle. Your other uncle is a Nazi . . ."

"Correction," John said. "He is a tsarist, which is not the same thing. He worked with Hitler, for a while, because he saw no other hope of bringing down Bolshevism."

"And you worked for him, with the same goal," Garrison said.

"For a while."

"And yet you fought with the Reds at the end. Hell, ain't you a Hero of the Soviet Union?"

"I am."

"Decorated by old Joe Stalin himself. Now there's a mixed-up life. I've heard of guys straddling the fence, but you seem to have four feet, and four separate camps to put them in."

"So?"

"Okay, wiseguy," Garrison said. "So you're George Hayman's stepson, and you think that puts you above the law. Maybe. What we want to know is, which foot are you leaning on, right this moment?"

"Being George Hayman's stepson doesn't put me above the law, Mr. Garrison," John said evenly. "But it does mean I don't have to be pushed around by thugs like you. So my answer to that one is, mind your own goddamned business."

Suddenly the friendly bear was back. Garrison smiled, and called for two coffees.

"So let's be friends. My guess is that you're not involved with the Reds. Or for the blackshirts, either. That you're one-hundred-percent American. I didn't believe it at first, but now I do."

"So?"

Once again the bear vanished. But this time Garrison was merely serious, rather than aggressive. "I'm also told that you're at loose ends Mr. Hayman. I'd say you've got too much going for you to be at loose ends."

John stared at him in utter incredulity. "You're offering me a *job?*"

"So what's so bad about that? You get to eat lunch in crummy joints like this at the government's expense. And to carry little bits of cardboard which nobody believes are real. There'd have to be some training, of course. There're codes and procedures. And we like our people to know something about looking after themselves." He grinned. "But I don't think we can teach too much to a guy who survived four years in the Pripet."

"You can't," John said. "And when I've done this training, I go hunting for gangsters? Life's too short."

"When you've done the training," Garrison said, "you help us to keep the good old U.S. of A. just the way it is. You're not a streetcorner man, Hayman, but you've got a knowledge of Russia and Russians that few people in this country possess. Now they may be your old buddies, but you should know as well as I do that they don't think Communism should stop at Brest-Litovsk. Or even at the English Channel. If you *don't* know that, well, the collected writings of Lenin and Trotsky, not to mention Uncle Joe himself, are a part of your training schedule. Now I can tell you that there are quite a few million people roaming around Europe at this moment, living in camps. People who have lost their homes, or been driven from their homes, and have to be resettled. People who in the main would like to come here in preference to going home. Okay, so we'll do what we can. But it just so happens that more than half of these people come from east of Prague—that is, from the part of Europe occupied by the Reds. And quite a few of them *are* Russians. Now don't get me wrong. Ninety-nine point nine percent of them are honest-to-goodness refugees, and the fact that they prefer us to the Reds rates them high in my estimation. But dressing some guy up as a refugee would be the simplest of all ways of getting an agent, or several agents, into the U.S. And the word we're getting from our people over there is that some of these refugees just fill that bill."

"So you turn them away," John suggested.

Garrison smiled slowly. "It ain't always that easy. And it ain't always entirely convenient."

John frowned at him. "You mean you *want* these people to come here?"

"Some."

"But why?"

"Because there are quite a few here already. Have been for some time. Okay, so all's fair in love and war. We have our people in Russia. But we never bothered too much about the Reds, before the war. Our enemy was organized crime. What happened in Europe, even what happened inside Hitler's Germany, didn't bother us a damn much before 1938; our business is internal security. Then everything changed and we were told to concentrate on the Japs and the Nazis. The Reds had a free hand. Next thing, they were our allies. But now, there's just them and us. Nobody else, Mr. Hayman. Great Britain and

France, Germany and Italy, even the Japs and the Chinks, ain't going to matter a damn next time the chips are down. And that's the scenario for a long time to come, in my book. Our business is to locate the Russian agents already in this country, and since some of them have been here for years, they could be anybody. But the new guys coming in have got to make contacts, join cells, receive orders, and transmit information. If we know who *they* are, we're halfway home."

"And how do we find that out?" John asked. "Ask them as they step off the boat?"

"I'm glad you said 'we.' No, Mr. Hayman, we burrow away, and we correlate information, and we use our heads, and we come up with some answers, and we hope we're right. It's in deciding what's right and what isn't that you can help us. It's not a glamorous job. You won't even carry a weapon. It's a matter of sitting at a desk and reading files, every file on every Russian or Pole or near-Russian who wants to come in, of looking at photographs and thinking about hard-luck stories, and looking out for anything, anything at all, that don't look quite kosher. We're not asking for miracles. Maybe four out of five will slip through. But if we can put a tag on every fifth man or woman, we're winning." He leaned back in his chair. "How about it?"

"Can I think?"

"Be my guest." Garrison called for some more coffee. "The money's poor. Hell, what government money isn't? But the hours, for your job, are regular."

For a while John said nothing. He supposed it was incredible but the idea attracted him. His feelings for Russia were indeed ambivalent. Certainly he could not hate a people at whose side he had fought for four years. However, he could now be quite certain that their way of life was not for him, and he could be equally certain that he did not wish to see it exported, not to anywhere he might be living.

What better, then, than to concentrate upon keeping them out of his country? Or at least, under control when *in* his country? It would certainly please both Sasha and Mother. It might even please Uncle Peter. He didn't know about George, who seemed willing to allow that even Communism might have its place in the historical scheme of things.

Garrison might have been able to read his thoughts. "There's just one thing," he said. "If you work for us, it has to be just between you and me. You don't tell anyone, not even your wife. Got me?"

"But . . . where would I work?"

"We'll fix you up with a cover. It'd be a nine-to-five job, just like any other. We'll even fix it so you can chat about the cover with your wife, and anybody else."

"Um." John still hesitated.

Garrison smiled at him. "I think you're going to say yes," he said.

"I might. There's something you ought to know, though."

"Try me."

"Well, I have a cousin named Gregory Nej."

"Son of Commissar Ivan Nej and Tatiana Borodina. Twenty-five years old. Captain in the NKVD. Planning to visit with your mother and stepfather for a while, early next year."

"Why, yes," John said. "You're very well informed."

"We're hoping to be better informed. What were you going to tell me about this character?"

"Only that he's coming to stay with my family. I'll be seeing a lot of him."

"You think that makes you a security risk?"

"Well . . . I wondered if maybe you want me to start my investigations with him."

"Forget it," Garrison said. "One thing I can tell you about the Reds you may not know, Hayman: they don't go spying wearing uniforms and medals and announcing that they're members of the NKVD. That would make life too simple, and our life ain't simple at all. You let us tell you who to investigate. You just worry about the how."

"Well, that's a relief," John said. "Gregory is coming as our guest. If I'd had to track him around with a magnifying glass I'd have had to say no."

"But now you'll say yes. Well, that's great." Garrison stood up and held out his hand. "So you go on home and resume work on your memoirs. I'll be in touch."

"Yeah." John had his hand gripped. "There's just one other thing."

"What?"

"Who put you on to me? And suggested I might be willing to work for you?"

"Like I said, this is a secret organization you're working for. So don't ask questions, except those we tell you to." He grinned. "But I can tell you that it was a friend. Of yours and ours, Hayman."

Chapter 4

"NERVOUS?" GEORGE HAYMAN POURED COFFEE.

"What makes you think I'm nervous?" Ilona stared out of
the window of the bedroom, situated high in the Dorchester
Hotel, across the snowy expanse of London's Hyde Park.

"It's just that you're not eating your breakfast," George
said. "The English pride themselves on their breakfasts. You'll
be upsetting the chef, and the entire hotel staff will go out on
strike."

"George!" Ilona admonished. But she was undoubtedly nervous. And not merely at the thought of meeting Michael Nej
again, he suspected; it was the prospect of entertaining her
brother that was mainly upsetting her. But she was also anxious,
as she had been throughout the trip, as she always was whenever
she had to be away from Felicity. They had tried to persuade
her to come with them, and she had refused pointblank. As a
result, Ilona had decided not to make the European tour he was
about to undertake, at the president's request, but was going
to return as soon as they had picked up Gregory.

"Just teasing." He squeezed her hand. "They really are very
nice people." He lifted his head as there came a knock on the
door. "Come in."

The waiter was deferential; he was well aware, from the
size of the tips, that the American was a millionaire, quite apart

from the fact that he was occupying the hotel's best rooms. "I beg your pardon, sir," he said, "but there are some people downstairs to meet you."

"Already? It's barely nine o'clock," George said.

"Shall I send them away, sir?" the waiter asked.

"Good lord, no," George said. "Mr. and Mrs. Nej, and a Captain Nej, is it?"

"Yes, sir," the waiter agreed, looking down his list. "And Miss Nej, and a Mrs. Petrov."

"Mrs. Petrov?" Ilona cried, and looked at George. "Judith?"

"Good Lord, it must be," George agreed. "Ask them to come up, will you, Carlos?" He and Ilona were already dressed.

"Did you write her?" Ilona asked.

"Never got around to it. But I'm glad she's turned up. It'll be quite a reunion. And we'll be killing two birds with one stone."

Ilona opened her mouth, and closed it again as she heard voices in the corridor; the waiter had been very quick. George hurried forward to open the door.

"Michael!" he cried. "Catherine! Nona!" He embraced the women, and reached past them to shake Gregory's hand. To his relief the young man was not in uniform. "Gregory! Great to see you again."

Gregory gravely shook hands, but George was already releasing him to gaze at Judith, the only woman who had ever threatened the serene happiness of his marriage.

"It is good to see you," he said at last.

"And you, George," she said, and stepped past him to greet Ilona. They had all known each other too long for either embarrassment or explanation. George thought it was remarkable and splendid, the way Ilona and Michael could sit together and discuss John, within minutes of meeting again after so long, mutually mutter about his prospects, with Catherine listening and adding her opinions—he wondered what Michael really thought about his son becoming an executive in a somewhat obscure Madison Avenue advertising firm, just about the most bourgeois of occupations; certainly Ilona had been taken aback at John's decision—or the way Judith and Nona could stand at the window, while Judith pointed out the distant Serpentine and talked of Peter Pan, almost as if Nona was the daughter *she* could so easily have had by Michael. What the Dorchester waiters, discovering themselves to be surrounded by a spate of Russian as they attempted to clear away the breakfast dishes, thought about it all, he couldn't possibly guess.

Only Gregory had little to say, glancing from face to face, as he listened to the conversation.

"What do you think of it?" George asked him. "London . . . this hotel . . . the people?"

Gregory considered. "This is a very nice hotel," he said. "I had not expected to find London so badly damaged, although the damage is not so terrible as in Leningrad, of course. But it rains all the time. And the people do not smile. Do they smile in America?"

"It's a better climate," George said. "We are really looking forward to having you over there, Gregory. My family is all quite excited."

Gregory looked embarrassed. He wore a brown suit which had certainly not been tailored in Savile Row, and he managed to give it a faintly villainous air. Or was that notion just an association of ideas? But it was impossible to imagine this cleancut young man being involved in any of the ghastly activities that were perpetrated in Lubianka.

"I am excited too," Gregory agreed. "In Russia, everyone is interested in America. We hear about it all the time. You do not mind my asking to stay with you?"

"We'd have been hurt if you'd stayed anywhere else."

"And I will not crowd your apartment? You can put me on the floor."

"Ah . . . we don't actually live in an apartment, Gregory. And I don't think you'll have to sleep on the floor. Your aunt will explain it all."

"But you must treat me as family," Gregory insisted. "Leave me to myself. I will explore, eh?"

"I'm sure you will. Do you drive a car?"

Gregory frowned. "No. I have never learned to drive. It is necessary?"

"It's a help," George said. "We'll have you learn, if you wish, when you get there. I've managed to get you and Ilona officers' berths on a troop carrier, at the end of the week."

"Ah. But you are not coming also?"

"I have to make a visit to Europe, on business. I'll be back in less than a month, though. You'll be staying some time, won't you?"

Strangely, the question seemed to embarrass Gregory. "If

I will not be a nuisance," he said.

"No chance of that," George assured him.

"Now," Michael said, "you must all come to the embassy for dinner tonight."

Ilona looked at George questioningly.

"Problem, Michael," George said. "Peter Borodin is coming *here* for dinner. Peter and Ruth, and this German fellow Ruth has married. So a better idea would be for you all to join us here."

They stared at him.

"But George," Ilona said, "if Peter sees Michael . . ." She glanced at him.

"I'm afraid she's right," Michael said. "The last time Peter saw me he all but seized me by the throat. Ribbentrop had to restrain him. My God, how long ago those people seem! But Gregory will dine with you, I am sure."

"He'd better," George said. "I've booked a room for him in the hotel. But don't you think Peter may have mellowed?"

"Peter will never mellow," Ilona said, and found herself looking to Judith for confirmation.

"He had not mellowed when I saw him last," Judith agreed. "And that was only last summer in Stockholm. But perhaps . . . George, you do realize that this German Ruth has married is Paul von Hassell?"

There was a moment's silence.

"Paul von Hassell?" Ilona asked at last. "The same man who was engaged to Svetlana?"

Judith nodded, her face a picture of misery.

"The SS man?" Ilona cried.

"Now, Ilona," George said soothingly. "Hassell left Minsk long before Svetlana's execution. He left Minsk *because* she had been arrested, as I understand it. He tried to free her, and was arrested himself."

"He was an SS officer," Ilona insisted, revealing a rare amount of passion. "Why hasn't he been hanged, or shot or something? Or at least put into jail?"

"Because he hasn't done anything *wrong*," Judith said. "Please believe that. He quit the moment he saw what the Nazis were really doing. He was imprisoned by them for nearly a year. And then he got himself involved in the plot against Hitler."

"He deserted poor Svetlana," Ilona said, bristling with righteous outrage. "And now he's married Ruth! My God! How could she *do* it?"

"He *didn't* desert Svetlana," Judith pleaded. "They were separated, and she was executed. That is why he turned against the Nazis. And then he saved Ruth's life. He saved both our lives. He got us out of Ravensbrück, got us to Sweden, and nearly died himself in doing so. He and Peter. He is a good man, Ilona. I promise you that. And after we got to Stockholm—well, we were all living in the same house, seeing each other all the time, and poor Ruth . . . she had had such a dreadful time—" She stopped abruptly; Ravensbrück was something she had intended never to talk about again.

Catherine Nej squeezed her hand. "And so they fell in love. I think that's wonderful. It is love we must look to now, not hate. Is that not true, Ilona?"

Ilona gazed back at her, her face momentarily rigid, while Gregory looked from one aunt to the other, uncertain which point of view he should be adopting.

But Ilona was already getting over her mood. "I suppose you're right, Catherine," she said. "I know what we'll do. If you all can't come to dinner, let's all go shopping together."

"Oh, that would be splendid," Catherine cried. "Will you take me to the Harrods? I have been told it is almost as good as GUM."

Ilona gazed at George for a moment, her eyebrows arched. Then she smiled. "Well, almost," she agreed. "You'll have to judge for yourself. If you men will just give us five minutes to get ready . . ."

"It sounds like you have a busy schedule," Michael remarked. He and George waited in the foyer of the hotel for the women to come downstairs; Gregory had been taken to his room by an undermanager.

"You're welcome to come tonight," George said, "if you think you can stand it."

Michael shook his head. "Better not. I am too old to be embarrassed. But I should not like to spoil Ilona's dinner party."

"Perhaps Peter *has* mellowed," George said. "It was all a very long time ago."

"Not to someone whose home was destroyed and who lost everything he possessed," Michael said.

"You mean you really *can* understand his point of view?"

George asked in amazement. "Even if you know that the first thing he would do, if he were ever Prince of Starogan again, would be to hang you?"

Michael smiled. "I think he would probably hang Ivan first." Then his face became serious. "You know that is a possibility. Certainly a firing squad."

George nodded. "It would restore my faith in Soviet justice."

Michael sighed. "I always knew Ivan was *capable* of doing something like that. But the point is, you know, that he truly loved Tatiana. He was just mad with jealousy when she left him. And until she actually announced her intention of leaving Russia, he always hoped she would come back to him. One cannot help but feel a little sorry for him. Not," he added hastily, "that I condone what he did in any way. But of course I can understand Peter's feelings. You cannot be someone's valet for long without getting to know him very well. Besides, I would feel the same way, in his position."

"Do you ever think of Starogan? The old days?"

Michael considered, and then shook his head. "I try not to. Starogan is like a previous existence." He flushed as he glanced at his friend, and George understood. Starogan was where the valet and the princess had grown up together, destined to become illicit lovers. Before the whole world had exploded. And had gone on exploding ever since.

"Besides," Michael said with a smile, "there is always the future to look forward to. One can never be old while there is still the future."

"Yes," George said.

"Like coming to live in America, perhaps. Catherine and I are to do that, you know, when the United Nations is established in New York. I can hardly believe that it is really going to happen, George. Will I like America?"

"*I* like it," George said. He was aware that they were only sparring, that Michael, who knew him every bit as well as he knew Peter Borodin, would certainly have deduced the most likely reason for George Hayman to be back in Europe only six months after going home, ostensibly for good.

"Well," Michael said, "I shall look forward to Gregory's report of it. He is very excited at the prospect."

"So he was telling me. I gathered from your letter that Premier Stalin isn't too pleased."

"Well, what would you expect? Apart from everything else,

Joseph Vissarionovich believes that the world comes to an end at the Vistula."

"Does he?" George asked, seizing his opportunity.

"It's a good, solid Russian point of view," Michael said, meeting his gaze.

"Nobody would believe that, you know," George remarked. "Not recently."

"George," Michael said, "we were invaded in 1941. You were there. You saw what happened. You cannot blame us for wanting it never to happen again. For wishing to make sure it *cannot* ever happen again."

"And that means bulldozing, or cajoling, all your immediate neighbors into Communism?"

"It means that we are happier surrounded by friends than by potential enemies. And why do you automatically suppose that the Bulgarians and the Yugoslavs were coerced? Can you not admit to yourself that they might *prefer* socialism to capitalism? Places like Rumania and Poland are not like France and England, you know. They do not have a long history of political involvement, and therefore a well-entrenched bourgeoisie. History has passed them by in that sense. Until 1939 they had a landholding and moneygrubbing aristocracy and a downtrodden peasantry that was pretty close to serfdom. Well, the aristocrats have been discredited by their flirtation with fascism, and the peasants want a bigger share in their country's wealth."

George could not help but take note of the presumably inadvertent mention of two countries that had not yet embraced Communism. "And the Red army is helping them to get it."

Michael shrugged. "The Red Army is there to keep the peace, and to see that the people—the *people,* George, not just the few at the top—get the sort of government that they want. Is that not what the Atlantic Charter is all about?"

George studied him.

Michael smiled. "And don't tell me that the United States has pulled all her troops back out of Europe, or seriously intends to do so."

"We're sure as hell not trying to influence any people in their choice of governments," George said.

"Is that a fact? Then can you tell me why there are no Communist governments in office where the Americans are occupying?"

"I don't think there's a short answer to that one," George admitted. "Okay, Michael, let's agree you have a point. But some of the tales that are coming out of Poland and Hungary and Czechoslovakia about the methods your men are using to keep the peace and let the people have their choice of governments are a little distressing."

"If you mean that we have had to lock up certain people, that is because we are maybe a little more sensitive about their past records than you seem to be. We are not separated from them by three thousand miles of ocean. The truth of the matter, George, is that your Mr. Truman has decided not to trust us anymore. It is the age-old story. Your government loved ours as long as we were fighting the Nazis, but now that that is over, you are remembering that we have a social system that is utterly opposed to the one in which a few dozen men become millionaires and assume all political power, while the rest starve."

"I hope you're going to take the time to have a good look at America when you come over," George said. "Mind you, you'll have to tread carefully, with all those starving bodies cluttering up the streets."

Michael flushed. "I was using a metaphor. We oppose the inequalities of wealth."

"But not of power?" It was George's turn to smile. "You'll not pretend that on your days off you rush down to Starogan to till a field with the rest of the commune."

"People have to be ruled. I will certainly admit that I am among the lucky ones. But it was not always so."

"I won't argue with that."

"The fact is, George, that for you not to trust us is an absurdity. *We* do not have an atomic bomb. You have it. But *you* do not trust *us*. Now if your government was to offer to share the atomic secrets..."

"Would yours, if the situation were reversed?"

Michael grinned. "Governments are always secretive about things like bombs. I do not blame yours. I am only asking you to look at the situation with an impartial eye. As I know you do. Tell Truman that we Russians are interested only in protecting Mother Russia, and living our lives in our own way. But we are determined to protect Mother Russia from another holocaust."

"I'll tell Truman," George said, "if you'll give me your

word that that's all Uncle Joe wants to do."

Michael gazed at him, and George remembered that this man had never been able to lie convincingly.

"I represent Joseph Vissarionovich, George," Michael said at last. "Therefore, whatever I say, he would say, were he here himself."

"And you've no objection if I take a tour through Czechoslovakia and Poland, and see for myself? Meet whoever I like?"

"I think that would be a splendid idea, George. You will go with my blessing. Officially. And then maybe you will believe me."

"And the Russian Jews? Judith's plans?"

Now the eyes were most definitely opaque, as if shutters had fallen into place. "There are close to two hundred million people in Russia, George, all struggling to exist, to better themselves, in a shattered country. Minorities, even Jewish minorities, must play their part in reconstructing the state, and take their proper places." Michael sighed. "If there is a God, one must pray to Him that Judith accepts this before... well—" He smiled. "—before she wastes too much more of her life."

And that, George thought, is the most interesting, and terrifying, thing you've said all morning, old friend, who is now definitely an enemy.

They went to Harrods, where Ilona was able to march an amazed Catherine and Michael through the endless display rooms of the great department store, while Gregory and Nona followed more slowly, and George and Judith more slowly yet. Before long they found themselves alone with the antique furniture.

"You must find Russia has changed after twenty-five years," George suggested. "I have an idea George junior might be interested in a series of articles."

"I'd never get them out of the country," Judith said.

"No," he agreed. "That is one aspect of the change, certainly."

"I thought you hadn't noticed."

"That Stalin has managed to create a dictatorship as tight as any the world has ever seen? With the aid of his Nejs and his Molotovs and his Berias."

"Not Michael," she said.

"You know, until this morning I'd have gone along with that. Now . . . he is certainly prepared to do what he is told, and say what he is told to say."

"I suppose you would have to put him down as an innocent," she said thoughtfully. "I mean, he genuinely believes in Communism. Well, who wouldn't, after the way he suffered at the hands of the tsar? But he believes in it so strongly that he also believes it should be possible to convince all the world it's the only way to live. Or at least, to be governed. The idea that people, even in Russia, may have to be *forced* into it is quite abhorrent to him."

"Yet he backs Stalin's regime all the way."

She shrugged. "Perhaps he is still hoping it will change to the idealistic concept everyone had in the beginning."

"And Boris?"

"Boris has never had any illusions about the regime, George. He just happens to be a patriotic Russian." She flushed. "That's why I love him."

"I have an idea that you are telling me this great thawing act is nothing more than propaganda."

"I would say that. Stalin uses words, ideas, emotions, to shape what he wants to happen the way you might use a hammer and nails and a screwdriver to build a rabbit hutch."

"Hm. And what about the visible evidences? Young Gregory on his way to America for a vacation, you traveling about, seeing what can be done for the Jews . . . but I gather it isn't all plain sailing in that direction."

She gazed reflectively at a Louis XV table. "Stalin refused pointblank to consider any general emigration scheme, or indeed any emigration scheme at all. But he said he'd reconsider in a year or two, and he seems quite prepared to let me do the necessary groundwork. Maybe he just likes me." She gave a guilty smile. "My return to Russia was big news. Heroine of the Revolution, and all that."

"And quite right, too. *Were* you with Rasputin the night he died, Judith?"

She raised her head to look at him. "You mean the night he was murdered. How come you never asked me that before, George?"

"Maybe I'm just realizing how many things I should've asked you before, and didn't. Don't get me wrong. I'm just happy to see you again, and to see you looking so well, and even so happy. I'm not going to ask you about Ravensbrück, either."

"And I wouldn't tell you about Ravensbrück, either. But I can tell you that if I were a cat, this is about my eleventh life. So why shouldn't I be happy? I've nothing left to lose."

"And Boris is the man?"

She met his gaze. "Boris has been the man for ten years, George. Longer than that."

"Yeah. How come he's not with you, if Catherine can accompany Michael?"

"Well, he ... he has work to do."

"You don't like that?"

She shrugged. "We haven't been married very long. All right, I admit he's been around for twelve years. He's still my first husband, and I'm still a bride. It would have been exciting to go to Palestine together."

"That's where you're going?"

"When I've talked to some people here."

George pulled his nose. "Do you remember getting agitated about Palestine—oh, a hell of a long time ago?"

"I should've gone then. Things would have been different."

"You might have used up a few more lives. They're still shooting over there. And since they've been at it for at least fifteen years, now, they're getting quite good at it."

"I've been shot at before," she said. "And it's going to happen, George. It must. Because there are enough people like me who are going to *make* it happen. If Hayman Newspapers were to come out on our side, it would be a great help."

"We're sympathetic. Do you mean to settle there yourself?"

"When I've got the Jews out of Russia. Those of them who wish to go."

"You don't think that might take a long time?"

"What else have I got to spend?"

He picked up her hand and squeezed it. "Will you take a word of advice?"

"From you? Of course."

"Don't ever go back to Russia."

"Don't—" She stared at him, her eyes enormous. "I have a job to do."

"You won't be doing it, so long as Stalin is alive and in power, Judith. Believe me—everything I've read, everything

I've heard on this trip, everything *you* have just told me, is convincing me that tsarism is back again, only without even the hope of the hereditary succession occasionally producing a weak or even a benevolent ruler. If Stalin is letting you roam, it is for some purpose of his, not to help your cause. When you go to Palestine, if you must, stay there. I'm sure they'll be happy to have you. And have Boris join you, just as soon as he can."

"But . . . how?"

"He must be in line for a vacation at some time. And surely he's entitled to spend his vacation with his wife. He doesn't have to tell anyone he's not coming back. You don't have to either, until he's beside you."

Judith attempted a smile. "Are you seriously trying to tell me that Palestine, where they're shooting at each other, is safer than Russia?"

"For you, Judith. As you've said, you're an important figure, a Heroine of the Revolution. If you start to make a noise, you'll be embarrassing the regime. But they can't publicly shut you up. You'd do well to remember poor Tattie."

"But . . . that was Ivan's jealousy." She stared at him. "Wasn't it?"

"Was it? Hell, I'm not happy about your being in Palestine. It would make far more sense to me for you to come back to America . . ."

Judith shook her head. "No, George. Quite definitely no. We tried that once before, remember?"

George sighed. "I guess you're right. But you can pick your spot. You worked for the paper before. I'll have George junior give you a job as correspondent, any place in the world you choose."

"It will be Palestine," she said, and attempted another smile. "Does this mean you won't be helping me to get the Jews out of Russia?"

"We'll back you. That's a promise. But *you* must get out and stay out. Are you going to be here when I get back from my tour? It's only going to be a couple of weeks."

She shook her head again. "I'm leaving on Friday."

"Well . . . what about tonight's supper party?"

Judith's mouth twisted. "I really haven't got the time, George. Not for a Borodin family get-together. Besides, I don't think it would be a good idea for me to meet Peter again, quite so soon. Do you?"

Prince Peter Borodin still carried himself with military erectness, while his silvery hair was as thick as it had ever been. He was, in fact, as handsome a man as his sisters were beautiful women—that was the Borodin tradition. George had first met him on that same day in 1904 that he had met the two girls, when he had ridden into Port Arthur with the besieging Japanese army so close behind. He had liked Peter from the start, just as he had adored the girls, had admired all the aristocratic and military qualities that the Borodin heir had inherited from generations of princely ancestors. That Peter's apparently mutual feeling of friendship should have been so far inhibited by pride, and awareness of position, as to make it impossible for him, then, to concede that his sister might possibly wish to marry the brash young American war correspondent, and that therefore they should have quarreled so deeply and so angrily, was irrelevant now. That was long in the past, and George had never felt anything less than sympathy for the young man, so imbued with ambition and traditional ideas of honor and glory, who had been pitchforked by his father's premature death into the Princedom of Starogan years before he had been ready for its responsibilities, only to have the whole thing torn from his grasp by the onset of the revolution. And when, as tonight, he was determined to be on his best behavior and to betray none of the intense anger that still permeated his personality, he could be perfectly charming.

He had even been charming to Gregory Nej—who had in fact enjoyed quite a triumph, George thought. He smiled at the three young people, who had been chatting together all evening. Another source of pleasure. And of great hope. Ruth Borodina, or Ruth von Hassell as she now was, had been imprisoned for two years by the NKVD—no doubt before Gregory Nej had ever been involved with that organization, but nonetheless at the whim of his father. She had then spent three years in Ravensbrück with her aunt. And she was the daughter of the most rabid anti-Communist in the world, as well as being half-Jewish. Yet she was sitting and talking on the one hand with a captain in the NKVD, and on the other with her husband, who had been, for a while, one of Hitler's brightest young men. Gregory was clearly cast in a different mold than his father, and Paul von Hassell had turned against the Nazi regime as soon as he had realized the full horrors of what it was practicing. But still, the two young men were natural enemies. Paul von Hassell was one of those who had invaded Gregory's homeland, despite being engaged to Gregory's sister. And that sister had died, horribly, as a result of that invasion.

Yet Paul himself was so likable that even Ilona, after a frosty beginning, had thawed, and smiled at him benevolently as she ate her dessert; they had had a private meal served in their suite.

And the youngsters made an attractive threesome, George thought—Gregory with his pronounced Nej nose and chin and short dark hair, Paul still with the bearing of a military man and with imposing blond good looks, and Ruth, a resplendently black-haired version of the Borodin beauty; of the traumas she had suffered in the past, the only obvious trace was a remoteness about her eyes. George doubted anyone had ever really known Ruth Borodina, since 1938. And he doubted anyone ever would, now. Not even Paul von Hassell.

But the three of them, he supposed, represented a good deal of what hope there was for the future of mankind, in their willingness to forgive and forget. After his gloomy meeting with Winston Churchill, no longer prime minister but still the man whose opinions George valued most, and the even gloomier conclusions he had been forced to draw from his chat with Michael Nej, this was the first ray of sunshine he had come across since landing in England.

"So Michael Nej is the Soviet ambassador to the United Nations. Well, well." Peter Borodin leaned back in his chair to light his cigar. The ladies had left them, and the four men were settling down to their port. "But then, he always had character. I spotted that early on. A man gets to know his servants very well, you know." He smiled at Gregory. "Just as I never doubted your character. You're Tattie through and through. I'm so pleased you've come out. Mind you, I always knew you'd do it. Certainly after what happened to your poor mother."

"Out?" Gregory asked.

George cleared his throat abruptly. "I think—"

"Out of Russia," Peter said. "Mind you, in my opinion

you're taking a bit of a chance hanging about here, even with George at your side. That father of yours is an unmitigated thug, you know. He'll be after you if he even suspects what you have in mind, even if he is in jail. Not that I believe he'll ever be convicted of anything." He narrowed his eyes at Gregory. "You'll have a bunch of Russians kidnapping you, if you're not careful."

"I think you should know, Peter," George said, "that Gregory is coming to the United States for a visit. He is not leaving Russia for good. Is that right, Gregory?"

"Oh, I . . ." Gregory was blushing. "Of course I know that you are all enemies of the Soviet, but are you suggesting I—"

"Of course you are going to defect," Peter said. "And it is the sensible thing to do." He gave a brief laugh. "The only *sane* thing to do. Within three years the Americans will have blown the Russians off the map."

"For God's sake, Peter—" George began.

"Well, my dear fellow, it stands to reason. Everyone can see how the Communists are trying to take over Europe. And everyone knows that it's their ultimate aim, anyway. Now is the time to settle the matter once and for all. Your people, George, have the atomic bomb. The Russians don't. A quick strike, and there it is."

"Do you know, sometimes I think you *are* nuts," George said.

"The trouble with people like you, George," Peter Borodin said, without anger, "is that you are quite incapable of making a painful decision, however necessary it may be. You prefer to muddle along, in the hope that the problem will go away. That is what caused the last war, you know—you people, and the British and the French, muddling along, hoping that Hitler would go away, when a preemptive strike in 1935 would have ended the whole thing there and then. Everyone knows, without a shadow of a doubt, that there is going to be a war between the United States and Soviet Russia, sooner or later. If you happen to want the United States to be sure of winning, as all of us here do . . ." He swept them with his gaze, lingering on Gregory's face. ". . . then it seems to me that it is criminal madness not to have the war at a time when the Americans are *certain* to be victorious. Don't make the mistake of imagining the Russians aren't going to have the bomb eventually. Our—

their scientists are just as brilliant as any Germans."

"You suggested some such crazy scheme to Roosevelt, before the war," George recalled.

"I did. And he chose to ignore me. Well, I don't condemn him out of hand. It is just possible that he possessed information I didn't, knew that the Germans would attack Russia, and thought it would be a good thing for the two of them to slug it out. But now—why, there can't be any argument at all."

George finished his port and set down the glass. "I think we should recall the ladies," he said.

"There you go," Peter said. "Pretending to take offense. That is just a form of cowardice, George. You know I am right. You *want* to agree with me. But some religious or ethical quirk in your background prevents you. Let us hope you keep on being fortunate, and will never live to regret your weakness."

"Let's hope." George smiled at Gregory. "I can only apologize for your uncle," he said, "and try to convince you that he represents nothing more than a lunatic fringe."

"But is there not some truth in what he says, Mr. Hayman?"

George frowned at him, pausing before the door. "I'm not sure I understand you."

"Well, if I were President Truman, I would certainly not wait until the Soviets got the bomb to fight a war."

George opened his mouth, and then shut it again. "But . . . you're . . ."

Gregory smiled. "They are my people," he said. "I have many friends there. But as to whether the Soviet way is the right way, for the world . . . I am a captain in the NKVD. You know that?"

"Of course."

"It is controlled by Lavrenti Beria. Before, it was controlled by my father. They do terrible things, sometimes, and command others to do terrible things for them. All in the name of the state."

"You'll *admit* that?" Prince Peter asked incredulously.

"It is unfortunately true, sir. So I would ask you this, Mr. Hayman: is there an NKVD in the United States?"

"Ah . . . no, I don't think the FBI quite comes into that category." George opened the door. "I think we *should* get the ladies in before one of us says something he might regret. Maybe we'll continue this conversation some other time."

"You look as if you've seen a ghost," Ilona remarked.

George sighed. "Thousands of them."

Peter left early. George gave a sigh of relief when the door had closed behind him. "With all due respect, Ruth," he said, "when I'm with your father, I never have any idea what's going to happen next. A preventive war! My God! And you, Gregory, playing along with him..." He glared at his nephew.

Gregory got up. "It is always interesting to hear other points of view, sir," he said. "I found Prince Peter's opinions most instructive. Now, if you will excuse me, I will retire. Aunt Ilona." He kissed her on the cheek. "Frau von Hassell. Herr von Hassell."

Ilona watched the door close. "Now you've offended him," she said. "Oh, George."

"He seems to be a mixed-up kid," George said. "Or a hypocrite. I don't go much for either type."

"He'll be all right when we get him home," Ilona said. "There's no—well..." She gazed at her niece.

"Intrigue over there," Ruth agreed.

"You're not saying that Peter is still actually involved in intrigue over here?" George asked. He had assumed that Peter's letter to John meant nothing more than that an aging man was going through the motions.

"Intrigue is all he lives for, really," Paul von Hassell said. "He is more than ever convinced that war between the Soviet Union and the West is inevitable, as he said this evening, and he would like to see it happen in his lifetime because he knows the West would win. At least, right now."

"My God!" Ilona exclaimed. "He's mad, you know. He always has been."

"I'm afraid I agree with you," George said. "And I told him so. But I have an uneasy feeling that there are quite a few people around who share his point of view."

"There are," Paul said. "He was invited back to England by an extreme right-wing group. He dreams of reviving that counterrevolutionary organization that he had before the war. And as you say, Mr. Hayman, when you think of all the Poles and the Czechs and the Hungarians who have fled to the West, and who all hate the Soviets, I don't think he's going to have any shortage of recruits."

"And where do you fit into this?" George asked.

Paul hesitated.

"Oh, yes," Ruth said, "Papa assumes Paul is going to be his right-hand man, entirely because he's married to me."

"Well—" Paul said.

"And he's not going to be," Ruth went on.

"Well—" Paul said again.

"Because I don't ever want to hear or see or speak with a Russian again, if I can help it," Ruth declared. "I'm sorry, Aunt Ilona, but there it is. Oh, Gregory Nej is very nice, but he gives me the creeps. And he makes me remember. I'll have nightmares tonight, I know it. I have better things to do with my life than battering my head against a brick wall, and so has Paul."

So bang goes that illusion of Peter's, George thought. But he had an idea that she was merely being the most honest among them.

"What things?" Ilona asked, with the quiet directness that was one of her most compelling characteristics.

"Well . . ." It was Ruth's turn to hesitate.

"It is a pity Mrs. *Petrov* did not come tonight," Paul said. "We would have enjoyed seeing her again."

"Judith is going to be in London for another day or two," George said. "And I'm sure she'd love to see you. But she's somewhat preoccupied with Palestine."

"It is Palestine we would like to discuss with her," Paul said.

"Don't tell me you're thinking of going there!" Ilona cried.

"Why not?" Ruth demanded. "I'm a Jew. Just like Aunt Judith."

"Yes, but . . ." Ilona gazed at Paul, her mouth open.

He smiled. "And I am an ex-Nazi." He looked at George. "But now I have a Swedish passport. Do you think they would refuse me entry, Mr. Hayman?"

"It's the British you'd have to apply to, not the Jews," George said. "But . . . mightn't you find it a little awkward."

"Awkward," Paul said, half to himself. "Yes. From time to time, in the past, I have found life a little awkward."

"And have you told your father of this decision?" Ilona asked Ruth.

The girl exchanged glances with her husband. "No, not yet," she said. "But we will, of course."

"It'll upset him," Ilona said.

"It'll break his heart," George said.

"He'll understand," Ruth said confidently. "He must. I cannot devote my entire life to his absurd causes. I've a life of my own to live. And causes of my own." She gazed from face to face, defiantly.

"Those poor children," Ilona said, after they had left. "My God, do you know, that's been my feeling since coming here? Pity for everybody. Isn't that terrible?"

"Not really," George said. "I feel the same way. Europe is a disaster area." He stood at the window and stared at the park. "I wonder how long it'll take them to settle down."

"George," she said. "Forget this wretched tour you're going to make. I'm sure you've heard enough, and seen enough. Come home with us."

"Now, my love," he said. "You don't have to worry that *I'll* become depressed. I've seen it all before, remember? So you get Gregory on that ship, and give him a good time. And just remember, too, once you set foot on American dockside, that disaster areas are far, far behind you."

"I'll say amen to that," Ilona said. "Oh, I'll say amen to that." She stood beside him and took his hand. "George? *You* don't have any plans to visit Palestine on this trip, do you?"

A flurry of snow swept across the afternoon, and the rented Buick skidded left and then right, as Anna Ragosina wrestled with the wheel. Driving had been a part of her training, but she was somewhat out of practice; there had been no cars in the Pripet. Fortunately, the causeway of the Cross Bay Boulevard was deserted on a January evening, and she could allow the vehicle to coast to a stop at the side of the road, while she took off her glasses to polish them. They were clear glasses, and quite unnecessary. But if she was going to act a role, she preferred to act it all the time.

She wore a voluminous cheap cloth coat with a fox-fur collar, which all but obliterated her, and a matching hat; cheap rings on her fingers and a black dress from Penney's completed the ensemble. With the glasses, and with her hair tucked up out of sight, she did not suppose she was worth a second glance from anyone. Which was what she intended.

She rolled down the window and grimaced at Jamaica Bay,

which stretched away on both sides of the road. In the distance she could make out the lights of Idlewild International Airport, and as she watched, blowing clouds of mist in front of her nose, she saw a huge four-engined airliner begin its descent into the maze of runways and hangars. She herself had flown in from Washington only two hours before. It seemed like an eternity.

But her destination could not be far now. She had chosen Rockaway Park just because it was close to the airport. And far from the city.

She put the car into gear, continued across the Cross Bay Bridge to Rockaway Park, and finally spotted the hotel sign on a side street just off the beach. It was a small hotel, no doubt busy enough in summer; in January it looked dingily deserted, and a shutter was banging. But Bogolzhin had recommended it for their first meeting. And Bogolzhin knew the ground better than she possibly could after only a few weeks. She had to believe this.

She stopped the car outside the front door, where there were several vacant parking spaces, went inside, hammered the bell on the reception desk, and watched as a somewhat stout peroxide blonde sauntered forward.

"Have you a room for me? My husband reserved."

The blonde looked her up and down. "You're the foreign lady?"

"That is correct," Anna said. "Will someone bring in my bag, please? And park the car?"

"Ain't your husband with you?" the blonde asked. She checked her diary. "It says here, a room for two. Mr. and Mrs."

"He has his own car," Anna said impatiently. "He will be here in a little while."

"He said on the telephone you was French," the blonde remarked. "You really French?"

"Of course. I am from Paris. But I . . . we are working in this country for a while."

"Paris," the blonde said. "I went to Paris once, before the war. Say, were you there in the war?"

"I was evacuated."

"Maybe you'd better sign the book," the blonde suggested, "since your husband ain't here."

Anna obliged.

"Chantal," the blonde said. "Say, I like that. It means singer, right?"

"Roughly," Anna said. "My father was in sewing machines." She had been told that Americans were a witty people, but the blonde didn't seem to know what she was talking about.

"How do you aim to pay?" she asked.

"With money," Anna said caustically.

"You mean cash? That'll be five dollars."

"You wish it now?"

"That's right, honey," the blonde said.

Anna paid. The blonde carefully counted the bills, and put them in a drawer.

"Well," she said, "I'll see what we can do about your bag. I have a husband too, although you wouldn't believe it. Goddamned layabout. Hey, Al," she bawled, emmitting a sudden gust of tremendous noise. "Lady has a bag. You wanna fetch it?"

Anna could not understand the reply, which appeared to come from some inner room.

"There is also the car," she said.

"It can stay where it is," the woman said. "It'll freeze there as good as anywhere. You'd better come see the room." She went up the stairs. "It's a walkup, see. I'm Frannie Hale."

Anna climbed the stairs behind her, and when they reached the top Mrs. Hale said, "This is number seven."

It was very small, with a sloping ceiling, a single window overlooking the backyard, rather than the street, and an ancient double bed with a pronounced sag in the middle. The yard, Anna concluded, was probably looking its best beneath a concealing layer of snow; the bedspread would probably also have been improved by a hole in the roof.

"This costs five dollars a night?" she asked.

"Mr. Chantal said you didn't want nothing expensive," said Mrs. Hale.

"It *does* have a bathroom?" Anna asked anxiously. Since discovering the delights of her little apartment in Washington, she had grown to appreciate some aspects of Western living.

"That door," Mrs. Hale said. "Al will bring your luggage up, sometime." She went to the door, and paused reflectively. "Try not to be in the tub when he gets here," she recommended. "He's a groper, Al is."

* * *

Anna sat in a corner of the hotel bar, and drank scotch. Her bath had been uncomfortable, and her dinner—a hamburger at the freezing corner drugstore a quarter of a mile away— unfilling. Since she was supposed to be French she hadn't risked asking for vodka at the bar; she had sufficiently surprised Al, who served the bar himself, by requesting her scotch neat.

Al, she thought, might well become a nuisance. She had tied up her hair in a handkerchief, and still wore her glasses, but without her bulky coat there was not a lot she could do about either her legs or her bust, and he was most definitely interested. There were surprisingly many people in the bar, and several other women; whatever its drawbacks as a hotel the place seemed some sort of a local rendezvous. Nevertheless, Al kept coming across to smile at her, and ask if she wanted a refill.

She looked at her watch. But there was no point in getting irritated until Bogolzhin actually appeared. The fact was, as she well understood, that for all of her utterly relaxed exterior, she was still unhappy at being out of Russia, and especially at moments like this. She was, she reflected, too used to being recognized as Anna Ragosina, whose very name would have people retreating nervously. Washington was fine. She had her new identity, and she was utterly fawned over by the ambassador, so much so that undoubtedly the rest of the embassy staff were of the opinion that he had imported his own mistress from Moscow—as, no doubt, he hoped he had.

But a clandestine meeting like this reminded her of her last foreign mission, that disastrous occasion when she had been sent by Ivan Nej to Berlin to assassinate Prince Peter Borodin. True, in the United States there was no Gestapo to worry about. But at least in Berlin she had been able to stay in a good hotel.

"Chantal!" Bogolzhin banged the door behind him and started across the room. He was a very tall, very thin man, with a hooked nose. Anna barely came up to his chin, but she stood on tiptoe to kiss him on each cheek, and to whisper in his ear, "Chantal is our surname, you fool. Call me Anna."

"Anna!" He kissed her again.

She pushed him away. "Get yourself something to drink, and put an icecube down your trousers," she recommended. She sat down and watched him. Beria had assured her he was a good man. She could only wait and see.

Bogolzhin, to her annoyance, returned with vodka, although

apparently it was necessary in this country to mix it with orange juice. He sat beside her and grinned at Al, who withdrew further down the bar.

"Well?" she asked. "What have you got for me?"

"A great deal."

"Do you speak French?"

"No," he said. "That is why I am stationed in America."

"They will listen to English, and we can hardly speak Russian," she said discontentedly. "We will go up to the room." She finished her drink, and got up.

"That is a good idea," he said.

"To talk," she said. She led him up the stairs, opened the door for him, and gestured him inside. "Sit down." She kicked off her shoes, pulled off her scarf to fluff out her hair, removed her glasses, and lay on the bed, where she watched him wandering round the room. "It is not wired," she said. "I have already looked. Besides . . ." She smiled. "I am told the Americans do not do that sort of thing without a good reason."

Bogolzhin grunted, stood by the window. He was definitely restless. No doubt, for all his dreams and his anticipations, he was now alarmed at finding himself alone in a bedroom with the famous Ragosina. "Sit down," she said again. "I am not going to bite you, comrade. I am not going to fuck you, either."

Bogolzhin gave a guilty start, and sat on the straight chair— the only furniture in the room other than the bed and dresser.

"I don't want to have to shout," she said, patting the bed beside her.

Bogolzhin got up again and cautiously sat beside her; their thighs touched.

"Well?"

"I have everything written down." He produced several sheets of paper from his pocket.

"Written *down?*" she demanded. "Have you had no training at all?"

"There are so many names," he explained.

"Oh, give them to me." She scanned the first list. Each name had a telephone number beside it, and in most cases an occupation as well. It was a professional job of supplying information, even if it was a most unprofessional act of spying. "These people," she remarked, "they are all Communists?"

Bogolzhin shook his head. "Not all of them. Most of them are sympathizers, even if they have not yet joined the Party.

Some of them are merely anti-atomic-bomb, and others anti-American-government, even if they work for it. And some, I think, are merely interested in money."

"Hm." Anna continued to study the list. "This man here. Has he really been supplying you with information since before the war?"

"He has been very faithful."

"What hold do you have on him? How secure?"

"I have no hold on him, comrade."

Anna stared at him. "You have no hold? No letters, no photographs?"

Bogolzhin shook his head. "He is a dedicated Communist. He is absolutely reliable. There are not too many of those. But enough. These people, for example..." he pointed out two more names, "are dissatisfied with the present regime here. I think—" He stopped talking as a knock sounded on the door. Anna hastily stuffed the lists beneath her pillow and took out the pistol that had been concealed there.

Desperately Bogolzhin shook his head.

"Mrs. Chantal?" It was Al Hale. "Are you in there, Mrs. Chantal?"

Anna put the pistol back under the pillow, placed her glasses on her nose, swung her legs off the bed, went to the door and opened it.

"Say, I'm sorry to disturb you, Mrs. Chantal..." Hale's gaze roamed past Anna to take in Bogolzhin, who had moved from the bed to the window, then came back to take in her loosened hair and stockinged feet. "I was just wondering if you wanted fruit juice in the morning with your coffee."

"That would be very nice," Anna said.

"And say, Mr. Chantal, you reckon you could sign the register as well as your wife?"

"I will do so in the morning," Bogolzhin said, "before we leave."

"Yeah," Hale agreed, and gave Anna another long look. "I'll be saying good night, then."

The door closed. Anna turned the key. "He suspects."

"Only that we are not married," Bogolzhin said.

Anna frowned at him. "Why is that any concern of his?"

"In America, comrade," Bogolzhin explained, "people are much more concerned with each other's morals than with whether or not they are foreign agents. For a man and a woman to check in at an out-of-season hotel, for one night, and arrive separately, must mean they are having an affair."

"An affair? What is that?"

"Well, that they are not married, comrade, but wish to sleep together."

Anna sat down, still frowning. "It is against the law to sleep together if you are not married? Why was I not told this?"

"I think it is against the law in certain states. But no one takes that very seriously. What is very much against the law would be for the landlord to *know* that we are not married. He might be accused of importing a prostitute for me to sleep with."

"I do not understand these people at all," Anna remarked. "And it is all your fault, for arriving so late."

"The roads, comrade, are very bad."

"I have driven on the roads," Anna pointed out acidly. "And I am not looking for excuses. Just efficiency. Now . . ." She retrieved the papers from beneath the pillow. "What is this other list?"

"Those are labor-union people who may be willing to work for us."

"None of them seem to be union officials," she complained.

Bogolzhin shrugged. "The officials are mostly very patriotic, and well paid. I do not think we will get anywhere with them. But these people . . . they speak well, and are therefore listened to by their fellow workers. And they are regarded as honest. The workers may well follow their lead. It does not matter whether or not we induce any *official* strikes, comrade, so long as we disrupt the work. That is what you said."

"And that is what I meant." Anna suddenly discovered that she was angry. With Al Hale, principally, but with the whole American nation. For having so much, and for being so pruriently absurd. "I have decided to sleep with you after all," she said, "if only to spite these people." She unbuttoned her blouse. "Come to bed."

Besides, she thought, she could always close her eyes and pretend he was Gregory. Because *he* would soon be here.

It had never before occurred to her that she might miss Gregory.

Chapter 5

KNUCKLES DRUMMED ON THE CABIN DOOR. "GREGORY? ARE you there? Gregory? We can see New York. Come up on deck. It's so exciting!"

"I'll be up in a moment, Aunt Ilona." Gregory Nej sat up, swung his feet from the bed to the deck, and inspected himself in the mirror as he shaved. Certainly he was excited, but less at the prospect of seeing New York than of being able to see Anna again. He had so much to tell her. Things he would not have believed possible.

Gregory was prepared to admit, at least to himself, that he had been decidedly skeptical when Lavrenti Beria had told him that the NKVD had certain knowledge that the Americans were preparing to launch a preventive war against Russia. He had thought such an apocalyptical view of the future was unnecessary, certainly unnecessary to convince *him* of what he had to do; he was a loyal Russian officer, and he was quite prepared to carry out whatever task was assigned, however distasteful it might be.

But that had been before he had met Prince Peter, had discovered that he was everything Father had ever claimed he was, and had realized that here was the true voice of the West speaking, that the majority of these people really did hate the Soviets, and were prepared to do anything to bring the Soviet state down. People like George Hayman, whose sentiments he was sure were genuine, and who wished only to see peace between the two power blocs, were the exceptions rather than the rule. He believed entirely in Uncle George's sincerity, placed him in the same class as Uncle Michael, who also did not understand the true forces at work. That both of these fine old gentlemen had to be deceived as much as anyone else was his only regret about what he had to do. Uncle Michael, of course, would eventually learn the truth, would understand that it had all been part of a plan vital to Soviet security.

But George Hayman would know the truth only when it was too late. Gregory was genuinely sorry about that. But in a war there had to be casualties—and undoubtedly this was a war, even if it was not yet being fought with bombs and bullets.

His only responsibility was to carry out his appointed task efficiently and well. He was disturbed at the careless way he had responded to Uncle Peter's outburst. Had George Hayman not been quite so inclined to accept him, he might have seriously jeopardized his own mission. He must learn to think carefully before speaking, to make himself oppose these people in most things, in the beginning, and only slowly to be won over to their ways and their points of view.

But he must not take *too* long about it. Anna had been very insistent about that. Oh, Anna, he thought, contact me soon.

He knotted his tie and went out on deck, to look at the skyscrapers rising out of the morning mist. And he was impressed, despite his new determination to remain skeptical about everything American. But even the huge ship seemed to be dwarfed by the towering buildings. He could not imagine being similarly impressed by entering either Leningrad or Sevastopol from the sea.

He was equally impressed by Ilona Hayman's reception, which meant his reception as well. But then, he had noticed throughout the voyage the deference with which she had been treated, the apparently automatic manner in which they had been seated at the captain's table. Now they were whisked through channels, greeted with great warmth by the various officials, who seemed to be expecting him and therefore stamped his passport without hesitation, while beyond Customs and Immigration there waited a huge, shiny Rolls-Royce, with a uniformed chauffeur eager to take command of the various porters who were transporting their luggage; Aunt Ilona, for a brief visit to England, travelled with a cabin trunk and four suitcases, while he, for a prolonged visit to the United States, had but a single case. And emerging from the back seat of the car was a young woman.

"This is your cousin Felicity," Ilona explained. "Felicity, this is Aunt Tattie's son, Gregory."

Gregory had forgotten to put on his gloves, however cold the air. Now he had to wait while Felicity Hayman slowly removed hers, to shake hands. But he was glad of the opportunity, because never in his life had he seen anyone quite so elegant, much less been introduced to her. Of course both Aunt Ilona and his own mother had always been ranked as the two most elegant women in Russia. But they were so *old*. And he had never actually left his motherland before this journey, to see the women of the outer world. In London people had been definitely drab; he might still have been in Leningrad. But here was height, and Borodin beauty, and overflowing feminine maturity, the whole encased in a sable fur coat with a matching hat, beneath which her hair was entirely concealed. On her right hand she wore a solitaire diamond ring.

She was a perfect specimen of American bourgeois degeneracy. She probably had never done a day's work in her life. Nor would she know one end of a pistol from another. Compared with Anna Ragosina she was a nothing.

How he would like to see Anna dressed like that, and wearing diamonds. She could be the most beautiful woman in the world.

Felicity shook hands. "Welcome to New York, Gregory," she said, her voice quiet, while he gazed into her startlingly blue eyes. They were sad eyes, and they had depths hardly in keeping with the rest of her. Perhaps, he thought, I have misjudged her, and she is aware of her degeneracy.

"You'll see better if you sit in the front, Gregory," Ilona said, and he obeyed reluctantly; he would have liked to sit next to the fur coat.

"Not that there's much to see," Felicity remarked, getting into the back beside her mother, while the chauffeur, whose name was apparently Rowntree, carefully negotiated his way through the traffic at the dock. "Excpet snow. I guess you're quite used to snow, Gregory."

"There is snow everywhere in Europe," he agreed, arranging himself, half turned, so that he could both see out and look

into the back seat of the enormous car. But he had little time
to look at the woman. They had emerged onto a street, and
never had he seen quite so much traffic, appearing from all
sides. Why there was not an immediate accident he could not
imagine. Some blocks later they crossed an enormous bridge,
far greater than any over the Moscow River, and far higher,
too, so that the half-frozen water beneath them seemed several
hundred feet away.

"This is called the Queensboro Bridge," Ilona explained.

"Will we go to Brooklyn?" Gregory asked. "I have heard
of Brooklyn."

"We'll skirt it. That is the East River we are crossing. We
go on up Long Island to a place called Cold Spring Harbor.
It's just beyond where the river becomes the Sound."

"You'll like it there," Felicity said. "It's nice and quiet."

Out of the corner of his eye Gregory watched her crossing
her knees, revealing a length of superb, silk-stockinged leg.
And suddenly he realized that he had never been so affected
by the first sight of a woman before.

But that was surely because he had been separated from
Anna for too long. And now they were in the same country
together. They would not be separated very much longer.

"Welcome to the United States." George Hayman, Jr., held
out his hand. "We've heard a lot about you."

Ilona was gratified; both her sons, and their families, had
braved the snow and ice to be on hand to greet their cousin,
who now gravely shook hands with Beth and Diana before
coming face to face with John.

"Hi," John Hayman said. "Remember me?"

"But of course," Gregory said. "I was there when you received your medal. From Comrade Stalin himself." He could
not keep the reverence out of his voice.

"It was quite an occasion," John agreed. "You'll remember
Sasha as well?"

Gregory kissed Natasha's hand. "I have seen you dance,"
he said. "You were magnificent, Madame Hayman."

"I think you should call me Sasha," Natasha suggested.
"Everyone else does." She held up her son. "This is Alex."

Gregory assumed the watchful expression most young men
do when confronted with a relative's child.

"I think Gregory will want to see his room," Ilona said.

"Harrison . . . ah, Harrison. Have the bags gone up?"

"Indeed they have, Mrs. Hayman," Harrison said.

"Then I'll take you up myself, Gregory. Come along."

"Mr. Harrison?" Gregory asked in a stage whisper. "Is he a cousin too?"

"Good heavens, no," Ilona said. "Harrison is the butler. You'll meet the rest of the servants later on. You don't *have* to remember all their names. Just smile at them and say good morning and they'll be quite happy."

George junior watched them climb the stairs, then glanced at John. "What do you think?"

"He's exactly as I remember him," John said.

"And are you still skeptical about him?"

"Skeptical? Good lord, no."

"What he means is," Natasha said, "that since he has gone into advertising, he is skeptical of everybody."

"And what do *you* think, sis?" George junior asked Felicity, who was, as usual, looking out of the window.

"About what?"

"About Cousin Greg, for crying out loud."

"I don't think anything about him," Felicity said. "He is a Russian." But John noted that she flushed as she spoke. He wondered why.

Joseph Stalin settled back in his chair and read the letter for the second time. Lavrenti Beria leaned forward eagerly, almost resting on the desk as he watched his master's reactions. But as usual, Stalin's expression never changed.

He laid the letter down. "Since Petrov is not to be allowed to leave the country," he said, "it would be better were he never to receive this."

"Of course, Joseph Vissarionovich. But . . . will Comrade Petrova not write again? Or even come back to see what is happening?" He paused uncertainly. "Or do you *wish* her to come back?"

"Judith Petrova will not come back," Stalin said. "She has no intention of ever coming back. That is obvious."

"Is it?" Beria was even more uncertain.

"Oh, indeed." Stalin tapped the sheet of paper. "She refers to having met George Hayman in London, and having talked with him. She says that Hayman has promised to back her campaign to 'free' the Russian Jews, as she puts it, and what else does she say . . . ?" He picked up the second sheet. "Ah, yes. 'George, as usual, has been full of good advice. He certainly thinks I should have your opinion on conditions here in Palestine, and as soon as possible. Do arrange a vacation—you must be due for one—and come to Tel Aviv. It need only be for a few days.' And the word few is underlined."

"Well," Beria said. "I do not see—"

"I know these people too well," Stalin said. "I have had dealings with them for years. Judith Petrova is quite shrewd, although she is not very bright, or she would not have written such a letter. She knows that I have no intention of allowing several million people, all of them talented and capable of hard work, simply to desert Russia because they have this absurd idea of taking some land from the Arabs for their own use. Even if I were sympathetic to their cause, I would regard that as an act of madness. Let the British have a war with the Arabs if they wish. I have no intention of getting involved. Petrova knows this, and thus has abandoned the idea of persuading me. She now hopes to force me to act in her favor, by adverse publicity. Thus she has enlisted the help of George Hayman, with all his newspapers. Well, they will be a nuisance. There is no use in denying that. And they will make Michael Nikolaievich's task more difficult. But they can have no effect here in Russia, where they are not read. But Petrova also knows that once such a campaign starts, she will have burned her bridges—I will never forgive her. Thus she knows she can never return to Russia, and she means to get Petrov out to join her, before the newspaper campaign begins. In a word, Lavrenti Pavlovich, they are intending to defect, under our very noses."

"I shall have her kidnapped and brought back," Beria said. "I shall—"

"Do nothing of the sort. That would make us look even worse. No, no." He gazed thoughtfully at the portrait of Lenin that hung on the wall opposite his desk. "Tell me. Is young Nej settled in, in America?"

Beria swelled with pride. He had been very nervous when Stalin had finally got around to listening to the detailed dispositions Anna had made, but to his relief and gratification his master had been pleased, in fact delighted, with the idea of using the Haymans' own cousin and nephew. "He is well settled in, Joseph Vissarionovich," he said, "as I understand it. The Hayman family has accepted him utterly. And Anna is doing well. Have you seen the news from there?"

"About the strikes? Of course. I am very pleased, very pleased. Comrade Ragosina has galvanized the situation. Half of American industry seems to be out."

"There is even talk of the strikes spreading to the mines and the railroads. People are speculating that the government would take them over and operate them with troops."

"That would certainly be the sensible thing for them to do," Stalin agreed. "But it will be divisive, and if the troops have to operate railroads and mine coal, they can hardly be doing anything else, eh? Oh, she has done splendidly. Now it is really a matter of young Nej and those atomic secrets."

"The atomic formulas will take time. But she has already made several important contacts."

"And Nej? When will he defect?"

"When we tell him to. I do not think Anna has contacted him yet. We must be very careful there. He must choose his moment with great care. I think he will wish to wait until Hayman returns from this so-called fact-finding mission. Then he will wish to link his decision to defect to some external event, perhaps. This is Ragosina's theory, at any rate."

"Yes," Stalin said. "Well, we do not want him waiting too long. No doubt he is living in the lap of luxury. We will give him an event that he can use to upset himself with, and at the same time solve our other problems. And show the Petrova that we are not such fools as she thinks we are. It is time to do something about Petrov."

"Oh, indeed," Beria agreed eagerly. "I shall have him arrested, and . . ."

"On what charge?"

"Well . . . is a charge necessary, Joseph Vissarionovich? In the past we always decided the charge from the contents of the confession."

Stalin sighed. "Times have changed, Lavrenti. I thought you understood that. Once upon a time the world regarded us as pariahs. Anyone who chose to live in the Soviet state deserved anything that happened to them. Then, within our own boundaries, we could do whatever we wished, whatever we decided was best for the state. Now, we are suddenly internationally important, and popular. We have taken on the might of Nazi Germany, the greatest war machine the world has ever seen, and we have smashed it. We have the most powerful army in the world. In the course of time I mean to see that we also have the most powerful navy in the world, and the most powerful air force as well. And when Anna Ragosina has completed her mission, and we have the atomic bomb as well, we shall be the most powerful nation in the world. But such power will mean that the eyes of the world are continually upon us."

"Does that matter?"

"It matters very much, because we *need* the rest of the world, as we never did before. We need their raw materials and we need export markets for our own industries. We can no longer exist in a vacuum, nor, if we are going to develop into the greatest nation in the world, can we produce here in Russia everything we require. But we cannot openly conquer other peoples, make colonies of them, as the British, and the French, and even the tsars were able to do in the old days. Then the Americans would *have* to react. Do you think I have forgotten the past? Historically, Poland belongs to us. So does most of Rumania, and Persia. So does Afghanistan. And so does Manchuria. We will have those places, in the course of time. We will re-create the tsarist empire at its peak. Perhaps we will be even bigger. But for the moment, we must proceed as we are proceeding here in Europe. Slowly. Step by step. We must prove to our neighbors that we are their good friends. Their best friends, in fact. People they can trust."

"We shall never make friends of the Americans," Beria grumbled.

"I know that. Which makes it even more important to be friends with the rest of the world. Thus the old days of arbitrary justice, of arresting people and holding them for several years without trial, are over. You must understand that, Lavrenti Pavlovich. Those are acts of tyranny, despotism, in the eyes of the world, and we must present ourselves as model rulers." He smiled benevolently. "Kindly men. Now, Ivan Nej was no problem, because he was clearly guilty of an atrocious crime, to set beside all his other atrocious crimes. That matter has been taken care of?"

"Ah . . . it has been taken care of, Joseph Vissarionovich."

"The world will soon forget about him. But this Jewish matter is entirely different. The Jews have everyone's sympathy, at the moment. And Judith Petrova is an international figure. Unfortunately, Petrov is another international figure—once our unofficial ambassador in Washington, then a prominent member of our Paris embassy, and more recently one of the heroic defenders of Leningrad. Were we to arrest him, on whatever charge, people would begin to say, look, here is another purge commencing. I do not wish that. Even less do I wish for them to side with the point of view Hayman is going to express in his papers. I wish them to side with us."

"Of course," Beria agreed uneasily, clearly out of his depths. He decided to stick to the main point. "But if we do not arrest him—"

"There are other ways of safely and usefully eliminating someone like Petrov," Stalin said.

"An accident," Beria said. "Of course. I will arrange it."

Stalin gave another sigh. "No, I do not mean an accident. Another accident, coming so soon after Tatiana Dimitrievna's, would be too suspicious. But suppose . . . Petrov has had a hard life. Anyone who fought throughout the Leningrad siege must have suffered a tremendous strain. Suppose Petrov were to go mad?"

Beria scratched his bald head. "I'm afraid he shows no signs of madness, Joseph."

Stalin appeared to be suppressing a powerful emotion. But his voice remained quiet. "That does not mean he is not mad, Lavrenti Pavlovich. He has been living alone since his wife departed on her travels. He may well have suffered a breakdown in the privacy of his apartment. He may be doing very odd things, things which could even endanger his life, but which have so far gone unnoticed. Mad people often attempt suicide. We cannot have that happen to a man of his stature. I think for his own good he should be committed to a mental asylum."

"Yes," Beria said, still uncertain exactly what they were talking about. "But will he not deny that anything is the matter with him? He will tell the doctors that he is perfectly sane."

Stalin carefully began filling his pipe; he seemed very close to snapping the briar between his fingers. "Mad people always claim that they are sane. It is one of the first symptoms of dementia."

"Oh? Ah, yes."

"It will all be very sad. It will be given maximum publicity. We shall all be very upset. And the world will sympathize."

"Yes, but . . . I do not see how this will forward our plans, Joseph Vissarionovich."

"It will accomplish everything we wish," Stalin said patiently, puffing smoke. He held up his hand, ticked off the points he made on his stubby fingers. "In the first place, Judith Petrova will learn that her husband has gone mad, and been committed to an asylum. It will be her duty to return here as rapidly as possible to be at his side. But she will know that Petrov is *not* mad, and that therefore it is a trap, into which she will be stepping if she does come back. If she does *not* come back, however, then she is revealing herself to the world as a heartless, ruthless Zionist, which is in fact what she is. But either way, she will be forced to reveal what she is really up to. And far more important, she will forfeit the respect of every woman in the world, and therefore she will be prevented from having any effect on world opinion, no matter how hard she squawks."

"She will go to Hayman for help."

"Let her. If he starts publishing statements that Petrov is not mad, without having actually come to see for himself, then he will just be revealing *him*self as a rabid anti-Soviet, and the rest of the world will draw their own conclusions."

"Yes," Beria said thoughtfully.

"And then young Gregory Nej can also draw certain conclusions. He will *appear* to draw certain conclusions, publicly. Because he will also know, and he will tell everyone who will listen, that Petrov is not mad, that the Soviet Union, which he has served so faithfully and well, is still ruled by the whim of one man, is still all that the Western press says it is. He will thus realize that he can no longer work for such a government, and he will have his reason for defection. A reason that everyone will believe. You have no doubt at all, Lavrenti Pavlovich, that he can be trusted? Bearing his father in mind."

"He can be trusted, Joseph. He hates his father for the death of his mother. And apart from his own certain patriotism, he is completely under the thumb of Anna Ragosina. If she were to tell him to shoot himself, he would do so without hesitation."

"We must hope that will never become necessary," Stalin said dryly. "Well, you had best get to work."

Beria stood up. But he still seemed uncertain.

"Yes?" Stalin asked.

"These conclusions, which you say Gregory Nej will be able to draw, for the American public . . . will they not be true?"

Stalin gazed at him. "Of course."

"Well, then . . ."

Stalin smiled. "How else *could* this country be ruled, La-vrenti Pavlovich? How else has it ever been ruled, success-fully?"

"But . . . the Americans will certainly believe him."

"That is the object of the exercise."

"And the rest of the world?"

Stalin shrugged. "Some of them, I suppose. But comrade, do you not realize when the time is right—when Nej is fully accepted by the Americans, and has thoroughly infiltrated the Pentagon—then we can discredit his reason for defection as mere hysteria, simply by producing Boris Petrov, alive and well. That will gain us much more than we can lose through his denunciations."

"But . . . will Petrov cooperate?"

Stalin's eyes were hooded. "I leave that to your people, Lavrenti Pavlovich. They have some time."

"You go down these steps here, Mr. Hayman," said the guide, showing George to the heavily worn-away stone stair-case. "And there is the corridor."

Cautiously George descended, and found himself holding his breath. The place, well below the ground, smelled of dis-infectant. But he would have held his breath anyway: Twenty-Five Sucha Avenue was where the Gestapo had had its head-quarters during the war.

Although he had not come to Warsaw to be told about the war, he would have wished to come *here,* even if his hosts had not been so insistent upon bringing him. Here was the true story of what this remarkable, heroic, talented, and yet self-destructive nation had suffered during the longest six years of its history. And although Judith was not a Pole, she was a Jew, and most of the men and women dragged down here had also been Jews. In witnessing the scene of their suffering, he could perhaps gain some insight into what she must have suffered. She and her amazing niece.

The guide indicated what appeared to be a schoolroom, with hard benches arranged in rows, facing a blank wall. "This they called the tram," he explained. "Prisoners brought down here were placed in these seats, to await interrogation. Often they sat here for forty-eight hours, without food or water, forbidden to move. If they moved, the guards beat them with their trun-cheons." He led George further along the corridor and opened a door. "In here they were finally interrogated. They were whipped and beaten, and given electrical treatment. And you will see that outside in the corridor there was a large radio. This was kept playing all the time, loudly, so that the screams would not be heard upstairs in the street." He led the way down a smaller corridor, leading away from the interrogation room. "After interrogation, they were put in these cells." He opened a door, showed George the rough cot, and also the pitted wall. "Sometimes they were executed right here. Those are bullet holes. They never knew when the window here would slide open, and a gun barrel come in. Here, do you see these inscriptions? They were carved on the walls by the prisoners."

George peered at the rough letters cut into the stone. "B–O–Z–E–J–A–K," he read. "And then, B—"

"Translated," the guide explained, "it says, 'Oh Lord, how they do beat.'" He opened another door. "Here is another one. This one reads, 'Nobody thinks of me and nobody knows I am so alone girl 21 years of age and must die guiltless 12:IX.43 Sunday Z R.'"

"Yes," George said suddenly. "I think I have actually seen enough. I should get back to the hotel. To prepare for my meeting with Mr. Osobka-Morawski."

"You are to meet with the premier?" The guide was impressed. He opened the door of the waiting limousine, while George stood on the pavement and inhaled the clean air, and allowed the late winter sun to warm his suddenly chilled flesh. Yet the whole of Warsaw made him feel chilled. The city had been utterly devastated, in a way not even Leningrad had suffered. It was now in the process of being rebuilt, and yet the Poles, with their passionate sense of history, were leaving several buildings exactly as they were, including this one on Sucha Avenue, as permanent reminders of what the war had meant to them. He got into the car and sat beside the guide as they drove through the empty streets. The only other car they passed contained two Russian army officers.

"Your saviors," George remarked, and watched the guide. The Pole's pockmarked face seemed to wrinkle.

"Or don't you consider them so?" George asked. He was not a newspaperman for nothing, even when officially retired.

"Before the Germans came," the guide said, "the Western nations told us we must accept Russian aid if we were to survive. But there is a saying in Poland: the Germans will take

our bodies, but the Russians will take our souls. Now . . ." He
shrugged. "The Germans took everything they could find." He
gave a wry smile. "And still the Russians found something to
take away themselves."

"But your new government, under Premier Osobka-Morawski, wishes to be friends with Russia," George prodded.

He shrugged again. "He spent the war inside Russia, Mr.
Hayman, so what do you expect? Anyway, when you are lying
down, and a lion is standing above you, it is wise to be friends
with the lion. The same thing applies to the bear."

"Do many Poles think like that?"

"All who have not spent the war in Russia," the guide said.
"And even some of those. But they are tired. You can have
no concept how tired, Mr. Hayman. One day they will be less
tired . . . and then it may be too late." The car was stopping.
"We have arrived. Mr. Hayman, I am an old man, and I talk
too much. Because I wanted you to know. But I would be
grateful if you were not to remember who said these things."

"You can count on that," George said. "Tomorrow?"

"Of course, sir. Tomorrow we go to Gdansk, to see the
shipyards."

George thrust his hands into his pockets as he slowly walked
into the hotel foyer. The guide had been recommended to him
by the government, and *he* had arrived here armed with letters
of recommendation from Michael Nej. Therefore the guide had
to be considered, at least by his employers, as a Russophile if
not perhaps a Communist.

But today had merely confirmed the impressions gained
during all the other days, the impressions he had gained before
he had ever left England. Ilona had been quite right: his journey
had not been necessary to confirm his opinions. Yet it had to
be undertaken, because if he was going to report to Truman
what he actually thought about the situation, then he was going
to be virtually recommending a war—not to be fought with
men and bullets, at least as yet, but certainly one that had to
be fought, with ideas and money and, above all, resolution.
The weapons the Russians were using.

That way lay a long, hard struggle. And since the Communist maggot preyed on poverty and disillusionment and dis-
satisfaction, it was difficult to see how it could be exterminated,
when every baby born meant a further diminution of mankind's
standard of living.

His head jerked. He was not naturally a pessimist, and he had promised Ilona that he would not become depressed by what he found here. No doubt it had to do with that dreadful torture chamber, or with the persistent and unthinkable thought that kept nibbling at the edges of his consciousness, that perhaps Peter Borodin might be right after all.

"Mr. Hayman, there is a cablegram for you, sir." The clerk handed him the envelope. "And a message from the premier's office." Like the guide, the clerk was clearly impressed. "A car will call for you at four o'clock."

George nodded absently, took the envelope and his key, and instinctively walked towards the elevator, even though it only worked one day in three, like most things in this hotel. He frowned as he saw that the cable had come from Tel Aviv. He slit the envelope and scanned the contents. The elevator car actually did arrive, the doors opened, and the boy looked for his passenger. But George was already hurrying back to the desk.

"I want to send an answer to this," he said. "And I want you to get me a flight, or a train seat, or whatever, to Tel Aviv. The very first available transport."

The boy goggled at him. "Tel Aviv? You mean, in *Palestine*, sir? But the car, at four o'clock—"

George was already filling in the cable form. "I'll have to make my apologies," he said. "I want to leave at once. So get to it."

It came to George, with a distinct feeling of surprise, as his aircraft dipped out of the sky above the sparkling blue of the Mediterranean and over the Plain of Sharon, that he had never been to Palestine before. His travels, and his main interests, had always been in Europe and North Asia, ever since he had first been horrified by the vast monolith of tsarist Russia, and fascinated by the diverse characters of the people of that crumbling empire. When he was courting Ilona Borodina before the First World War, when Lenin was an anonymous pamphleteer and no one in America but himself had even heard the names of Nej, and Stalin, this historic plain, the age-old corridor from Asia to the wealth of Egypt, belonged to the equally crumbling Turkish Empire. During and immediately after that war it remained a sideshow, despite the historic announcement in 1917 by the British foreign minister, Arthur Balfour, that the British intended to reestablish the Jews in their original home.

His first interest had been aroused by Judith, when she had embarked upon her long campaign. He had talked her out of coming here then, had done so selfishly and unwisely, in view of everything that had happened since. But all the time the pragmatic newsman in him had recognized that here was going to be an unceasing canker, eating away at the peace of the world, however much one might sympathize with the point of view of one side or the other, or of the unfortunate British, who were attempting to cope with one of the most unfortunate of all the legacies of their imperial past.

Tel Aviv was, perhaps, a very typical British colonial town, hot and dusty, and yet remarkably clean and well behaved, saved from mediocrity at once by its evident history—dating from the days when it was called Jaffa and had mail-clad Crusaders walking its streets—and by the brilliant waters lapping at its beaches. There *were* evidences of unrest, he observed, in that the policemen wore khaki to suggest they were a paramilitary force, and in most un-British fashion carried sidearms. They were also, he decided, a peculiarly hardbitten body of men, volunteers for a supremely difficult task—that of maintaining the peace between two hostile factions living side by side, both of whom hated *them* with a single-minded intensity. And yet they were utterly polite when they examined his passport, and inquired his business.

"Visiting a friend," he had said. "I'll only be here two days at the outside."

But the news that George Hayman, president of Hayman Newspapers, was to be in Tel Aviv had spread, and he was soon surrounded by a horde of reporters, Arab as well as Jewish as well as British, wishing to know just what he was doing, what he thought about the local situation, and which side he was prepared to support. His reply that he was on a purely personal visit was naturally received with skepticism, and he was glad to escape into the temporary privacy of a taxi, although a glance through the rear window warned him that several were still following him.

"You have a room for me," he told the desk clerk when he arrived at the hotel.

"Mr. Hayman. Yes, indeed." The young man grinned. "Mrs. Petrov is waiting for you, sir."

"Right. And you can keep those vultures off my back by

not giving them the number," George said, hurrying for the elevator. A moment later he was closing the bedroom door behind him, and looking at her across the room.

"I'm glad you waited," he said.

She shrugged. "I'm good at waiting. But you should not have come. I should not have let you come. Ilona..." Her eyes were dry, and there was no evidence that she had cried at all. But he suspected that Judith had used up all her tears, years ago.

He kissed her on the forehead. "Ilona will understand, Judith."

"But what can you *do?* What can anyone do? I simply must go back."

He half pushed her into a chair and took a seat himself. "Don't fly off the handle, but I have to get some facts straight. I don't suppose there is any chance that Boris *could* have had a breakdown?"

"Boris? Oh, George..."

"I said, I had to find out," George said.

"Boris is the most sane, level-headed man I have ever met. And that includes you, George."

"There are people who manage to preserve that façade, and are actually a jumble of fears and uncertainties inside." He thought of his own daughter.

"If you think that of Boris, then you certainly can't help us."

"I can't if you won't let me. But if you're absolutely sure he's sane, then you *can't* go back to Russia."

"I must. How can I stay away?"

"Because if you go back they'll have you in a lunatic asylum alongside him."

"I can't believe it," she said. "I just can't! Why? In the name of God, *why?*"

"That's what I mean to find out. But I have a terrible feeling..." He got up, walked to the window, and looked down at the crowded street. "Did you write him, as I suggested?"

"Yes. Almost the moment I got here."

"Then I'm right. Your letter was opened by Beria, or one of his henchmen, and they worked out what you were really saying. You were discreet?"

"Of course I was. I just asked him to come down here for a holiday, whenever he could."

"Yes," George said. "Well . . . believe me, I feel guilty for suggesting it, although this proves I was right in the first place about your safety. But we'll get him out, Judith. That's a promise."

"But why, George? Tell me *why?*"

He sighed. "The why is that Russia hasn't changed a bit from 1937, Judith. We all thought it had. We all thought it *must* have, after everything they have gone through, after their troops had fought virtually shoulder to shoulder with ours. We all thought that, because we *wanted* it to be like that. But it isn't, and maybe it never will be. Old Joe is still in charge, and a complete dictator. And he's still as paranoic as he was after Kirov's murder. For some reason he doesn't like what you're doing, or he suspects you're up to something, and—"

"But he gave me his support."

"Judith, what Stalin says to your face and what he does behind your back are two completely different things. Believe me, we're just coming to grips with that fact now, on a world-wide basis. Now you listen to me. I'm going to do everything I can. I can't promise how soon we'll get results, but we're going to get results. But you must sit tight here."

"How can I do that, George? How *can* I?"

"Because you have more guts and determination than any woman I've ever known. You survived the tsar's Okhrana, you survived Siberia, and you survived the Gestapo and Ravensbrück. Are you going to give in now? Anyway, you have a job to do, remember?"

"Such as what? My job is the Russian Jews."

"Your job is being a Jew. Aren't they glad to have you here?"

"Of course they are. They're delighted. But—"

"Then delight them some more. Have you heard from Ruth?"

She frowned at him. "No. And I don't expect to. She didn't approve of my leaving her father and going back to Russia. That's why I didn't want to see her in London. I thought maybe you'd guessed."

"I had an idea. But I still think you may be hearing from her, one of these days. Now Judith, everything is going to be all *right*. Believe me." He held her hands, and pulled her to her feet. "Let's go get something to eat, I want to get back to London right away. I have a lot to do."

"George!" Michael Nej had his own office in the Russian embassy, just off Kensington Gardens, a large, bright room dominated by an outsize oak desk. Now he hurried round it, arms outstretched, and clasped his friend's hands. "My dear George, what are we to do with you? Not even you can . . . how do you say it? Stand up a premier."

"I sent my apologies," George said. "It was an urgent matter."

"Premiers are inclined to regard themselves as the most urgent matters in the world, George. Osobka-Morawski is deeply offended."

"I'll write him a letter," George said. "You haven't asked what the urgent matter was."

Michael Nej's face seemed to close. "Has it to do with me? Ilona? Something has happened to John?"

"No. But it has to do with you," George said grimly. "Boris Petrov has been sent to a lunatic asylum."

Michael stared at him; that he was genuinely astonished could not be doubted. "Boris? I cannot believe it."

"Your old friend Boris," George said. "The man who fought with you in Leningrad. The man to whom both you and I, Michael, owe a hell of a lot for looking after Judith when we couldn't."

"Judith! She will be devastated." Michael stepped back behind his desk, sat down, brought out a bottle of brandy and two glasses, and poured. "She has gone back to Russia?"

"She isn't going back to Russia."

Michael took a sip of brandy and frowned. "I'm afraid I do not understand you."

"You don't seriously suppose that Boris *has* gone mad? Or has even had a nervous breakdown."

Michael's frown deepened. "But you said—"

"That he had been locked up in an asylum. And you said that you could not believe it. Neither do I. Neither will anyone else."

"I do not like what you seem to be suggesting, George."

"I don't like it either. But you damn well know that Boris is not mad, Michael. That he could not possibly be mad. He's been locked up because Judith wrote and asked him to join her in Palestine, for a holiday. Your boss is so convinced everyone in the world is trying to do him in that he's virtually mad himself."

"I am bound to resent that remark, George."

"You can resent anything you like, Michael. I am here to tell you that the Hayman newspapers are going to make a stink about this, and are going to continue making a stink until Boris is let out of that hospital, and is given the normal rights of any human being. And that includes being able to join his wife on a vacation." His finger stabbed the air. "And you can tell Joe Stalin just what I've said, with my compliments."

"George?" Peter Borodin stood back from the apartment door. "Come in, my dear fellow. Come in. I had no idea you were returning to London so soon."

"I've decided to cut short my tour," George explained.

"Well, you could have seen nothing you did not already know," Peter said, taking George's hat and coat. The sight of this man, who as a young man had never even lit his own cigarette because of the hordes of servants around him, now more or less fending for himself never ceased to amaze George. "You'll stay for lunch?"

"Can't, old man," George said. "I'm leaving today for home."

"Are you? Which boat?"

George walked beside him down the short corridor towards the lounge; the apartment was situated in Knightsbridge—not far, indeed, from the Russian embassy—and was more comfortable than George had expected, even if, as in most houses in postwar London, there were damp patches on the walls and a general air of neglect. "I'm not going by ship. I'm flying."

"Flying?" Peter looked scandalized. "Is that not very dangerous?"

"It's not dangerous at all."

"But—the fuel?" Peter had stopped in the living room doorway.

"No problem. We fly from Croydon to Shannon in Ireland, refuel there, fly from Shannon to Gander in Newfoundland—that's the long hop, but these big planes can do it comfortably—refuel there, and then on down to Idlewild. Takes about twenty hours."

"Still sounds a dangerous trip to me." Peter shrugged, dismissing the subject. "Ruth," he called, "George Hayman is here."

"Uncle George." Ruth came out of the kitchen, wiping her hands on a towel, and put up her cheek for a kiss.

"Paul here?"

"He's out, right now," Ruth von Hassell said. "But he'll soon be home. You'll stay to lunch?"

"George is flying back to New York today," her father explained. "He's just dropped by..." For the first time it seemed to occur to him that George might have had a reason for dropping by.

"To see you Ruth," George said. "When we last talked, you had plans."

"Oh." Ruth glanced at her father. "Yes."

"Ah, yes," Peter agreed. "About charging off to Palestine behind Judith?"

George sighed with relief. "You have discussed it, then. Thank God for that."

"It's an absurd idea," Peter said. "A Borodin princess..."

"Papa," Ruth said. "I am *not* a princess. Not anymore."

"My dear girl," Peter pointed out, "one cannot be a princess one moment, and not a princess the next. You were born a princess, and no matter what happens, you will die a princess. And the idea, as I am saying, of a Borodin working on a kibbutz is farcical."

"I am going," Ruth said, a touch of steel in her voice.

"When?" George asked.

"Well..." She flushed. "There are difficulties over obtaining Paul's visa. It's taking an awfully long time. But we will get there."

"It's not a question of funds, is it? If you don't mind my asking."

"Ha," Peter said. "We manage, George. I am still in demand for lectures and newspaper articles."

"Yes. But..." He looked at Ruth.

Her flush deepened. "Paul feels our situation very much, Uncle George. Which is another reason for our emigrating."

"No reason at all," Peter declared. "I have offered him a job. That way he would at least be earning some of the money— my money—that it takes to keep him."

Ruth bit her lip.

"Well, I think you should get to Palestine as quickly as you can," George said. "And if a loan will help matters, then I'm available any time. But your aunt needs you, Ruth. Badly."

"Aunt Judith? What's happened?"

George told them. Peter went to the sideboard and poured three glasses of sherry. "They are bastards, George. All of them. Michael Nej included. Now perhaps you'll agree there is some truth in what I have always said."

"Oh, I'll agree," George said. "Even if I can't agree with your suggested remedy. The fact is, though, Ruth—Judith *does* need you."

"And we'll get over there as fast as we can, Uncle George," she said.

"Write her and tell her that."

"I'll do that, right away."

"Good girl. And give my love to Paul. I must dash." He finished his drink.

Peter came with him to the door. "I know you imagine you're the most broadminded man on earth, George," he said. "But if you ever trust a Bolshevik, any Bolshevik, after this, you need your head examined."

The horses galloped across the sand, yellow spray flicking away from their hooves, unerringly picking their way in and out of gullies, splashing through pools left by the last tide, never putting a foot wrong, leaving their riders to manage as best they could. Gregory Nej clung on for dear life. He had always counted himself quite a good horseman, for his mother had tried as often as possible to re-create the atmosphere of her own youth on Starogan, a prerevolution paradise of which he had only heard, and had taken both him and his sister Svetlana into the country whenever possible, and attempted to let them live like aristocrats, however briefly. But he was willing to admit that he was an absolute tyro compared with his cousin. On the back of a horse, Felicity Hayman was a true Borodin, might have been born in the saddle; she even came to life and laughed as she urged her mount even faster.

As usual, she was flawlessly dressed, from highly polished black boots past thigh-clinging white breeches to blue jacket, and then blue hard hat, which, also as usual with her hats, concealed the last vestige of her lovely blond hair, which she wore in what the Americans called a pageboy. Her hair was the only disappointing thing about her physical appearance. It should have been truly long and flowing, like Mother's or Aunt Ilona's. For the rest, she remained the most perfect woman he had ever encountered—physically. But except on rare occasions, as now, she paid him little attention, and performed her duties as guide—instigated by her mother—with an air less distracted than bored. Of course, he was seven years her junior, and undoubtedly she considered him a very callow youth. Nor had he made any serious attempts to break through her reserve. She was an enemy, as all these people were his enemies.

But he could not stop himself from having erotic thoughts, even erotic dreams, about her. He told himself it was merely because he had not had a woman in too long, and was condemned to spend so much time in this woman's company. He had never imagined life with the Haymans would be anything like this, had not been able to visualize life in the United States at all. He had anticipated an apartment larger than any one in Moscow, certainly, together with much eating in restaurants and cafés, and a continual round of parties at which he would meet people and learn something more about the country and its society, just as he had also envisaged being able to take long, private walks through the streets of New York, observing, stopping whenever he wished, speaking with whomever he wished, feeling the real pulse of America.

Instead he lived in this luxurious mansion, miles from the city. He supposed people *did* walk in New York; nobody walked around the Hayman estate in Cold Spring Harbor if they could help it. If it was a matter of going to the store in the tiny town hardly half a mile away, Ilona and Felicity still drove, or were driven by Rowntree. The servants, from Harrison the butler and the chauffeur down, were not worth talking to; they were entirely committed to the Haymans. And Felicity hardly ever talked at all. Ilona almost every day suggested a drive they might take, and Felicity responded readily enough. Often enough these were into the city. He had been to the top of the Empire State Building, and to the Metropolitan Museum, and to Radio City, but with Felicity at his side he had hardly exchanged a word with a soul. Ilona hinted that things would be different when George returned, and when spring arrived. Then they would be throwing some parties, and they would be taking him on a tour of some other parts of the country. But he had no idea when George was going to return, and in any event, he did not see things changing very much with George at his side instead of Felicity.

Thus he was gaining most of his impressions about America from listening to the radio, and watching this strange thing called television, in which one could actually see the man who was reading the news, or the singers who were attempting to entertain, rather like having a tiny cinema screen in one's own living room. This he found fascinating. But then, he had to admit that he found all he had seen of America fascinating, from the house and its magnificent surroundings to the cities and the freeways. England had been much as he had expected. It's historical greatness was obvious, in the buildings and the pomp and circumstance with which every official action seemed surrounded. But that the greatness was all in the past was also fairly obvious. Although London was not as badly damaged as Leningrad, the people had looked even more desperately unhappy; there were as many shortages and just as much rationing as in Russia. True, the range of goods in places like Harrods had been much vaster than in the Moscow GUM, and also had been available to ordinary people spending English pounds, instead of only to those with foreign currency; but everyone knew that was because Britain was being supported by America, was in fact hardly more than an American satellite, however much people like Mr. Churchill might talk loudly about his country's strength and responsibilities.

But America was another world. Again, he had been warned what to expect, reminded that the entire economy was in the hands of a small group of capitalists, mainly Jewish, who held the rest of the nation in a vise of debt. He had seen nothing as yet to suggest that this appraisal might be incorrect. Obviously the Haymans were outside the normal situation; they belonged to the select group. And while he was being treated as an honored and important guest, there was very little prospect of his getting to know any of the ordinary people at all well.

But he had to concede that they were the most aggressively, confidently, cheerful people he had ever observed. And even if every wage earner *was* working simply to pay the interest on his mortgage and his installment loan, he had done well out of the deal, as could be gathered by a glance at the number of automobiles on the streets, the crowds in the restaurants or at the theaters. And in a few months, as he had been told, there would be crowds on these Long Island beaches.

Americans did not seem particularly warlike. But then, the average German was not particularly warlike. People did what their leaders told them to do. That was the trouble. And these people could be no different from any others. It was not his business either to feel sympathy for them, or to envy them. He was here to work.

And so far it was proving singularly difficult to get down to it. He blamed Anna. He had been here several weeks now, and she had not attempted to make contact. She had left him entirely to his own devices. He had no idea what was happening, when he was supposed to make his move . . . He was in limbo, helpless.

Felicity had slowed her horse to a trot as the roof of the house came in sight, looming over the dunes. Gregory kicked his mount in the ribs to catch up with her, and noticed a woman standing on the high sand to his left, absolutely still, looking down on the two riders.

He knew it was Anna.

He recognized Anna instinctively, even though he could not properly see her face, nor was there anything identifiable about the voluminous coat she was wearing, and her hair was concealed beneath an equally cheap hat. But it was Anna.

He could hardly contain himself, as he rode with Felicity into the stableyard behind the house, or as he sat with her and her mother over the light luncheon they invariably ate. Anna was here! She was here, and she would wait until he was free. After all these weeks, she was here. He would be able to touch her, to hold her in his arms, to be himself instead of constantly acting a role.

"Well," Ilona said. "What are your plans for the afternoon?"

She smiled brightly at her daughter as she spoke. Aunt Ilona was undoubtedly pleased with the way things were turning out; she had explained to Gregory about Felicity's problems. Aunt Ilona was delighted that she had at last found, in him, an excuse to force Felicity out of the house, and today, for the first time, she had got her onto the back of a horse. Apparently horseback riding had formerly been Felicity's favorite pastime, but she had not done any riding for years.

Well, he was pleased too, to have brought a little good into the world, even if it was clearly wasted on such a creature. Now that he knew her sad eyes were merely a result of her inability to cope with tragedy, he had lost a lot of his initial respect for her. How would she fare if she had lost both a mother and a sister, as violently and cruelly as he had?

But it was good to see Aunt Ilona looking happy.

Certainly any sympathy would be wasted on Felicity. The brief spurt of cheerful energy she had revealed that morning was already spent. "I think a siesta," she said. "I'm quite exhausted."

But today her depression was just what he required. "I think that is a good idea," he agreed. "To ride a long way, after not having done so for some time, is very hard on the muscles."

Felicity shot him a glance, and he wondered if he might have said the wrong thing.

"I think *I* will take a walk," he continued hurriedly. "Now that the weather is turning fine."

"On the beach," Ilona said enthusiastically. "There are lovely walks on the beach. Felicity knows some splendid rambles."

He realized he had made a mistake, as usual, by being too forthright. He should have waited for them àctually to retire.

But he need not have worried; Felicity had apparently decided that he had been poking fun at her. "I am going to rest," she said again, quite firmly, and left the table.

"She is so *moody*," Ilona said. "I'm sorry, Gregory. Would you like me to come with you?"

"Of course not, Aunt Ilona," he said. "I shall just take a little walk. I shall not be long."

He escaped the house before any other alternative could be found. He walked slowly at first, while he remained in sight of the upstairs windows of the house, just in case someone was watching, but quickened his pace as soon as he was sure he was out of sight, heart beginning to pound now, sand crunching beneath his shoes, mind whirling with anticipated pleasure, wondering exactly where she would be, and yet he came upon her quite unexpectedly. She sat on a folding stool, and had erected a folding easel in front of herself, on which was a square of canvas, lightly marked with paint.

She did not turn her head, but continued gently to stir her oils. "I had nearly decided you did not see me," she remarked.

"They are difficult people to escape," he explained. He stood behind her, looked at her hair, escaping in straggles from beneath her hat, and at her glasses . . . glasses?

"The girl, you mean," she said, still without turning her head, and leaning forward to add a dab of pale blue to her sky. "Is she one of your cousins?"

"Yes," he said. "A gloomy person." He held her shoulders. "Anna—"

"She did not look gloomy to me."

"Well, she likes riding horses. Anna . . . I never knew you wore glasses."

At last she laid down her palette and brush, and turned, taking off the glasses as she did so. "I do not. But they make a convenient change in my appearance."

He waited for her to move towards him, but she did not, so he looked at the canvas. "I didn't know you could paint, either," he said, and realized that she couldn't.

"I have been taking lessons," she said. "This also makes a good cover. I come here to Cold Spring Harbor to paint, you see. And then, whenever I am here—and I can give you no indication of how often that will be—you can come to see me."

"But how will I know you are here?"

"You will come for walks on this beach. Every day. As you are doing now."

"I don't think I can, every day. Sometimes we go into New York, for the entire day."

"'We' being you and your gloomy cousin."

He knew he was flushing. "Well . . . yes. Sometimes Aunt Ilona comes as well."

"Then I will have to be patient," she said, her face coldly expressionless. "You will walk here as often as you can. Every afternoon, if possible. If I come and I do not see you, then I will spend a day or two painting, until I do."

"Oh," he said. "Yes, that sounds all right." It did not, however, sound at all like Anna Ragosina. "But Anna, it is so good to see you. Anna . . ." He took her hands, tried to draw her upwards from the stool, and found he could not. He was roughly twice her size, but he doubted he was actually any stronger. "Anna," he said. "There is nobody on this beach in the afternoons. We could lie over there, on that soft sand, where there are the bushes. Nobody could possibly see us."

Anna freed her hands, leaving him standing helplessly with his arms dangling at his sides, realizing that this was a side of

Anna he had never seen before. Could she possibly be jealous? Anna Ragosina? And of Felicity Hayman?

"I did not come all the way out here for a fuck, either," she said. "I have come to give you your orders. It is time for you to stop flirting with your so gloomy cousin, and get to work, Gregory Ivanovich. I have received orders from Moscow."

George junior was at the airport to meet his father when the plane touched down from Washington; the president had wished to see George right away on his return from Europe, and George had wanted to see the president. But clearly the meeting had not gone well. It was unusual for anyone to see George Hayman looking upset, but he was looking so today.

"Not pleased?" George junior asked, as he drove out of the parking lot.

"With what I had to say?" George asked. "Well, who would be? It's too close to the opinions that have been forming in Washington."

"So?" George junior frowned at the road.

"So the business is to be handled with kid gloves, for the moment," George said. "Apparently Truman feels we still don't have enough proof of what Stalin is up to. He's disturbed about Churchill's speech in Missouri—it was a humdinger, from what I read in the European press—"

"It certainly was," George junior agreed. "He accused the Russians of erecting an iron curtain across Eastern Europe, behind which they are busily enslaving half a dozen populations."

"Well," George said, "It seems a good many people dismissed it as just the old bulldog pounding his outdated anti-Russian theme. So the president is afraid that by taking too firm a stance against the Reds right this minute, we might alienate more people than will support us. He wants the Soviets to commit some overt act on which we can seize. He's sure they're going to do that, sometime soon. Well, I think old Joe and his gang are a hell of a lot smarter than they're given credit for. I also happen to think that there are a hell of a lot of men holding down the big jobs in Washington who are a damn sight too sympathetic to Moscow's point of view."

"Well," George junior said, putting his foot down as they reached a clear stretch of highway, "I wouldn't know about that. But Truman could just be right as far as public opinion is concerned. It's just too soon after the fighting stopped to go calling our allies enemies."

"You think so?" George snorted. "He doesn't want Stalin upset in *any* way at the moment."

George junior shot him a glance.

His father went on. "It seems that according to our embassy in Moscow, Petrov could well have suffered some kind of a breakdown. Apparently there is well-supported evidence of queer behavior and strange noises coming from his apartment. I tried to tell the president that of course the Reds would make sure the evidence was supported, but he said that until we could *prove* it was a put-up job we'd just be laying ourselves open to the same charge as was made against Churchill—mere anti-Russianism."

"Well," George junior said with some relief, "he could be right."

"He also isn't eager to see any pro-Jewish newspaper campaign, at least in regard to the mass emigration of the Russian Jews. He says we have to take the Palestine problem slowly. To win our point, and have five million immigrants suddenly appear in Tel Aviv, would set everything on its ears."

"He could have a point," George junior said.

"You think so? Do you honestly suppose that if Stalin gave his approval tomorrow, any of those people would get to Palestine the day after? Or that they could possibly all arrive together?"

"Now, Dad, I know you promised Judith—"

"Yes. I promised Judith. And everything she's done has been on my advice. So what do I tell her now?"

His son sighed. "Well, if you're dead set on doing it, not even Harry Truman can stop us. This *isn't* Russia yet, thank God."

"Hell, I won't go bucking the president," George said. "Not when he thinks his whole Russian policy is at stake. I'll just have to explain the situation to Judith as best I can. But you know what?" he muttered darkly. "I think your Uncle Peter may just have a point. The administration *is* keeping its eyes shut to a lot of things, and particularly Palestine, and hoping everything will just go away, given time. Or, as regards Palestine, that the British will somehow be able to resolve the situation. I hope to God they're right, and that one day it doesn't blow up in their faces."

"Amen." George junior swung the car into the driveway; they had made very good time.

"George!" Ilona stood on the steps to take him in her arms. "You've lost weight."

"Which can't be altogether a bad thing." He kissed her. "About Tel Aviv—"

"Oh, I understand about that, George. There was nothing else you could do. What has happened to Boris is shocking." She held his hand as they went into the house, leaving Rowntree and Harrison to help George junior with the baggage. "I'm also worried about Gregory, at the moment."

"Gregory? He's not sick?"

"No. But he seems more upset than anyone about the news of Boris. George . . . he wants to have a chat with you. Do you think he wants to go home? It's been so lovely, having him here."

"I don't suppose he *wants* to go home," George said. "But of course he has to, sometime. He's had a pretty extended leave of absence as it is." He frowned. "But I can't see why he needs to discuss it with me."

Chapter 6

"PENNY FOR THEM," ILONA HAYMAN SAID.

George lay on his back with his hands beneath his head, and stared into the darkness. "I didn't know you were awake," he said.

"Well, I was quite sure you were," she said. "I feel I've been sleeping on a roller coaster."

"Sorry. I'll settle down."

"Is it Judith? Or Gregory?"

"Bit of both, I suppose," he confessed. "When I think of her, sitting all alone in Tel Aviv, just waiting for news..."

"I thought she was moving out to a kibbutz or something."

"Well, you know what I mean."

"As I understand the setup in those places, she's hardly likely to be all alone. Anyway, don't you think Michael will be able to help?"

"It's a chance, I suppose. What a Goddamned mess."

"And now you can't make up your mind what to do about Gregory, is that it?"

"What *can* I do? Here's a captain in the NKVD, who tells me he's disgusted with what's happening inside Russia and wants political asylum. And who also tells me he's willing to buy it, with information. As I say, that doesn't leave me with too many choices. Tomorrow I contact J. Edgar Hoover."

"And that doesn't make you happy? I'm very happy that he's made that choice. How I wish Tattie and Svetlana could have come out before . . . well, everything, I guess."

"I know," George said.

"But you're unhappy about Gregory. Surely you don't think he's not genuine?"

"I wish to hell I knew," George said. "I keep on remembering a conversation he had with Peter, in London."

"What about?"

"About defection. Peter, predictably I suppose, assumed that was what he was going to do—and you know, Gregory didn't get offended."

"Maybe he *was* considering it, even then."

"And just needed this Petrov business to push him over the edge? I guess you could be right." He raised himself on his elbow, and kissed her on the nose. "Anyway, one thing's for sure. Washington is going to be as pleased as punch. So will George junior. It's the scoop of the decade."

"If I have too many more of these pizzas," John Hayman remarked, "I'm going to sink like a stone next time I go swimming."

"So stay on the shore," Arthur Garrison recommended. "All well?"

They drank beer, as usual.

"It seems to be working," John said. "I tuck my little briefcase under my arm every morning, and I bring it home again at night."

"And the little woman never suspects? Never asks about your day at the office?"

"Of course she does. She's interested. But I have a chat about the advertising business with Mr. Forbush every afternoon, and my briefcase is always packed with marketing news and prospective layouts, so I can carry on a fairly coherent conversation on the subject. Your people are very thorough."

"That's what we're here for. And the word is *our* people, remember?"

"Not that I enjoy deceiving my wife," John added. "I feel pretty much of a louse, if you must know. But presumably I will be able to tell her what I'm really doing, sometime."

"Sometime," Garrison agreed vaguely. "How about the rest of the family?"

"Well, my mother doesn't like it at all. I . . . well, I suspect she thinks advertising is not quite respectable."

"That figures. So what do you tell *her?*"

John shrugged. "The usual guff, about a man making his own way. I must say, George seems to understand."

"That's the old man, eh?" Garrison did not seem interested. "What about your brother and sister?"

"Well . . . my brother is amused by the whole thing, I think. And Felicity . . . it's difficult to decide what Felicity thinks. She doesn't say much. Anyway, for weeks she's been spending most of her time driving Gregory Nej around, showing him things. That's what I want to talk to you about."

"What?" Garrison suddenly picked up his pizza again and began chewing intently.

"Gregory Nej. My cousin. I caught his radio talk. Well, I knew that was in the works. You people arrange it?"

"We thought it'd be good propaganda material. 'Red Secret Policeman Defects.' Hell, we ain't never had anything that good before."

"And now you're done with him, he just has to survive as best he can, is that it?"

"Not by a long shot. He's our baby. There's even talk about finding him a job inside the organization. Something like yours. He'd be useful at that. But the boss figured he could do with a nice long holiday first. And—what the hell, you may as well know—the Pentagon is interested in him too."

"Did they get anything out of him?"

"A hell of a lot."

"I meant, anything worthwhile?"

Garrison shrugged. "Who knows? It takes time to evaluate all the information you get in a rush like that. But I can tell you that he confirms everything your stepfather had to tell us. You know he was sent on a fact-finding tour by the president?"

John nodded.

"Well, it was his opinion that the bear is still the bear, as proved by his talks with Michael Nej, and by the Soviets' treatment of that Petrov character. Well, this Gregory Nej has just about confirmed that point of view, as well as supplying information about other things. They're calling him the most valuable defector we've ever had."

"I know that," John said. "I read it in the papers. My brother's paper."

"Oh, sure. Well, he claimed exclusive rights to the story. Naturally, with his old man actually bringing the guy out of England."

"I assume I'd be right in thinking that he now means to stay?" John said.

"Gregory Nej? If he wants to keep breathing, he ain't never going to leave this country again."

"That makes him an immigrant," John pointed out. "A Russian immigrant. How come I still haven't had anything on him?"

"Why should you have a file on him?"

"For God's sake," John said. "I've been given a file on every single East European immigrant over the past six months, and told to make *some* comment on it. Now we have the most important Russian immigrant we have ever had, since my Uncle Peter, and I haven't even been asked to *read* a file on him."

"I told you once before, we didn't think it was necessary," Garrison explained. "Hell, the guy was brought in by your own stepfather."

"And you don't think that is an interesting fact?"

"You accusing George Hayman of playing about with the Soviets?"

"Of course I'm not. But George is a political innocent. Believe me."

"You think so? And what about this Nej character? You wouldn't say he's sticking his neck out, a captain in the NKVD, going on radio and television to tell all America what a lousy bunch the Russians are? You think he's a nut?"

"No," John said thoughtfully. "I don't think he's a nut."

"So what are you trying to tell me? That you don't like the guy?"

"I like him very much. He's a very likable fellow. I knew him before, you know, when I was in Russia."

"Great. Maybe you'll tell me what's eating you."

"I don't know, for certain. I only know that if his name wasn't Nej, but Ivan Ivanski, and he'd been brought into this country by his uncle John Doe, who's a long-established and important figure here in the U.S., and he was also claiming to be a defector, you'd have given me the file and I'd have bounced it right back at you and said, Don't touch this with a ten-foot pole."

"And it would all be instinct, eh? Like Sherlock Holmes."

"Sherlock Holmes was deduction. Mine's instinct, yes."

"Well, Johnnie my boy, I'll note your comments, and pass them on. But remember that what you are being paid for is just that: your comments. The detective work belongs to another department. Division of labor. That's what makes a society great."

"I'll remember," John agreed. "But will you do one little thing for me?"

"Such as what?"

"There's a high-ranking officer in the NKVD, a woman named Anna Ragosina. Maybe you've heard the name."

"Sure I've heard the name. I've been reading your memoirs in The *People*."

"Well, I think it would be a good thing for all of us if you could find out exactly what Comrade Ragosina is doing now."

"How am I supposed to do that?"

"Oh, come on now," John said. "You have contacts in Russia."

"And what's so important about this dame, except that she seems to have been pretty good at killing Nazis during the war?"

"She's pretty good at a few other things as well. One of them was training and commanding NKVD suicide squads. And among the people she trained was Gregory Nej." He paused, but Garrison did not seem overly impressed. "You don't think that might be significant?"

"How? We knew all along that Nej was an officer in the NKVD. He'd have had to be trained by somebody."

"Seems I can't win," John said. "But will you try to find out just where she is now? What she's doing?"

"Okay. If it'll make you happy, I'll see what I can do. But since you obviously don't have *enough* to do, I've got a real juicy one here for you." He placed the file on the table. "Study that one, and let us have your comments. *Your* comments now."

John picked up the file and stared at the name in disbelief: Igor Borodin.

"Sit down, Mr. Hayman." J. Edgar Hoover leaned back in his chair and surveyed the young man in front of him. "I've heard nothing but good reports about you."

"Thank you, sir." John glanced at Arthur Garrison, who gave him a reassuring smile. This time they were meeting in a hotel bedroom, but it was a good hotel, and the desk clerk was apparently quite used to having one of his rooms hired for the afternoon by hard-faced men. Unless he supposed they were all homosexuals, John thought.

"And now you've got hold of something big, I'm told," Hoover remarked.

"Well, sir, I don't know about that. It could all be perfectly genuine. This man Borodin certainly fits the bill as my cousin, if all the information he has supplied is genuine."

"Such as?"

"Well, he claims to be the son of Viktor Borodin. Now, Viktor was a first cousin of my mother. He was apparently pretty leftist in his thinking, despite being a prince, and in fact he joined the Bolshevik movement in 1917, and remained in it for a while, although his parents, and his brother and sister, were all murdered in the revolution."

"You said 'for a while.'"

"Well, the family lost touch with him, of course, but when my mother and George returned to Russia in 1922, Viktor made contact with them, and told them that he was actually working as a White counterrevolutionary agent for my Uncle Peter, who was his cousin as well, of course."

"Your folks believe him?"

"I don't know whether *they* did or not. The Soviets certainly did. They shot him."

"Did he have time to mention a wife, or a son, to your mother?"

John shook his head. "That's the odd part. Mind you, they weren't together very long before he was arrested. Mother was arrested too, just for talking to him."

"I remember the flak." Hoover glanced at the file. "This guy claims to be twenty-five years old. He would have been one when his father was executed. And he was brought up in one of the state orphanages, put into the Red army, fought right through the war, and has now decided to desert to the West, and wants political asylum here in the U.S. Presently held in West Germany, I see. What do you think? You say he *is* probably a cousin of yours?"

"I'd have to talk with him to be sure. But I think it's at least likely."

"Yeah. Now tell me this—if he can put down all the facts about his ancestry, he must know there are aunts and uncles and cousins scattered about the place, and that at least one of them is in a position to do him a hell of a lot of good here in the U.S. So why hasn't he written to your mother in the first place? Has he made any attempt to contact *any* of your family?"

"Not to my knowledge."

"I think it stinks," Hoover said. "I mean, look at Gregory Nej. He says quite frankly that he wouldn't have come over here if his family wasn't here already. He didn't try to sneak in from West Germany."

"Yes," John said doubtfully. He glanced at Garrison, and received a quick shake of the head accompanied by a frown. Obviously this wasn't the place to air any of his reservations about Gregory Nej. "So you're going to turn him down?"

"Like hell we are. Let me tell you something, Hayman. We've known for some time that the Russians are attempting to build up their strength over here. It's evident in the increase of activity, the approaches being made to people in key positions, the infiltration of our industries. But we have also known that there is to be a new supremo, a kingpin who will actually be running the whole show. When I say new, I'm speaking figuratively, because the Soviets have never had much of an organization here in the past, and have never had a supremo at all. But now there has to be an area commander, either already installed, or on his way—the mere increase in the number of agents demands it. Question is, who? We've got people inside the Soviet Union working on it, and though they haven't come up with any concrete answers yet, they *have* managed to catch a whisper that it will be someone very well connected, and also somewhat young for the job. Now, it seems to me that this Igor Borodin fills that bill."

"You wouldn't say that Gregory Nej also fills it?"

Hoover frowned at him, and then looked at Garrison.

Garrison cleared his throat. "Hayman won't be convinced that this Nej guy is genuine."

"For Christ's sake," Hoover said. "He's defected. He's been spilling the beans all over the place. There was no subterfuge about him. *And* he's Ivan Nej's son. Do you know who Ivan Nej is? Or was, maybe. He seems to have disappeared in true Russki style."

"I know Ivan Nej," John said.

"Can you see anyone, even a Russian, sending his own son to a possible date with the electric chair?"

"I don't think Ivan Nej had anything to do with Gregory's being here," John said. "And knowing the NKVD—"

"Ivan Nej had everything to do with that boy being here, and defecting," Hoover said. "It was the murder of his mother that sent him over here, and he came with at least some idea of defecting in the first place. He admits it freely. The Soviet system got to him. But he couldn't bring himself to do it, because he's a decent guy, until he heard about this Boris Petrov being sent to a loony bin just for opposing the Kremlin policy on the Jews."

Hoover pointed with his pencil. "Everything this Gregory Nej has done has been straightforward and aboveboard, and he's sat through over a week of intensive grilling, without putting a foot wrong. I believe in him. So does everyone else who's come into contact with him. And so does your own stepfather. So you have a gut feeling. That's good. I like my people to have gut feelings. But I don't like them to become obsessions. It's this Borodin I want to concentrate on right now. And I'm making him your pigeon, Hayman. Garrison has told me about how you've hinted at wanting to get out into the field. Well, I'm going to give you that chance. Borodin will get his papers, and we'll arrange for you to bump into him accidentally when he gets over here. He's a cousin. You'll be friends. But remember, you have to give him enough rope to hang himself—and as many of his people as we can manage. Think you can do it?"

"Even if it means becoming a Commie yourself," Garrison smiled. "We'll vouch for you, when it's time to quit."

"It's an important assignment, Hayman," Hoover said. "Think you can handle it?"

"What's the program for today?" Felicity asked, buttering her toast.

"Ah . . ." Gregory Nej looked left and right, from George at one end of the table to Ilona at the other. "I thought I'd spend a lazy one."

"And why not?" Ilona said. "I'm sure you need some quiet time. Your uncle and I are going into town. But Felicity will be here, won't you, love?"

"I expect I shall," Felicity said, and waited. She knew exactly what he was going to say. And do.

He flushed. Predictably. And said, "Oh, I don't think I shall trouble Felicity this morning. I thought I'd take a long walk."

"Of course," Ilona agreed.

"I'm not sure that's a good idea," George said. "You can't be exactly the most popular man in Russia, at this moment."

"But I am not in Russia, Uncle George," Gregory pointed out.

"The NKVD has a long arm. You may as well know that the FBI wanted to put a twenty-four-hour guard on you. I've persuaded them that it isn't necessary, out here, and they've settled for having a man in the town who can check out odd arrivals and generally keep an eye on the area. But the deal is that you stick close to the house."

"Good heavens," Ilona said. "It never occurred to me that Gregory might be in any danger here."

"I don't think he is, but we can't be too careful," George said.

Gregory smiled. "Then I will be careful, Uncle George. But you must not forget that I was an officer in the NKVD myself. An instructor, too. I know more about what they are likely to do than they do themselves, I should think." He leaned across the table to squeeze Ilona's hand. "But I shall stay close to the house, I promise."

Felicity continued to look at him, but now he was concentrating on his waffle; apparently he had never had waffles until coming to America, and had developed a taste for them. Yet he knew she was looking at him; the tops of his ears were glowing.

He was an odd fellow. Well, she supposed all Russians were odd. Every tale she had ever heard about her Borodin ancestors indicated that they had been extremely odd. And he was a defector, and therefore, for all his pretended confidence, probably afraid, and even still a little uncertain about what he had done. No matter how much of a monster his father was supposed to be, Gregory was still a Russian, and had deserted his country.

She found him more ambiguous, and therefore more interesting, than any human being she had ever met. He was extremely earthy. In the beginning she had been rather appalled by that. The first time they had gone into New York alone together, on the way home he had requested her to stop the car so that he could relieve himself at the roadside, and she had been so embarrassed she had been unable to speak. But then she had reflected that this was probably the way it was done in Russia, just as his eating habits were not really geared to a separate fork for each course, or to linen napkins, and he looked at women, or certainly at her, with hungry eyes, his gaze drifting from thighs to breasts and then back again, again in a way she had never known before. She had been too young to notice how Daniel Rourke had looked at her, and David Cassidy had always been the perfect gentleman; since David's death the only men with whom she had come into any regular contact were members of her own family.

As was Gregory Nej. The realization made her feel quite uneasy.

But certainly he admired her body, and despite herself, she had to admit she found this exciting. Just as, when they were together, whether going through a museum or eating a hamburger, he genuinely seemed to like her company. What was even more important, he was utterly natural with her, neither gave her the exaggerated sympathy she had come to expect, and dread, from her family, nor the equally exaggerated respect she received from strangers, merely because she was George Hayman's daughter.

For all these reasons, she was quite prepared to like him. She felt that here was someone she could talk to, someone who obviously felt as dissatisfied with the end of the political and ideological scale Russia represented as she was with the other end of the scale as represented by America; otherwise he would not have defected in the first place. It might even be possible to share with him her innermost thoughts, the beginnings of her philosophy.

Since he was so much younger than herself, she had reasoned, there was not the slightest risk of sex actually obtruding upon their relationship. Of course he found her physically attractive; she found *him* equally so. All relationships started with simple attraction like that. But the best ones were surely those in which that starting point developed into a meeting of the minds.

Having decided, with almost conscious decision, that she would be his friend, she had been quite taken aback when, in recent weeks—since his defection, in fact—he had more and more chosen to be on his own. She quite understood, and even sympathized. But she regretted it, especially since she was sure no dislike of her was involved. Quite the reverse—and perhaps that was the problem: he still looked at her with those hungry eyes. Undoubtedly sex had come into it, after all. The poor boy was falling in love with her. It was quite absurd, in view of the difference in their ages, as well as the nearness of their blood relationship—as he was well aware, judging by the sudden fence he was trying to build between them. What he was doing made sense. Intimacy between them would be incredibly stupid, and even more so for her, since she was the older, and also the one with the set ideals she was determined to maintain.

But it was a position she had never been in before.

"You've heard nothing from the State Department about employment?" George asked, folding his newspaper and finishing his coffee.

Gregory shook his head. "Should I apply?"

"I wouldn't. They'll get to you when they're ready. I was wondering how you're situated for funds."

"Funds? Money? Oh, they gave me some. I still have it. I do not seem to need any."

"That's fine. Just remember that if you ever do need any, I'm always here." He kissed Ilona and left the room.

"I must go and put on my walking shoes," Gregory said, and also left the table.

"It's so good to see him happier," Ilona remarked. "And he's good for you, too, Felicity. You know, I have never seen you looking so—well, *interested*. At least, not for a long time."

Felicity drank some coffee. "I assure you, Mother, that I am not in the least interested in Gregory Nej. He's only a boy."

Ilona gazed at her for several seconds. "Yes," she said at last. "I'd forgotten. But he... well, he's exciting. Wouldn't you say so, darling?"

Natasha fussed about the apartment, putting out bowls of salted peanuts and pretzels. "I don't really understand why we have to take him up," she grumbled.

John checked over his bar, arranged the bottles, and filled the ice bucket. "You sound just like Mother. He's a relative, my darling. The very last blood relative we have, in Russia."

"He's not in Russia now," she pointed out. "And I don't see how you can know he's the last. Anyway, he's... well..."

"As you say, he's left Russia now," John said. "And he

lived there for less time than you did, you know."

She kissed him on the cheek. "Forgive me. I'm just nervous, if you must know."

"I do know. Although I can't really understand why."

"Well, it's because, I suppose . . . I just don't want to be reminded of what I've escaped. Maybe I feel guilty about it. I've got everything, just by marrying you. And those poor people back in Russia . . . like Boris Petrov. It makes my blood curdle."

"From what George was telling me, it's probably making Petrov's blood curdle as well. But I agree. It's quite unbelievable that if you earn the dislike of someone senior to yourself, he can have you shut up in a nuthouse even if there's nothing the matter with you. Tell me, when you were living in Russia, did you suspect things like that went on?"

"You don't really think about them. You're conditioned not to. I mean, I *knew* what opposing the Soviets involved. My parents were murdered by Ivan Nej and that Ragosina horror, remember? And the whole farm was razed to the ground. Just because my father was making a good profit."

John squeezed her hand. "I didn't mean to bring that back."

"It's never been away. But after that, after Tattie adopted me, the memory was, well . . . sort of dull. I was too afraid to consider any real feelings about it. I just wanted to survive. And I knew that I could, with Tattie's help. That I could even prosper. The fact that she was Ivan Nej's wife, even if she had left him, just made the whole world too crazy to understand. I think one is inclined to turn inwards, in the Soviet Union. There is the government, the state, which includes people like Ivan Nej and Anna Ragosina, but it's almost as though you take their presence for granted, like diseases and illnesses and injuries. There is nothing you can do about them, except walk very carefully, and breathe very slowly, and keep your eyes fixed on your own business. Then maybe they won't trouble *you*." She shrugged. "I guess I'm talking about a coward. A whole nation of cowards."

"No one can say that, after this last war," he objected. "Least of all about you."

"Oh, that." She walked away from him to look out the window. "When I killed those Germans, it was sheer instinct— reaction to being raped, I think. And beaten. I think the beating was worse than the rape. More humiliating. I just wanted to hurt somebody, anybody, the way I'd been hurt. But do you know . . . I've never confessed this to anyone before, John. Do you remember that morning, when the farm was first overrun, and we were all gathered there, Tattie and the girls, and you and me, to meet Colonel . . . what was his name?"

"I can't remember either. Spicheren, or something like that."

"He was such a nice old fellow. And his men were so pleasant, too. I thought to myself, then, Glory be, they're going to tear down the whole rotten Soviet system, and maybe shoot Stalin, and Ivan Nej, and . . ." She glanced at him. "I guess I included your father in the general hate."

"I don't blame you for that."

She turned to face him. "And you know what? I have an idea there were quite a few Russians who felt exactly the same way I did. Maybe millions. If Hitler had had the sense to let the regular army get on with the job, instead of sending in the SS and the Gestapo, he might have won that war. He certainly wouldn't have had all those partisans to contend with. Would you have gone into the marshes if they hadn't assaulted me?"

"I guess I wouldn't," he agreed. "It's a thought. Ah!" The bell was ringing. "Somebody's here." He opened the door and greeted Beth with a kiss.

"Where's the long-lost cousin?" George junior wanted to know.

"Hasn't arrived yet. But he's coming. He said he was anyway."

"Maybe he'll change his mind, and we can have a family get-together." Beth hugged Natasha.

"That's what we *are* having," John pointed out. "Martinis?"

"Can't be bad." George sat down and stretched his legs. "Ma and Pa coming in?"

"That's right."

"With Gregory?"

"As far as I know. And, believe it or not, Felicity is coming too."

"Yeah?" George sipped, and nodded approvingly. "I'll believe that when I see it."

"This will probably be them now," John said, as the bell rang again. He opened the door, and gazed at the tall, thin young man who stood there, wearing an ill-fitting suit, and with lank fair hair which badly needed cutting. "Igor! Come in."

Igor Borodin stepped cautiously into the room, blinking at the other three people. His shoulders were hunched, and his hands twined together.

"This is my brother George," John explained. "And this is his wife Elizabeth. And this is Natasha, my wife."

Igor Borodin licked his lips. "Madame Brusilova," he said, and kissed her hand. "I saw you dance once, in Leningrad."

"Oh." Natasha flushed, and glanced at her husband. "I hope you enjoyed it."

"You were wonderful," Igor Borodin said. "I was only a boy, but I shall never forget it. The entire orphanage was taken to see you dance."

"It's good of you to remember. Well, I'm retired now. I'm sure you'd like a drink."

"Martinis," John said, and poured.

Igor peered into the glass, and sniffed suspiciously. "Martinis?"

"Mainly gin. Much stronger than vodka. Your health."

"And yours, comrade." He flushed, and glanced left and right. "I apologize. I should have said, friend. Or cousin."

"You needn't apologize," George junior told him. "Come and sit down, and tell us what you are doing."

"I have a job," Igor said.

"As?"

"I am a guard in a bank," Igor explained importantly.

"A . . ." Beth closed her mouth with a snap.

"That is how I met John," Igor told her. "I could find no work when I first came to America, and then suddenly this bank gave me a job, as guard. And the amazing thing is, it is the same bank where John keeps, how do you say, his account? We bumped into each other on my second day."

"He didn't recognize me," John confessed. "But I knew right away he had to be Russian, and he looked remarkably like a Borodin. So I asked him." He looked around the room, a trifle defiantly. "And here we are."

"Banking," George junior said. "Do you find it interesting?"

"Of course," Igor said. "I never knew there was so much money in the world. And I meet a great number of interesting people."

"I'm sure you do. But wouldn't you prefer something different? A little more rewarding, perhaps."

Igor shrugged. "I have no trade."

"Have you ever thought of writing?"

Igor frowned at him. "Writing? Writing what?"

"About Russia, for example. We could use a series of articles about life for the ordinary person in Russia." He glanced at John. "I had some hopes of Gregory, but he's so much under wraps at the State Department, he's not allowed to write a thing for publication. Not even for the family newspaper."

"You never asked *me* for any articles," Natasha said.

"Ah, no. But to be fair, Sasha, the life of a prima ballerina isn't man-in-the-street stuff. It might give entirely the wrong impression of what life in Russia is really like."

"What he means is," Beth said, "that The *People* is really a propaganda sheet, dedicated to demonstrating to the great American public just how obnoxious the Soviet regime really is."

"We don't have to demonstrate anything," George junior said, without heat. "We just print the truth. How about it, Igor?"

"Write about Russia? I could not do that."

"Why not?"

"Well . . . the NKVD. They would get to me."

"Oh, come now. You're in the United States of America. In New York City. Not Moscow."

Igor shook his head. "You do not know them, Mr. Hayman. They are terrible people. They would get to me. They would kill me."

"That I can't believe. What do you think, John?"

"They're here." John opened the door, kissed his mother on the cheek, and shook Gregory's hand. "How's Washington?"

"Very warm," Gregory said.

"Well, I'll turn up the air-conditioner. Now then, Igor, this is my mother, who is your cousin too, I think. And this is our other cousin, Gregory Nej. And this is . . ." He stood back to allow George and Felicity into the room.

Igor stared at Gregory. "Nej? Gregory Nej?" He pointed. "He is an officer in the NKVD."

"Was," George junior pointed out. "He's decided to come and live here, too. You must have read about it."

"He is Gregory Nej," Igor shouted again. "His father is Ivan Nej. His father had my father shot." With a howl of mingled anger and despair, he hurled himself at Gregory.

Gregory's reactions were instinctive. His hands came up, and caught Igor a blow on the side of the face that sent him tumbling to the floor.

"For God's sake!" Beth shouted.

"Gregory!" Ilona protested.

"Grab Igor," George snapped, and George junior and John each took an arm as they helped the panting young man to his feet.

"He attacked me," Gregory pointed out.

"Yes, he did," Felicity agreed. She peered at Igor. "Are you really one of our cousins?"

Igor looked from one to the other. John and George junior released him, although they remained standing beside him, and Igor pointed. "That man is *evil,*" he said.

"Oh, come now," George said, and held out his hand. "I'm George Hayman. I knew your father well, and I'm terribly sorry about what happened to him. But it was a long time ago, before Gregory was even born."

Igor straightened his tie and stood very straight, heels together. "I apologize," he said. "It has been a great privilege to meet you, Aunt Ilona, Mr. Hayman." His gaze swept the room. "To meet you all, after so long. But I cannot remain in the room with that man. I shall say good night." He closed the apartment door behind him.

The Haymans stared at each other.

"That was a brief party," Natasha remarked.

"I am sorry," Gregory said. "I seem to have spoiled the evening."

"Nonsense," George said. "I suppose something like this had to happen, sometime."

"As I said," Beth said brightly, "now we can have a family get-together."

"What do you think of all that?" George junior asked John, joining him at the bar. "Are you going to get in touch with him again? I kind of feel one of us should."

"Yeah," John said thoughtfully. "One of us should certainly keep in touch with him." He clapped his half-brother on the shoulder. "I found him. You leave him to me."

* * *

The fisherman stood in the shallows, hidden from the road by an outcropping of rock and the line of dunes, and cast his line with purposeful determination. He was a very tall man, which was not as conspicuous in America as it would be in Russia, Gregory supposed, and he had rounded shoulders and an enormous hooked nose. He was clean-shaven, wore a sweater, slacks tucked into his waders, and a brown slouch hat. He smoked a pipe, and appeared entirely at peace with the world.

Gregory's heart began to pound. Certainly he was disappointed that this man wasn't Anna Ragosina, but at least he was someone—it had been months since he'd seen anyone at the appointed spot. Lonely, desperate months. And he would be risking nothing by suggesting the password.

"Good afternoon," he said. "Are they biting?"

The man never turned his head. "Only the big ones," he replied.

"I am not very good at fishing," Gregory said. "Perhaps you will teach me where these big ones are."

"It will be my pleasure." Now at last Bogolzhin looked at him. "Are there people about?"

"Not one," Gregory said.

"That is good." Bogolzhin reeled in his line, took it to where his knapsack and basket waited at the foot of the dunes, sat down with a sigh, and began to peel off his waders. "Fishing bores me," he said, shifting to Russian.

Gregory sat beside him. "Why has not Anna come herself?" he asked. "Is she ill?"

Bogolzhin studied him. "Comrade Ragosina is very busy," he said at last. "It is also very dangerous to come here now."

"You are here," Gregory pointed out.

"I am not as important as Comrade Ragosina," Bogolzhin reminded him. "But it is dangerous for me, too. Do you know, at the hotel where I am staying, my room was searched last night? Fortunately, I did not leave anything incriminating in it. Not even a weapon." He continued to study the young man, appreciating his disappointment. "But Comrade Ragosina sends you a message. She is pleased with your progress. She said to tell you this. She is impressed with what you have accomplished. I am impressed too, because you are so young. You are *very* young."

"Were you not told this?"

"I was told you were young," Bogolzhin said. "But I did not understand how young."

"Age is not relevant," Gregory said, "as long as you know what has to be done, and are prepared to do it."

Bogolzhin knocked out his pipe.

"What have you got for me?" Gregory asked.

Bogolzhin got to work with a little penknife, scouring the bowl. "I have prepared lists of what Comrade Ragosina requires." His gaze flickered up. "You understand, comrade, that if these lists were to fall into the hands of the FBI—"

"And who do you think it was that searched your room last night?" Gregory demanded. "It is against all our training to write things down. I will burn these as soon as I have memorized them." He took the papers, glanced at them, and folded them into his hip pocket. "But I have no contacts as yet."

Bogolzhin filled his pipe, slowly and carefully. "You will have, Comrade Nej. We have been informed that you will be offered a post inside military intelligence. Inside the Pentagon itself. We have this on very good authority."

"Whose authority?"

"That is no concern of yours. We have certain people who are in a position to know. But you will be in the Pentagon. We have never had someone actually inside the Pentagon."

"And do you suppose they are going to show me any classified material? I am a defector."

"In the beginning, we understand, they will want you to teach them the methods the NKVD uses for interrogation and political control. This is for their own agents' safety and training. But they will also know that as an officer in the NKVD you will have had access to both military and industrial plans . . ."

"I have had very little such access, comrade," Gregory said.

Bogolzhin smiled. "Oh yes, you have, comrade. Study those papers I gave you. You have had a very privileged career, because you are Ivan Nej's son. The fund of information at your disposal is amazing. Certainly it will amaze the Americans. You will tell them everything they wish to know. Everything. And it will all be true. That over the next few weeks there will be a general redistribution of our most important military and industrial centers is just their bad luck. The information can be proved to be true when they receive it. This will serve two purposes. First, by the very questions they ask you, we will be able to gain some insight into *their* plans. Second, they will very soon begin to trust you absolutely. Then you may well have access to classified material."

"And you expect me to start passing such material to you immediately? That will be crazy."

"Nonetheless," Bogolzhin said, "it must be done. This has high priority, Comrade Nej. We want access to material relating to the American plans for the atomic bombs, as quickly as possible. Especially, we want material relating to the bomb itself."

"That is quite impossible," Gregory said. "It must be the most closely guarded secret in the country."

"No doubt it is. But we must have it. And you must not just sit back and wait to be shown it. You must make your opportunities. We know there are people involved who have serious doubts as to the morality of possessing such a weapon, and certainly of ever using it. People who feel that for the United States alone to possess such an awesome power is wrong, and may well involve the world in an unimaginable tyranny. You will locate such people, comrade. Promise them what you like. *Give* them what you like. For this purpose you have but to requisition, and whatever you need shall be yours." He smiled again. "We recommend—Comrade Ragosina and I recommend—a homosexual approach. Americans are terrified of being discovered to be homosexuals. If you can make them fall in love with you, you can blackmail them for the rest of their lives. And you are a handsome fellow; it should not be difficult. But however you do it, we expect results."

"And you expect me to do all this while living in the Hayman house?"

"That is the best cover in the world," Bogolzhin said.

"It will be very difficult."

"I do not think Comrade Ragosina is interested in your problems," Bogolzhin said. "She wants results." He got up. "I must go."

"When can I see Comrade Ragosina?" Gregory asked.

Bogolzhin frowned at him. "You wish to object to your instructions?"

"I wish to see my area commander. I am entitled to do that."

"I do not think you are."

"But I wish to see her. I *need* to see her," Gregory insisted. "Tell her that. We have known each other a long time. And I have not . . ." He flushed, and bit his lip. "Tell her it is most urgent."

Once again Bogolzhin submitted him to an appraising gaze. "Ah," he said at last. "She has a way with her, has Comrade Ragosina."

"I have no idea what you mean."

Bogolzhin smiled. "But that was in Moscow, comrade. Things are different in America. Here she is area commander." He clapped Gregory on the shoulder. "And here, perhaps, she has discovered the difference between men and boys."

Gregory stared at him, as a dreadful suspicion began to seep through his mind. This man? She would have contacted him almost the moment she reached America, and that was some time ago. She would have been seeing him regularly ever since, no doubt clandestinely . . . but it could not be true. He could not let it be true.

And even if it was, he could not let it interfere with his assignment, or the things he had to do to protect himself. He was too well trained for that.

By Anna Ragosina herself.

"It is most urgent," he said again.

This time Bogolzhin's frown was genuine. "Then you had better tell me, and I will tell Comrade Ragosina."

Gregory hesitated, but only for a moment. What had happened was too important *not* to be told. He related the events of John and Natasha's party.

Bogolzhin's frown deepened. "When did this happen?"

"Three days ago."

"Hm." Bogolzhin stroked his chin. "Do you think this Borodin is genuine?"

"Everyone else does. He could make life very difficult for me."

"Oh, indeed," Bogolzhin agreed. "If his father *was* Viktor Borodin, who was a very well-known White agent, then the odds are he is also involved in counterrevolutionary activities. Why, he could even be working for your Uncle Peter, the so-called Prince of Starogan. Yes, indeed. Something will have to be done about this Igor Borodin."

Gregory realized that he might just have condemned Igor to death. "Perhaps it will not be so serious as all that," he said. "I suppose there is no chance he could have been sent by Lavrenti Beria, to *increase* my cover."

"I doubt that," Bogolzhin said. "But I will discuss the matter with Anna, and see what she has to say."

"And then you will discuss it with me again," Gregory said. "I want no overt action taken until it has been discussed with me again."

"I have said, I will discuss the matter with Comrade Ragosina. We will let you know what we decide." He picked up his fishing gear, turned round, and gazed at Felicity Hayman.

She wore a loose slacks suit, in pale pink, had her hair secured by a headband. Suddenly she seemed to have shed ten years; but she was very rapidly putting them on again as she gazed at Bogolzhin.

He was equally disconcerted, and quickly looked past her as if to see how many policemen she had in tow. Then he realized that she had just come round the nearest dune, by herself, and he raised his hat. "Good morning," he said, and walked away.

At least, Gregory reflected, he had remembered to speak English. But the rat was running out, when the only thing to be done . . . suddenly he was appalled at his thoughts. It was the way he had been taught to think, by Anna. But to relate death to this sadly beautiful woman, on this sadly beautiful beach, in this so secure world of wealth and privilege, was impossible.

He got up, and waited. Felicity continued to watch Bogolzhin's retreating back. Then she said, "The papers he gave you are sticking out of your pocket."

Gregory started guiltily, looked down, and hastily crammed the lists out of sight. "How long have you been there?"

"I have been watching you from the top of the dune for ten minutes."

Once again, he could only wait.

Felicity sat down. "What are you going to do? I suppose what you *should* do is kill me. Would you like to do that?"

He stared at her in consternation, and she smiled. Hastily he sat down beside her. "Why should I want to do that?"

"Because you're a spy."

"For God's sake. I came for a walk, and met this man, who was fishing—"

"This Russian man," she said. "I could tell he was Russian at a glance."

"Well . . . of course he is a Russian. And he knew who I was. He had heard me on the radio, and seen my picture in the newspapers. So when we discovered we were both Russian emigrés, we sat down to talk."

"And exchange papers?"

Gregory's face hardened. "What *are* you going to do?"

"If you don't kill me?" She lay down, her hands beneath her head, and stared at the sky. He watched her blouse rise and fall as she breathed. "I don't know. Will you show me those papers?"

"I'd rather not." He was still desperately trying to normalize the situation. "Why did you follow me?"

"I felt like a walk myself?" But there was color suddenly flaring into her pale throat. "There is nobody at home," she explained, "except the servants. Dad is playing golf and Mother has gone into town."

He lay beside her, propping himself on his elbow. Her eyes were shut. Strands of blond hair drifted away from the head-band.

"Well," he said. "Now we must either be great friends, or great enemies." His body felt light, as if he had no stomach. He knew what was going to happen, what she had come out here to have happen. That thought alone would have induced the lightness. But now, neither of them could face what might happen afterwards.

"What would happen to you," she asked, "if I told Dad what I had seen, and he made you give him the papers to hand over to the FBI?"

"I would be shot," he said. "I beg your pardon. In New York, I would be sent to the electric chair."

Her eyes opened. "I think they would just send you back to Russia, since you're not an American citizen."

"If I am sent back to Russia," he said, "without having succeeded in my mission, I will still be executed."

She raised herself on her elbow so that their gazes were level. Her face was only inches away. "So then," she said, "you *have* to kill me."

He leaned forward and brushed her lips with his own. They parted before him. For how long had she waited to be kissed like this? And he had been taught how to kiss by Anna Ragosina.

He trembled as he allowed his free hand to rest on her hip, and slide upwards, under the blouse, to touch the velvet of her flesh.

She turned her head away, and he felt as if he had been kicked in the stomach. But she only said. "Not here. Please not here. There is nobody at home, except the servants."

"At home?"

She sat up. "I promise. If one of us has to die . . . we'll talk about it afterwards. I promise."

She was incredibly naïve, incredibly youthful. For all her years, she had actually *lived* very little, and her life had been so very sheltered she could still view it as a series of relationships, which could be controlled by mutual respect, mutual understanding, mutual desire. She did not realize that there were things—beliefs, ideals, duties—that transcended the human factor.

But was he being any less naïve in believing it could wait? Because he was also rising to his knees. He wanted her with a desperation he had never known before, at least partly because he wanted Anna so very badly, and could not have her. And she was his for the taking. If he demurred, if he threw her on her back here and now, her protests would be no more than formal. He knew that, and thus there could be no risk, either to himself or his mission. He could satisfy himself, and then drown her. No one would ever know how it had really happened. He had all the time in the world to concoct an unbreakable story; the servants would know she had left the house in search of him, but they might never have met each other at all.

That was how Anna would handle it.

But he was walking beside her back along the beach, brushing sand from his pants.

It was quite a distance back to the house. They half-ran, half-walked, and it took them fifteen minutes. They did not say a word, but after a few seconds his hand brushed against hers, and they remained hand in hand until they reached the house. He wished he could tell what she was thinking, but when he looked at her, she looked away. Yet her pace never slackened.

She ran up the stairs in front of him, brushed the always

excited dogs out of the way, and gave a quick smile to the butler, who emerged to see who had entered the house. By the time Gregory came in she was at the top of the staircase, and Harrison was still there. Gregory climbed the stairs more slowly. It was utterly absurd. The man knew what they were up to.

He paused at the top. All the bedroom doors were closed, and his was at the opposite end of the hall from Felicity's. But she must have gone to hers. He stood outside her door, looked at his watch, and saw to his amazement that it was just two o'clock in the afternoon. Somehow that seemed an impossible hour to be having an affair.

He opened the door and stepped inside. Felicity stood at the window looking out. She was still fully dressed.

"Would you like me to leave?" It was probably a silly question, but he thought perhaps she might have changed her mind, without in any way knowing what he would do if she had. Then he saw that she was unbuttoning her blouse, throwing it on the chair, and still facing away from him.

He closed the door and watched her unfasten her brassiere. If his mother had ever looked like this, he thought, he could for the first time understand how she had turned the heads of half of Europe. Felicity was now turning to look at him, heavy breasts spilling from her brassiere. She kicked off her shoes, released her zipper, then stepped out of her pants.

She stood still, waiting for him. He removed his own clothing as rapidly as he could. They moved together, to meet at the foot of the bed. They were nearly the same height, matched each other lip for lip, belly for belly, knee for knee. He opened his mouth, and she kissed him before he could speak, half pulled him to the bed, lay beneath him and yet possessed him, moaned with pain and yet never relaxed her grip on his shoulders, and he knew that he would carry the marks of her nails for a considerable time. But that was irrelevant, compared with what he was doing, had done, as he came in surging rakes up and down her body, aware that he had discovered only a fraction of her, that there was so much more to be felt and enjoyed, inhaled and tasted.

And yet, it was the most important part of her that had become his. He pushed himself up, gazed at her face, flushed and open-mouthed in abandon. "I did not know," he said.

Felicity held his head to pull him down to her again.

Chapter 7

IT WAS SILENT EXCEPT FOR THE SOUND OF BREATHING. BUT COULD they not also hear their thoughts? Each other's thoughts?

"I did not mean to hurt you," Gregory said into her ear.

"I'm glad you did," she said. "I'm glad it was you." She kissed him. "It won't hurt the next time."

"Do you wish there to be a next time?"

She moved his hand, got out of bed, and reached for her robe.

"No," he said.

She hesitated.

"Don't put it on," he said. "I wish to look at you." Oh, how he wished to look at her, at every bead of sweat on the shell-pink skin, at every dimple of muscle in back or leg, at every secret valley or tumescent hillock.

He had never intended to get involved with her. He had dared not get involved with her. And the situation had not changed, only his attitude had. This woman was too dangerous to live, unless she could be conquered, absolutely.

Was she thinking something similar, about him?

She glanced at him, went to the window, and stood in front of it, the gentle breeze rippling through her hair, drying the sweat. "Will you show me the papers?"

"If you wish. Do you read Russian?"

She turned her head. "No."

"Then I will have to read them to you."

"Would you do that?"

"Would you believe what I said?"

She came back to him, and sat beside him on the bed. "I am betraying my country."

He held her hands. "You are half Russian."

She shook her head. "I am an American. I was born here, I believe in America. At least, I believe in what America could be. The Russians murdered my grandparents. Your Soviet system is abhorrent to me."

"You don't know anything about it."

"I have read a great deal."

"Written by American authors."

"Well, then, I have heard a great deal. From both Mother and Dad. You'll not deny that your Joseph Stalin has been responsible for thousands of deaths, perhaps millions. Executions *your* father carried out."

Gregory gazed at her. She would be more difficult to convince than an ordinary girl, because she was Ilona Hayman's daughter. He could only proceed as Anna would have done.

"They were necessary. I am sure Mr. Hayman's ancestors were responsible for quite a few deaths in your famous Civil War. Do you blame him for those?"

"That was a *war,* Gregory."

"And so was ours a war. A civil war that lasted for too long, and in which many more people were killed than in yours. But it is over now."

"The killing went on long after it was over," she pointed out. "You cannot just kill people for opposing you, whether or not they have arms in their hands. Oh, I suppose *you* can; decent people don't."

"Will you believe that I have never actually killed anyone in my entire life? Not even a German?"

"Oh, I didn't mean you personally, Gregory."

He sat up and held her against him. "Listen to me, Felicity. There is an enormous struggle going on at this moment. It is a struggle for the entire future of the world. We of the Soviet Union had a long and hard and bitter struggle in the first place, to achieve what we have done, our own system of society and government. It may not be your ideal, but it suits us. And if you know so much about Russian history, you will know that it has to be better than life under the tsars. Even your mother would have to admit that."

"Well . . ." Her arms were tight around him. Because of her so-long-deferred grasp at even a semblance of love, he had all the advantages. But they were advantages which would last only so long as they were in this room together.

"We do not wish to impose our system upon any other country," he said. "Believe me."

She gazed at him. "That's not what my father says."

Gregory released her, and got up to stand in front of her. "Felicity, I hate to say this, but your father is not guiltless."

She frowned at him. "I don't know what you are talking about."

He knelt, his hands on her naked thighs. "Listen to me. Your people, your government, your own family, regard the Soviet state as their natural enemy, because our system is in opposition to yours. But *we* know there is room in the world for the two systems to live, side by side. We are afraid of you. Of course we are. You have things like atomic bombs, where we have only bullets. But we hope, we intend, to live in peace with you—with all the world. We do not mean to wage war on you, not now, not ever."

"And do you think we have any desire to fight *you?*"

"The plans are already laid for a preemptive military strike against the Soviet Union. The orders are ready to be given."

"That's absolute rubbish," she said. "It has to be."

"Do you really believe that?"

She bit her lip. "We aren't governed by criminals, Gregory."

"I would be quite happy for you to discuss this with your father, Felicity. Without saying what I have told you, of course."

"With Dad? But—"

"Of course he will deny that there are such plans. But I would like you to find out from him if such a thing has ever been considered."

"To find out?"

"Not for me. I know the truth. But for yourself."

She gazed at him, and he waited. Curiously, he was not afraid, even if he knew that he could never kill her, now. He was too confident of success.

She held his face between her hands. "Did you seduce me?" she asked.

"I am in love with you," he said. "You must have known that. As you said, I should have killed you, back there on the beach. Had I been the sort of person you apparently think all Soviets are, would I not have done so? I am an officer in the NKVD. Do not your people equate us with the Gestapo? I love you, Felicity. I fell in love with you almost the moment I saw you. But I had to tell myself that it was absurd. You are so beautiful, so sophisticated—"

"So old," she said. "How can you love someone seven years older than yourself?"

"Because I do," he insisted, this time with the utmost sincerity, for Anna was *ten* years older than himself.

Once again she gazed at him, her eyes filled with tears. "I could love *you*," she said. "It's stupid. It's wrong."

"Why is it stupid and wrong?"

"Because . . . it is impossible for two people like us to fall in love. We are enemies. We are also first cousins, which in most people's eyes would make our affair unnatural."

He got up and took her in his arms as he scooped her from the bed, then laid her down again, on her back. "When two people love," he said, "things like that are not important."

"And because you *are* seducing me," she whispered.

He covered her. "And myself. With your beauty."

"And because you are asking me to betray my country."

"No," he said. "There is no betrayal. I am asking you to help me prevent your country from committing a terrible crime. But I am only asking. You must make up your own mind. After you have spoken with your father."

They played squash, Arthur Garrison hitting the little ball with tremendous but not always effective power, John Hayman scoring with deft flicks varied with occasional hard drives.

"I'm getting too old for this game," Garrison grumbled as John won again. He toweled himself, and looked up to make sure there was no one on the balcony overlooking the wooden court. "So what do you think?"

"That Igor's assault was genuine."

"And therefore that he's genuine, eh?"

"I don't see how he can be anything else," John pointed out. "He's not going to uncover any state secrets working in a bank, especially when you put him there in the first place."

"Yeah," Garrison said. "But you have to think like the

Soviets think. They play a lot of chess. Say, you used to play chess."

John sighed. "However did it slip your mind?"

"Well," Garrison said thoughtfully, "as I understand it, chess is a matter of outfoxing the other guy. It's all there in the open, what you're doing, but you have to make him think you're doing something else. Right?"

"Not entirely. But you're close."

"Yeah, well now, let's see. The fact is that this guy Igor only turned up *after* your other cousin defected to our side. That's the salient point. So this Igor has appeared as utterly destitute, without a friend in the world, apparently, without even wishing to look up the family he has over here. But, looking at it like a chessplayer—" Garrison ticked the points off his fingers. "The Soviets know that we screen every immigrant pretty closely, especially the ones coming from Russia. So they will be sure we will learn all about this guy, and his background, and his family connections. Therefore they will reason that if we let this Igor in at all, we'll make sure that he contacts his family. Which is exactly what we have done."

"Why should *they* figure on that happening?" John asked. "They don't know I'm working for you. Or at least I hope they don't."

"Not relevant. We'd still want him to make contact, just to find out if he's genuine."

"Why?"

"Well . . . because we'd regard it as a doublecheck on this Gregory character. It all fits. And the Soviets will know there's no other way of getting access to Gregory, except through your family. When he's not with you people, he's always with one of us."

"You're losing me," John confessed. "If you believe Gregory is genuine, and you say you do, why do you figure the Russians want to contact him? To make him change his mind about defecting? It's a bit late for that."

"For Christ's sake, they don't want to *contact* him. They want to eliminate him."

John stared at him. "And you think Igor Borodin was sent here to assassinate Gregory? His own cousin?"

"It fits the Russian pattern, son. They're ruthless as hell."

"I just can't accept that. Anyway, wouldn't he blow the whole thing by taking a swing at him, in my apartment?"

Garrison shook his head. "You gotta think like the Russkis, John. They're deep. This Igor couldn't pull out a gun and start blasting with all of you there, now could he? Not if he hoped to live afterwards. He has to play it smart, infiltrate, and look for the time when he gets invited out to Cold Spring Harbor, and Gregory is there too, and maybe they get to take long lonely walks on these beaches of yours, to talk over Mother Russia."

"I just can't believe..." John paused. He was reflecting that his mother, having been reluctant to meet Igor at all in the beginning, had now gone the other way, and had suggested that the way to make him realize that Gregory was not an ogre, and to bring the poor mixed-up fellow back into the family circle, would be to invite him out to the house for a weekend. "After all," she had said, "he *is* poor Viktor's son."

"Yeah," Garrison agreed. "Worth thinking about, eh? So you want to remember that he's *your* baby. And that whenever he's out at the family place, Gregory's safety is your baby too. You don't want to forget that for a minute." He grinned. "And leave it to J. Edgar and me to decide what Uncle Joe Stalin is going to think of next."

Joseph Stalin closed the file folder and leaned back in the chair behind the huge desk. "This is good," he said. "You are once again to be congratulated. Lavrenti Pavlovich. So is Comrade Ragosina. And so is Comrade Nej, to be sure. Yes, indeed. It is all working very well. But they still have not achieved any concrete results. You must keep on top of them. Comrade Nej in particular is there to work, not merely to enjoy the limelight, and slander me."

"Be sure I shall keep a careful watch on the situation, Joseph Vissarionovich," Beria agreed.

"I was sure you would," Stalin said. "Now, tell me what you are doing about Judith Petrova."

"Judith Petrova?"

"You have not forgotten her, I hope."

"Of course not, Joseph Vissarionovich. But...she is in Palestine."

"Doing what?"

"Well..." Beria polished his pince-nez. "Doing very little, so far as I can ascertain. She seems to have accepted the situation, has officially adopted Jewish nationality, and works on one of those communal farms of theirs, what they call a kibbutz. And now she is being joined by her niece, according to my information."

Stalin frowned. "Her niece?"

Beria nodded. "Prince Peter Borodin's daughter. She and her husband are to join Petrova on this kibbutz."

"And you do not find all this strange?"

"That she should work in a kibbutz? It is what the Jews are expected to do."

"I know that, Lavrenti Pavlovich. What I find strange is that Judith Petrova should be content to sit there, working away in a kibbutz, without making a sound about her husband's incarceration."

"Well . . . perhaps she is leaving the whole business to Michael Nej. I have been bombarded with letters and telegrams from him, some of them quite offensive, Joseph Vissarionovich, even *demanding* Petrov's release. I had meant to speak to you about it before."

"My dear Lavrenti Pavlovich, Michael Nikolaievich will certainly keep on writing you letters and sending you telegrams, and you will keep on ignoring them. And Judith Petrova knows that this will happen. Yet she does nothing. Now she is being joined by her niece, the daughter of our bitterest enemy in the world. Even more important, and to my mind, more sinister, George Hayman is doing nothing. What is more, he has not apparently even done anything about what he saw and heard while in Europe. The *American People* has not even carried a single article by him on that tour. That is unusual. In fact it is unique, in my experience of Hayman. There has been almost no publicity given to Petrov's madness in the West, and we have accomplished nothing towards discrediting Petrova. This is all not only very annoying, it is sinister. I do not like it at all. Something is cooking."

"Well . . ." Beria began doubtfully.

"And we must find out what it is."

"Ah. Yes. Well, perhaps Gregory Nej—"

"Gregory Nej has been given an assignment. I do not wish it tampered with. The person we need to find out from is Judith Petrova. She will undoubtedly know what Hayman is up to, because she will be up to it herself."

"Yes. But you said, Joseph Vissarionovich, that she was to be left alone."

"Circumstances have changed," Stalin pointed out. "They often do. A wise man, an efficient man, allows for this and is ready to change his plans. I want Judith Petrova back here in Russia. And quickly."

"Here? But—"

"She has not reacted at all as we expected her to do. Therefore we are obtaining nothing of value in having her remain in Palestine. Fetch her back. I do not care how you do it. Once she is back, we can give out the story that she has returned to see her sick husband, as she should have done months ago. But I want her here. I want to know what she is cooking up. Never forget, Lavrenti Pavlovich, that this woman did as much as anyone, I admit it freely, to bring down the tsars. She is a born conspirator. I want her here."

"It will be difficult," Beria said. "Technically, while she is in Palestine she is under British protection. And after this fuss they are making in Canada about our activities there . . . as you yourself have said, we wish to be friends with these people, at least for the time being."

"I am not suggesting you kidnap her, unless it can be done without publicity." Stalin's voice was quiet. "But I am sure you have someone who could *persuade* her to return."

"Judith Petrova? She is not an easy woman to persuade, Joseph. She is not an easy woman to frighten. Perhaps, if we were to recall Anna Ragosina from America—"

"Ragosina stays in America," Stalin said. "She is far too valuable there. But I can think of someone who might frighten Judith Petrova."

Beria frowned at him.

"I am thinking of Ivan Nej," Stalin said, his voice now hardly more than a whisper.

"Ivan Nej? But he is . . ." Beria's face went very red.

"Alive and well and residing in cell number forty-seven."

Beria stared at his master, who smiled.

"It is my business to know what goes on, Lavrenti Pavlovich. I know I should be very angry with you. I know that perhaps I should even consider that you have been guilty of treason against the state." He paused to let his words sink in, and watch the sudden color draining from Beria's face as rapidly as it had arisen. "But sometimes all things turn out for the best. Ivan Nej is really too valuable to be killed. And by now the world will have forgotten all about him. He has been suitably punished, in any event. And he will be punished even more, by his demotion to the level of a mere field operative. But Judith Petrova will not have forgotten Ivan Nej. He executed her parents. And he has done various other things, as well, of which she is aware." He leaned forward. "I suggest you take Ivan Nikolaievich out of his cell, Lavrenti Pavlovich, and send him to Palestine, with a suitable passport and a suitable reason for going there, and tell him to come back with Judith Petrova, if he wants his old position back."

"I adore croquet." Natasha Hayman bent over her wood, judging the distance to the next hoop, the lie of the worm casts on the lawn. "I think it is the finest game in the world."

"It allows you to give vent to your worst passions," Ilona smiled.

"Of course. But also because it is very skillful, on a good lawn. One day John and I will have a house in the country, like this, and a croquet lawn. I am determined on that." She smiled. "When he is made a partner in his firm."

"When?" Ilona repeated.

"It will happen. I am sure of it." Natasha positioned herself, the mallet swinging between her legs, brushing back her summer dress. "John has too much talent not to reach the top. Oh, darn it."

The mallet had not hit true, and the ball was slicing to the right, missing hoop and waiting black. "You will have to rescue me, Beth."

Summer Sundays in Cold Spring Harbor. George thought there could be nothing finer in the world. He leaned back in his deck chair, straw hat pulled down over his eyes, and watched the players—George junior was partnering his mother—watched Gregory sitting next to little Diana, opposite him on the far side of the lawn, watched Felicity and John strolling by the rose bushes, deep in conversation—he wondered if she was tackling her brother on the same question she had been asking him a few days ago—watched little Alexander on the grass, playing with his toys. He wondered if any man had ever known such simple but perfect happiness, in his declining years, enjoying his family, watching them at play.

Perhaps a Borodin, at some time in the past. Perhaps old Prince Peter, Ilona's grandfather, the man George had seen only as a corpse lying in state, on his first visit to Russia, after he had viewed the Russian debacle at Port Arthur. After that the family had never been truly united again except in direst tragedy. Ilona would have been eleven when the Russians leased Port Arthur from the Chinese, so presumably she had many memories of Starogan in the golden days, even of croquet on the lawn, with little Tatiana no doubt screaming about the place and cousin Tigran carefully stroking his incipient moustache—had he stroked that moustache the day Dora Ulyanova, the revolutionary, had rushed into his Petrograd office and shot him through the heart?—and cousin Xenia preening herself, and Uncle Igor glaring at everyone with the universal disapproval he invariably exuded.

It was a memory they never discussed, although when they had first met, in Manchuria, Ilona had made him fall in love with the place before he had even seen it, by telling him of the peace and beauty there. It had not been a memory, then, but rather an anticipation. When he actually got there, with old Prince Peter and his heir both dead, with young Prince Peter a Japanese prisoner of war, with the empire being torn apart by defeat and dissension, the beauty was still transcendant, but the peace was already sliding into oblivion. .

To be re-created here, seven thousand miles away, on a lawn overlooking Long Island Sound. He thought, as his eyes closed and he drifted into a pleasant sleep, that as long as memory was there, to gather and retain, and eventually, even forty years later, to re-create, there was nothing to fear from the future.

Not even when that future was suddenly so clouded? But as long as the country was aware of those clouds, and kept itself guarded against them, catastrophe could be avoided. He was only sorry, terribly sorry, that at the end of their lives he and Michael should have had to quarrel.

"I like you," Diana confided to Gregory.

"Why?" He watched Felicity even as he smiled at the girl.

"Oh, I know that I shouldn't. I mean, well . . . but you're so nice. And if I'm meant to like Sasha, why can't I like you too?"

"What do you mean, you shouldn't?"

"Well, Mother and Daddy . . . oh, you know what I mean."

"But I am virtually an American myself, now," he protested.

"I am applying for citizenship. And I have been given a job, helping your government. Doesn't that make me a friend?"

"Of course it does," she agreed. "Mother and Daddy are awfully old-fashioned. And I would like you anyway, because Felicity likes you so very much."

He frowned at her. "What makes you think that Felicity likes me so very much?"

"Well . . . the way she looks at you." Diana flushed, as Felicity herself knelt beside them, having left John. "You do."

"I do what?"

"Like Gregory. Don't you?"

"Of course I do." Felicity smiled. When she smiled she was quite lovely. But it was a sad smile, twisted with thoughts of calamity. Now she ignored her niece to gaze at the man.

"Well?" he asked.

"I . . . I don't know. It's too horrible to contemplate."

"It'll never happen," Gregory promised. "We'll make sure it never happens."

"What will never happen?" Diana wanted to know.

"Nothing," Felicity said.

At that moment Beth laid her ball expertly alongside her sister-in-law's, just brushing the wood, then adjusted them for a roquet. "I have never seen Felicity looking so good," she remarked, producing another perfect shot, which carried Natasha's ball closer to the hoop, while hers rolled across to touch George junior's. "So happy." She arranged another roquet.

"For heaven's sake," George junior remarked, as his ball was sent rolling into the bushes. "There's no need to be vicious." Sadly he walked behind it.

"Or so well," Beth said, lining up her continuation shot.

"Yes," Ilona said, absently watching her daughter.

"I think Gregory is doing her a world of good," Beth persisted, making yet another good stroke, which carried her ball to the very center of the next hoop, and hurrying behind it.

Ilona preferred to remain where she was, next to Natasha. "It's something I should like to talk to you about," she said, speaking very quietly.

"What?"

"Well . . ." Ilona bit her lip. She was not very good at this sort of discussion. But she was at least sure that Natasha would hold a similar point of view, whereas Beth, with her Bohemian outlook, might well approve of the whole thing. "I think that they're, well . . . that they're having an affair," she said, dropping her voice to a whisper.

Natasha frowned. "I find that hard to believe. Felicity is seven years older than Gregory."

"Yes," Ilona said grimly. "It is quite absurd."

"And what makes you think so, anyway? I mean, he's away all week, isn't he? At the Pentagon down in Washington?"

"He's home every weekend. And Felicity meets him, every Friday evening, just like a housewife. Then they're together just about every moment that he's home. And . . . well . . . I've seen him coming out of her room. At six in the morning."

Natasha's eyes widened.

"Isn't that proof?" Ilona demanded.

"Well . . . I guess it'd stand up in a divorce court. But . . . my God! Felicity—"

"Oh, I don't *blame* her," Ilona said. "She's had such a miserable life. And I did rather throw them . . . the thing is, Sasha, what are we going to do?"

"Is it that you don't like the idea of Felicity having an affair with a Russian defector? Well, I suppose—"

"Oh, what has that got to do with it?" Ilona asked. "He's her first cousin—my sister's son. And there's the age difference. Suppose they want to get married?"

"I don't think they can, legally," Natasha said. "You'll have to get advice on that."

"But suppose she gets pregnant?" Ilona's voice rose, and she looked guiltily left and right. But no one had heard; Beth and George junior were still searching for his ball, Felicity and Diana and Gregory were deep in conversation on one side of the lawn, as were John and George on the other. "My God, she probably will get pregnant," she whispered. "I doubt that Felicity knows the first thing about contraceptives."

"Then hadn't you better tell her?"

"But that would be to condone the affair!"

Natasha kissed her mother-in-law on the cheek. "They're happy. Perhaps that is all that matters. Have you discussed it with George?"

Ilona shook her head. "He has enough on his mind."

"Well, I'll talk to John," Natasha promised. "But don't *worry*." She followed her ball.

* * *

John lowered himself into the deck chair beside his step-father.

"How's the advertising business?" George asked.

John gave him a quick glance. Sometimes George used a tone of voice that suggested he knew every secret in the world. But his eyes were still shut.

"It's a living."

"I want to congratulate you," George said, "on those final chapters of your memoirs. They were amazing."

"It was an amazing time," John said. "But I'm glad they're done."

"The time, or the memoirs?" George opened his eyes when John didn't immediately reply. "Times like those are often good, to look back upon."

"Oh, sure," John agreed. "You either love war, or you hate it. You sure as hell can't be indifferent to it. Real war. This cold stuff gives me the shivers."

"Very clever," George said. "But it has to be one degree better than actually shooting."

"Presumably Truman is basing a lot of his anti-Communist actions on what you told him, George."

"He has far better sources of information. But he's right. I had hoped . . . No, he's right, John. And so are you. You only deal with the Soviets by carrying a very big stick, and letting them know it's available for use."

"Yeah. You know, Felicity was asking me a lot of very odd questions, just now."

"About whether it *will* ever become a shooting event?"

"In effect."

"And what did you tell her?"

"That I don't know anything about it. But that if such a war did happen, we would win it." He gazed across the lawn. "That there are those who say we shouldn't wait, but should blast the Reds right now. There are, you know."

"I know," George said. "Your Uncle Peter is one of them. I told her the same thing, but it didn't seem to reassure her."

"Do you suppose Gregory put her up to it?" John mused.

"Gregory? What's he got to do with it?"

"Haven't you noticed how close they've become? When do you last remember Felicity coming down to a croquet party?"

George sat up. "You've got a point. You don't approve?"

"Me? Well . . . oh, for heaven's sake, George, what have

I got to do with it? Felicity's thirty-three years old, and she's had a pretty rotten life. If Gregory can make her smile like she's smiling now, then it's all right with me. It's just—"

"That you don't actually cotton to Gregory. Now, I *have* noticed that."

"I'm sorry," John said. "I hope I haven't offended anyone."

"I don't think anyone else has noticed. But I'd like to hear your reasons."

"For not liking him? Well—"

"Not here," George said, as Natasha hit her wood against the winning post with a great shout of delight. "Play golf with me tomorrow. That advertising agency must give you *some* time off."

"Tomorrow?" John shook his head. "I'm sorry, George. It'll have to be some other time. I have an appointment tomorrow. Anyway, what I think isn't important. Maybe I'm just worried about what's likely to happen next weekend."

"When Igor comes down? You're sure he's going to do that?"

"I had a long chat with him. He seems to have simmered down. But God knows how he'll react. Two whole days."

George smiled, and lay back in his chair. "It'll make for an interesting weekend."

Felicity Hayman soaked in her bath, her hair gathered on top of her head. It was ten in the evening, and dinner had been over only half an hour; the family was undoubtedly still downstairs, enjoying their liqueurs, chatting...but it was established that Felicity always went to bed early.

That she should have a bath every night before going to bed was a new pattern, but it was not one any other member of the family should be concerned with, except Gregory.

And he *was* a member of the family. She was surprised that this should be the aspect of her situation which most worried her, but it was so. He was her cousin, a figure out of her Russian past, an aspect of life with which she had always determined never to be involved.

But once again, she *knew,* and most certainly this had to be for the last time. As to when she had become certain, she couldn't be sure. But it was before that wild tumultuous day when they had first become lovers. That was the important fact. Perhaps she had known from the moment of their first meeting. Certainly the knowledge had come very early in their acquaintance, had established itself even as she had been resolutely resisting it. Because she had known, too, that something was wrong. Unlike the rest of the family, who had observed him only at mealtimes or in public, she had watched him in his off-duty moments, so to speak. As indeed they had been off-duty moments, for him. He had probably not tried to impress a young woman who was in any event reputed to be rather self-absorbed.

And instead he had fallen in love with her, although she doubted whether, in the beginning, it was really herself he had fallen in love with. He had been swept off his feet by the sheer sophistication of New York, but even more by the woman who had acted as his guide. She knew she was beautiful; she could tell that every time she looked in a mirror. She had always delighted in dressing well, however depressed she might have been feeling. Oh, certainly he had never had a chance.

But it was *her* feelings that really mattered. She had not wanted even to like him. And to feel anything more than liking for a Russian officer had been ridiculous; she could not say for a Russian defector, because she knew now that she had suspected his motives from the beginning. Yet the attraction he held for her had been equal to that she held for him. It was because of his natural, easygoing attitude, because he was totally unlike everything she had expected him to be, and because she had soon become aware of his interest in her. This last was the most compelling reason of all.

At first his interest had only amused her. And perhaps intrigued her. Nothing more than that. When she had followed him that afternoon, it had been entirely on impulse. She had suddenly realized how lonely and how bored she had been with keeping herself shut up in this great house day after day, how much she had enjoyed the last few months, driving Gregory all over New York and Connecticut, and that he was probably equally bored, equally seeking more from their relationship, and equally uncertain how to secure it. Her intention had been to do nothing more than walk, and talk.

And instead she had stumbled upon a spy exchange. She was still, when she considered it, amazed at her reaction. At the way she had walked up to the two men instead of turning and running back along the beach. Easy to say that Felicity Hayman had never had to run away from anything in her whole

life. It was far more accurate to say that she had known she
was in no danger, not because she was Felicity Hayman, but
because Gregory was in love with her. The realization that her
instincts had been entirely right had put the seal on her latent
desire. She had realized that above everything else, she wanted
to be loved, physically as well as emotionally, and that her
only reservation was that the man should love her first. After
that there had been no reason for holding back. She had only
wished that he was not so closely related to her by blood, never
that he was not a Russian spy. That consideration had come
later, and been as quickly discarded, because everything he
had said was true. There *was* no way the Soviet Union could
harm the United States of America. There was no way the
Soviets could even *reach* America, quite apart from the absurdity of pitting TNT against atomic bombs, and it *was* wrong
for the United States to have an absolute monopoly of power.
She had read enough history and philosophy to be sure of that.
Lord Acton's famous aphorism—all power corrupts, and absolute power corrupts absolutely—was as true now as fifty
years ago. She could see it happening. And her fears, and
Gregory's fears, had been confirmed by the talks she had had
with her father and with John. They had both tried to slide
round the question, but they had answered her by their very
evasion. Of course America had nothing to fear from a war
with Russia, they had said reassuringly. As to whether America
would ever *go* to war with Russia, well, Dad had said with his
gentle smile, that depends on the Soviets. But be sure if we
do, he had said, we'll smash them in seconds.

As Hiroshima, and then Nagasaki, had been smashed in
seconds? There might have been some reason for Hiroshima,
although she would never concede it. She doubted even Truman
could explain away Nagasaki.

Thus the time had come for her to make up her mind. Or
it would come soon, when he came to her room.

She glanced at her watch and got out of the bath, toweled
herself, slowly and thoughtfully. But her heart was already
pounding, and she could see in the mirror the rose-pink blush
spreading over her body. They had made love five times since
that first afternoon, and each time had been different; therefore
tonight would be different again—some new facet of sharing,
some new use to be made of their bodies, which she would
find initially shocking and even repulsive, but which, having

submitted to, she would discover to be the most marvelous sensation in the world. He was terribly experienced, yet it was not something she resented, or regretted. She was the beneficiary. His touch was the gentlest she had ever known, his desire the most irresistible. His strength was remarkable—to look at, in the row of rippling muscles that illuminated his every movement, and to feel, as it overpowered her own weakness with such infinite care, such utter enjoyment. That he adored her body in equal proportion was certain. She inhaled to force her breasts away from her chest, sucked her belly flat, tensed her thigh muscles to compress her buttocks into hard balls. It was a body to be loved, to be possessed—and it was his in a way he could never be hers. Oddly enough, though, the fact that she had been a virgin had seemed to distress him.

It had not distressed her. His greatest attraction was that he had come from nowhere; there were no childhood or college memories to be shared, to distort the present and influence the future, as there had been with both Daniel Rourke and David Cassidy. Thus there could be an utter lack of inhibition. If *only* they didn't share the same family background. But this was no longer relevant, as she wished to allow herself to belong, more and more, to his demanding manhood, often in direct contradiction to her own instincts. She was surrendering slowly, because his desire to suck her nipples, gently taking them between his lips and into his mouth without ever allowing his teeth to touch her flesh, or to kiss between her legs, using his tongue almost like a weapon, but the softest and gentlest weapon she could possibly imagine, or to stroke her with his fingers, with equal care, always surprised and shocked her in the first instance. Thus relaxation came reluctantly, and thus, she knew, she had not yet obtained the maximum from their lovemaking. What she sought, what she knew was there, would be hers. She never doubted it.

If she wanted it. But that took her back to the beginning. It would be hers, if she maintained their relationship. If she acquiesced in his spying against her country. And if she could truly accept the fact that he was her first cousin.

She lay on the bed, naked. This was the way Gregory liked to see her every moment he was in her room. She looked again at her watch. He would soon be here.

She should be *doing* something. It was absurd to be lying here, panting for a twenty-five-year-old boy. Or was that only hidebound propriety asserting itself, morality, uncertainty, plain age-old American prudery? She had never been so happy. She was never going to be so happy, as in Gregory's arms. Did it matter if he knew it? For he most certainly did know.

But he still needed to be sure of *her*. She could not blame him for this. He was utterly at her mercy; a single word to her father . . . no, there was no way that Gregory could be as sure of her love as she was of his. Unless she made him sure, convinced him that she would never betray him . . . but would betray her country instead. Or was that just more patriotic nonsense? Of course it was. The world was not full of nations. It was full of men and women. If they were foolish enough to combine into nations, and allow their leaders to whip up hate towards other nations, then they were wrong. It was the people like Gregory and herself, who could reach across the barriers of nationality and ideology and past antagonisms, to a mutual love, who were the true hope of mankind.

Had not Dad said the very same thing, to the assembled family, on the day they had been told that Gregory was coming?

The door opened, and he stepped inside. He had been to his own room and changed into a robe, might have been on his way to the bathroom if anyone saw him—except that all the bedrooms in this house had their own baths. But it was late enough for no one to worry about what he might be doing.

He closed the door behind himself and shrugged the robe from his shoulders in the same movement. Neither of them spoke. Words were quite unnecessary at moments like this, when they both knew what they wanted, and knew too that it would happen.

He sat beside her, leaned over her to kiss her on the lips. Then she was in his arms, sitting up, while his fingers traced light patterns up and down her back and shoulders, slid around to touch her breasts, slipped down her tensed stomach to her silk-coated groin. She waited—for something different, some new tearing down of all the barriers of suppressed desire that had accumulated during more than thirty years of spinsterhood.

He stood up, carrying her with him, and gently turned her away from him. "Kneel," he whispered. "On the bed."

She obeyed, instinctively spreading her legs, afraid to consider what he really intended, certain only that it would be experience, and sheer animal pleasure, and thus everything she wanted. And she felt him, more than ever before, because everything was new. His groin was against her buttocks, as if molded to them, his hands were closed on her breasts, his lips were nuzzling the nape of her neck.

But most of all she felt him inside her as she had never done before. Filling her, seeming to reach beyond her vagina to enter her very womb, and create within her an immense sense of well-being.

Their bodies swayed together, back and forth on the bed—again, a new experience, for always before he had moved in and out of her. Now he hardly seemed to move at all inside her, instead remained swelling and swelling, driving out the well-being she usually felt and replacing it with a building sensation, something she had never known before, had never suspected to exist, in her wildest dreams, a release of passion and emotion and desire that began inside her and then raced away to reach her toes and her fingers; even her nose seemed suddenly to glow, and she gave a shriek of sheer ecstasy as her knees gave way and she fell on her face, crushed into the bedclothes by his weight, but now moving by herself, carrying him with her, unable to keep still, determined not to keep still, until she had wrested the very last surge of passion from her orgasm.

He was panting into her ear. "Do you think anyone heard?"

"Hm?" His weight was gone, and she rolled over onto her back, aware of the most delicious relaxation she had ever known. "Was I very loud?"

He smiled. "Loud enough."

"Well, I don't care. I don't care who heard." She raised herself on her elbow. "Will it happen again?"

"Of course," he promised. "If you wish it to."

"Oh, I wish it to. Oh, my darling . . ." She lay against him, her head crooked in his arm and shoulder. "I love you. Oh, how I love you. I have waited my whole life for you, without knowing if you would ever come."

"Then I must be careful not to go away again," he said.

It was the closest he would ever come to asking a direct question, as she knew. Yet the question had been asked, and must now be answered.

"I would never betray you, Gregory," she said. "You know that." She smiled into his flesh. "You knew that from the beginning."

"I need your help."

She raised her head. *"My* help?"

He waited for a few seconds, then he said, "The man I met on the beach requires certain information from me." It would not be wise to mention even the existence of Anna Ragosina. "Information about American imperialism, American plans to destroy Soviet Russia. It is *my* job—*our* job—to make sure such a thing can never happen. This means that I must have a constant method of communication with my contact. But despite my acceptance by your family, by the American public, I am still very much on trial. I must be careful not to arouse their suspicions in any way, even more so now that I have been given this job at the Pentagon, lecturing your army officers on Soviet methods and tactics. For me even to meet my contact again would be extremely risky. I need a go-between."

Her eyes were enormous. "You wish *me* to do that?"

Gregory ran his fingers over her back in a way she adored, and then up to thrust into her hair and massage her scalp, another utter delight.

"What do you want?" she asked. "What do you really want?"

"The atomic secrets," he said, and her breath rushed against his face.

She removed his hand, and sat up.

"That is the only sure defense," he said. "—For your government to understand that the Soviet government is its equal in strength. In time we will discover how to create our own atom bomb. But it will take time. Until Hiroshima it never occurred to our scientists to devote themselves to such a weapon of destruction. But now we know that every day we do not have that knowledge increases the risk of your country attacking mine. Therefore we must obtain the formulas as rapidly as possible."

Felicity went to the window and stared out at the summer night. "How can you possibly get them?" she asked.

"We are working on it."

"By seducing people, the way you seduced me?"

"Is that what you believe, Felicity?"

She turned to face him. "No." She smiled. "Yes. Of course you did. Oh, thank God you did."

"Even if you had not discovered me receiving those papers," he said, "I would have told you eventually. I do not wish to have any secrets from you. I do *not* have any secrets from you, now. And I shall never have any secrets from you, I swear."

"Oh, my darling, darling boy." She sat beside him and hugged his head between her breasts. "And I shall never have any from you. Will you do something for me?"

"Anything you ask."

"Will you swear to me, by everything you hold sacred, that Russia will never, *never* use the atom bomb, except in self-defense?"

"Willingly. We are not in the business of mass destruction. We shall never use the bomb until one is dropped on our own territory."

"Tell me what you want me to do," she said.

"Take a walk with me, tomorrow."

"To see this contact of yours?"

"To introduce you to Bogolzhin."

John Hayman drove his Studebaker slowly down East Seventh Street. It was not a good neighborhood, but it was apparently where Igor liked to be; John had offered to find him somewhere better to live, but he had refused. He was about the most mixed-up guy John had ever met. It was impossible to think there could be anything sinister about him; if it was all an act, then he was in an Academy Award class of his own.

Besides, Igor was the least of his worries, now. What Sasha had told him about Felicity and Gregory had taken him entirely by surprise. He still could not accept that it was true. And what the hell was he to do about it? His attitude was complicated by the fact that he still could not bring himself to like Gregory—or at least, to believe in him. On the surface, he was the most plausible, likable, innocent of men. But John had spent four years watching Anna Ragosina at work, and he simply could not forget that she had trained Gregory. Not that he would ever be able to do anything about it, unless he could actually catch the guy red-handed passing secrets to some Russian agent, and that was an unlikely prospect, simply because he *had* been trained by Anna Ragosina. His superiors, and even George, seemed to accept Gregory without question; obviously, they wanted to. He was a propaganda catch, and in their excitement they had forgotten the old adage about bewaring a Greek, or in this case a Russian, bearing gifts.

Presumably it was not his responsibility. In fact, his responsibility had suddenly developed into keeping Gregory alive and well—so that he could continue having an affair with Felicity.

But in that sense, he thought, as he slowed even further and began looking for numbers, this Felicity business had to be reassuring. Gregory would certainly never have risked an affair with her if he was playing a double game; his superiors would think he had lost his mind.

And Felicity would never dream of having an affair with a man she didn't believe in, utterly. So he was probably quite wrong.

But what advice was he to give Mother about the whole thing?

He became aware, as he pulled up to the curb, that he was parking behind a police car, and that another police car was parked beyond that, and that quite a crowd was gathered outside the seedy-looking house in which Igor rented his apartment.

A uniformed officer stood at his window. "You got business here, buddy?"

John frowned at him, a curiously breathless sensation seemed to take over his mind. "I have a cousin who lives here," he said. "I've come to pick him up."

It was the policeman's turn to frown. "A cousin? You'd better give me your name."

"My name is John Hayman."

"Hayman? Say, you the son of the newspaperman?"

"George Hayman is my stepfather, yes."

"What do you know." The policeman looked up. "Hey, sarge," he called. "I have John Hayman over here."

The sergeant came across. "Mr. Hayman? The people inside tell us you knew this character Igor Borodin."

"He's my cousin," John explained, opening his door and getting out; now his stomach felt definitely light. "What's the matter? Has something happened to him?"

"You could say that," the sergeant agreed. "He fell from his apartment fire escape, about an hour ago. Broke his neck. Your cousin is dead, Mr. Hayman."

Arthur Garrison pulled his car in behind the Studebaker. The quiet back road north of New Rochelle was empty.

"This had better be good," Garrison said. "That telephone number is for use only in an emergency. And on a Saturday morning—"

"Early this morning," John said, speaking very evenly, "Igor Borodin fell from his apartment window and broke his neck."

"You don't say? Now, why would he do a thing like that?"

"What makes you think *he* did anything?"

"Well . . . you've been telling us he's a pretty depressed character."

"And you've been telling me he's a Russian assassin."

"Even assassins get depressed. Maybe he figured he'd blown his mission, like you suggested."

"*If* he was a Russian assassin," John said, "he was just about getting set to *complete* his mission. I was on my way to pick him up and drive him out to Cold Spring Harbor for a weekend with the family. A weekend with Gregory."

"Oh, yeah, that's right," Garrison agreed. "I'd forgotten. Now that's something, eh? Oh, well. You win some, you lose some. You'd better do the right thing by your long-lost cousin, and then go back to work. Now, I have to rush. I'm playing golf."

"For Christ's sake," John shouted. "Do you really think he jumped?"

"How the hell do I know? Maybe he fell. Some of these Russkis hit the vodka pretty early in the morning. Finding out exactly how it happened is a forensic job."

"And you don't suppose he might have been pushed."

Garrison, already opening the door of his car, stopped, and turned his head. "Pushed? Why the hell should anyone want to push him?"

"Well . . . just suppose *I* happened to be right about Gregory, all along, and he's really a plant rather than a defector. Along comes this cousin who might know something about him. That would make the Russians pretty anxious."

Garrison closed the car door and came back across the road. "Your problem, son, is that you read too many thrillers. In the first place, only you have ever had any doubts about your cousin Nej. In the second place, this Igor sure didn't know anything more about him than the rest of your family does. And in the third place, what Russian even knew he was here? That's assuming *he* was an innocent bystander. As he seems to have been. If he was an NKVD agent, as I thought he was, the only people who might have been interested in bumping him off would have been us, and we're a bit more subtle than throwing people out of windows. At least, we try to be."

"He was innocent," John said. "And of course the Russians knew he was here and who he was. Don't you think they know just as much about us as we do about them? Besides, Gregory certainly knew he was here."

"Which takes us back to square one. Let me ask you something. Suppose, just suppose, this Gregory *is* a double agent, if such people really exist. How's he working with the Reds over here? He's either in Washington, being watched like a hawk, or he's in Cold Spring Harbor, being watched like a hawk. He doesn't write letters, and he doesn't make telephone calls. Who's he contacting, and how?"

"He has a lot of time to himself, in Cold Spring Harbor," John said.

"Not really," Garrison said. "He spends just about every moment of the day in the company of your sister, according to our agents on the spot. I don't want you to take offense, son, but *that's* what you should be brooding about, them being first cousins and all."

John flushed, and decided to try another approach. "Did you ever manage to dig up any information on Anna Ragosina for me?" he asked.

"Not a lot. Seems the word in Moscow is that she's been sent down to the Crimea, or some such place. Nobody knows for sure. So you can't even link *her* to this chap's death."

"Nobody knows for sure," John echoed. "What you mean is that she isn't in Moscow and her bosses have leaked word that she's in the Crimea. She could be anywhere in the world. She could be right here in New York."

"Doing what? Shopping on Fifth Avenue?"

"Pulling the strings," John said. But he felt he was hitting his head against a brick wall. "She's the best they have."

"Is that a fact? Well, buddy, I'll tell you what. You produce this Ragosina dame here in New York, or anywhere in the country, and I'll believe you have something on Gregory Nej. Until then, for Christ's sake cool down." He gave a sympathetic smile. "Don't take this thing personally. Hell, I know it's easy to do—first field assignment and all. But we're a busy organization, as you should know by now. We have enough to do handling the real subversives, the real crimes, the real spies and drug pushers, without dreaming them up. Igor Borodin is a police job. If they find he was pushed, then we'll start thinking about who might have done it. If they find that he jumped or fell, then we'll just forget about him. And so will you."

* * *

John ran up the front steps and into the house.

"Why, John, darling." Ilona was just coming down the inner staircase. "Where're Sasha and Alex?"

"She's coming down in her own car," John said.

"And Igor? Don't tell me he's changed his mind?"

"I'm afraid he has. Mother . . . where's George?"

"In his study." Ilona kissed her son on the cheek, then peered into his eyes. "What's happened? You look as if you've seen a ghost."

"I . . . I have to have a word with George. Excuse me just a moment, Mother." He hurried down the hall, knocked, and opened the study door. George Hayman was on the telephone, his high forehead deeply corrugated, copying a message onto one of his desk pads. He looked up as John entered and waved him to a chair.

John sat down, beginning to get his breathing under control. There was no point in getting all steamed up over what had happened, however much he was determined to do something about it, or have George do something about it.

He realized, not for the first time, what a comforting figure George Hayman was, with his wealth, and the power represented by his newspapers.

"Yes," George said. "I've got that. Thank you." He replaced the receiver and looked at what he had written down. He seemed to have aged in a matter of seconds.

"George?" John asked. "Is something wrong?"

"That was a telegram from Judith," George said, slowly getting up. "She and Ruth are in deep trouble."

Chapter 8

THE AFTERNOON WAS HOT. BUT THEN, THE AFTERNOONS IN
Palestine were always hot. It was incredible, Judith thought,
that two peoples should wish to fight each other for possession
of so sunbaked and basically infertile a strip of land, and suddenly she wondered if she was too cosmopolitan to make a true
Zionist.

Yet she was here to stay. She had first wanted to come to
Palestine in 1921. Now it was the autumn of 1946. Hers had
been a long odyssey.

She patted sweat from her lips and forehead, blotted her
neck with the handkerchief, and looked down at her sodden
cotton blouse as the jeep came to a halt, immediately overtaken
by its own cloud of dust.

"It'll settle," the driver said. He was a young Englishman,
whose name was Nigel Brent. He wore the khaki shorts and
bush jacket, the khaki stockings with the blue tops, the khaki
sun helmet with its blue band, and the Sam Browne leather
belts of a British colonial police officer. And since he was
stationed in Palestine, he carried a loaded revolver in a holster
at his waist, in contrast to British police officers everywhere
else in the world. Like her, he was a recent arrival; he had

spent the previous five years fighting Germans and Italians, and was now pitchforked into a situation where both sides regarded him as a nuisance, in the way of the crossfire—and neither side was particularly concerned about his getting hurt.

Judith wondered what he thought about it all. He was an attractive man, young enough to be her son; not handsome, but with large, friendly features that went well with his large body; his exposed legs were those of an athlete. The amazing thing was that he was friendly to Jews and Arabs alike. That, judging by the official statistics, at least one person in every twenty he met might be secretly plotting his murder, and that, again using the statistics, someone was likely to succeed if he stayed here another six months, was apparently irrelevant beside the fact of doing what he considered to be his duty. To leave his relatively cool office and drive a middle-aged female Russian emissary across a desert in the middle of the afternoon was also apparently no more than a pleasant break in routine.

He winked as the dust finally settled and they could see where they were, then pointed. "There's the kibbutz."

The houses gleamed white in the distance. The fields were closer at hand. At least, Judith thought, she was enough of a Zionist to feel pride at the achievement of people who could carve fertility from the very sand, and to feel resentment at the desert nomads who would oppose this simplest and best of man's occupations.

"Where on earth does the irrigation come from, in this desert?" she asked.

"That windmill, basically. There is water, even in the desert, if you know where to dig and are prepared to dig deep enough. These people are always prepared to do that. I must say, you have to admire them."

"Yes," Judith agreed.

Brent glanced at her. Since he was in charge of security for this district, he would have a file on her; she had had to apply for permission to come this far north.

"I'm afraid you'll have to walk," he said.

"Doesn't the road go into the village?"

"Indeed it does. But Rabbi Yanowski is more often found in the fields than in the synagogue." He swept his field glasses from side to side as he looked into the valley below the car, then handed them to Judith. "Down there."

Judith squinted into the glare, and gazed at the short, heavy figure with the rifle slung across his shoulders.

"*That* is Menachem Yanowski?"

"I thought you said you knew him."

"A long time ago. Twenty years. I cannot imagine him ever carrying a gun."

"He has a permit. The fact is, Mrs. Petrov, this is a very isolated kibbutz, and up here in the north we're not all that far from Syria." He pointed at the blue haze of hills in the distance. "Those are the Golan Heights. They actually are inside Syria."

"I see. It seems such a crazy world, doesn't it? What harm can a rabbi cultivating his tomatoes do to anyone, anywhere?"

"Good point." He got out of the car, came around, and helped her out. "Would you like me to come down with you?"

She shook her head. "If you don't mind."

"Not in the slightest. I'll wait here. Do give him a shout." He smiled at her. "I mean, don't sneak up on him."

"You mean he has actually shot somebody?"

"Not to my knowledge. But there is always a first time."

Judith walked down the slope, stones crunching beneath her feet, hot desert wind flicking at her skirt and blouse and the bandanna she wore on her head. Then the ground softened where the water had reached it, and the breeze dropped, as she sank below the level of the hill, and picked her way between the plants, heavy with tomatoes, huge and bulbous and almost ripe, red and succulent.

"Menachem," she shouted. "Menachem Yanowski."

The rabbi straightened, and turned, one hand instinctively reaching for the trigger guard, the other shading his eyes. He was an old man. But then, she remembered, I am almost an old woman.

"Who are you?" he asked.

"I am Judith Petrov. Judith Stein, remember, Menachem? Do you not remember, from New York?"

"Judith? Judith Stein?"

She was in his arms, and he was kissing her on each cheek. His hair was as white as his beard. She remembered the vigorous man to whom she had turned for advice when first she had wanted to come here, more than twenty years before. Despite his utter dedication to Zionism, he had dissuaded her. It was crucial, he had argued, for her to remain in New York and work for Hayman Newspapers, because at that time her friendship with George was potentially of more value to the cause of her people than tilling a field in the desert. Undoubtedly he had been right, even if he had not been able to foresee the affair that had so nearly blasted both her and George's lives.

But that was a long time in the past, and now they had both come home.

"Judith Stein," he said. "I had heard a rumor that you were in Palestine. But Judith . . ." He looked at her ring finger.

"Petrov. Do you remember Boris Petrov?"

"I remember the name. But he is not here with you?"

"No, Menachem." She would not say more than that. She was not a woman who shared her tragedies. Nor was she a woman who despaired. Boris would survive, as she had survived. And one day they would be united again.

"Ah." He seemed to sigh. "But you . . . I had heard . . . you mean you are alive, and well?"

"It was Ravensbrück, Menachem. Not a death camp."

"But still people died."

"There was a war on, Menachem. People were dying everywhere."

"And you are not bitter," he observed. "No, you would never be bitter, Judith. And now you have come to stay with us?"

She walked beside him, up the hill towards the waiting jeep. "I have applied for permission to stay. But I hope to do more than just till the land. I hope to bring many of our people from Russia."

"From Russia? You have been back there?" Menachem Yanowski had been born and had grown to manhood in Brest-Litovsk, before a tsarist pogrom had sent him fleeing across the Atlantic.

"I have been living there with my husband."

"You? In Russia again? After all these years? With *Stalin?*"

"It is Stalin who will let our people go, eventually."

"Do you believe that?"

"I must believe it, Menachem. I have friends who will bring pressure to bear, and I will bring pressure to bear myself, in time. I have been working with our leaders in Tel Aviv. But when my residential permission comes, I want to live here. Would you like that?"

"I would like that more than anything else in the world," he said.

"I am glad. But Menachem . . . I wish to ask you something. There is no one else I know well enough to ask it of. I did not know what to do, until I heard you were here."

"Of course I shall help you, Judith—with advice, at least." He smiled. "I have never been able to offer you anything more than advice. Which you did not always take."

"I need more than advice now, Menachem."

"Then tell me what you wish."

"Do you remember my sister, Rachel?"

"Rachel? She married the Prince of Starogan."

"And died young."

"Yes. It was very sad. There was a daughter."

"Her name is Ruth, and she is on her way here, now. She also wishes to live and work with our people."

"She is one of us," Yanowski said. "She is entitled to come here, and she will be welcome."

"Yes," Judith said. "She is entitled to come here."

The rabbi stopped walking, and frowned at her. "She has suffered?"

"She was with me at Ravensbrück. That is not important now. But she has a husband."

"Ah. She also has married a gentile. Will he come with her?"

"If he can."

"Then he too will be welcome."

"He is a German," Judith said.

The frown was back.

"He travels under a Swedish passport, now," Judith said. "His name is Paul Hassell. But once it was von Hassell."

"He was a Nazi?"

"Yes," Judith said. "But that must be a secret between you and me, Menachem. I am relying on that."

Yanowski gazed at her. "He was a Nazi, and your niece could marry him?"

"He rebelled against the Nazis when he realized the horror of what they were doing. Menachem, he helped Ruth and me escape from Ravensbrück. If he had not done that we would certainly have died. He is a good man, Menachem, and he knows how to fight. He was trained as a soldier. He would fight for us now. There is going to be a fight, Menachem. You know that."

Yanowski sighed. "There already is a fight, Judith. Yes.

Soldiers are necessary, and will be more necessary than ever when we have driven out the British."

"If Ruth and her husband come to your kibbutz, to be with me, would you make them welcome?"

Yanowski looked at the sky, and then down at his tomatoes. "If they come to live with us, and work with us, and die with us, then they will be welcome. As you are welcome. We will go into the village now. My friends would like to meet you. That I know."

Judith pointed at the jeep.

"Ah, yes," Yanowski said. "Inspector Brent. Well, he will be welcome too."

"Just now you spoke of driving the British out."

"That is something we have to do," Yanowski explained. "It is not essential for us to hate them. Inspector Brent I happen to like. He will be welcome too."

The line of people moved very slowly; the crowd of them increased the heat inside the immigration shed. The windows were shut, and dusty; through them Ruth Hassell could just make out the wharves at which they had disembarked, the blue waters of the Mediterranean, the ships at anchor. From those ships, Tel Aviv had looked a beautiful city; she had not suspected that there would be this limbo before they could actually set foot on Palestinian soil.

Everywhere there were British soldiers, and policemen, dressed in dull khaki uniforms, rifles tucked under their arms, surveying the new arrivals with watchful eyes.

"As if we were criminals," Sylvia Levin said. "It is *our* land, and they treat us as if we were criminals."

Sylvia was short and plump; she hardly came to Ruth's shoulder, and clearly had never missed a meal in her life; even onboard ship her supply of chocolates and Turkish Delight had been apparently inexhaustible. The remarkable thing about her was that she was English, born and bred in London, and had lived there throughout the blitz and therefore considered herself a veteran of warfare, and yet in the fervor of her newly awakened religious zeal, she regarded her countrymen, who had fought and gained the victory, as hereditary enemies. Now she bristled with righteous indignation. They had become friends onboard the ship; the Cockney had been able to recognize the aristocrat, with all the possible benefits such a friendship might include. And Sylvia had been one of the very few of this batch of immigrants who had not regarded Paul as some sort of a pariah, not for being a German, of course—no one knew that, or could ever know it, Ruth prayed—but for being a gentile intruding upon this most emotional of homecomings. But in spite of their friendship, Ruth was glad she and Paul were ahead in the line; she could just see Sylvia rubbing the immigration officer the wrong way.

Paul was before the desk, his passport being thumbed. The Englishman raised his head.

"You were born in Berlin."

"A long time ago," Paul said easily. He was not a man who ever showed fear, or even apprehension.

"And you have come here to live? You are not a Jew."

"They are my wife's people," Paul said.

The stamp thudded down, and it was Ruth's turn. No questions here, just a long stare. Then Sylvia.

"You'd think we was carrying bombs, or something," Sylvia remarked.

Heads turned, and the room seemed to freeze. The immigrants exchanged glances, unable to understand the sudden hostility which filled the air.

"Yes," the immigration officer agreed. "You would think that, Miss Levin." He stamped her passport, and they were through, into the customs hall, able to look beyond the barriers at the crowd waiting to welcome them; the room was filled with cries of recognition, wails of pleasure . . . but here too the guards were ubiquitous, standing on balconies overlooking the throng beneath; not even the exercise yard at Ravensbrück had given Ruth such a feeling of imminent disaster.

"There's Judith," Paul said, peering from face to face.

"Thank heaven for that," Ruth said, and waved.

Judith stood away from the throng, an official beside her. She was evidently a VIP. And now she was pointing, and the man beside her had come inside the barrier, and was speaking to one of the customs officers. Immediately Ruth and Paul were being attended to.

"You've nothing to declare?" This man smiled at them. "No weapons or explosives?"

Paul shook his head.

"Then you may go through."

Ruth started to move, then looked over her shoulder at

Sylvia, standing suddenly isolated, lips twisting.

"There are three of us," she said.

"This young lady as well? Through you go."

"Aunt Judith." Ruth gave Judith a hug and a kiss. "Oh, it is so good to be here."

"It is so good to see you. So good to know you have come to join me." Judith smiled through her tears. "I had thought—"

"Never," Ruth said. "I knew you were doing the right thing in marrying Mr. Petrov. But I . . . I had to stay with Papa. At least for a while. You do understand that?"

"Of course I do, my darling girl. Now, I have a taxi waiting. Paul, you are looking well. How was the ship?"

"Crowded."

"This is a friend, Sylvia Levin," Ruth explained.

Judith shook hands. "You are being met?"

"I . . . no. I don't know anyone here, Mrs. Petrov."

Judith glanced at Ruth, who conveyed what she could with her eyes.

"Then you had better come along with us, for the time being," Judith said. "I have two rooms at a hotel. You can share with me, Miss Levin."

She escorted them towards the door, and the sunshine—and more British soldiers.

"You'd think there was a real shooting war going on," Paul observed.

"There is, to all intents and purposes," Judith said. "Of course, you would not have heard. A few days ago the King David Hotel in Jerusalem was blown up by a bomb."

"An entire hotel?" Sylvia cried.

"Well, most of it. They are saying that nearly a hundred people were killed. English officers, mainly. It was their headquarters in the city."

"My God," Paul said. "And they're afraid the Arabs might try it here in Tel Aviv?"

"It was not the work of the Arabs, Paul," Judith said quietly, showing them to the waiting taxi. "It was the work of Jewish extremists."

"But . . ." They stared at her in horror.

"Yes," she said. "The soldiers are wondering how many of the people on your ship will also turn out to be terrorists."

Paul had opened the door for her, and she got in, slid across the seat, gazed out the far window at the sidewalk on the opposite side of the street—at Ivan Nej.

"It was him. I know it." Judith stood at the window of the hotel bedroom and stared down at the street beneath her. "Didn't you recognize him, Ruth?"

Ruth shook her head. "I have never seen him, to my knowledge."

"But you were—"

"Imprisoned by the NKVD? Yes, but they kept me blindfolded until I was in my cell, and then I saw only Anna Ragosina." The room was silent. No one, least of all Judith, had really meant to remind her of those two years. "But it cannot have been him at the dock, Aunt Judith," Ruth said. "Ivan Nej is in prison in Russia, awaiting trial for the murder of Aunt Tattie."

"It was Ivan Nej," Judith said stubbornly. "Do you think I could ever forget him? He murdered my parents."

"But here, in Tel Aviv?" Paul asked. "What on earth can he want here? If it *was* him."

Sylvia Levin sat in a corner, fingers wrapped around her glass, looking from one to the other. Suddenly she had moved into a world beyond her experience.

"Oh, God knows," Judith said. "He works for Stalin. And *he* has fingers in every pie in the world. And he was standing there, waiting for us to come out, waiting for me to see him. Ivan Nej. He *wanted* me to see him. Me!"

"Knowing that you must hate him more than almost anyone else in the world," Paul said.

The telephone jangled. All four heads turned as one; three of them, at least, had known it would ring. Judith walked across the room and picked up the receiver. "Yes?"

"Comrade Petrova?"

"I am she," she said.

"I should like to speak to my niece, please."

"To . . . are you mad, comrade? She has no desire to speak with you. And if you try anything—"

"I am not going to harm her," Ivan Nej said. "I am surely entitled to speak with my niece. It is a very urgent family matter. I will wait for her down here, in the lobby of this hotel. It is broad daylight. Besides, you have my word." He waited, perhaps for a comment, but Ruth did not speak. "Tell her to come down now," Ivan said. "It is a matter of life and death. Perhaps for us all." The telephone went dead.

"What does he want?" Ruth asked.

"To speak with you." Judith stared at her.

"Is he mad?" Paul demanded.

"Downstairs, in the lobby," Judith said. "But why with *you?*"

Ruth returned her gaze. Ivan Nej had come all the way to Tel Aviv, to meet *her?* The man who had had her kidnapped from Berlin, held her for two years in solitary confinement, and then handed her over to the Nazis, all to strike at her father? No matter that it had been Ivan's evil succubus, Anna Ragosina, who had carried out the actual imprisoning. Anna had been working for her master. And if Ivan Nej was here, Anna might well be here also, waiting in the shadows to do his bidding.

Anna Ragosina, Ruth thought. When she had been arrested, and shut up in cell number forty-seven, with no light and no air and no company, Anna Ragosina had been her jailer. She had not understood why, or how, it had happened, and Anna had not been forthcoming. But for two years Anna had been her only companion, and at the end of that two years, when she had believed she was being set free, she had instead been returned to Berlin, where Himmler had already been informed that her mother was a Jew. That had been the final cruelty she received from Anna Ragosina.

And now Anna's master was here, in Tel Aviv, waiting for her, aiming to terrify her into submission by his very presence.

And about to fail, she realized. She took no pride in the understanding that she could no longer be afraid of Ivan Nej. After what he had had done to her, and after three years in the Ravensbrück brothel, she could not be afraid of any man, ever again. But she could recognize how dangerous he still was, to Aunt Judith at least.

"It can do no harm to listen to him," she said.

"Even his words are poisonous," Judith said, and flushed, as if understanding how melodramatic she must have sounded. But she could not believe it was happening, that Stalin should actually have sent after her—and that he should have sent Ivan Nej.

"There can be no danger, downstairs in the lobby," Ruth said. "There are British soldiers everywhere."

Paul gazed at her for some seconds. But he had been married to her long enough to understand something of her courage, and her determination, too. "All right," he decided. *"We'll* talk with him. I'll come down with you. I'm anxious to see what this famous monster looks like."

"He may not speak, if you are there," Ruth said.

"I won't butt in. I'll wait for you on the far side of the room. But I'm certainly not going to let you see him alone, even if the entire British army is standing around."

Ruth hesitated, then nodded, went to the door, and smiled back at Judith and a still overwhelmed Sylvia Levin. "I won't be long."

There was nobody else in the elevator, and they didn't speak until they reached the ground floor. Then Paul squeezed her hand. "Scared?"

"I'm glad you're with me." She stepped out of the elevator, looked over the palm trees and the comfortable chairs in the hotel lobby. There were a lot of people, and there were the inevitable British soldiers. And, on a leather-upholstered bench against the far wall, apparently reading a magazine, sat a little man in a white summer suit and a white straw hat. Ruth had no doubts about his identity; she had seen plenty of pictures. His sharp features seemed to quiver as he saw her, like a mouse smelling cheese.

"There he is," she said.

"Not quite what I'd expected," Paul remarked. "I'll stay over here. But I'll be watching everything that happens."

Ruth nodded and walked across the floor, her heels sounding very loud on the marble floor. Ivan looked up, and smiled, then stood up.

"Ruth," he said. "Ruth Borodina. Ruth Hassell. You have not changed as much as I would have expected."

"It is only five years since I left your cell," Ruth said, keeping her voice even with an effort. So he *had* seen her, even though she had never met him before today.

"And in that time you have suffered a great deal." Ivan sat down again, and Ruth took a chair beside him. "Do you hate me very much?"

"I despise you," Ruth said.

Ivan gazed at her. "I do not blame you," he said. "I did what I had to do. Will you believe that when I was told to send you back to Germany, I wept?"

"Does it matter?" Ruth asked, "—whether I believe you or not?" How incredible, she thought, that I should be sitting here, exchanging pleasantries with a mass murderer, a man who once had me chained to a stone floor.

He was again giving her an appraising stare. "But now you are happy," he said. "And that is your husband over there, watching us? He is a fine-looking man."

Ruth said nothing.

"You were in Sweden when the war ended," Ivan said. "And then you went to England to be with your father. Is that right?"

Ruth looked down at her hand; Ivan's had fallen on top of it. Carefully she drew the fingers away, and clasped them on her lap. "You had something to say to me. Something important."

"Indeed I do," Ivan said. "It concerns your Aunt Judith. You are fond of her?"

"She is the most important woman in the world to me," Ruth said. "If anything were to happen to her—"

"That is why I am here," Ivan said. "You know she has been acting as a Soviet emissary, officially, with a view to discovering what Russian Jews can be accommodated here?"

"Yes." Ruth frowned.

"Well, it has come to the attention of my superiors in Moscow that she is actually engaging in anti-Soviet activities."

"Aunt Judith is no longer working for your superiors," Ruth pointed out.

"*They* do not know that," Ivan said, "since she has not actually told them so. Thus their suspicions. And you know that suspicions are often enough to condemn a person."

Ruth's frown deepened. "And you have come all the way to Tel Aviv, to tell me this?"

Ivan smiled. "Hardly. I have come to invite your aunt to return to Russia with me, and answer these undoubtedly unfounded suspicions."

"And you really suppose she will do that?"

Ivan's spectacles seemed to glint. "I think, if she will see me, that I may be able to persuade her that such a course of action would be in her own best interests. And the best interests of others. You will know that her husband has been taken ill?"

"So I have been told."

"Well, he is getting no better. It is even feared that he may never recover at all. It is an illness he seems to have contracted in Leningrad during the war. There are several others who are suffering from the same complaint, all commissars, but all men with a weakness, perhaps. The others are all Jews, and it is supposed that their religion inclined them to think more of the Jews than of the Russians, and that they might even have been so deluded as to communicate with the Germans from time to time, offering such things as a surrender of the city in exchange for a better treatment of their people in occupied Europe."

"Boris Petrov is not a Jew," Ruth said.

Ivan shrugged. "And thus at the time he was above suspicion. But now that he is married to a Jew, who is acting so very unpatriotically, it is remembered that Comrade Petrov has always been very sympathetic towards the Jews. Ruth, I have to tell you that this disease could well prove fatal. It has already proved fatal to at least one of the people I was speaking of." Once again he picked up her hand, and gave it a gentle squeeze. "He needs help. He needs the help of his wife. You ask your aunt to think about what I have told you. I will be going from here to Jerusalem. I have always wanted to see Jerusalem. Tell her to contact me there, at the International Hotel. Tomorrow."

Ruth shook her head. "She cannot possibly come to Jerusalem tomorrow. Tomorrow we are leaving Tel Aviv."

"Well, then, as soon as she can. I will be in Jerusalem for several days. But she should not delay for *too* long. Every day poor Boris gets more and more ill. Every day is precious." Ivan smiled sadly. "You tell her that."

Judith paced the bedroom floor, fingers twisting together. "I must go," she said. "That is a direct threat to Boris's life. And more. Why did he approach you, instead of me, directly? He is threatening your life, as well."

"You cannot go," Ruth insisted, for the fourth time. "Then you will be held too. Perhaps even executed. Uncle George was right about that. Ivan Nej approached me because he imagined that considering what happened in 1939, I would be terrified at the very sight of him, and that that would terrify you, too. But I assure you, he can no longer harm me."

"I'll see to that," Paul agreed.

"Just as he can no longer harm you, either, Aunt Judith. Unless you let him. He is laying an elaborate trap. He doesn't dare do anything openly against you. You *have* to go to him, of your own free will. Once you do that, he can perhaps force you to accompany him back to Russia. Until you do that, he is helpless."

Judith stared at them, chewing her lip.

"Do things like this really *happen?*" Sylvia inquired.

"In Russia they do," Ruth said, and gazed at Paul.

"And in some other countries as well, from time to time," Paul said.

"You expect me just to sit here, or on the kibbutz, and do *nothing?*" Judith demanded. "I have been doing that for months. And now they will execute Boris."

"It is a *trap,*" Ruth shouted.

"I had hoped, I had prayed," Judith said, as if her niece had not spoken, "that Michael would be able to intervene. Even that I would be able to resume what I came here to do—to help my people. My Russian people. How can that be anti-Soviet? And once again I have failed. All my life I have just stumbled from failure to failure."

"That isn't true," Ruth said.

"You've survived, Judith," Paul said. "And in this century of ours, that is quite an achievement in itself."

"So I abandon Boris, and I go on surviving, a fugitive, no use to a soul, for the rest of my life," Judith said bitterly.

"How can you be a fugitive, here in Palestine? This is your home, far more than Russia ever was, or England, or America."

"Oh . . ." She walked to the window, and stared out at the night. They had argued all afternoon, taken their meals in the bedroom so as not to interrupt the debate. "Then you believe what Ivan Nej had to say?"

Ruth gazed at Paul. "There is no reason to *dis*believe him. Why should he come all this way to see us, and then tell me some lie? He has been sent to frighten you into returning to Russia. It is as simple as that. But you must not let him succeed."

Judith forced a smile. "I will sleep on it," she said.

"And we'll get some sleep as well," Paul said, escorting Ruth into the second room, and throwing himself across the bed. "I have never been so exhausted in my life. And I had thought that coming to Palestine would mean an end to all the horrors. I knew there would be danger, but *this* . . ."

Ruth sat beside him and propped herself on her elbow to look into his face. "It will be an end. It's home. Believe me, I'm terribly sorry Judith hasn't found her rest yet. But she will. I think that her getting here at all is the luckiest thing that has happened to her. Of course I'm sorry about poor Mr. Petrov. But we simply can't let her go back."

"I have an idea your Aunt Judith will make up her own mind." He sighed. "You don't think that some people are like the Flying Dutchman? Born to roam, with never a rest in their entire lives?"

"Judith?"

"Perhaps. I was actually thinking of you and me."

"Us?"

"Well . . . with this Nej man trotting at your heels, the weight of what the Borodins were, and what they did, hanging around your neck all the while . . . I'm not complaining. I have it coming, I suppose. Don't shake your head. I *was* a Nazi."

"You're suggesting that seventy percent of the people in Germany are never going to have any rest."

"Could be right."

"That's nonsense. And what about me?"

"*You*—you've never done anything wrong in your entire life, and yet you have lived one long agony almost from the day you were born. It doesn't seem right."

"It's over now," she said, "for both of us. We are here, and we are never going to wander again. Promise me?"

"Certainly not if I can help it."

"Then that's agreed." She pushed herself up and took off her blouse. "Are we going to celebrate our arrival? Or are you still thinking about Ivan Nej?"

He caught her wrist and pulled her down into his arms. "Never Ivan Nej."

Ruth shivered. "Despite what I told Judith, you know, he *does* scare me. I hope I never have to see him again. I won't ever have to see him again, Paul, will I?"

"Not if you're right, and this is to be our home, my dearest one. The Ivan Nejs of this world have no place on a kibbutz. And I promise you this: he will never harm you again, either. No one will ever do that, while I live and breathe."

The hall was crowded. It occurred to Ruth that everyone in the kibbutz must be here tonight, to greet the new arrivals. Of course curiosity would have a great deal to do with it, but everyone appeared very friendly. And there had to be more than mere curiosity involved. She had been quite disturbed by the realization of just how complete a community a kibbutz was. It was not merely the communal eating, the total commitment of everyone to the village's labor, the obvious sense of independence; this kibbutz had been here for twenty years, and the older residents had shared a great deal, from childbirth to sudden death. It was more than anything else the intimacy of isolation. The nearest real town was fifteen miles away, across the desert. The road that led south just disappeared from sight, at the first hill after the end of the village street, in stony desolation, while to the north the distant hills brooded, the epitome of hostility.

It was as if she had stepped off the world, and into this community. Here she was, and here, eventually, she would die—in the company of these people.

She wondered if Paul felt the same, but he was, as usual, relaxed and apparently confident. It was a part of his training, his upbringing, she knew. He had not spent his life running from one antagonism, one unbearable situation, to another. He had had a difficult childhood, certainly, for he could remember the dreadful days in the early twenties in Germany when a wheelbarrowful of marks had not been sufficient to buy a loaf of bread. But after that he had found, as he and so many others had supposed, his salvation, in the dream of a resurrected Germany as promised by the Nazi Party. In that world of black and red and gold, of marching feet and stirring songs, of unrelieved death and glory, there had been no room for doubt, in the beginning. When he *had* doubted, when he had realized the true horror of what he and his fellows were doing, he had broken away, with all the desperate decisiveness of his character. Then he had become a fugitive, like her. But his flight had always been accompanied by the powerful self-confidence of the professional soldier.

She supposed it was her admiration of that self-confidence—so unlike anything she had known in her childhood—which had made her his wife. He had saved her life by rescuing her and Judith from Ravensbrück, and had been seriously wounded in the effort. Thus she had known gratitude, and intimacy, as she had nursed him back to health. That the pair of them, utterly adrift on the sea of life, should have gravitated more and more towards each other, had been natural, especially since she was the first cousin of his previous fiancée, the girl he had had to abandon to the most terrible of deaths. They had sought different objectives. To her, he was strength, and comfort; in his company she had for the first time in her life felt an absence of fear. That he was a man was almost irrelevant.

The years in a military brothel had made that unavoidable.

And he had understood that, which was the most splendid thing about him. He loved her, and if that love meant that he desired her, then she was happy that her body should belong to him. But she herself could no longer feel physical passion, no matter how hard she tried, and the fact that that did not anger or disturb him as it would have so many other men, was a miracle. Paul's greatest gift was that of understanding, and of gentleness.

But now that she had stopped running, perhaps it *would* be possible to feel again, she thought. Perhaps it would be possible to forget, every time he covered her with his body, how many other men had done just that.

Her thoughts rushed back to the present, for a young man was bending over her, and she was accepting his invitation to dance. The gramophone, to her surprise, was playing western music, and nearly all the young people were dancing, while their elders sat around the walls and watched, or conversed, exchanged tales of their adventures during the past six years, remembered old friends and even older enemies. Judith was deep in conversation with her friend the rabbi, and several of his friends. Paul, lazily watching her, was talking with the English police inspector, Nigel Brent.

To Ruth it was clear that these people regarded the British as their natural enemies, simply because they were *there;* in the three days that she had been on the kibbutz, Ruth had heard not a single word of regret for the people who had died in Jerusalem. Yet they invited the police officer to their social evening. And they could hardly be unaware that the British were the reason the Arabs stayed up in those hills, most of the time.

The man Brent could hardly be unaware of these facts either. But he matched Paul in his utter, casual confidence as they talked. Did he know all about both of them?

"You will have children?" the young man asked. She gathered he had been speaking to her for several minutes, and she had not been listening. Now he smiled at her. "We need lots of children, here in Palestine. We are creating a nation."

She presumed he was quoting someone.

"No," she said. "I don't think I will have children." She wondered what he would say if she told him why.

"That is a great pity," he said. "A beautiful woman like

you, a handsome man like your husband, that is a shame. Your husband is Swedish, is he not?"

"Yes," Ruth said, immediately watchful.

"It must be a beautiful country, Sweden," the young man said. "I would very much like to go there, one day."

"Then you should," Ruth said.

He frowned at her. "But my place is here, Mrs. Hassell. This is the place for all of us."

The music was stopping, to her great relief. She turned towards the chairs, and faced the policeman.

"Mrs. Hassell," he said. "Your husband has been kind enough to allow me to ask you to dance."

"Oh, I . . ." She glanced at the young Jew, who gave a quick bow and sidled away.

Brent smiled at her. "I'm afraid I do have that effect upon some people."

The music was starting again, and she was in his arms; it was a slow foxtrot.

"You'll be telling me next that he is a criminal, Mr. Brent."

"That depends entirely upon one's point of view. The people here would describe him as a fervent Zionist."

"But to you he is a terrorist."

"If I *knew* that, Mrs. Hassell, I would have him behind bars."

"Then you are using a policeman's instincts?"

"Perhaps. Do I detect a certain dislike for policemen, in your voice?"

"Since we are talking around the subject, Mr. Brent, I would have to say that from now on I must surely be as fervent a Zionist as the next man or woman."

He nodded. "I agree. You do realize that you have chosen rather a bed of nails?"

"Would you not say that about all these people?"

"I would. But some are more suited to it than others."

"Meaning I am not?"

"Meaning you and your husband, Mrs. Hassell."

Their heads turned together; Paul was deep in conversation with her former dancing partner.

"Your husband is a gentile," Brent remarked.

"So everyone keeps reminding me."

"I'm sorry. I'm trying to be helpful, really I am."

"In what way?"

"Well . . . there are quite a few gentiles who have emigrated to Palestine, of course. They are sympathetic to the Jews, or they have links with them, such as marriage, as in your case. They are valuable, and valued, additions to the community. But because they are gentiles, they often feel it necessary to try even harder than your people. And because they are gentiles, certain sections of the Jewish population feel that they *should* try harder. And of course, certain gentiles are more vulnerable than others."

Her head went back as she gazed at him. He does know, she thought. My God, he does know.

He continued to smile. "I hope I am not giving offense, Mrs. Hassell. I would hate to do that. I would just ask you to mention this possibility to your husband. And ask him, too, from me, to be careful of the company he keeps."

Once again their heads turned together, to watch Paul leaving the hall, in the company of her previous dancing partner.

"It is cooler outside," the young man said. "At this time of the year the nights are warm, eh?"

"You can say that again," Paul agreed.

"In the winters, it is cooler. Never cold, you understand." He continued to walk, hands thrust into his jacket pockets. "My name is Benjamin Cohen."

"Paul Hassell."

"That I know. Cigarette?"

Paul accepted, and bent his head for the match. The hall had faded into the night, together with the sounds of the music.

"What did you wish to discuss?" Paul asked. "You said it has to do with my wife."

"She is a beautiful woman," Cohen remarked. "And she has had a hard life. I have been told that she was in Ravensbrück. Is this true?"

"I'm afraid it is," Paul said. He was no more than normally wary. That both their pasts would be a continuing source of inquiry to their new neighbors was inevitable.

"Did you meet her there?"

Paul smiled as he shook his head. "Ravensbrück was for women only, my friend."

"But there were men there, from time to time," Cohen said. "There must have been guards, and doctors, and people like that."

"I am sure there were," Paul agreed. "You will understand that it is something I have never discussed with my wife. I am sure she would rather forget all about it. And I should be offended were anyone else to attempt to remind her of those years, too."

"Were you not one of those guards, or doctors, Herr von Hassell?" Cohen asked.

Paul's head came up, at the same time as he was aware of movement, behind him and to either side. There were four other young men, appearing out of the darkness.

"Will you deny that your name was von Hassell?" Cohen asked. "That you served with the SS at the beginning of the war?"

It occurred to Paul that he might be in some physical danger; in their antagonism to the British these young men, or others like them, had not shown any great concern for human life. He was not afraid of them; he regarded himself, anyway, as living on borrowed time, and was content to take each day as it came. But it made no sense to be killed, or even beaten up, when Ruth depended on him for so much.

"At the beginning of the war, Mr. Cohen," he said. "If you know so much about me, you will also know that in 1942 I was placed under arrest by the Gestapo, and—"

"You were arrested," Cohen said. "And were then released."

Paul continued to gaze at him. "And that from the moment of my release, six months later, I was involved in the plot against Hitler. As a result of which I was forced to flee Germany."

"You were arrested by the Gestapo, and released," one of the other young men repeated.

"I was not released. I escaped," Paul said.

"Every German who survived the war claims to have been involved in the plot against Hitler," Cohen remarked.

"In my case it happens to be true."

"You are a German, a Nazi, a natural enemy of us Jews," said one of the other men. "Why are you here?"

They were very close; he could smell them. And they were not afraid, either of him or of what they might have to do to him. With an effort, he made himself keep still.

"My wife is a Jew," he said. "So you see, I am not really your natural enemy."

"Bah," said one of the men.

"You are not welcome here," Cohen said.

"Well, I *am* here," Paul pointed out. "So I am very afraid you will have to put up with the idea."

"Life can be very unpleasant for those who are not welcome," Cohen said. "We are engaged in a struggle for survival. When we have driven out the British, then we are going to have to defeat the Arabs, for the right to live. We shall do these things. But we cannot have any people living in Palestine who are not prepared to support us in every way."

"Try me," Paul said.

"Having a Jewish wife is not enough," Cohen went on. "Rather, it is the Jewish wife who then becomes an object of suspicion, who is thought worthy of sharing the fate of her husband, should he prove to be a traitor."

"I said, try me," Paul repeated. "But let me give you a piece of advice. Lay a finger on my wife, and I will break your neck."

Cohen's hand moved, emerging from his jacket pocket with a pistol wrapped in his fingers.

"Even if you have a gun," Paul said, "you can try me there, too."

The two men stared at each other, eyes only a faint gleam in the darkness, while the others waited.

"So you are a brave man," Cohen said at last. "I did not doubt that. I am looking for a brave man. Will you join us?"

"In doing what?"

"Fighting the British."

"You mean, murdering them when their backs are turned?"

Cohen shrugged. "War is a nasty business. But you must once have hated the British as much as any German."

"I don't hate any man, enough to murder him. Not any more."

"You *must* hate the British," Cohen said, "if you are going to be with us. We must drive them out, don't you see? And quickly. Once they are gone, we will settle with the Arabs."

"And you think murdering a few British soldiers will make them leave?"

"It will. Soon enough. You will work with us?"

Paul shook his head. "I will work with you and fight with you if anyone comes to destroy this kibbutz. Then I will kill for you. I will not murder for you."

Cohen stared at him for some seconds, and Paul became

aware that the other men were even closer.

"You have no choice," Cohen said. "Otherwise your life will become very unpleasant. Very unpleasant for your wife as well. You may threaten me. You may even kill me. But there are too many of us. Our women support us, Mr. von Hassell. You will not be able to kill them. And they are the ones who make life unbearable for your wife. They will drive her to despair, Mr. von Hassell, and I would say that she has had enough despair in her life already. Whereas, if you support us, if you will work with us, your wife will be a very happy woman. She will be looked after by all the community. And if anything should ever happen to you, in the course of your duty, she will be the heroine of the kibbutz. Think about these things, Herr von Hassell."

Paul gazed at him, alarm bells jangling in his brain but constantly being dulled by despair. As he had tried to say to Ruth in Tel Aviv, he hadn't really expected anything different than what he was hearing; he was a man condemned by the fact of what he had once been. His only reason for living was to preserve Ruth, and give her some happiness.

"In Palestine," said one of the other men, "it is all or nothing. You must understand this, Herr von Hassell."

Paul nodded thoughtfully. "I don't have a hell of a lot of choice," he said. "No doubt you fellows will let me know what you want me to do."

"Your first target is already chosen," Cohen said. "It will be an easy one for you. This man Brent is becoming a nuisance, and is far too friendly with the rabbi. You will have to kill him for us. We will tell you how, and when. But it will be soon. And then you will be one of us."

Ruth Hassell turned in her husband's arms, sighed, and awoke as he kissed her forehead.

"Paul?" She always asked this, as if afraid that he might have mysteriously disappeared while she slept.

"I'm here, my darling."

"But not sleeping? You are always lying awake."

"Perhaps I do not need as much sleep as other men." He gazed through the window, at the moonlight swathing across the desert, and listened to a dog barking.

"Or perhaps you are worrying," she said. "What do you have to worry about, Paul? Here we are safe, as you always said we would be. Could we be as safe, anywhere else?"

He kissed her again. "And you are happy here?"

"Oh, yes, Paul. I have never been so happy in my life. The people are so kind..." She sat up and tossed strands of hair from her eyes. "But *you* are not happy? Are they not being kind to you, too?"

"They are being very kind to me," he said.

"Well, then..."

"So I lie here and think," he said, "that perhaps I do not deserve such kindness."

"Oh, Paul," she said, and lay down again, head pillowed on his shoulder. "You deserve everything, and more than everything. And these people want you here. You can see that. They *need* you. You are a natural leader."

"Perhaps," he said. "Is Judith really going in to Jerusalem next week to see Ivan Nej?"

Ruth sighed. "So she says. I cannot persuade her otherwise. And I can understand that it is something she feels she must do, that she can leave no stone unturned if there is a chance of helping her husband. She has promised not to allow herself to be hoodwinked. And I don't think that anything can happen to her. That British police officer is driving her in. I really am very grateful to him. He's a nice man."

"Yes," Paul agreed again. "He is a nice man."

"And with him along, not even Ivan Nej would dream of trying anything funny," Ruth asserted. "Ivan Nej is at heart a coward. Believe me."

"I am sure you're right. But I am sorry she is going next week, because I shall also be away."

Once again Ruth sat up. "You? Where are *you* going?"

"Now, I told you, my love. I am a soldier, and the people here wish me to fight with them in the war that is coming with the Arabs. They wish me to lead them, as you said. So the young men from the village must train, and they wish me to train with them. Six of us are going on a three-day exercise next week. I'm afraid I'll be away at the same time as Judith."

"Oh," she said, and lay down again. "Well, I'll manage. Sylvia will keep me company. But six men... what sort of an exercise can six men have?"

"We will be linking up with others," Paul said without hesitation.

"Which six? I have not heard anyone else speaking of this."

"Of course not. In military matters it pays to keep things secret. I shouldn't even have told you, so you must promise me not to discuss it with anyone, not even Judith. And certainly not with Miss Levin."

"Oh, I won't," she said. "I promise. But can't you tell *me* who you're going with?"

"Ben Cohen and his friends."

"Oh, *them*," she said. "That's all right. I was afraid you might be getting mixed up with some of the extremists. Ben's all right. I think he's rather sweet."

"Yes," Paul agreed, for a third time. "I am sure he is."

"Comrade Petrova!" Ivan Nej stood in the doorway of the hotel bedroom and beamed. "It is good to see you again, after so long."

She evaded the arms that would have embraced her, stepped past him into the room, sat down, and fanned herself. Jerusalem was even hotter than the desert. And she was more nervous than she had supposed she was going to be. Or merely more alert, she told herself reassuringly, and noted that there was a door leading to an adjoining room, presently closed. But this was a large, international hotel, and Nigel Brent was waiting for her just round the corner. She had nothing to be nervous about.

Ivan offered her a cigarette, and took one himself when she shook her head. "You have been living in the north, eh?" He wagged his finger at her. "That is very dangerous."

Judith gazed at him. "May I remind you, *Comrade* Nej, that I am not responsible to you, or to anyone? As it happens, and as you well know, I am sure, my niece is settling in the north, and I wished to spend some time with her."

"Of course you did, Comrade Petrova," Ivan said soothingly. "Nor would I dream of questioning your actions. And your niece is now . . . settled?"

"I think so," Judith said.

"Good. Good. Then you will be glad to return home."

Judith frowned at him. His assurance had taken her by surprise. "Return home?"

"Of course. Everyone returns home eventually, comrade. That is why I sent for you to come to Jerusalem. I have your ticket here, and some funds for traveling. But I shall be going with you, of course. You are booked on a flight leaving this afternoon."

"Leaving this afternoon?" Judith hated herself for her sudden inability to think straight. But Ivan Nej always had that effect upon people.

"At four o'clock," he explained. "I suggest we lunch together, and then I will drive you to the airport myself."

Judith pulled herself together. "I came here to discuss the *possibility* of my returning home, Comrade Nej," she said. "I have no intention of leaving Palestine without adequate safeguards for my husband as well as myself."

"Ah, Comrade Petrov. Are you not in a hurry to be reunited with poor Boris? Be sure that he has great need of you." Ivan tapped his temple gently. "It is the strain, of course. Everyone in Russia is under great strain, trying to end the ravages of war, to launch the new five-year plan. And those in positions of authority are under greater strains than others."

Judith leaned forward, hands on the desk. "There is nothing the matter with Boris. You know that as well as I."

Ivan smiled at her, as reassuring as ever. "He has had a breakdown. That is all I know. But he is in a psychiatric hospital, where he can be looked after. Where you will be able to see him, and reassure him."

Judith drew a long breath—there was no more point in losing her temper than there was in being frightened. "Comrade Nej," she said, "I want my husband released from that place. I want a letter signed by Lavrenti Beria to the effect that Boris is not ill, and has never been ill, that his arrest was merely a means of forcing me to return to Russia. That letter I will lodge in a safe place, to be used in case of need. Then I will return. I do not know *why* I am wanted, but I will return and answer any charges against me. When I have that letter."

"I can see that you are disturbed and upset," Ivan said kindly. "This does not surprise me in the least. I sometimes think it is more difficult on the wives than on the men themselves, when something like this happens. I will get you a pick-me-up, eh?" He pressed a bell, and the door behind Judith opened. "Comrade Petrova would like a small glass of brandy," he said, and beamed at her. "These things always sound much worse than they really are, Comrade Petrova. When Boris sees you, he will feel much better."

A young woman stood beside Judith, the glass in her hand, a smile on her face. Instinctively Judith reached for the drink, because she did feel like a pick-me-up, and then checked herself. Ivan was smiling too, and waiting. Once she drank whatever was in that glass, she was theirs.

She looked over her shoulder, at the open door. Open, but not empty; two men stood there. They too were smiling at her. She was trapped. It was incredible, that she should be in the very center of Jerusalem, with armed British soldiers on every side, with Nigel Brent practically within earshot...and she could reach none of them.

But that was absurd. She had come here today just because of those safeguards.

"Come along, Comrade Petrova," Ivan said. "The drink will make you feel better."

She wondered what it would do to her. Would she pass out, and be taken to the airport as ill? Or would she merely lose all the will to resist them? She rather thought the latter; they would not wish to risk an incident—which was exactly where her safety lay.

"I think you should know that you are making a fool of yourself, Ivan Nikolaievich," she said. "Did you really suppose I would come here without making adequate preparations? There is a British police officer waiting for me now." She looked at her wristwatch. "If I am not with him in ten minutes, he is going to come up here to get me. So I am sure you will agree that it would be best for us all if I were to leave now. But my offer stands. Let me have that letter, and I will come to Russia of my own free will—after Boris has been released from prison."

Ivan smiled at her. "I am afraid that Comrade Petrova seems to be suffering from the same hallucinatory symptoms of her poor husband," he said. "But she has given us convincing reasons for making haste. Assist Comrade Petrova to drink her brandy, Sonya. You will help too, Vassily. I wish her out of here in five minutes."

Judith realized that she was not going to talk herself out of this room; that, as at Ravensbrück, it was necessary to *do,* if she would survive. If only she did not feel so old, so tired. Yet the determined impulse was already on its way from her brain, the will to survive. She propelled herself from her chair, struck the woman Sonya in the stomach with her shoulder, sent the glass flying with her free hand, and found herself against the wall. She turned to face them, panting, wishing that she could bare her teeth, like a rat.

Ivan sighed. "As I feared," he said. "She has become violent. We will need an injection. You will prepare one, Sonya. Tigran, you will assist Vassily. Comrade Petrova will have to be restrained."

The men came towards Judith slowly. They were still between her and the door. There remained the window. But the Russian suite was on the fifth floor of the hotel. Did that mean she would have to commit suicide? She certainly did not intend to do that. But she did not intend to surrender, either. Not now, and not ever.

She drew a long breath, turned, and threw herself at the window.

"Stop her," Ivan shouted.

The two men ran forward, but Judith was already half out, one foot finding a lodgment on the narrow ledge that ran around the building, two feet beneath the window sill, realizing that it *was* a narrow ledge, not more than six inches wide, and hesitating. Vassily grasped her sleeve, and she jerked herself away from him with such force she nearly fell. With an immense effort she pressed herself against the wall of the building while swinging her other leg onto the ledge. She closed her eyes, immediately lost her balance, and opened them again. Hands came out of the window, grasping for her, and she made herself move sideways, back pressed against the wall, staring down at the street, fifty feet beneath her. It did not look so very far. If she were to jump, she might escape with a broken leg. She might.

If only someone would look up! They would if she screamed. She began to inhale, slowly and carefully, afraid that a sudden gush of air from her lungs might force her away from the wall, stared over the houses at the rounded dome of the Church of the Holy Sepulcher, and its matching counterpart on the Mosque of Omar, twin symbols of the reasons she was here.

Ivan's head emerged from the window. "You are being incredibly stupid, Comrade Petrova," he said. "Next thing you will fall, and be seriously injured. Now, Vassily has gone for a rope, which we will attach to you, and then we will be able to bring you back to safety."

How hot it was. The midday sun seemed to be beating straight down on her; there was not enough breeze even to rustle her skirt. Her voice would carry a long way, if she could just use it.

"Help me," she shouted. "Help me."

It was a thin, lifeless sound, immediately lost in the growl of the traffic. No one looked up.

"That was very silly of you," Ivan said severely. "Behavior like this will have to go into my report, you know, Comrade Petrova. It will be held against you."

"If you come near me, I'll jump," Judith whispered. "So help me God, I'll jump."

Her foot slipped. Desperately she pressed herself against the wall, kicking as she did so. Her shoe came off, and she watched it spiraling downwards, with infinite slowness. Oh God, she prayed. Oh, God. Let it hit someone. Let it—

The shoe hit a policeman on the shoulder.

A woman screamed. Heads turned, and people started moving towards the corner of the street; the scream had come from beyond there.

Nigel Brent sighed, considered getting out from behind the wheel of the parked jeep, and decided against it. Undoubtedly there had been some act of terrorism committed, but this was not his patch, and he was off duty; he was not even in uniform.

He had come into Jerusalem to do some shopping, and to give Judith Petrov a lift. The latter was far more important, although he would have been hard put to pin down the reason. She was old enough to be his mother, and the ravages of her past had caught up with her, left her handsome face gaunt, sewn thick strands of gray in the still-rich black hair. But she was Judith Petrov, who had once been Judith Stein, and as his file told him, she had stood on a Moscow barricade, rifle in hand, just as she had reportedly helped Rasputin to his execution. She would have been beautiful, then. And utterly vital.

The vitality remained. It had even survived a Nazi concentration camp. He supposed, in her past, and in her present, she epitomized all the Jews who were determined to fight so hard for their right to be a nation, for a land of their own, and for their own land. He admired them as much as he hated his job. But it was a job he did because someone else might be unable to understand, might oppose defiance merely with harshness.

He was required to be harsh, often enough. Just as he and his policemen defended the Jews from Arab fear and anger, so he also arrested them when they broke the laws imposed by his superiors, and when they broke the laws badly enough, he sent them here to Jerusalem, where he knew they would be hanged, after due process of law. He could do nothing about that, once the crime had been committed. But in his friendship with Rabbi Yanowski, and with most of the people in that single kibbutz, as well as in the others which came under his jurisdiction, he felt he was making progress towards alleviating the worst results of this generations-old conflict. If it could be possible to reconcile the two nations to living beside each other, then everything would have been worthwhile. His only fear was the growing rumor that the London government was getting fed up with the expense and revulsion involved in such an unpleasant task, and was considering giving up the mandate and pulling out. That was what the Jews and the Arabs wanted to happen. *He* could see it in no terms other than catastrophe, at least for the Jews.

It would mean a desertion of people who desperately needed help. Of Judith Petrov, and of her niece. Dangerous to think of the niece. In Ruth Hassell he could see all of the burgeoning beauty, and the innate strength, of body no less than mind, which must have belonged to Judith in her time, which had been absolutely necessary for her survival from disaster after disaster after disaster. This girl, according to the file, had also suffered her disasters. And survived. Married to an ex-Nazi. There was a secret they would have to guard. It also indicated that there might be other secrets in their lives, which had not reached even his file. Which but made them the more interesting, the more attractive.

The more to be helped. But only the aunt. It was no business of his to become involved in the marital affairs of these refugees.

There was definitely something happening around the corner; more and more people were running, and now an ambulance rushed by, siren wailing, and he suddenly remembered that while Judith had asked him to meet her here, the hotel where this Russian *chargé d'affaires* had set up shop was in the next street, where the commotion was coming from. She could well have become involved in some sort of disturbance.

He got out of the jeep, joined the throng, rounded the corner, and stared, with everyone else, at the woman flattened against the wall, feet clinging precariously to the ledge, high above him. For a moment he could not believe his eyes, then he ran forward, thrusting Arabs and Jews and Europeans left and right in his haste, keeping his gaze fixed on the woman, taking in the people who were leaning out of the nearest window, apparently trying to attach a rope to her, from which she was shrinking.

But now a fire engine had been brought into position beneath her, and the ladder was being slowly extended. It took him only a moment to make his decision; the Russians might easily bar entry into their suite. He ran forward, broke through the cordon of policemen who were holding back the crowd, and flashed his badge at them.

"You can't come up here," protested the fire officer, as he climbed on to the engine.

"I'm a police officer," Nigel said. "And that woman is in my care."

"Well . . ." The man scratched his head, and Nigel stepped past him and began the ascent.

"Just hold on," he said, as the top of the ladder came to rest beside Judith. "Just hold on, Mrs. Petrov."

Judith stared down at him. "Mr. Brent?" she asked. "Oh, thank God, Mr. Brent."

He was immediately beneath her, and she was coming forward, into his arms. The crowd broke into a storm of applause, and Ivan Nej, leaning out of the window, clapped politely.

"That was well done, young man," he said. "My people are coming downstairs now, to help you. We will look after her."

"No," Judith whispered, against Nigel's ear, as he slowly began his descent. "Do not let them take me, Mr. Brent. Please. They wish to send me back to Russia, to prison."

Ivan could see her speaking, could guess what she was saying. "That is a Soviet citizen," he shouted. "Be careful what you do, Englishman."

Nigel looked down into Judith's face, and then up at the angry Russian. "Bugger off," he said.

Judith sipped brandy, shivered, and sipped again. She looked left and right around the little bar, and seemed to hug herself. But it was a small bar, and there were only three other people in it. And one of those was sitting beside her. Nigel Brent.

Finally she spoke. "I don't know what to say."

"Then why say anything?"

"But . . . won't you get into trouble?"

"Nothing I can't handle. You have applied for the necessary permission to stay here, and you are Jewish, so I can't see a problem. As for Comrade Nej—well, he is unlikely to make much of a protest, since he was trying to kidnap you in the first place. I imagine he will be catching that plane back to Russia as fast as he can, together with his goons."

"It's just so unbelievable," she said, "that such a thing could happen here, in broad daylight."

He squeezed her hand. "It didn't happen," he reminded her. "It only tried to happen. Now, if you'd like to finish your drink, I'll drive you out to the kibbutz."

"But . . . the police . . ."

"I told you, Mrs. Petrov, I've sorted them out. You have been released into my custody, pending an investigation of what happened at the hotel. I will make an official report as soon as I get home, but that will indict Nej, not you. So don't worry." Another squeeze of the hand. "Shall we go?"

She finished her drink, stood up, and gazed at the door to the bar and the three young men who stood there. Remarkably, on such a hot day, they wore scarves. But of course, from their dress they had just come in from the desert, and had not yet fully appreciated that they were away from the dust and the worst of the flies—the scarves were still loosely draped around the lower parts of their faces, rendering them effectively disguised. But there was something familiar about one of them.

Then she saw the guns. Her heart seemed to give a great leap, as the first young man fired. She saw the flash of red, but did not hear the sound of the explosion as she threw herself sideways to the floor, and listened to shouts of alarm from the other two customers in the bar, then found herself gazing at Nigel Brent, who had drawn an automatic pistol from inside his jacket and was returning fire. She heard a scream from one of the attackers who had been hit, twisted her head, and gazed at the middle of the three men. His scarf had fallen away from his face as he leveled his pistol, and she realized that it was Paul von Hassell.

Chapter 9

THE CLODS OF EARTH FELL DULLY ONTO THE WOODEN COFFIN, and the mourners turned away. They were a small group—the Hayman family, and two of the other guards from the bank where Igor Borodin had worked. These last were embarrassed at the exalted company in which they found themselves, and were eager to hurry away from the graveside. They had hardly known the dead man, anyway.

The family followed more slowly. But had they known him any better than his workmates? John Hayman wondered. He gazed at Gregory, walking beside Ilona and Felicity, and no taller than either of the women; he looked as sad as any other member of the family. But then, they were an emotional family. And why not? John suddenly realized that of this last two generations of Borodins, not one had yet managed to die naturally, in bed. That was an unthinkable thought, when applied to someone like his mother, but it was true.

On the far side of the cemetery, beyond the railings, a dark blue Buick was parked. Garrison always did things by the book, had no doubt attended the funeral in the hope that someone might attend who would be worth following up. But he would not be weeping. It was all a great jigsaw puzzle, to Garrison; none of the pieces actually had any life to them.

John found himself beside George, as he had intended.

"Poor Igor," George said. "He never had a chance."

"No," John agreed. "I managed to get hold of an autopsy report."

"So did I," George said.

They looked at each other.

"But I meant, life never gave him a chance," George said.

"And you think it all adds up?"

"That he was full of vodka, that it was even spilled on his clothes? Why shouldn't it all add up?"

"It was all in his stomach," John said, "not anywhere near the kidneys or bladder. He must have drunk it immediately before falling. Did you ever hear of anyone getting drunk to commit suicide?"

"As a matter of fact, yes. And who said it was suicide? The police think he just got so steamed up about the prospect of visiting with us last weekend, that he drank himself silly to make himself come with you at all, and then wandered to the open window and fell out."

"Past the fire escape," John said.

George frowned at him. "What's on your mind?"

"I wish I knew," John confessed. "Maybe I'm just inclined to be suspicious."

George continued to gaze at him for some seconds, then looked up as Ilona left Felicity and Gregory to come across to them. "I wish you weren't rushing off," she said.

"Now, my love, you know I have to."

"But what can you *do?*" Ilona asked. "Paul Hassell was taken with a gun in his hand. Of all the senseless things to do—to try to kill a British police officer . . ."

"I'm afraid I agree with Mother, George," John said.

"Because you fought against him in the war?"

"Because of the *facts*. Okay, maybe I could never forgive him for what happened to Svetlana. Maybe I can never forget that he was trained as a killer, to hold life cheap. But as Mother says, no one is attempting to dispute the fact of what happened."

"Well, I still think I have to go and have a look," George said. "I advised them to go there in the first place."

"But you can't be responsible for them for all the rest of their lives," Ilona protested.

"Agreed. Yet I can't just let them down, now. And there *are* things in Paul's favor, you know. From what I gather, he had this policeman in his sights, and didn't fire."

"Because Judith was there," John suggested. "He would have fired if she hadn't been."

"We don't *know* that," George said.

"Anyway, merely by carrying firearms in Palestine, without authority, he was subject to the death penalty." George junior had joined them.

"I *must* go," George said, looking from face to face. "God, how that family has suffered. I must go. Now. Those two women are entirely alone."

Ilona sighed. "Of course you must go, George. But for God's sake, hurry back." She waved to Felicity, who was driving Gregory home. "We have problems of our own."

They drove back from Idlewild Airport, slowly, Felicity behind the wheel, Ilona in the middle, Gregory on the far side.

Ilona sighed. "He feels he has a duty to those women. He has felt that since 1914. Well, I suppose in a way he has. No one could possibly have suffered more than the Steins. But then, in the last hundred years, no one could have suffered more than the Jews as a whole. They seem to attract misfortune, and they meet it with such determination, such courage. You have to admire them."

The others did not reply, and the car fell silent.

"I suppose," Ilona said, after a while, "that we Borodins have had our share of misfortune. But we have always seemed to land on our feet."

"How can you say that?" Gregory asked. "After what happened to Mother? And now poor Igor. And all the rest of the family."

"I suppose I was thinking of the Haymans, really," Ilona said quietly. "The Borodins, the rest of them . . . it is quite incredible to me how some families seem predestined to catastrophe. When you think of those brothers, Tigran and Viktor, and Xenia, so beautiful, so vivacious . . . in 1913 they had the world at their feet. So what happens? Tigran is shot to death in his office, Xenia is torn to pieces by a mob, and Viktor is shot by the Bolsheviks . . ." She glanced at Gregory. "I'm sorry. But it did happen."

"Yes," Gregory said. "It did happen. That is why I am here, and not in Russia."

"And then Viktor's son struggles up from nothing, and

manages to reach us here, and then commits suicide."

"Now, Mother," Felicity said. "You don't know it was suicide. No one knows that. The police say he got drunk, and fell."

Ilona sighed again. "I don't suppose we shall ever know the truth. It makes you wonder why *we* should be so happy . . ."

"Yes," Felicity said, staring ahead, down the road. "One should always grasp happiness whenever one can."

"Oh, yes," Ilona agreed, and bit her lip as she realized she might have fallen into a trap. She had been intending to use George's absence as an opportunity to have a heart-to-heart talk with Felicity and Gregory, if possible—he was *her* nephew, not George's—but this chat was going in the wrong direction.

Felicity was guiding the car in and out of traffic with expert ease. "I know it's a bad time," she said. "With all this misfortune happening to Judith and Ruth, and Father having to go away . . . but would you have any great objections if . . . well . . ." She glanced across the car at Gregory.

"The fact is, Aunt Ilona," Gregory said, "now that I am working at the Pentagon, I think it would be far more convenient if I were to take an apartment in Washington, and consider it my home. Of course, I'd come up here as often as I could," Gregory said hastily. "But really, I have so little time there, anyway—"

"Yes," Ilona agreed with sudden enthusiasm, as she realized that he was proposing a solution to all her problems. "Yes, that *might* be a sensible idea. Don't you think it might be a sensible idea, Felicity?"

Felicity continued to watch the road in front of her. "I would like to . . . to help Gregory with his apartment, Mother."

Anna Ragosina stood beneath the cherry trees on Haines Point and looked across the river at the airport. "I think you are mad," she remarked. "Next you will be telling me that you are in love with this girl."

"Of course I am not in love with her," Gregory said. "But she provides a most superb cover."

"You call drawing attention to yourself by creating a scandal and by quarreling with your family, good cover?"

"Of course. The best. I am behaving as if nothing else in the world matters to me but Felicity. She believes this, and her family believes it. They think we are in love. They do not approve. My aunt was very upset. I thought she was going to faint. She even called in Felicity's brother, George junior, to talk to Felicity. And then the half-brother, John Hayman. They talked, and they argued, but Felicity was adamant. And the important thing is that the family is at last convinced that I am genuine."

"The family has been convinced from the beginning, surely," Anna pointed out.

Gregory shook his head. "No. I thought they were, in the beginning. But now that I look back on it, I am not sure."

Anna frowned at him. "What makes you say that?"

"Little things. Snatches of conversation. Oh, I do not think George Hayman or Aunt Ilona ever had any doubts, but I think George junior was not sure, and I feel that John Hayman was definitely suspicious. He is not important, of course. He is the least important member of the family."

"He is a Hero of the Soviet Union," Anna pointed out, somewhat stiffly.

"That is in the past. Now he works in advertising. Even his own relatives do not think much of that. It is George junior I worried about. And that business about Igor . . . It is something I wished to discuss with you, Anna. I think such extreme action was quite uncalled for. I cannot believe he was so serious a threat to me."

"Are you questioning my decisions." Anna demanded quietly.

"I am saying that I think it was an unnecessary decision. It might have spoiled everything. It could even have aroused doubts in Felicity's mind."

"Did it?"

"She believes what the police said, that he got drunk and fell."

"She seems to be a very gullible woman," Anna remarked.

"She is lonely, and she is confused. She cannot bring herself to believe that she deserves to be a Hayman, with all the wealth and power they enjoy. Thus she is prepared to believe in socialism. She is also desperate for love, and she has found in me someone to love. For me, she has broken with her family, her friends—no one speaks to her anymore. She is living in sin—".

"You will make me weep in a moment," Anna said coldly.

"Well, comrade, you may argue as much as you like, and make
as many excuses as you like, but I think that *you* have made
a mistake. That woman should have been eliminated the moment she came upon you and Bogolzhin. To avoid doing that,
and then to tell her the truth—my God! I suppose you have
told her about me, as well."

"Of course I have not done that, Anna," Gregory protested.

"You mean you have not gone *quite* mad, as yet. And I
cannot even do anything about it, now. To have her eliminated
at this stage would attract even more attention."

"To—If you were to lay a finger on her, Anna—"

Anna's head half turned. "You would do what? You seem
to be forgetting that you are under my command. And without
referring to me, you have virtually recruited an agent, and are
using her as a go-between."

"It was what I was told to do," Gregory said.

"You were not told to get into any emotional involvement."

"Bogolzhin suggested that too," Gregory reminded her. "He
recommended a homosexual relationship. Well, I have done
better."

"You think so? Homosexuals can be blackmailed. This girl
is working with you and for you entirely because she believes
herself to be in love with you. Have you considered what
happens when this affair ends?"

"Why should it ever end? Felicity *is* in love with me."

"She is infatuated," Anna said contemptuously. "And of
course the affair will end. All affairs end. And when it does,
this woman will take a completely different look at life, and
at you, and at what she has been doing. Then she will *have*
to be eliminated. You must be very clear in your mind about
this."

"When that time comes," Gregory said, "if it ever does, I
will do what needs to be done."

"And get yourself sent to the electric chair?" Anna's voice
was again filled with contempt. "*I* will decide what needs to
be done, and when, and how. Remember that. Now, we have
spoken long enough. Do not ask to see me again. It is too
dangerous, and I absolutely forbid it. In any event, I have no
desire to see *you* under the present circumstances. And do not
ever reveal more to this woman than you have already done.
Since she has met Bogolzhin, you may continue to use her as
a courier. But nothing more. And she must *never* learn of my

existence. That I will regard as treachery."

She turned away, and Gregory caught her arm. "You are angry with me."

"Yes," she said. "I am very angry with you."

"And do you realize that none of this would have happened, had you allowed me to see you from time to time? Had you not turned away from me?"

"Silly boy," she said. "We are here to work, not to make love." She thrust her hands into her pockets, and walked away.

Ivan Nej hunched in his chair before the huge desk, eyes flickering from face to face. "I was unlucky," he said. "I laid my plans very carefully. I forced Petrova into a position where she would *have* to come to me. But there were factors present that I could not possibly foresee. How was I to know that she would have made a friend of a British policeman, that he would actually drive her into Jerusalem? And even that, Joseph Vissarionovich, I was prepared to overcome. My plans were already laid to waylay them on their way back to the kibbutz. I would have had the woman on that plane. I swear it. But how could I foresee the assassination attempt? From that moment on, they were both entirely surrounded by policemen, for days on end. To have attempted anything further would have been to risk an international incident." He stared at Stalin, eyes glinting behind his glasses. "But now that the furor has settled down—"

"As you say," Stalin said, not unkindly, "you were unlucky, Ivan Nikolaievich. That is sad. No man can entirely control his luck. But when a man's luck runs out—why, then he seldom accomplishes much."

"I tried," Ivan said miserably. "I could not foresee ... Do not be harsh with me, Joseph Vissarionovich."

Stalin smiled. "Why should I be harsh with you, Ivan Nikolaievich? As you say, you tried, and no man can do more than that. You will not be punished again. I am sure that Lavrenti Pavlovich here can find you a position in keeping with your talents, and your lack of luck."

"It will be difficult," Beria said.

"I was thinking of Tomsk, or some such place," Stalin said. "I am sure there is room for a man like Ivan Nikolaievich in Tomsk."

Ivan swallowed. *"Tomsk?"*

"It is a place," Stalin said reassuringly, "where luck is of little relevance. The sun rises in Tomsk, and the sun sets. In the winter it snows, and in the summer it bakes. Not a great deal else happens. You will prosper in Tomsk, Ivan Nikolaievich."

"Tomsk," Ivan muttered miserably. His head rose again. "I would fetch that Jewess back for you, Joseph Vissarionovich," he said. "I would fetch her back, no matter what the cost."

"Yes," Stalin agreed dryly. "You will do well in Tomsk. I think the sooner you leave, the better."

Ivan stared at him, then looked at Beria, then realized that the interview was at an end. Slowly he got up, then squared his shoulders. "I should like to see my son, Gregory," he said, "before I leave. I . . . I have not seen him since before his mother died. He is all the family I have left now. He is very dear to me. I should like to see him."

"That is impossible," Stalin said.

Ivan frowned at his master. "You have executed him?"

"Of course I have not executed him," Stalin said.

"You have sent him to a labor camp," Ivan accused. "There was no need for that. He is a good Communist. He worships the Soviet state."

"He has not been sent to a labor camp," Stalin said. "He is being employed in work of a confidential nature. He is doing very well. But it will not be possible for you to see him. Good day to you, Ivan Nikolaievich."

Ivan looked at Beria, then left the room.

"You are kind to him," Beria said. "He is a fool and a bungler. He commanded a team of three, and yet they could not prevent Petrova from escaping. That is the very height of inefficiency."

"He certainly seems to have mismanaged things," Stalin agreed. "But he is really a faithful little man. He can come to no harm, down in Tomsk."

"And when he learns the truth about his son?"

Stalin leaned back. "How can he do that? We have never released the news of Captain Nej's defection here in Russia, and as it is now months since it happened, his very existence has been forgotten. There is no risk of any of our Russian Embassy people saying anything about it. As for Michael Nikolaievich . . . he is too shocked by the whole thing. There is absolutely no risk of Ivan Nej finding out about it, especially in a place like Tomsk."

"I meant, when he learns that Gregory has been executed. He will have to be told that, eventually."

"But Gregory Ivanovich has *not* been executed," Stalin said patiently. "Nor do I think he should be."

"Ragosina is of the opinion that Gregory Nej may well turn out to be a bad risk, since his liaison with this Hayman woman. She has asked specifically for permission to terminate his assignment. Together with the woman, of course. And, although she did not mention it, I am very afraid that Bogolzhin is also involved. I hate to bother you with departmental matters, Joseph Vissarionovich, but in view of the interest you have taken in this whole project . . ."

"I am very glad you did bother me, Lavrenti Pavlovich," Stalin said. "I have read Comrade Ragosina's report very carefully, and I think she is being hasty. That is the trouble with employing women. Even women like Anna Ragosina. She is perhaps our finest agent; I am quite willing to agree with that. But she is still inclined to become emotionally involved. This is a clear case of jealousy. As for young Nej, is he not returning information?"

"A trickle. He is still finding his feet. There can be no doubt that he is well placed," Beria agreed, anxious to agree with his master, "and that if he can make this woman into a faithful accomplice she too may be of great value."

"Exactly," Stalin said. "You will tell Anna Ragosina that we think the present situation has immense possibilities, and that she is to do nothing about it for the time being. You will also remind her that her primary objective is the formula for the atom bomb. Why has nothing yet been accomplished in that direction? She has been in America nearly a year."

"There are difficulties, Joseph Vissarionovich. And she is having some problems deciding who can be used and who cannot. America is composed of so many diverse elements. For example, she has made contact with a man who works for the state, and definitely claims to have access to material relating to this bomb. But Ragosina cannot bring herself to trust him, because he is of German descent."

"For God's sake," Stalin said. "Half of the people in Eu-

ropean Russia are of German descent. Certainly those born
west of Smolensk. She could well have a German grandmother
herself, the stupid girl. You will tell her to proceed with this
man, and anyone else who can possibly be of help to us. We
must obtain those secrets, Lavrenti Pavlovich, and very
quickly. There are signs that Truman is at last adopting a firmer
attitude towards our successes in Europe. There is a distinct
hardening of opinion against us, just for example, in Greece.
And I cannot bring myself to trust this scoundrel Tito, however
much lip service he pays us. The Yugoslavs are an unreliable
lot. They always have been. They live in their mountains and
think they own the earth." He seemed to realize that he was
rambling. "So time is running out, comrade. And that girl is
just sitting on her ass in some comfortable Washington apartment and suffering fits of jealousy because one of her operatives
has found himself a woman. Shake her up."

Beria nodded, and got up. "And Judith Petrova?"

"She will have to be forgotten for the time being. Besides,
if what Ivan Nikolaievich had to tell us was true, she is of less
importance than I had supposed."

"There is no doubt that she is writing articles for Hayman
Newspapers," Beria reminded him.

"I do not think Judith Petrova can tell George Hayman
anything about us that he does not already know, comrade. In
any event, his papers have been very noncommittal about us
this last year. As for Petrova, I can tell you that if this Nazi
storm trooper her niece has married is really going to be hanged
by the British, she will have more than enough to think about.
He *is* going to be hanged?"

"I should think he will be hanged, comrade," Beria agreed.
"That is what the British do to terrorists."

"Down there are the tomatoes," Judith said, pointing. "That
is our principal crop. And they are fine tomatoes, George. The
finest in the world. You wait until you taste one. Do you see
that windmill? That raises water from the table beneath the
sand. Twelve feet, it has to be raised. To turn this dry gulch
into a fertile valley."

"I'm impressed," George said. He wiped sweat from his
neck and adjusted his dark glasses; the glare, arising equally
from the white buildings behind him and the shimmering desert

to either side, was tremendous. "And this is to be your home for the rest of your life?"

She glanced at him, and flushed, traced designs in the sand of the road with the toe of her sandal. "You make it sound so, well . . . meager."

"I didn't mean to, believe me. I meant, can you be happy here?"

"I thought so, George. Oh, I thought so. Even with Boris . . ." She sighed.

"Is there no news of him?"

"Only that he is alive. Or he was up to the time Ivan Nej tried to kidnap me."

"I'd like you to tell me about that," George said.

She shrugged. "It was partly my own fault. I was over-confident."

"I'd like to punch him on the nose."

She almost smiled. "You did once, remember? Anyway, Boris . . . I must just wait, and pray. But Paul . . . I suppose one doesn't ever really know a man. I liked him. You know I liked him, George. But I guess he was educated to be a killer, and thus he *is* a killer. Poor Ruth is absolutely shattered."

"Where is she?" George asked.

Judith pointed into the fields. There were several women down there, working. "Ruth is the one in the white headscarf. That is her friend, Sylvia Levin, beside her. Thank God for Sylvia. I think Ruth might have gone mad without her."

"Ruth has never struck me as the going-mad variety."

"But can you imagine? She came here looking for peace, looking for security, and first of all there was that thing with Ivan Nej, and then *this*. The trouble is that she cannot bring herself to blame Paul. She . . . well, she just seems to have gone numb."

"Has it occurred to you," George said gently, "that Paul may *not* be guilty?"

Judith stared at him, frowning. "George, I was *there*. I saw him standing in front of me, with a pistol in his hand."

"But not firing it."

"No, well, I suppose he lost his nerve, or something."

"If you are so convinced of his guilt," George said, "why did you send for me?"

"I'm sorry, George. Believe me. I wasn't ever going to call

on you again. But . . . I just had to shout for help. For Ruth. To wake up and discover that your husband is a mur- derer—"

"Judith, in my opinion, there is at least an even chance that Paul was recruited to do what he did, and that he therefore considers himself to be part of an army."

"You mean the Stern Gang? Or Haganah? But to go around killing people—"

"They may regard it as necessary."

She held his hand. "Then you'll help us?"

"I'll see what can be done," he agreed. "But I can't stay long." His face twisted. "Even the George Haymans of this world have their problems."

"George?" Her grip tightened. "Ilona isn't ill?"

"Not physically. But there was a telegram awaiting me in Tel Aviv. Felicity has run off with Gregory Nej."

"Felicity? And Gregory?"

"I don't mean that they've got married. But they've appar- ently set up house together."

"Oh, *George*. And Ilona—"

"Is horrified. But helpless. Felicity is thirty-three years old."

"But . . . what are you going to do?"

"Try to talk some sense into them, as soon as I get back. But I'll see what can be done in Jerusalem first."

"George, I feel terrible. Dragging you over here when there's something like that going on at home—"

"Nobody's on trial for his life, at home," George said. "It's you I want to put straight, Judith. I have an idea Paul *had* to do what he did, and if that is the case, he was working for you and for Ruth as much as for anyone else. I don't hold with murder any more than you do, but the circumstances here are peculiar. I recommended you come here. I am proud of the way you are sticking it out. I regret most bitterly that I haven't been able to do anything about Boris. But Judith, if you are going to stay here and live with these people, they have to be *your* people. There can be no halfway measures. I suspect Paul has found that out the hard way. Now, I'd better be getting on."

She gazed at the rented Land Rover, waiting in the dust of the road. Nothing but the best for George Hayman. There would never be anything but the best for George Hayman.

"George," she said. "Will I see you again?"

"I'll come back out tomorrow, to tell you what happened. I'd like to see Ruth then, too."

"Of course," she said. "George, I wish I could tell you how grateful I am—*we* are."

"I'm not promising anything."

"Just being here. Tomorrow . . . will you be able to stay the night?" She flushed. "There are so many people I'd like you to meet."

He hesitated, then shook his head. "Ilona needs me." He held her hands, leaned forward, and kissed her on the forehead. "Just remember what I said. These are your people now, Judith. You can't go halfway with them. Not any more."

"Mr. Hayman." The police commissioner stood up to shake George's hand. "This is quite an honor. Do sit down."

George sat down facing the desk; through the open window he could smell and hear Jerusalem. It was a city he had intended to bring Ilona to visit, one day. Now that day suddenly seemed to have receded far into the future. "You know why I'm here?"

The commissioner nodded. "It is a sad case."

"But a foregone conclusion, in your opinion?"

The commissioner shrugged. "There is very little to be done about it. The man Hassell was taken with a weapon in his hand, in the very act of firing at one of my officers."

"I understood that he did not actually fire the pistol."

"He did not have time. Inspector Brent is very quick, and very accurate. He hit one of the attackers with his first shot, and the other two seem to have lost their nerve. One ran away, and in fact has so far managed to escape arrest. Hassell just stood there, and surrendered."

"Hardly in character, don't you think?" George suggested. "For a man who served in the SS, and survived the plot against Hitler? If he had intended to kill this man Brent, he would have done so."

The commissioner sighed. "You may well be right, which is why I referred to it as a sad case. Certainly Brent thinks that. He is very reluctant to give evidence against this fellow. And he is a policeman, as well as the intended victim. Of course, there are other factors involved. Brent has made the mistake of becoming friendly with Mrs. Hassell, and with her aunt—"

"How on earth can it be a mistake to be friends with someone?" George demanded.

"Mr. Hayman, we have a difficult task here in Palestine. The Arabs don't want the Jews here, and the Jews want the country all for themselves. We just have to stand in the middle and try to keep the two sides from massacring each other, and in the process we are attacked and murdered in cold blood by the extremists on both sides. Yet we have to try to deal with them all, Arabs and Jews, as fairly as we can. It is an aspect of what Kipling called the white man's burden. I suspect he really meant the Englishman's burden, because we seem to have managed to get ourselves into unholy messes like this more often than any other colonial power. But what is certain is that we cannot afford to take sides. Becoming friendly with a Jewish family amounts to that. It makes the job that much harder, as Brent is discovering."

"Yes." George was really not interested in Nigel Brent's problems. "What are the prospects for Hassell?"

"I'm afraid that is largely up to him. He has been formally charged and committed for trial. The trial itself will not take place until well into next year. But I am afraid there can be little doubt as to the verdict, if he persists in his present attitude."

"And if he is convicted, he will he hanged?"

"That is the legal penalty for terrorism, yes."

"Even if he never actually *committed* such an act, but just happened to be there."

"Mr. Hayman, I don't know anything about American jurisprudence, but in English law, if two men set out to commit a crime, say a larceny, and one of them carries a pistol, and the pair are challenged by a policeman, even if this challenge takes place *before* the larceny has occurred, and the man with the gun fires and kills the policeman, then *both* are guilty of murder. Hassell not only set out to commit an act of terrorism, he carried a weapon for use in that act. All three of those men are equally guilty, before the law."

George reminded himself that this patient, and probably well-intentioned man did not make the law. He merely enforced it. "You said, if he persisted in his present attitude. What exactly did you mean?"

"I meant that it is within Hassell's power to save his neck, if he wishes. As I say, one of the gunmen has got away. And undoubtedly the three of them are a part of a much larger organization. We have invited Hassell to cooperate with us, to give us, first, the name of the third man, and second, to give us information on the entire group. But so far he has refused such cooperation."

"You really expect him to give you that information? To betray his compatriots?"

"I have some hope of it, once he understands the situation he is in. He is not a Jew himself. There was no reason for him to become involved."

"He is married to a Jew."

"I cannot believe that Mrs. Hassell really wishes her husband to hang, Mr. Hayman."

"I was thinking more of their having to live here, Colonel Wilson."

"I agree that would be impossible. But we'd ship them back out. And give them protection until they could be safely away." A wintry smile spread across the clipped features. "That would surely be preferable to *dying* here." The smile faded, and Wilson leaned across the desk. "If you want to help Hassell, Mr. Hayman, my advice would be to have a chat with him, make him realize how serious his situation is and show him that he can still save his neck. But only *he* can do that. It's up to him."

Ruth Hassell slowly lowered herself into the straight chair, rested her elbows on the plain table, and waited. This was her third visit, and she still felt she was in some kind of dream.

She had felt she was in a dream ever since that dreadful day. This was her refuge, into which she had learned to retire so often during the horrors of the past seven years. She had hoped never to need it again.

And this time it was hardly proving effective, because this was too much of a nightmare. An eternal, unending nightmare. With the most peculiar aspects. In the kibbutz she was suddenly being treated like a queen. No one, and especially the other women, could do enough for her. It was because they were all involved—as involved as she was, without her even understanding what had happened. It had taken Uncle George, with his clear-headed common-sense, to make her see what *was* happening, that Paul was actually in danger of his life.

But how was she to make anyone else see that?

The door opened, and she looked up. Paul wore an open-necked shirt and light trousers, looked as calm and as relaxed as ever. His suntan was beginning to fade, but apart from that he looked healthy, and was obviously well fed.

The guard came in with him and stood against the wall. He was an Englishman, and did not appear the least hostile. But he was watchful.

Paul sat down, and they could touch fingers across the table. She wanted to do nothing more than this, and he could understand that, whatever his own feelings.

"Did you see Uncle George?" she asked.

"I did. He is quite a forceful gentleman, when he wants to be."

"He has gone back to the U.S. now," Ruth said. "He has troubles of his own. His daughter has run off with that Russian cousin of theirs—you remember him, Gregory Nej? Ivan's son? Maybe he told you."

"Good Lord," Paul said. "No, he didn't tell me anything about that."

"It is causing a terrible scandal, of course."

For a moment the room was almost normal. They could have been having tea together, engrossed in family gossip. Families like the Borodins were always having scandals.

But there was nothing normal about this room. She leaned forward. "Did you talk with him?"

"I did."

"Did he give you some advice?"

"He gave me the same advice the British have been giving me, since my arrest," Paul said. "But he didn't expect me to take it. He told me as much."

"Paul . . ." Her fingers tightened on his. "You must do it. You *must*. Or you will be hanged."

"I cannot do it, my own dear love, and you know that I cannot."

Her lips tightened. "Then I will do it," she said.

"You?"

"I know the name of at least one of them. That boy—"

"Shut up," he snapped, his voice suddenly filled with steel. Ruth's head jerked. He had never spoken to her like that before. Then she looked at the guard, who was watching and listening with interest.

"You know nothing," Paul said. "Nothing at all."

"Paul," she said, "you are going to *hang*."

"Listen to me," he said. "We decided to come to Palestine to join the Jewish people. Your people, Ruth. To *join* them. That means to share their lives, and when it became necessary, to share their deaths, as well. You knew we could not come here and just sit on the sidelines, and watch what was happening. We came to *join*."

"Paul..."

"Listen to me," he said again. "I am a soldier. I know no other profession. I knew, when I came here, that I would have to continue being a soldier, because I knew that was what they would require of me. Soldiers fight, my darling, and some of them get killed. I have been very lucky to survive this far. I should have been killed in the war. I should have been executed by the Gestapo, and I should have died from that wound outside Ravensbrück. Instead I survived, and I have enjoyed a few extra years of happiness, with you. But I also made you a promise. That I would bring you home. Somewhere for you to live, away from harm, away from fear, away from people like Ivan Nej. You cannot betray that home, anymore than I can."

"Paul," she said, "you are going to *die*. How can I sit back and watch that happen?" Her eyes were filled with tears. It was the first time he had ever seen Ruth's eyes fill with tears; he had always supposed that she had shed all her tears, either in Lubianka or in Ravensbrück.

He squeezed her hand. "I have not yet been convicted. While there is life there is hope, eh? And I will tell you something, in the strictest confidence, my darling. I do not think I am *going* to be convicted. I do not think my... associates will ever let that happen. They know my value, my increasing value in the times to come. And they know I have played my part as I said I would. Have faith in them, Ruth. But no matter *what* happens, you must look to the future. These are your people. You must live with them, and fight with them. They *will* have to fight, you know, merely to survive. And you must stay by Judith's side, because she needs you."

"You are sacrificing yourself," she said, "so that Judith and I will be accepted. While all the time that—"

"That nobody," he said. "Remember that. Whatever I told you, I told you in confidence. You must *never* repeat it to a soul."

"And you expect me to live with him, seeing him every

day? He once asked me to dance. My God!"

"He is fighting for your people, Ruth. And in time he may well die for them, too. You *must* remember that."

Judith Petrova picked tomatoes, slowly releasing each round, succulent red fruit from its stem, and placing it carefully in the basket she carried over her arm. It was winter, and quite cool; although the sun seemed as warm as ever, the breeze drifting down from the Golan Heights was chilly.

She wore an old dress and a loose sweater, and her hair was bound up in a headscarf. She was, in fact, indistinguishable from any of the other women in the tomato field. That was as she wished to be. As, she had realized these past few months, she had always wanted to be. She had never wanted to lead, to be in the forefront of affairs. She had wanted to swim with the great tide of history, to take part, no more than that. When she had jumped on the barricade surrounding the Kitai-Gorod in Moscow on that unforgettable day in October 1905, she had not known that the man standing beside her, with the short-cropped red hair and the jutting chin, would one day call himself Lenin, and rule all Russia. She had been seventeen years old then, afire with the desire to help her people, all her people; she had not even thought of herself as a Jew as opposed to a gentile. But that day, together with that chance meeting with Princess Ilona Roditcheva, had launched her upon a life in which she had always seemed to hold the center of the stage, as she still did, despite her present anonymity. It was not something she could change, apparently, no matter how hard she wished.

She straightened, and watched the rabbi hurrying down the slope towards her. "Is there news?" she asked.

Menachem Yanowski's face was bright. "Great news," he said. "The conference has ended. The British proposed to divide Palestine into two, with the Arabs in one half and us in the other, and the Arabs have refused to consider it."

Judith peered at him. "Is that good news?"

"Of course. The British have shot their bolt. We did not even send a delegation to this conference, as you know. We refused. And I will tell you frankly that, after our boycott, if the Arabs had accepted the British plan, we would have been isolated. But now that the *Arabs* have rejected it . . . there is a rumor that the British intend to hand the whole business over to the United Nations."

"Do you think that will mean an improvement in the situation?" Judith asked as they walked back towards the village.

"Indeed it will. The United Nations is almost certain to put forward the British plan all over again, because it was really an American plan in the first place. And this time *we* will accept it, and it will be the Arabs who will appear to be in the wrong. It is all working out very well."

"I am afraid I do not understand international diplomacy," Judith said.

Yanowski chuckled. "The Arabs, the Jordanians, the Syrians, and the Egyptians are saying that they will destroy us, if the British pull out. I should like to see them try."

Judith stopped walking and grasped his arm. "Did you say, if the British pull out? Are they going to do that?"

"There is talk of their ending the mandate, yes. That is what I have been telling you. That they are considering handing the whole thing over to the United Nations. It has proved very costly for them, and they are quite unable to solve the problem."

"But . . . if they pull out . . . ?"

Some of the contentment left Yanowski's face. "It will not happen for some time, Judith. At least a year."

"Yes, but, if the British *know* they are leaving, then perhaps Paul—"

"They will still regard terrorism as terrorism, up to the day they leave. The trial date has been set. It will be in March."

"Another four months," she said, and resumed walking.

"Yes," Yanowski agreed. "It would have been so much better for everyone had Hassell been shot down. And had he taken Inspector Brent with him."

"Menachem," Judith cried. "How can you say that? Do you support terrorism?"

Yanowski flushed. "We are at war, Judith. There is no use in hiding from that fact. And Hassell—well, is he not making you and Ruth utterly miserable, lying in that cell in Jerusalem? Of course you would have been miserable had he been shot down, but that would have been over and done with. There would have been none of this long-drawn-out agony. And it is agony for him too, you know. For all of us. There is always the risk he will break down and implicate others."

"I wish he would," Judith said fiercely. "Why should he be the only one to suffer? God knows, I hate the thought of what he did. I even hated *him,* when I saw him standing there with a gun. But I cannot believe those people he was associated with, whoever they were, will just let him die. He went with them, he acted with them, they owe him their help. If only I knew who they were, how he became involved. And *why?* He had only been here a few days. How did they manage to pick on him so quickly? How did they even know he was a soldier? Menachem, could they have been people from the village?"

She looked at her friend, and realized with a start of horror that his eyes could become quite as opaque as ever Michael Nej's had been.

"You do know," she said. "I am sure you do. And I have the oddest feeling that Ruth knows too, and yet she does nothing about it. But Menachem, you must help us. You cannot just stand by and watch that boy die."

"There is nothing I can do, Judith," he said. "Nothing any of us can do, but remember."

"Menachem!" She took his hands. "Paul saved my life. And Ruth's. He took us out of Ravensbrück. We would surely have died had we remained there. He took us out. We must help him."

"We cannot."

"Well . . . at least tell me who they are. How they knew he was a German. Because they must have known that. They must have used that knowledge to make him work for them, and no one knew, except—" Her voice trailed away.

"Yes, Judith," Yanowski said. "No one knew, except me. Paul von Hassell was a German, and a Nazi. He had a great debt to pay to our people. And he has paid it, and is paying it. It is the finest thing he has ever done. We will remember him with honor."

Judith stared at him, and slowly released his hands.

"That is all any of us can do, Judith," Yanowski said. "Die for our people and our country. That is something we are all going to have to be prepared to do, when the British pull out."

Police Commissioner Wilson leaned back in his chair and allowed the sheet of paper he had been reading to fall to the blotting pad. He raised his head to stare at the young officer in front of him. "This is a total absurdity, Brent, and you know it."

Nigel Brent stood at attention, staring straight ahead. "It is my decision, sir."

"To resign from the force? What do you suppose that is going to accomplish? You will still have to give evidence at Hassell's trial, you know."

"I accept that, sir."

"And he is still going to be convicted, and sentenced to death, and hanged. Nothing on the face of this earth can change that, now. Unless he turns state's evidence, and there is no indication that he is prepared to do that."

"He dares not do that, sir."

The commissioner shrugged. "That may be so. We are interested in the facts of the case, not the emotions."

"I find it impossible to separate the two, sir," Nigel said. "Which is why I am resigning."

Wilson leaned forward. "This man, this German, this *Nazi*, came to Jerusalem to *kill* you, Brent."

"I think he was forced to come, sir. I think pressure was brought to bear on him because of his background, and because of his wife's background as well."

Wilson frowned at him. "You think the terrorist group is actually in the village?"

"Yes, sir, I do. But that is not the point."

"I'm afraid it is very much the point. It may be the lead we have been waiting for. If we can nail some more of these scum—"

"I also find it impossible to regard them as scum, sir," Nigel said. "I understand much of their feelings. God knows I don't go along with murder, but these are people who regard almost the entire world as being against them. I cannot hate them. I cannot stop myself admiring them. I can no longer continue arresting them and marching them to the gallows."

Wilson stared at him. "If you have any information, Inspector Brent, any suspicions, even, it is your duty to reveal them."

"Would that save Hassell's life?"

"Of course not. *He* has not cooperated."

"Then, sir, I have nothing to offer."

"Brent, you are placing your entire career in jeopardy."

"Colonel Wilson, I have just terminated my career as a policeman."

Wilson picked up the letter of resignation, looked at it, and put it down again. "Once I accept this, there can be no changing your mind. You do understand that?"

"I do, sir."

"Nor will I allow you to remain in Palestine. Do you understand *that?*"

"Why should I not remain here, sir?"

"Because you have allowed yourself to become emotionally involved with these people. With Hassell and his wife. With Mrs. Petrov. It is as plain as a pikestaff. And you know too much of our methods, of what is in our files, for me to allow you to associate with them after leaving the force. If I accept this resignation, I am going to put you into protective custody until the trial, and the moment you have given your evidence you will be deported. I wish you to understand that, very clearly. And an order will be made forbidding you to return to Palestine, at any time and for any reason. Do you understand that?"

"I understand that you have that power, sir," Nigel said.

"So you will be serving no purpose whatsoever by taking this absurd attitude. Now, shall I tear up this letter?"

"No, sir," Nigel said. "I wish the letter to stand. Whatever the consequences."

Ilona sat behind the wheel of the Rolls-Royce, gloved hands tight on the spokes. "Shall I come up with you?" she asked.

George hesitated, and then shook his head. "Better not. If things work out, I'll come down for you."

"What are you going to say? What are you going to *do?*"

He shrugged. "I have no idea. Play it by ear, I guess." He leaned across the seat to kiss her on the cheek. "Keep the heater on," he recommended, and got out. He just could not make himself become as upset as Ilona obviously was. But that was dangerous thinking. He *was* going to play it by ear, and that meant permitting no preconceived opinions.

The apartment was a walk-up. Felicity, of course, had her own bank account, and Gregory was presumably being paid by the Pentagon, but rents in Arlington were high. This was probably the best they could afford. He reached the landing only slightly out of breath, rang the bell, and waited.

"Who is it?" But she was obviously peering through the Judas window. "Daddy?" The chain scraped, and the door swung in. "Oh, Daddy!"

He took her in his arms, realized that the woman he was holding exuded more vitality than he had ever seen in her. At least, since 1941. He kissed her forehead and looked past her into the little living room. Felicity had always been careless in the condition of her room at Cold Spring Harbor. But here everything was neat and clean, and she herself, clearly in the midst of her morning's chores, was wearing lipstick and nail varnish, and had her hair neatly caught up in a coif. He held her at arm's length. "You're growing your hair."

"Well . . ." She flushed. "Gregory says all Borodin women should have long hair. I guess he means Hayman women as well."

George released her and went into the room. She closed the door and replaced the chain. "Would you like a cup of coffee?"

"That sounds good." He followed her into the small kitchen, watched her prepare the percolater. It was difficult to remember the old Felicity summoning the energy to butter a slice of toast.

"Gregory at work?" he asked.

"That's right." Her head half-turned. "He will be sorry to have missed you. If you'd let us know you were home—"

"It's you I wanted to see," George said.

She poured, arranged the cups on the tray with the sugar bowl and milk pitcher, and led him back into the living room. "That's strange," she remarked. "No other member of the family has wanted to see me at all."

"Well . . ." He sat down and stirred his coffee. "I guess you took them by surprise. And then . . . well . . . let's say it's a rather unusual setup."

"Why?" she challenged.

"Well . . . to begin with, you *are* first cousins."

"What has that got to do with it?" she demanded, her voice tight.

"Let's say it's frowned upon, by church and by society. By doctors, too."

"Only the doctors make any sense," she said. "And we understand that. We aren't going to have any children. That's a promise."

"There *are* laws against incest," George said, mildly.

"To protect teen-age girls from lecherous uncles and fathers," she said. "Gregory and I happen to be adults. Sure, I guess you could bring charges against us, if you wanted to, maybe have us sent to jail. But what would that prove, Dad? Nobody else wants to know. Oh, I guess there were a few raised eyebrows at the Pentagon, but Gregory's proving so valuable to them, they'll never make trouble. And anyway, you don't *know,* nobody *knows,* that we sleep together. I'm keeping house for my cousin, that's all. If you want to put another construction on that, then that's your business."

George finished his coffee and leaned back. "I'm anxious to be on your side, Felicity. The hostility isn't necessary. Not yet, anyway. Do you think you could tell me why?"

She gazed at him for several seconds. "In confidence, Dad. If you'd tell me something, afterwards."

"I promise."

"We love each other. In confidence, we do sleep together. I . . . I guess I woke up one morning and realized just how much of my life I had wasted by always looking over my shoulder. And there was nothing I could do about it, I thought. And then along came Gregory. We fought it. Believe me, we did. But it's just one of those things. When you fall in love, when the chemistry goes *bang,* things like blood relationships don't mean a thing."

"And you're happy?" George asked.

She met his eyes. "Yes," she said. "I'm the happiest woman in the world, I think." Nor did he suppose for a moment, from the way her eyes shone, that she was not telling the truth. "Now, you tell me," she said. "Why is everyone so against Gregory?"

"Nobody is against him, my darling girl. But he *is* your cousin."

"I think that is nonsense. I think all of you are against him because he is a Russian. Because he is Ivan Nej's son. Because he used to be in the NKVD. And because he's a defector. Can't you convince them all how wrong that is? Gregory is a man who wants to help us all, Russians as well as Americans, to live in peace. He wants to bring us together, if that is possible. And he's got the guts to try. That's a reason for admiration, not dislike."

"And you are *really* happy?" he asked.

"Oh, yes, Daddy. As I said, I don't think that any other woman can ever have known what real happiness is."

George nodded, and got up. "Then be happy, my dearest Felicity. There's not much happiness about, right now." He kissed her again, and went to the door. "I'll talk to your mother."

Chapter 10

THE COURTROOM WAS HUSHED AS THE JURY FILED IN TO take their places. They had only been out for half an hour.

It was a well-chosen group of men: four Arabs, four Jews, and four Englishmen. They looked sad, the Jews no sadder than any of the others. But there was nothing they could do with the facts of the case as presented to them, and not denied by the defense.

The foreman stood up, facing the judge's bench and the clerk standing in front of it. The dock was to the right, where the accused stood, very straight, close-cropped hair brushed straight back from his forehead. He looked very German, as perhaps he intended to look, today.

"Foreman of the jury," said the clerk, "have you reached a verdict?"

"We have," the Englishman said.

"Will you let me have it, please."

The Englishman held out the slip of paper, and it was passed to the clerk, who unfolded it, and read what was written. Then he raised his head. "How do you find the prisoner? Is he guilty or not guilty?"

The Englishman drew a long breath. "Guilty."

It was as if the entire courtroom had been holding its breath, such was the hiss of expelled air.

"And that is the unanimous verdict of you all?" asked the clerk.

"It is," the Englishman said, and sat down.

The paper had arrived at the chief justice's desk, and now he looked at Paul, the white curls of his wig seeming to flicker as a shaft of sunlight drifted through the opened window to play on him. "Prisoner at the bar," the judge said, "you have been tried, and found guilty, of the crime of terrorism. Have you anything to say before I pass sentence upon you?"

Paul's head turned, and he looked over the seated barristers, the solicitors behind them, and into the gallery of the court. There he could see Ruth, with Judith to one side of her and Sylvia on the other. They were flanked by two other women from the kibbutz, lending their support, their strength, he hoped. Further along, he could make out the figure of Nigel Brent, wearing civilian clothes, as he had done when giving evidence. The fact of his resignation had been brought out in cross-examination, but had contributed nothing to the case for the defense. Neither Menachem Yanowski nor Benjamin Cohen was in court.

"I have nothing to say, my lord," Paul said.

"Then you must understand that you have been convicted of a most serious crime, that of terrorism against the State— of, in effect, armed rebellion. It is a crime which is cowardly and distasteful in its conception, as it necessitates attacks upon the lives of men who are not by design your enemies, but are merely attempting to do a job. It is a crime for which there can be no justification, in law. You must understand this. Your able advocate has made much of the circumstances, peculiar to your case alone, by which you have found yourself in this court. We have been reminded of your unusual war record, and it has been pointed out to us that you have proved yourself something of a hero. It has been suggested that you joined the terrorist ranks to improve the chances of your wife and yourself being accepted here, and it has been further suggested that there is something honorable in such a course of action. I have to tell you that there is nothing honorable about murder, in the eyes of honorable men. Some play has also been made of the fact that you did not actually fire the weapon with which you were armed, although you had the opportunity. It may be, and

I am prepared to hope that this was indeed the case, that at the vital moment you did experience a pang of honor, and if you did, then it will be a solace to you and your loved ones, and, one hopes and prays, may rebound to your credit when you meet your maker. But the act of pulling the trigger on a pistol does not make a terrorist. It is the act of carrying the pistol in the first place, with the *intention* of pulling the trigger, that has brought you here today, and that obliges me now to pass sentence upon you, a sentence decreed by law, and beyond the power of any man to mitigate." He paused, and turned his head to look at his clerk, who stood next to his chair, carrying a crimson cushion, on which there was a square of black cloth.

Ruth Hassell glanced at the policeman who was opening the door for her, then stepped past him into the little room just off the courtroom itself. She halted instinctively, immediately inside the still open door, heard it close behind her, and gazed at Nigel Brent, who stood by the small window. He had been looking out. Now he turned at her entry. Between them were a table and two small chairs; there was no other furniture. The room, she thought, was exactly like those in which she habitually met Paul, except that there were no bars on the window.

"I . . ." Nigel drew a long breath. "I wanted to say good-bye. I . . . I am being deported this afternoon."

"Because of Paul?"

He shrugged. "Because of a great many things. Paul was just the climax." He attempted a smile. "I am accused of being too friendly to the Jews."

Her face remained grave. It occurred to him that he had seen her smile only once. But what on earth did she have to smile about?

"I am sorry," she said.

"That I should favor your side?"

"That you should be punished for it. We are very grateful to you, Mr. Brent. All of us. Aunt Judith, for saving her from the NKVD. And Paul and I, for . . . for all you tried to do."

"Which wasn't very much. You will be seeing Paul?"

"Of course."

"And he will be appealing?"

She sighed. "His lawyers intend to. I cannot see they will achieve anything. He has been convicted as much for being a Nazi as for trying to kill you."

"Ruth . . ." He checked whatever he had been going to say.
"I want you to understand that I reacted instinctively. I drew
my weapon and shot that young man, and I guess I would have
shot Paul, had he not surrendered. It was the way I have been
trained to react, I'm afraid."

"Of course we understand that," she said. "We do not blame
you for anything. I told you, we thank you, for trying so hard
to put things right." She raised her head. "What will you do?"

"Do? Oh, you mean when I get home. I'll find something."
This time his smile was genuine. "I won't starve. I've been
offered a thousand pounds by a Sunday newspaper for my story.
But Ruth . . ." He came closer. "I intend to return to Palestine
just as soon as I can."

She frowned at him. "To Palestine? But . . . can you? After
being deported?"

"Not legally. Not at all, while the British control the country.
But there is no doubt at all now that they are going to surrender
the mandate. And the moment they do that, I will be back."

Still she frowned. "But why?"

"To . . ." He bit his lip. "To help your people. They will
need all the help they can get. I would like to play a part in
what lies ahead. Will you tell Paul that? That I will fight his
fight for him, as soon as I can?"

She gazed at him for several seconds. "I am glad," she said.
"Perhaps I'll be able to see you again."

"I would like that."

A tinge of rose appeared in her cheeks. Then she held out
her hand. "Good luck," she said. "Until we meet again."

The cell door opened, and Paul turned his head. He had
finished his breakfast, had been staring through the small barred
window high in the wall at the deep blue of the early morning
sky.

"Time, Hassell," said the prison governor.

Nothing from London, he thought. No reprieve. But why
should they reprieve an ex-Nazi? And how could they reprieve
one terrorist without reprieving them all?

He felt no bitterness. Indeed, he felt nothing at all but a
curious anticipatory breathlessness—a sense of suspension, he
thought wryly, a feeling that he was done with one life, and
there was no use in feeling anything else, until he was able to
begin whatever came next.

He got up without a word, relieved to find that his legs were not weak. He had feared that. He walked between the jailers, out into the corridor, the parson beside him. The parson was reading something from the Bible, but Paul did not listen to him. Since he was not a believer, there probably *was* no next thing for him. He had been a believer once. He had believed in the greatness of Germany, the *right* of Germany to dominate Europe, and through Europe the world, the dream of omnipotent power and unending glory as projected by Adolf Hitler. No doubt he should have died in defense of that dream, as had so many of his friends. Instead, when he had realized the filth upon which the dream had rested, the filth out of which it had sprung, he had turned away from it. And survived. No man could reasonably expect more, even if the survival had been for a shorter time than he had hoped, and expected.

But the truth of the matter was that he still did not believe this was happening, that it would be carried to its unthinkable conclusion. He had played his part, as he had been asked to do. He had not actually been able to make himself shoot Brent, not because of Judith's presence, but because he was not a murderer. But he had accepted his fate, betrayed no one. Cohen could not just let him die, surely. There had to be some dramatic last-minute intervention, which would at least commute his sentence to life imprisonment, until the British left. If he ceased to believe in that, then he would be unable to walk a step.

The prison was silent, the only sounds the clicking of the heels of the little party. Most of the prisoners in this cellblock were also Jewish, and a fair number of them were awaiting trial for terrorism. They had nothing to say about this old enemy whom they had in effect condemned to death before the British put manacles on his wrists. He wondered where Ruth was. She had visited him yesterday for the last time, and he had then told her not to stay in Jerusalem for this morning. But he supposed she had stayed. She was his wife.

He thought they had been happy during their three years together. *She* had been happy. At least, as happy as Ruth could ever be. Of course she had never *loved* him. Ruth had never been allowed to love any man. Her life had been a long misfortune, and if he was proud of anything he had ever done, it was the fact of those three years, that he had been able, first, to save her life, without even knowing who she was, and then that he had been able to make her smile.

He was aware of the first trace of bitterness, of anger, of resentment, as they entered the final doorway, immediately followed by a surge of all those emotions. The hope was, after all, only a fantasy. Cohen did not care whether he lived or died; he was merely a weapon that had broken. Thus he had merely sacrificed himself for Ruth, and for Judith. He did not regret this. But it was all so *unnecessary*. The British *were* pulling out. There was going to be a Jewish state, and that state was going to have to fight for its existence. He would have had so much to offer. It would have been so magnificent to end his life in battle, in victorious battle, for he did not doubt the outcome.

He realized that he had been placed in position, and that someone was holding a black hood ready to drop over his head.

"Have you anything to say, Hassell?" asked the prison governor.

Paul gazed at him. "It is a waste," he said. "Has anyone the right to waste anything of such value as a human life?"

The hood dropped over his head.

"Mr. Hayman. Both Mr. Haymans." Harry Truman gave one of his rare smiles. "Sit down. Sit down. I haven't met you before," he said to George junior. "But you look like a chip off the old block."

"Thank you, sir," George junior said. He did not seem the least overawed at finding himself inside the Oval Office. But then, George reflected, his son was not an easily overawed man.

"I don't know if you've met George Marshall," the president said. "Your stepfather has, of course. And Dean Acheson." George had not seen the general since their last meeting at the White House.

They shook hands, and waited. There had to be a reason for their being summoned here.

Truman placed his elbows on his desk and brought his fingers together; they exactly obscured his bow tie. "I wanted to talk to you two first," he said, "because you were in on the beginning of this business—at least, you were, Hayman," he said to George. "And therefore you have a right to know, and because, hell, I'm going to need all the help I can get. You've got a Republican paper, and you've given this administration a few hard knocks, but when the chips are down I think we both mean the same thing. I'm talking about the Reds."

And about next year's election? George wondered. But he didn't say it. Instead he said, "You know our views there, Mr. President."

"Yep," Truman agreed. "And there was a time when maybe I didn't share them. Now, I'm not saying things have changed. In fact, I'm admitting that you were maybe closer to the mark than I was, all along. What I am saying is that it's time we did something about it. I'm afraid what we're looking at is the slow but sure Communization of all Eastern Europe." He held up his hand. "All right. You told me it was happening, over a year ago. At that time I thought we had to go through diplomatic channels, and the U.N. Now I can see that's not working. So I aim to do more. The problem is, *attitudes* haven't changed that much. Our people can still remember the last war too well, and they sure as hell don't have any wish to get involved in another shooting war. That's why I'm going to need all the newspaper support I can get, from both sides of the fence." He paused.

"May we ask what you have in mind, sir?" George junior said.

Truman took a long breath. "First thing, I mean to concentrate on the area that is most vulnerable. It seems to me we may have already lost the Balkans. That's too bad, but we can't change it now, short of that shooting I was talking about. But Greece and Turkey are still on our side, despite the pressure the Reds are putting on them. Now, my guess is that if we were to lose Turkey, we'd lose the whole damn Mideast. And that's going to become a trouble spot, anyway, over the next few years, when the British abandon their mandate for Palestine. So my first aim is to keep Turkey and Greece on our side. I'm going before Congress next week to make a speech, in which I'm going to propose that this country give the Greeks and the Turks all they need, not only in the way of weapons, but in help with their industries and their schools, to raise their entire standard of living, to beat back this Communist threat. I'm going to ask for a lot of money. And with a little bit of help from my friends, I'm going to get it."

"What do you suppose the Russians' reaction will be to that, sir?" George asked.

"They're not going to like it," Truman agreed. "But there's nothing they can do about it, unless *they* mean to start shooting, and when it comes to that, we've still got the drop on them. No, sir, I'm more concerned about what's said here at home." He glanced at Marshall. "Hell, George, they may as well know it. I'm not even sure I can carry my cabinet unanimously. But I'm sure as hell going to try." He leaned forward. "Will you back me?"

"We'll back you," George said.

"We'll call it the Truman Doctrine," George junior said. "How's that, Mr. President? That this country will resist the Red tide wherever it's flowing."

Truman grinned.

"But I'm not sure just shoring up the Greeks and the Turks is going to be enough," George said.

"You couldn't be more right," the President agreed. "So we've got a few more plans. They're George's babies. Tell the Haymans, George."

General Marshall cleared his throat. "As you say, Hayman, Southeast Europe is only one half of the business. The Reds are infiltrating Western Europe as well, because the countries there just can't get back on their feet. Sure, maybe we ended Lend Lease a year too soon. That was what the public wanted. And even now our people are inclined to ask why the British and the French can't work just a little bit harder. But right now, we're interested in results. My idea is that we give Western Europe the same kind of help as we're going to give Greece and Turkey."

"Now *that* will take a bit of selling," George junior said.

"Right," Marshall agreed, and smiled as he looked at the president. "That's why it's going to be my baby, at first. I'll propose it in a speech and see what sort of a reaction we get. But there's no harm in finding out in advance, as far as we can."

"You've got us on your side," George junior said. "Every Hayman paper, worldwide."

"You don't look quite as enthusiastic, Hayman," Truman remarked.

"I think it's a great idea," George said. "I'm just a little bothered about the implications for the future, and the questions that are going to be asked. There'll be those who say we're taking on Western Europe as a permanent dependency. There'll be Britishers and Frenchmen as well who'll object to that suggestion."

Truman turned to Marshall. "George?"

"Right again," Marshall said. "So we have to look beyond the mere business of pumping money into European economies. We have to make *them* believe in the future. And that means their ability to stand up to the Russians. Now I know there's a lot of talk going on about European unity and what have you. Churchill is all for it, and Schumann in France. And it may just happen. Trouble is, neither of them happens to be in office, so it's going to take time. Even economic union is going to take time. Political union within that bunch, who've spent the last thousand years killing each other, is going to take a *life*time. But *military* unity now, that's not only a possibility within the next five years, but an essential, I'd say. And they can see that."

"You mean a pooling of the British and French armies and navies, just as during the war?" George asked.

"Right," Marshall said.

"You think Attlee and Bevin would agree to that?"

"I do. They're Socialists, not Communists. They know where the danger lies."

"I doubt that even Britain and France, working together, could oppose the Soviets," George junior said. "Not without help."

"I agree." It was Marshall's turn to take a long breath. "But there're also the Germans."

The room was silent for several seconds.

"The *Germans?*" George asked at last. "You seriously mean to rearm the Wehrmacht?"

"That'll send Stalin straight through the roof," George junior said.

"We won't be able to call it the Wehrmacht," Truman said. "But the Germans, the West Germans, anyway, have to have some sort of defense force. And the fact is, if we ever come to a shooting war with the Reds, and the Germans *aren't* with us, it's going to be a hell of a hard job winning it, in Europe."

"And there can be no doubt," Acheson said, joining the discussion for the first time, "that the best hope we have of keeping the Germans from pulling a third stunt like the other two *is* to integrate them as part of a general West European army. Don't worry, we intend to take part as well. And we've some hope of the Canadians, and the Italians, as well as some of the smaller countries, like Belgium and Holland."

"And you wouldn't call that committing yourself to Europe for the foreseeable future?" George junior persisted.

"I would say we are already committed in a military sense," Truman pointed out. "We could never let the Reds take over Britain and France, anyway. This is just being realistic about it."

"What about the bomb?" George asked.

"We are obliged to share our know-how with Britain and France," Truman said. "And as a matter of fact, the British are pretty close to exploding their own device. The French won't be too far behind. But I am not considering arming the Europeans with nuclear weapons, at least not as things stand at present, and I'm sure London and Paris will go along with that point of view. Besides, since it'll be our money and we'll be supplying the bulk of the personnel for the next few years, it's our prerogative to name the commanding general. I'm thinking of Dwight Eisenhower. He knows the ground and he knows the people. If anyone can make this thing work, Ike can. Would you go along with that?"

"We'll go along with all of that," George said, speaking slowly, "if you'll tell us what you're doing about right here."

Truman sat bolt upright. "You'd better say what you have in mind."

"I meant Communism right here in the U.S."

"To some people," Marshall said quietly, "Communism is a belief as basic and as important as Christianity."

"You're not going to tell me American Communists don't take their orders from the Kremlin," George said.

"There's no proof of that," Marshall objected.

"What do you want, a signed confession from every member of the Party in this country?"

"Maybe you're right, Hayman," the President said soothingly. "But what do you suggest we do? Free speech, freedom of worship, freedom of thought, freedom from persecution, those are the things we preach, the things we live by."

"So we give Communist sympathizers or believers or even Party members jobs in the State Department? And in our key industries?"

Truman flushed, and glanced at Marshall. "There's not a

hell of a lot we can do about it."

"There is, you know," George said.

"Well . . . is that the price of your support?"

"Some better screening of applicants for jobs of importance, either in government or in industry. Some discouragement of the activities of those already there."

Truman frowned at him. "Just how high are you going?"

George met his gaze. "Just now, Mr. President, you pointed out that you might not be able to carry your cabinet with you unanimously."

Truman stared at him for some seconds. Then he nodded. "Okay, Mr. Hayman. We'll have the FBI step up their surveillance and their screening. There's no need for us to fall out over this. Our objectives are the same." He stood up and held out his hand. "It's been good to talk."

The riverbank was dark, and obscured by a light summer drizzle. There was no moon, and it was difficult to see far; the road was slippery. Anna Ragosina was glad to be able to switch off the engine and coast to the side of the road to park behind the big Lincoln. And to sit there, and listen to the silence, blanketed by the light patter of the rain on the roof of her car. She shivered, and wondered if she was afraid.

The door of the Lincoln closed, her own passenger door opened, and Bogolzhin sat beside her. "You are early," he commented.

"It pays not to be on time," she said. "How long have *you* been here?"

"Ten minutes."

"*I* should not be here at all," she grumbled. "It is against the rules."

"He will deal with no one but you," Bogolzhin explained.

"Me?"

"The boss, he says. He has no idea who you are, of course."

"And you could not convince him it was you he should deal with?"

"No," Bogolzhin said. "Since I made the first contact, he knows that it cannot be me."

"And you think what he has may be valuable?"

"The most valuable yet," Bogolzhin said. "All the rest was as nothing."

"I hope you are right, comrade," Anna said skeptically. "I hope you are right. It is not a part of my job to make these assignations."

"You are not afraid?" Bogolzhin sounded genuinely concerned.

"Of course I am not afraid," Anna snapped. "I fought in the Pripet, against the Germans. Against the SS. How can I be afraid?"

Bogolzhin chose not to answer that one. He looked along the rainswept road, at the dimmed headlights of a car, slowly approaching. "Kiss me," he said.

"Here?" Anna inquired. "Now? Is that all you ever think about, Dimitri Igorovich?"

"It may be the police," Bogolzhin said, and took her in his arms.

He knew that she would not resist him, Anna thought. That she would want it as much as he. She had, in fact, been guilty of a serious breach of professional conduct, since coming to America. Not in sleeping with this man. That she should use her body, and his desire for possession of it, to its best advantage, was part of her stock in trade, her weaponry. But that she should enjoy it was not. She never had before. She had enjoyed the mastery, just as she had enjoyed casting the man aside, afterwards. Until Bogolzhin.

It was not, of course, love. It was impossible for any woman to love a lecherous cretin like Bogolzhin. It was pure physical satisfaction, at the size of him, and the stamina he possessed. Bogolzhin could even exhaust *her*, and still look for more. In the beginning, she had been at once amazed and somewhat disgusted—this, she had thought, was less a man than a machine; and besides, she had feared that his bouncing up and down, hour after hour, would awake everyone in that silly little seaside hotel, quite apart from the risk to her ribs. Then, she had looked forward to the arrival of Gregory Nej.

But that phase had passed quickly enough. She had not loved Gregory Nej, either. Anna Ragosina was not a woman who loved, and she was proud of it. The only man she had ever wanted to love, John Hayman, had rejected her. Since that disappointment, possession had been the key, especially of Gregory Nej, because he was her master's son.

But he was a boy. He had been a virgin when they first slept together, and she had therefore taught him just about everything he knew, but he still took diffidently, seeking her approval. Presumably this was his attitude to the Hayman woman, as well. That affair had angered her. It had angered her enough to kill. But it had been the losing possession of him, not necessarily the losing of *him*. In any event, her recommendation to Beria had been based upon sound common sense and the best principles of espionage. There had been nothing personal in it, nothing that could be detected in Russia, although she would have liked to carry out the executions herself, and to have taken her time about it.

But Beria had said no. He had been prepared to risk the consequences of Gregory's behavior, and thus risk her, as well. She had been angry about that, too. But Beria might well have been right. For all the apparent folly of Gregory's behavior, the situation was working out very well. Gregory's information might not contain anything of spectacular value, but it was always useful, it was consistent, and it would certainly grow in importance, since he was more and more accepted by his new employers. He was in fact a born spy, because of his transparent honesty, his openness, his willingness to please. Of course progress was necessarily going to be slow, because he was finding it difficult to make any contacts within the Pentagon itself. She had never supposed he would discover any Communist sympathizers within that stronghold of American militarism, had pinned her faith on blackmail. But of course it was difficult for a young man who has just caused a scandal by setting up housekeeping with his own cousin to strike up a homosexual relationship.

And in fact Gregory had come up with some significant information. It was as yet pure deduction, but it could be very important in the future. He had been asked to pinpoint various military and economic sites inside Russia that would be obvious places for an American bombing strike in the event of war. This in itself was not sensational, but by keeping his ears open he had discovered that these strikes would not be launched from England or France or some European ally of the Americans, but from the United States itself. That meant that the rocket experiments of Dr. von Braun and his associates were to be put to a military use, if necessary—and must be nearing fruition if the military was getting down to concrete plans.

Gregory had also got hold of the idea, by listening to the various allusions made by his superiors, that the Pentagon was planning the development and deployment of a whole arsenal of atomic weapons, mounted on these rockets, which would be stored in underground silos so as to be invulnerable to attack and yet would be able to reach and dominate almost all the world, and certainly all of European Russia. Hence those sites to be pinpointed.

But if Gregory could possibly find out where the rocket silos were to be situated in the United States, then he would have justified all their patience. If he lasted that long.

But he would last that long, because the most amazing thing of all was that the woman was proving as faithful as he had promised she would be. She loved, with an apparently unceasing passion. That could only be based on physical desire. Physical technique. Which *she* had taught him. She supposed she should be proud of her pupil. Which did not mean that when he had eventually outlived his usefulness, or more likely, a quarrel with his mistress made them both security risks, she would not enjoy putting a bullet in each of their bellies.

But Gregory's information had made securing the atomic secrets even more urgent a matter. Moscow had been quite strident in its demands for results, had seemed at times almost to carp at her for inaction, to forget the enormous success she had had in organizing strikes which had cost United States industry no less than a hundred million working days during the past year, as compared with no more than two million secured by her fellow agents in Great Britain. A poor reward for all her work.

But she would show them that she was worth twice as much as they thought. About that she was determined. And tonight... Even as she stroked her tongue against Bogolzhin's, she watched the car slowing, and pulling in beside them, and realized that her heart was thumping. But the vehicle had none of the flashing lights of a police patrol.

Bogolzhin released her reluctantly, allowing his fingertips to drag across her back and then her breasts as he liked doing, and as he knew she also enjoyed. He rolled down the window, and she saw to her relief that he had in the same movement drawn his pistol. But then, so had she.

"Good evening," said the man who had left the parked car. "Isn't the rain warm."

"For the time of year," Bogolzhin agreed, while Anna

sighed. She hated these silly password games.

"Well?" asked the man. "Where is he?"

"This is my principal," Bogolzhin said.

The man peered into the gloom of the car. "That is a woman."

"So?"

"Tell her to get out, so that I can look at her," the man said.

"You will get to look at her," Bogolzhin said, "after you have got in here."

"In there? You think I'm some kind of nut?"

"Get in," Anna snapped, her voice suddenly hard and crisp.

The man hesitated, then got into the back seat. Bogolzhin turned around to face him, showing the pistol, while Anna started the engine.

"Say, what *is* this?" the man protested.

"We mean you no harm," Anna said, turning onto the road. "We only mean to make sure that you cannot harm us. You have the information?"

"I have some information," the man said. "I can get more."

"I see. You do not trust us."

"You're just a girl," the man said.

"I am flattered, my friend," Anna said. "And you do not like dealing with girls?"

"I deal only with principals," the man said. "I told this goon so."

"I am the principal with whom you will deal," Anna said.

"Prove it," the man said.

Anna frowned. It had not previously occurred to her that she might need to prove anything. "How would you like me to do that, my friend?" she asked.

"Well, hell . . . If you're the principal, you're pretty high up, I reckon."

"That is correct," Anna said.

"You'd have to be a friend of Joe Stalin's, then," the man said.

"I am employed by Marshal Stalin," Anna agreed cautiously.

"Yeah? Well, if you are, lady, you bring me a personal message from Uncle Joe, and I'll go along with you."

"Are you mad? Marshal Stalin cannot become involved in this operation. You are dissatisfied with what we are offering?

Well, I am prepared to add another five thousand dollars. But not a penny more until I have had an opportunity to evaluate this information."

"The money's fine. Hell, what's money, lady, when the world is rushing to an end? Listen, Uncle Joe doesn't have to become involved. He makes speeches fairly regularly, right?"

"Yes," Anna said, totally mystified.

"Well, the next time he makes a major international speech, one I'll be able to pick up on my radio—I speak Russian, you know, I listen to all the big speeches—you have him say something like, 'I send greetings to all the Joes in the world.'" The man chuckled. "My name is Joe, too, you see. I just want to be sure *he* knows that."

Anna braked, pulled the car over to the side of the road, and turned her head. *"That* is what you wish?"

"That's right."

"Let me see what you have brought with you."

The man gave her a tiny slip of microfilm, carefully laying it in her palm. "You have that blown up, and show it to any competent physicist, and he'll know it's the goods."

"And what else do you have?"

"Everything," he said. "I've been photographing for months, bit by bit, everything that came my way. And most things do. I may not make the headlines, but it's people like me who do all the actual work. Your man here supplied me with the camera, and that's all I needed." He grinned. "I'm a great one for working late."

"And how did you get the film out? There must be a great deal of it. Our information is that security is very tight."

"Sure it is," the man agreed. "You couldn't smuggle a pinhead out of that office. They make you strip, and they go through your clothing inch by inch."

"But you walked out with several rolls of microfilm in your pocket."

"The formula, data on the experiments, observations—you name it, I've got it."

"You will have to tell me how you did that," Anna said.

"Simple. Like I told you, I've been working on this for months. So I made myself a capsule, like a pill, see, only out of plastic, so it wouldn't dissolve. Then, whenever I completed a roll of film, I put it in the capsule, and an hour before I was due out on a weekend pass, I swallowed it. Then, as soon as I got home, I took a laxative."

Anna almost recoiled from the film she held in her palm. "And you have been doing this for months, accumulating this information, with the intention of selling it to us? Or to anyone?"

"I'm dealing with you," the man said.

"And the money is right?"

"Sure."

"What about the rest?"

"I'll bring it along when I hear from Uncle Joe."

Anna shrugged. "If that is what you wish. I will have to send this back to Russia for examination by my experts. If they say it is genuine, then you have a deal. It will not take long. I will drive you back now."

She turned the car, drove back to where the other cars were parked, let the man out, and gazed at Bogolzhin.

"I am going to have to laugh," she said. "He genuinely wants to *give* us the atomic formulas, just to know he's working for his 'Uncle Joe.' I will never understand these people."

"He is an idealist," Bogolzhin said. "He believes that Communism is the hope of the future."

"I will *never* understand these people," Anna said again.

Joseph Stalin finished reading the report, raised his head, and gazed at Lavrenti Beria. "This is from Gregory Nej?"

Beria nodded.

"And he is sure of his facts?"

"It is only rumor, of course. But apparently it is being widely discussed in the Pentagon. And Comrade Ragosina, you will see, has added a note that she had also seen a rumor of it in the newspapers."

"This is madness," Stalin said. "Utter madness. I always thought that Roosevelt was soft in the head. But this man Truman is positively dangerous. Rearm the Wehrmacht?" He wagged his finger. "That is directed against us, you know. There can be no other reason for such an action."

Beria nodded.

"Those formulas Ragosina sent," Stalin said. "Have they been evaluated?"

"Oh, indeed, Joseph Vissarionovich. Our people are of the

opinion that it is undoubtedly just what we are looking for. That woman is a treasure. In fact..." He hesitated. He was well aware that his master had not forgiven Anna for making him fit that absurd greeting into his last major speech, even if the formulas she had thereby obtained *were* genuine. "I would say that she has completed her mission. I would like to bring her out of there."

"At a time like this? That is nonsense, Lavrenti Pavlovich. Ragosina stays where she can do the most good. We are going to need every bit of information she can supply, if we are to tackle this problem. Now we must decide what to do about it. Vyacheslav Mikhailovich?" He looked at the third man in the room.

Molotov cleared his throat. "I would say things are moving in our favor."

"You would say so," Stalin observed. "Nobody else."

Molotov raised his hand and ticked off the fingers. "We have got a formula at last for the bomb. That is something we can count on. When?"

"It will still take some time," Beria said.

"Nonetheless, it is in the works," Molotov said. "It is something we can look forward to. Now, the Americans are taking active steps, but steps which will alarm many people, not only here in Russia. This should mean a gain of sympathy for our position. I think now is the time to force the issue."

"Now?" Stalin demanded. *"Before* we have manufactured the bomb?"

"We are safer now than we will be then, Joseph." Molotov insisted. "To drop an atomic bomb on Russia would forfeit the Americans the good will of everyone on earth. Now is the time to make them either pull in their horns altogether, maybe even leave Europe altogether, or take that overt step. I promise you, they will pull in their horns."

"How do we make them do that?"

"They are attempting to force a unilateral solution of the German question. That is obvious. Well, we must take countermeasures. If they are going to arm the Wehrmacht, we must expel them from Berlin."

"Expel them?"

"That would be openly breaking the treaties," Beria objected.

Molotov gave one of his very brief smiles. "Persuade them to leave, comrades. I can tell you that there is continuous British and French and American traffic using the autobahn from Hanover to West Berlin. This is because they bring in all the food and oil and coal supplies for the city by road transport. But that autobahn passes through the Russian sector. Suppose we close it to traffic? I am sure we can think of a reason. Their garrisons in West Berlin will be like cut flowers in a vase. They will *have* to be pulled out, or starve. Oh, they will shout and rave and threaten, but they will not *do* anything. And now that the United Nations is about to open in New York, Michael Nikolaievich can be putting our case to all the non-aligned nations. *We* are not playing a dangerous game; the Americans are, because only a rearmed Germany presents any threat to world peace. That is the line to take."

"But . . . if they pull out of Berlin," Beria said, "what have we achieved?"

"Of course they are not going to pull out of Berlin," Molotov said. "It is an emotional point, and the Americans are emotional people. And when they can no longer maintain themselves, short of using force, we say to them, it is very simple: you abandon your absurd plans for the Wehrmacht, and we will reopen the autobahn."

"Hm," Stalin said. "Hm. That might work, you know. It might just work. Mind you, it will have to be carefully timed."

"Again, things are working in our favor," Molotov said. "We have but to wait a few months, until the new year, in fact, because next year is an election year in America. Truman is going to have to be very mindful of public opinion over there throughout next year, and according to Anna Ragosina, public opinion is almost wholly against the bomb, or *any* sort of confrontation with us. That is point number one. Point number two is that the British have now announced they are definitely surrendering their mandate over Palestine next May. The day the British pull out, that area is going to explode."

"We don't know for certain what will happen there," Beria objected.

"It is surely our business—*your* business, Lavrenti Pavlovich—to make sure that it does explode. The Arabs are not going to require a great deal of prodding. So all the British and American attention is going to be centered in the Middle East.

I would say we make our move next spring, comrades." He leaned back to smile at them again. "I think next year is going to be a good year for the Soviet Union."

Felicity Hayman painted her toenails, slowly and carefully. She sat on her bed, with her right leg drawn up and her skirt folded back across her lap; thus both legs were totally exposed.

Gregory Nej sat opposite her, and watched her, as he liked doing, and as she liked him to do. It was one of the endless fascinations of their relationship, she thought, that they never tired of each other, of looking at each other, of touching each other, of being together. They loved. She could imagine no couple in history who had ever loved as they did, so completely and without reservation.

That they were working together, in pursuit of a mutual ideal, only added to their magnificent intimacy. The element of risk—because undoubtedly there *was* an element of risk, even if she could not convince herself that it was very great—gave their lives a spice that might otherwise have been lacking, might even have introduced the boredom of overfamiliarity, because they had no social life at all. The officers with whom Gregory worked at the Pentagon had shown no desire to make friends with him, partly because he was a Russian, partly because of the professional soldier's ingrained abhorrence of the traitor, and at least partly because of his peculiar domestic arrangements. Thus they very seldom went out. She went shopping every morning, and then returned to the apartment to do her chores, and to wait for him to come home from his lecturing duties. Then they would sit up in bed together and discuss what he had learned during the day, and decide, together and mutually, what was worth passing on to his superiors, through the man Bogolzhin. The actual passing on was her responsibility. Since they had moved to Washington, Gregory had abstained from all contact with his control, as he called it. Thus, even if he was under constant surveillance by the FBI, as he had recently concluded he was, they could never catch him in a single indiscretion. Instead, every Friday morning, Bogolzhin went shopping at the same supermarket she did, and the information was passed from one shopping basket to the next, without their even exchanging a word or a look. It was as simple as that. And no one would think to place George Hayman's daughter under surveillance, in any event.

The information came in a steady trickle. Because he was employed mainly in revealing Russian secrets to the Americans, Gregory actually obtained a great deal of utterly secret information in return. He had first learned of the guided-missile project, for example, because he had been required to supply a list of worthwhile Russian targets for the missiles . . . Felicity had been shocked by that. But everything that was happening, every single piece of information that he brought home, only confirmed what he had said in the beginning, that America, her own country, was getting set to dominate the world by force of arms. It was a horrifying thought.

The really upsetting thing was that she did not think they were going to be able to stop it, anymore. Gregory insisted that they would, but she did not see how telling the men in the Kremlin what the Americans were planning to do could stop them from doing it, until the Russians had a bomb of their own to set against it, and there was no sign of that happening yet. She would have preferred a much more direct course of action, such as sabotaging the missile sites as fast as they were built—not that any had yet been built; it was all still on the drawing board—or better yet, blowing up the Pentagon itself. But Gregory had firmly set himself against anything quite so dramatic, or risky. We are not here to take risks, he would say. We are here to do a job.

As dictated by Bogolzhin? Having met the man, Felicity did not think so. In any event, Gregory himself let slip, occasionally, that there was someone right here in America far superior to Bogolzhin, who actually gave the orders. And it wasn't the ambassador. Once upon a time she had been upset that she had not been allowed to meet this mysterious string-puller who ruled Gregory's life, and therefore hers as well. But it really wasn't important. The man, whoever he was, knew of *her*, and of her part in the great project; Gregory had assured her of this.

But Felicity could not help but feel, sometimes, that she was far more serious about the project than Gregory was. To her it was the most important thing in life, after his embrace. *He* sometimes showed a distressing levity, even suggested occasionally that they go out to a nightclub. Of course he was still very young. But she could imagine nothing more un-Russian and totally American, and with every day she was growing more and more anti-American. These people had so much,

compared with the unending hardship of life in Russia, as
related by Gregory. To wish to dominate the world as well
made them into ogres. In this class she even placed her own
family.

In fact, she classed them as the biggest ogres of all. Not
her father, of course. He always meant well, even if he was
totally committed, by reason of his birth and upbringing, to
capitalism. But the rest . . . They had refused to speak to her
for some time. Now they had decided to let bygones be bygones—what an act of magnanimity!

She raised her head. "I don't think we should go," she said.
"I think we should let them stew in their own juice a while
longer."

He smiled patiently, and got up to hand her her dress. "They
are your family," he pointed out.

"Ugh," she said. "They are capitalist swine." She had been
reading Lenin.

Gregory took her hands. "My darling," he said, "your father
has been working on this reunion for months. It has taken him
a great deal of time and effort. I do not think we can let him
down now. Besides, it is Christmas, and at such a time family
is very important. In Russia, family is the most important thing
in the world, and at Christmas it is more important than ever."

"Not here," she said. "Christmas in the United States is an
overcommercialized spending spree. As for spending two days
at Cold Spring Harbor . . . it is going to be boring, and uncomfortable. Mother will sit and stare at me. Beth will go on and
on about her latest exhibition. Diana will say that she likes us,
as if she is bestowing a great favor. George junior will tell us
everything that is wrong with the world, and how *he* would
put it right. Natasha will talk nothing but babies, and about
how John is working such long hours she hardly ever sees him
anymore. So how did she get pregnant again, I'd like to know?
And John himself will sit and stare at you."

Chapter 11

GREGORY KISSED HER ON THE NOSE, AND PULLED UP THE ZIPPER on her dress. "They are family. And they are part of the scene, my darling. A scene that we have created, and therefore that we must belong to, too. Always. Because that is part of our *job*."

As April turned into May, the weather in Palestine became very hot. One sweated all the time, and became more aware of the flies, even in the north, beneath the brooding presence of the Golan Heights.

But Spring in this year of 1948, Ruth Hassell thought as she harvested tomatoes, was the worst time she had ever known. It was the best time of the year, almost everywhere in the northern hemisphere. It signified a final end to winter, a final leap into the promise of summer, a time when buds burst into flower and tomatoes became ripe, when even the desert beyond the irrigation supplied by the windmill started to look almost green. And a time where she could not forget the day an innocent young man had been hanged by the neck until he was dead.

Remarkably, she blamed her own people more than the British. The British stood, as they had stood for centuries, for an absurd pragmatism. They quite honestly believed that what they had to offer the world was better than had ever been offered before by any other conquering power. If their sole reason for empire was the fattening of the coffers of various merchant adventurers in Liverpool and Bristol, and most of all in London, they had carried Christianity, law, and order, according to the British pattern, with them to all the far corners of the globe, and they had never doubted that English law was infinitely preferable to the happy-go-lucky anarchism of so many of the systems they had replaced. Themselves once described by an eighteenth-century visitor as the most ungovernable of peoples, they had by a peculiar inversion come to regard themselves as the most eminently suitable of all people *to* govern. One had to respect a nation so entirely steeped in their own self-esteem, however one might loathe the result of their coldly impersonal approach to life, or death, because one knew that they would, and did, apply the same rules to their own people as to those of their subject countries.

One could never accuse the Jews of being coldly impersonal. In the fight for existence, no holds were to be barred. That was because their fight here in Palestine was not for the difference between being number-one nation or number-two, or even between being rich and being poor; in the coming war with the Arabs they were faced with the simple choice between winning or dying, men, women, and children. In such a conflict one used whatever came to hand, to its best possible advantage. And when it had been used, one cast it aside, without sentiment. No one had played false with Paul. If he had succeeded, he would have lived and been honored as a hero, and protected as one, too. The decision *not* to fire, and to be taken, had been *his* decision. And since he had betrayed none of his associates, they had kept their word as regards his widow. There was no woman in the kibbutz more honored than Ruth Hassell.

Thus she and Aunt Judith had stayed. That they had no alternative, now, was neither here nor there. That they might both be utterly miserable was neither here nor there. As Paul had sacrificed himself, so Judith had sacrificed her husband, for this garden created out of the desert. Judith, Ruth thought, was the more unfortunate of them, in that she did not even know for certain whether Boris lived or died. But this was their home, now and forever.

And whatever happened, after the British pulled out tomorrow, they would share in it.

But even such loyalty, loyalty of despair, could not make her look at Benjamin Cohen without shuddering, could not make her wish that somehow things might not have been different.

She raised her head to watch the bus from Jerusalem pulling to a stop on the road above her, and saw the man get down. She stared, and flicked sweat from around her eyes to see better. Then she put her basket on the ground and ran up the slope.

"Nigel!" she shouted. "Nigel Brent!"

"Ruth!" Nigel Brent held out his arms, and for a moment she nearly entered them. Then they both recollected themselves, and shook hands.

Nigel inhaled sharply. "It's good to be back."

She gazed at his dusty civilian clothes, his slouch hat. "But . . . how?"

"I pulled strings," he said. "Besides, as of tomorrow—"

"Yes," she said. "I know." She turned, because other people had left the fields and were climbing the slope to the road, to surround the new arrival.

"Good morning, Rabbi Yanowski," Nigel said, with cheerful confidence. "Mrs. Petrov? How good to see you."

They also peered at his civilian clothes.

"What are you doing here, Mr. Brent?" Yanowski asked.

"Visiting you. But I'm hoping to stay."

"To stay? Here? Where . . . ?"

"Where I was once a policeman? I am a policeman no longer, Rabbi. I have not been a policeman for quite a while."

Yanowski nodded. "I know that. We honor your decision. But here . . ."

"You may need me," Nigel pointed out. "Tomorrow is the day the last British soldiers leave. You have heard what the Arabs are saying?"

"Talk," Yanowski said. He turned to look at the blue of the Golan Heights. "Just talk."

"Let's hope so. They are taking the talk pretty seriously in Tel Aviv and in Jerusalem."

"Then why have the Arabs not attacked already?" Judith asked. "The last soldiers left up here a week ago." She too stared at the distant hills.

"Possibly because they don't want to face us with the crisis of conscience," Nigel said. "Once we're out, we're out, and we won't be coming back, no matter what happens. But if they started massacring your people while we were still actually in the country, we'd *have* to react. But more likely, I think, they are waiting to see what you do. If you go ahead with declaring the State of Israel—"

"We will go ahead," Yanowski said. "It is to happen tonight."

"Well, then, as I said, you may need all the able-bodied men you can raise, by tomorrow."

"We do not need *you*," Benjamin Cohen said. "We will never need you, *Inspector* Brent."

Nigel gazed into his eyes. "Well, you've got me, Mr. Cohen. Or are you going to try murdering me one more time?"

"Ladies and gentlemen! Friends!" Rabbi Yanowski smiled at Judith. "Comrades! Let us toast Chaim Weizmann, and David Ben-Gurion."

The crowded hall became filled with murmured assents. "President Weizmann. Prime Minister Ben-Gurion."

Every person in the kibbutz was here tonight, Ruth thought, even the children. She stood, as usual, next to Sylvia, with Judith on her other side. And in many ways the evening reminded her of her first here, nearly two years ago now. Then, as now, she was on the threshold of something new, and then, as now, she had been vaguely apprehensive of what the coming days might bring. The difference was that then she and Paul had been isolated, alone in their apprehensions, alone in their beginnings. Tonight, she and Judith were a part of something greater than self. She wondered how many people in all history had been privileged to be present at the actual birth of a nation. She wished that she could have felt a more positive reaction, a more certain feeling that it was *her* nation.

There was another difference to a year and a half ago. Then the English policeman had held the center of the stage with easy confidence, sure in the support of his constables, and of the might of the British army behind even them, of the immense power wielded by his imperial masters, whose fiat he was enforcing. Tonight, *he* was the man alone. And yet, as Paul had, he still exuded that same confidence, stood next to the rabbi and raised his glass with the rest of them.

The music began, and the dancing. But Ruth refused all

invitations, as she had refused so many invitations this last year. In the beginning she had been left largely to herself, because she was a widow and still in mourning. But that had been well over a year ago. And despite all that she had suffered, she was only twenty-seven, by far the best-looking woman in the village. She could appreciate the feelings of the many unmarried young men in the kibbutz, that it was absurd she should wish to remain a widow forever.

She was conscious of this herself, even if she had absolutely no desire to marry again, to share herself with any other man. But then, she had never really wanted to share herself even with Paul. And there lay the difficulty. Paul had understood, because he had *known*. The men in the kibbutz were aware that she had spent some time in a concentration camp, they had seen the numbers burned into the flesh of her forearm—she was far from being the only woman in the village so marked. But since she had survived without any apparent injury, they did not know in exactly what way she had suffered. The fact that she had emerged whole, at least externally, would make any man believe she could be a good and comforting wife.

That she might wish to scream every time she felt a naked body against hers, because of all the hundreds of naked bodies that had devoured hers during her years in the Ravensbrück brothel, would not occur to any of these men. And if it did, each man, being a man, would suppose that it would be *his* caress, *his* brand of lovemaking, that would make her forget the past. And each man, being a man, would turn against her when he discovered that there was *no* brand of lovemaking that could accomplish that.

So she smiled at them, and gently refused, and prepared to slip easily into the role undertaken by the elderly women of the village, the other widows and the grandmothers—and suddenly she looked up and realized that this particular man bending over her was Nigel Brent.

"I'm told that you no longer indulge," he said. "But you did, once. And it will do you good. Tonight is a special occasion."

She hesitated, then stood up. "This will not make you popular with the other men," she told him.

"I have a vague suspicion that I'm not, in any event," he smiled, and took her in his arms as the music began. "But I think they're going to have too much on their minds to worry about me, over the next few weeks."

She raised her head to look at him. "You genuinely think there's going to be trouble?"

"I have no doubt of it at all," he said. "I only wish I could persuade your people of it. I've asked your rabbi to put out a couple of guards, at least during the night, and he says he doesn't think it's necessary. He says you have occasionally been sniped at in the fields, but you've never had to withstand a serious attack. And it didn't do any good to remind him that *we* were here then."

"But why should the Arabs wish to attack this place?" she asked. "This was only desert, before we came. The Arabs did not use it for anything. Should they not be pleased that we have cultivated it?"

"They happen to regard it as their land," he reminded her, and held her hand as the music died, to lead her outside into the comparative cool of the evening. As usual, in the desert, a wind had sprung up out of the north, strong enough to rustle her dress. "Too cold for you?" he asked.

"I like it." She pushed hair from her eyes, walked to the edge of the wide porch which fringed the hall, and gazed into the blackness. "This place is so peaceful," she said. "So . . . so much an example of how men were *meant* to live. It is terrible to remember that it was created out of violence, to think that there may be people out there planning more violence. Even our destruction."

"Isn't that nature's way?" he asked. "Life and death, a constant cycle, a constant struggle for survival?"

She turned to look at him. "If you're so sure there is going to be trouble," she asked, "why did you come back? These aren't your people. Most of them do not even like you. Why should you risk your life for them?"

"I didn't come back to risk my neck for *them*," he said quietly.

She stared at him. Nigel Brent, she thought. An English equivalent of Paul. A man to be trusted, certainly, even with the hideous secrets that lay locked in her heart. Or was she deluding herself, taken in by that quiet smile, that confident manner?

"I did not mean to blurt it out quite so soon," he said.

She was grateful for the semidarkness, which hid the color in her cheeks. "Pity is no basis for a relationship, Mr. Brent," she said.

"I have never pitied you, Ruth. I think, rather, I have envied your strength and your courage."

"Strength," she said. "Courage. Resignation, you mean. You know too little about me, Mr. Brent."

"I think I know more than you might think," he said. "I was a police officer."

"And the thought of me in a German brothel fascinates you?" she said, and hated herself.

"The thought of *you* makes me realize how fortunate a man Hassell was, even if only for a short time," he said. "Ruth . . . as I said, I did not mean to bring this up so soon. But as it has been brought up, we cannot pretend differently. Ruth, I cannot presume to take Paul's place. I have no right to do so. I can only say that I have thought of no one but you for the past year, and I knew the moment I returned I would *have* to say something. I love you, Ruth. I think I have loved you almost from the moment I met you. I . . ." He sighed. "At least say you do not hate me."

She began to turn again, to look at him, and stopped, as from out of the darkness there came a sudden flash of red, followed by a most tremendous explosion.

Ruth sprawled on the floor of the porch, having been pushed there by Nigel. Her ears were singing, and she was covered with a fine white dust, and the entire night seemed to be filled with screams of pain and terror and booming crashes still echoing about her.

She raised her head to stare at the man whose face was only inches away from hers. His mouth was open, and he was clearly speaking, but she could not hear what he was saying, was only reassured when she felt his hand again, pushing her flat once more, while the earth close by trembled. And she realized, with a feeling of pure horror, that despite everything she had experienced, this was the first time she had ever been at *war*.

Feet kicked her, and she looked up again. A man had staggered from the hall, tripped over her, and gone rolling down the shallow steps that edged the porch. She could not see him clearly in the gloom—all the lights in the kibbutz had gone out—but she could tell that he was unconscious. And then she realized he was probably dead.

Nigel was on his knees, and pulling her up as well, scooping her into his arms and then half-climbing, half-falling over the balustrade at the end of the porch to come to rest on the soft earth of the flowerbed beyond. She landed on top of him, rolled away, and was caught by his hand and pressed flat again. She smelled burning, and looked up at flames gushing from the roof of the hall, which had been hit at least twice.

Nigel was on his knees again, pushing her along the wall of the building, pointing to the far side, the side away from the desert. She didn't really want to move. She seemed to have no strength in her legs, and her brain was a gigantic surge of terror. She wanted only to lie there, with her arms over her head, and preferably his body covering hers, to feel his strength and that so-reassuring confidence. But he kept pushing her, and pointing, and she did not feel that she could let him down by just lying there and screaming, as she wanted to do.

Hearing was returning to her stunned ears, as she rounded the building, and could at last collapse, in the company of several others, with him beside her.

"What is that?" Rabbi Yanowski was asking. "What is happening?" He sounded utterly confused, for a whine and another enormous thud shook the entire village, and brought a fresh shower of dust and a fresh chorus of screams.

"Mortars," Nigel said. "Those are mortars."

Judith Petrov pushed herself to her feet. "There are people still inside," she said. "Children. They will burn to death."

"You cannot help them now, Mrs. Petrov," Nigel said. "For God's sake, get down."

"Get down," Ruth said, pulling on her aunt's hand, while tears of relief flooded down her face that Judith had thus far survived. "Oh, get down."

Judith fell to her knees, head slumping onto her chest.

"What are we to do?" Yanowski asked. "My God, what are we to do?"

"We can do nothing," Nigel said, "until the bombardment stops. But they will not attack until then, either. You have weapons?"

"We have some rifles," the rabbi said. "We have no mortars."

"Machine guns?"

The rabbi looked at Benjamin Cohen, who also crouched in the shelter of the building.

"For God's sake, man," Nigel shouted, "now's not the time to play silly buggers. We're going to need those guns, the moment the bombardment stops."

They stared at him, because his shouting was suddenly very loud; the bombardment had stopped.

Nigel was on his feet. "Those rifles," he snapped.

"Yes," Rabbi Yanowski agreed. "Benjamin, break out the guns and ammunition. Round up whoever you can."

Cohen hesitated for an instant, then ran across the street. Several other young men ran beside him.

"I will need you, Rabbi," Nigel said. "They won't take orders from me."

Yanowski nodded. He at least was prepared to accept that here was a man trained to command.

"Good," Nigel said. "Do you have a shortwave?"

Yanowski nodded again.

"Then have someone get through to Jerusalem and tell them we are under mortar bombardment and expect an attack very shortly. Hurry, Mr. Yanowski."

The rabbi ran into the gloom.

"We must get in there and help those people," Judith said. "Sylvia? Sylvia, where are you?"

There was no reply.

"Ruth, come with me," Judith said.

It was Ruth's turn to hesitate. "What are you going to do?" she asked Nigel.

"Form a perimeter," he told her, "just as quickly as I can, and hope to throw back any assault. You help your aunt. But Ruth . . . Arabs are . . ."

She stared at him.

"Just take care," he said. "For God's sake take care."

Judith was already hurrying around to the door of the hall. The flames still burned brightly, lighting up the night. Ruth saw several women gathered there, some armed with blankets, others only with aprons, trying desperately to beat down the flames.

"Water," Judith said. "We must have water."

"The mill is down," someone said. "They hit that first."

"And the generator is dead," said another.

The night filled with noise, dull, shallow cracks. Someone gave a shriek and half turned before falling heavily to the ground.

"Down," Judith screamed. "Take cover. Where are the men?"

Forty years ago she stood on the Moscow barricades, Ruth remembered. What memories this must evoke.

"There," she said, and watched Nigel running past them, followed by Benjamin Cohen and several others. They carried rifles and revolvers and boxes of ammunition, and two of them carted an old Lewis gun, smuggled in from sympathetic Frenchmen in Lebanon.

"Take care," she shouted, and then got up and ran behind them. If she was going to be killed, if she was going to be taken and mutilated by some Arab, she wanted it to be at his side, because suddenly she knew that if she was going to survive, it would have to be at his side, too; there was no other way.

They had formed a line at the end of the street, where the desert began, lying on their bellies, rifles pushed in front of them, while Nigel and Ben erected the machine gun. Now Ruth could see the spurts of red light in the night as the rifles were fired out in the desert, and instinctively she dropped to her own knees, and crawled up to them.

"The belt goes here," Nigel said. "Come along, boy, you're all thumbs. There we go." He sat behind the gun, and fired a burst into the darkness. "That's better. Hold your fire," he bawled, as the young men about him also started shooting. "We don't have bullets to waste. Let them come to us. They will." He seemed to realize for the first time that Ruth was lying beside him. "What in the name of God are you doing here?"

"Helping you," she explained.

He seemed about to say something, then looked past her at Rabbi Yanowski, crawling up the street, his rifle banging on his back.

"Did you get through?"

"Yes," Yanowski gasped. "But . . . it is very bad."

"What?"

"There is fighting in Jerusalem too. The Jordanians have invaded. There is fighting everywhere. They can spare us no help before tomorrow. They say we must manage on our own."

* * *

Suddenly it was light. Twilight did not linger, in the desert. Ruth woke with a start, aware that she had been dozing.

And there had been no Arab attack.

Now it was cold, and still. The shooting had only been intermittent for the last few hours, and the Israelis had seldom bothered to reply.

She raised her head, and discovered to her alarm that Nigel no longer lay beside her. Instead it was Ben Cohen, and another man. "Where—?"

"He is inspecting our defenses," Cohen said, and offered her a drink of water from a bottle.

"He is your captain." She could not resist saying it.

"He is a professional soldier," Cohen said, without embarrassment. "He fought in Burma against the Japanese. He understands tactics."

She looked back at the burned-out hall, where Judith and the other women were still working, moving charred furniture, and dragging out even more charred bodies. That was where she should be.

She got up, attempted to smooth dust and sand from her dress. Her very best dress.

She stood beside her aunt. Now there was a stench, but as yet only of burned flesh, sickly sweet. The real horror would come later on today. And so many of the bodies were so very small.

"Twenty-four dead," Judith said. "And half of them were children."

"Twenty-four dead, so far," said one of the other women.

Ruth looked down the street. Several of the houses had been hit. She did not know if the house she shared with Judith and Sylvia, and another family, was damaged, and she did not wish to go and see. Not now.

"Sylvia!" She looked at Judith questioningly.

Judith pointed. Blankets or aprons had been thrown over the burned bodies, and only the legs showed. Sylvia's legs were easily recognizable; she had been proud of her tiny feet.

"Oh, God," Ruth said. "Why? Oh, God, why? When will it end? When?"

"When we have proved to those people that we will not be driven out," Rabbi Yanowski said. "We knew it was going to be hard. We knew we were going to have to fight. Perhaps we thought it was going to be a business of ultimatums and declarations, of conferences and votes, and even perhaps, finally, of professional soldiers. But we are all front-line soldiers here, Ruth."

She watched Nigel hurrying down the street. He had taken off his jacket and his tie, and unbuttoned his shirt; an automatic pistol was strapped to his waist. Incredibly, he looked happy.

"But thank God," Judith muttered, "for the professional -soldiers."

"Do you think they have gone away?" Rabbi Yanowski asked hopefully, belying his own words of a moment before.

Nigel shook his head. "I think they're waiting for reinforcements. They'll know we're not getting any for a while. I've an idea they didn't expect us to be so well armed, though."

"We'll throw them back, whenever they come," Cohen declared. He had joined the impromptu council of war.

"I wouldn't count on it," Nigel said. "Not if, for example, they happen to be expecting one or two tanks. Has everyone breakfasted?"

"All who wanted." Cohen seemed to have recovered a good deal of his courage.

"Well, we must attack *them* now," Nigel said.

They stared at him, and then turned, to look at the desert.

"Attack the Arabs?" Yanowski was incredulous.

"Passive defense never won anything," Nigel said. "If they are awaiting reinforcements, we simply have to destroy or disperse them before the reinforcements arrive. Ben, how many men do we muster?"

"We have sixty-two carrying arms," Ben said, "and three wounded."

Only three men wounded, Ruth thought. But twelve children dead.

"Um," Nigel said. "We could have done with a few more. Well . . . we'll have to leave half the men to hold the perimeter, just in case things go wrong. That leaves us thirty-one . . ."

"But—what do we attack?" Yanowski asked, still staring at the apparently empty desert.

"They aren't far," Nigel assured him. "Those mortars don't have much of a range. What we have to do is pinpoint their exact position. Now, last night the main weight of their attack came from out there. They only sniped to the south and east.

I suspect they're still right there. If they'd tried to move the mortars in daylight we'd have seen the dust, and it would have been damn near impossible to position them accurately in the dark. But we'll make sure. Ben, I want you to take six men and run down to the windmill. Sure it's blown down, but you'll carry tools as if you were going to repair it. The Arabs will buy that one; they know how essential water is. That'll draw their fire and enable us to decide exactly where their main strength is located."

"But . . ." Cohen looked down the slope. It was four hundred yards to the windmill, and the way was totally exposed.

"So you'll be a hero," Nigel told him. "We can't all be that lucky. Anyway, as soon as they open up you can go to ground."

"And you will lead the assault?" Yanowski asked. "Over open ground? That will be suicide."

Nigel pointed at the bed of the dry streambed that seeped into the hills away from the northeastern side of the village. "We'll use that wadi for cover. I'm surprised the Arabs haven't thought of doing that yet. But they will if we leave them to think about it. So let's beat them to it." He slapped Ben on the shoulder. "It's better to die doing, than sitting. I wish we had more people, but there it is."

Ruth gazed at him. From the moment the first mortar bomb had landed last night, she had done absolutely nothing, because she had not been able to identify with these people. She had never been able to do that. Nigel had only arrived here yesterday, and already he was totally committed. While she . . . but they were *her* people. And if she was ever going to be worthy of living here, or of this man's love—or any man's love—then it was time to stop reliving the past, stop looking over her shoulder, and start living, and dying, in earnest.

"You have more people," she said.

They looked at her.

"There are more than fifty women in this village," she said. "We'll man the defenses. You go and kill the enemy."

Ruth crouched behind the machine gun, Judith beside her, while the other women settled themselves with their rifles. They were used to guns; they had been carrying them in the fields for years. But they had never felt so close to the reality of killing anyone before.

Nigel crawled towards them. "Now, remember," he said.

"When you hear us, hold your fire."

She nodded.

He smiled at her. "I don't have to tell you what to do, I think."

And she smiled back, to her own surprise. "Good luck," she said. "Remember, if you fail, we all fail."

"I'll keep that in mind. Time, Benjamin."

Cohen had also been crouching close by, his six volunteers behind him, clutching their weapons. Now the sun was looming high over the hills to the east, and it was easy to see how pale their faces were. They had dreamed of days like this, had boasted of what they would do when the moment arrived. But the moment was somehow different from what they had expected—there was real lead in those rifles out in the desert, and the people lying in an orderly row behind them were really dead.

Cohen took a long breath and rose to his feet. "Let's go," he said, and ran from the shelter of the houses, down the slope into the valley; that had to be traversed before he could reach the hill where the gaunt remains of the windmill stood.

"Wait," Nigel said. "Hold your fire. Wait."

Ruth discovered she was hardly breathing. She watched the seven young men gallop through the first of the tomatoes, so recently harvested, waiting in round red splendor in the packing sheds at the back of the village for transportation to the coast; the men scattered the green stalks as they ran. There was no sound at all, apart from their fading gasps. The desert might have been empty. Perhaps, she thought, it *is* empty. Perhaps the Arabs *have* gone away. Oh, if only that could be so.

A shot rang out, and then another. One of Cohen's little band fell, the others immediately hit the ground, nestling amid the tomato plants, while from the ridge about half a mile from the village they could see the flashes of light.

"Return fire," Nigel snapped, and immediately set off, bending double as he ran, past the houses and into the shallow wadi that led northeast from the village. The forty men in his assault force hurried behind him; there had not been sufficient rifles to go around and still leave the women capable of defending themselves, so half of the men carried machetes or hatchets or even ancient swords.

But the women were putting their weapons to good use, as they blazed away at the distant ridge, and Ruth sent several bursts of machine-gun fire in that direction also, while Judith fed the bullets into the outdated, overheated gun. The firing became general, as Ben and his band also returned fire; the morning glowed with sound and heat and anger; bullets whined amid the houses and ricocheted from wall to wall; someone moaned as she was hit and another shrieked and dropped her rifle. Nigel and his assault force had disappeared as if the desert had swallowed them up.

Then there came another burst of firing from away to the right, and a new series of yells and shrieks. "Cease firing," Ruth shouted, and the cry was taken up. The firing died from the village as they listened to the noise from in front of them, wiped sweat and hair from their faces as they realized that their fates were being decided in a place they could not even see. Long minutes later they gave a great cry of joy as first one and then another of their husbands appeared on the ridge, waving captured guns, while some thoughtful man had even unfurled a gigantic blue flag bearing a yellow Star of David in its center.

The women left the safety of the houses and ran over the sand, shouting and cheering, gaining the ridge to embrace their loved ones, to stare at the dozen dead Arabs, at the captured mortars, at the dust of their fleeing enemies as they drove their jeeps and their camels back towards the safety of the hills.

"A first victory," Rabbi Yanowski announced. "A first victory. Thanks to you, Nigel." He shook the Englishman's hand, while Judith embraced him. "Thanks to you."

"Well, we must use the time well, before they come back with their friends, to . . ." He checked, as all the noise of celebration died, as they listened to the clanking of tractors, and turned, slowly, to watch the squadron of tanks, a dozen in number, emerging from behind the village.

"Oh, my God," Judith said. "Oh, my God."

"He has delivered us," Yanowski shouted. "He has delivered us."

For flying above the first tank was another Star of David.

"He has delivered us," Ruth murmured, and felt Nigel's arms go around her.

Chapter 12

JOHN HAYMAN SIGHED, AND WATCHED THE RAINDROPS DRIFTING past his office window, catching the reflection of the neon lighting across the street. As usual, he was working late.

He had in fact been working overtime for the last six months; Christmas had been a very attenuated holiday for him, and Easter even more so. Nor did mid-summer indicate any relief. Not that he had any reason to carp. This stepping-up of activity was something he had sought ever since he had entered the service, an active rather than a merely contemplative approach to the situation. But quite apart from the interference it was causing in his social and domestic life—to Sasha's quite obvious concern—for him personally it was tiresome and basically unrewarding work, and at times he could not help but feel that he, and the entire service, were attempting to grasp a large and very slippery fish, made of rubber, which was no sooner pinned down in one place than it managed to pop up again somewhere else.

The Communists had in fact been given an enormous head start. Worse, it was difficult for any reasonable man, brought up in the American traditions of free thought and free speech, to condemn another man merely for believing in a different system, and undoubtedly there were a large number of good Americans who considered capitalism to be a greater evil than socialism, and were prepared to say so, to join groups and clubs to put forward their point of view. They would have been horrified to find themselves under investigation by the FBI, or to realize that in certain quarters they were considered as virtual traitors, just as undoubtedly they were quite unable to understand why, over the last six months, they had been refused certain jobs, and in a growing number of instances had been fired from jobs they already held.

It was because of the small proportion who took their orders from Moscow, or were merely anarchists at heart, dedicated to the disruption of any organized society, whatever its political color.

The difficulty, and the injustice, lay in deciding where the one ended and the other began. His misfortune was that it was not his decision. He was merely given an increasing number of files, of photographs, of newspaper cuttings, and of reports submitted by FBI field agents who had infiltrated various left-wing groups. Out of this mass of names and places and faces and snatches of conversation it was his job to pick out anything that struck him as being in the least suspicious. But he could not help but be aware that whereas, when he had first begun to work for J. Edgar Hoover, his suspicions had always been treated with a good deal of reserve, now that the official attitude had hardened, he had merely to hint at a feeling of disquiet, and that unfortunate individual became the object of a most intensive investigation into every aspect of his private life.

At least he had been able to assuage, even to his own satisfaction, the lingering suspicions toward Gregory Nej. Having accepted him without reservation, the FBI had decided to place both him and Felicity under the severest surveillance, without being able to discover the slightest suggestion that they were anything different to what they claimed. Gregory went nowhere, except to the Pentagon and home again. Felicity went nowhere, except to the local supermarket to shop. That the supermarket was also used by a certain Bogolzhin—about whom the service had considerable suspicions, although mainly because he was not only of Russian extraction, but because he was a known associate of several of the labor leaders who had provoked the strikes of last year—had caused a stir, but in all the six months they had been under surveillance there had been no indication that they had ever met, much less that they were communicating with each other, which was a great relief.

But the fact was, he was coming to believe in Gregory himself. There *was* something utterly innocent about that easygoing young man, just as there was something utterly ingenuous about his domestic arrangements. Besides, it was impossible to think of his own sister as a possible traitor, and it was equally impossible to imagine any couple sharing as much as she and Gregory obviously did without also sharing their political beliefs. He could not help but admire the way they had pursued their love, without flinching before the storm of criticism it had aroused, criticism in which he had shared to the full. But he was so happy it was over; this past winter the pair of them had joined the family at Cold Spring Harbor at least one weekend a month. Even Mother was visibly thawing towards them, while George had always behaved with his invariable open-mindedness.

Wearily he opened another file, aware that his concentration had been drifting. The worst feeling of all, the deadweight that seemed present in his mind all the time, was the certainty that *he* was accomplishing nothing, that the whole department was accomplishing nothing. They were snipping at the fringes of their gigantic fish, causing untold distress and hardship, and yet making no progress at all towards solving their problems. In all their investigations, they had not yet turned up a single confessed Russian agent from whom some of these smaller fry might conceivably be taking their orders; they lacked enough evidence to arrest people like this Bogolzhin character. In any event, they were reluctant to pull people like him in; there was always the chance that he might one day lead them to someone important. Until that happened, there was simply no hope of ever ending the Soviet penetration of American society. Nor did he see, he thought, as he glanced at the inked lettering on the file cover, that they were ever going to get any further by taking dozens of secret photographs at a Russian embassy reception in Washington. Their enemies were certainly not going to invite any of their own agents to an embassy cocktail party.

Yet the photographs had to be examined with a magnifying glass for any face, or any action, that could be construed as suspicious. Those were orders from Hoover himself.

John pulled the arm light lower, picked up his glass, and began going over the pictures, one after the other, face after face after face, hand after hand after hand, even buttonholes and pockets, women's corsages, every movement, placing each unrewarding photo in a neat pile before looking at the next, working with painstaking care, without any spark of anticipation that he might find anything worthwhile.

And on the seventh photo he realized, with a slow increase of his heartbeat, that he was staring at the face of Anna Ragosina.

Slowly he put down the photograph, and blinked. He got up, poured himself a glass of water, then returned to his desk, polished the magnifying glass, and picked up the print again.

It was not a good photograph. None of the photos were good, for they had been snapped with some new invention one of the department's tinkerers had come up with, a miniature camera that looked just like a wristwatch. The agent who had been planted on the guest list had merely snapped in every direction, every time he could reasonably shoot his cuffs. And on this occasion he had taken a group standing in a corner, four men and a woman, and the woman was half-turned away.

Yet John could not doubt that it was Anna Ragosina. He had spent three years living beside her, eating beside her, sleeping beside her—and killing beside her, in the Pripet Marshes. The image of her face was burned into his brain as much as the memory of her soft voice or her hard-muscled body.

Hurriedly he went through the rest of the photographs. It was possible he had made a mistake. Did he wish to have made a mistake?

There was another shot of the group in the corner, taken as it was splitting up, and this time the woman was looking straight into the camera. There was no mistake.

John laid down the second photo and leaned back in his chair. Anna Ragosina was here, in the United States. The most famous woman officer in the NKVD had been photographed at an embassy cocktail party in the heart of Washington. So obviously she had entered the country as a member of the embassy staff, and under an assumed name; that was the only way she could have avoided turning up on his desk before now. There was no telling how long she had been in the country.

Anna Ragosina! The knowledge that she was here suddenly made sense out of every little nagging disquiet that had haunted him for the past year. To pinpoint her would make everything he had set out to do since joining the service worthwhile. But what exactly would pinpointing her involve? If she was a member of the embassy staff, the best they could do would be to demand her expulsion from the country. Even if, as seemed likely, she was the commander of all Russian operations in the country, the hiatus would only be temporary, for the operations.

But what about the *operatives?* Garrison had once said, "Find me a link, here in the United States, between Anna Ragosina and Gregory Nej, and we'll think again." So Gregory had been officially cleared, for the second time, in the recent investigation. But what closer link could anyone ask, than that commander and pupil both be in the same country? Indeed, now that Gregory was living in Arlington and working at the Pentagon, both just across the river from Washington proper, they were virtually within a stone's throw of each other.

So was Felicity.

John got up to pace the office floor. That was an impossible thought. It had to be, because if Gregory was really working for Anna, and Felicity knew about it—and she *had* to, since she lived with him—then that made her a Russian agent, too. A traitor to her country.

But she, like Gregory, had been utterly cleared. Except that no one could be considered cleared now that Anna had turned up. He thought of the man Bogolzhin. He knew nothing about him, because Bogolzhin had been an American citizen since before the war, and therefore had never come under his scrutiny. The name had only cropped up because he had been observed at meetings with immigrants who were still under investigation, and because he was known as a labor agitator. There was nothing truly sinister about any of those facts, unless one added another totally unsinister fact: he used the same supermarket as Felicity Hayman. And then came the additional fact that Anna Ragosina was in Washington.

What was he to do? What *could* he do, but present the facts to his superiors? He had sworn an oath, and it was his country, as well, that he must think of. But it was also his sister, whom he would be condemning to a lifetime in prison, if not the electric chair.

Never had he felt so alone. There was nobody he could discuss his dilemma with—not even Sasha—without breaking the oath of secrecy. But if he did nothing, just passed these photographs as he passed so many photographs, with the stamp *No Comment,* was he not equally breaking the oath of loyalty? Gregory worked at the Pentagon, where he undoubtedly had access to classified material. Certainly he could not be allowed to go on working there. So, if he went to see him, told him the facts, told him to resign, for whatever reasons, told him to refuse all further connection with the State Department . . . No, that was schoolboy thinking. Gregory was a trained officer in the NKVD.

Trained by Anna Ragosina.

Well, then . . . go to see Anna? Tell *her* to get out, and to take Gregory with her, or he would expose them both? *That* was kindergarten thinking. Anna Ragosina? Probably the most deadly woman in the world?

And would not either of those courses be equal violations of his oath?

He supposed he could go to see Felicity. A brother was entitled to talk things over with his sister. But if he warned her, she would be able to warn Gregory, who would warn Anna . . . For Christ's sake, he thought, shaking his head as if by doing that he could empty his mind of absurdities. That would make him as much a traitor as either Gregory or Felicity.

His hand hovered over the telephone. Garrison, for all his manner, was basically a decent guy. Hard, but decent. He could at least be sounded out as to the best course to follow.

In any event, there was nobody else.

John dialed, and waited.

"Yes?"

"I must see you. It is very important."

"Yeah? It'll have to keep. Have you heard the news?"

John frowned into the receiver. "What news?"

"All hell is busting loose, that's what news. Uncle Joe has closed the autobahn from Hanover to West Berlin, put the city virtually under siege. We could be shooting by this time to-morrow."

Harry Truman's face was grim, as he greeted his Secretary of State. "Well?"

"I'm afraid there's no doubt about it," General Marshall said. "We thought at first that maybe it was just another holdup, there've been so many this last month, but Clay informs me that all traffic has been brought to a complete standstill, and that no further movement is to be allowed for the foreseeable future. *Nothing* is being allowed through."

"You've seen the ambassador?"

"I have. He says it's a technical matter and he has no information at the moment. He says undoubtedly it will all be cleared up in a day or two. In any event, he says that when

Ambassador Nej arrives here next month, he will be in a position to explain everything."

"A day or two? Next month?" The president snorted. "That's
nothing but doubletalk. As for this Ambassador Nej, I have a
damned good mind to refuse him entry."

"He's coming to represent the Soviet Union at the United
Nations. You *can't* refuse him entry."

"I know that. George, these damned Reds have caught us
with our pants down. Why didn't we guess they might try
something like this?"

"I'll take the blame," Marshall said. "I'll confess I didn't
think they'd ever have the nerve."

"For God's sake, I'm not looking to blame anybody. I'm
looking for answers. Is Hayman here?"

"Outside."

"Bring him in." Truman arranged himself behind his desk,
sitting absolutely straight, hands clasped together before his
chin, as he liked to appear to the public, and watched the
doorway. "Hayman! Good of you to come. We appear to have
a man-sized crisis on our hands."

"I'll agree with that." George shook hands and sat down.

"You know these people better than any other American.
You know this Michael Nej. What's it all about?"

"It's their way of protesting against your decision to rearm
the Wehrmacht, I would say."

"So they don't like it. Do they think that gives them the
right unilaterally to ignore treaty arrangements? Don't they
realize we could blast them from here to kingdom come?"

"But you're not going to," George pointed out.

Truman glared at him. "And they know that?"

"They're prepared to take a calculated risk. But is it really
a risk? Could you possibly justify declaring war on the Soviet
Union because of Berlin, much less throwing an atomic bomb
at them?"

"So we just fold up our tents and steal away?"

"They know you're not going to do that either. My guess
is that Michael Nej is coming with a brief to negotiate: no
rearmed Wehrmacht, no Berlin blockade."

"And if we tell him no dice?"

"Then they'll probably sit it out. People describe the Russians as great chess players. They're even better at five-card
stud."

Truman looked at Marshall. "How long have we got?"

"Not more than two weeks."

"Two *weeks?*"

"There's more than just our people involved, Mr. President. Our transport supplies all of West Berlin with food. The entire population will be starving at the end of two weeks. There's nothing coming in from East Germany."

"By God," Truman said. "How can they *do* this? We're the most powerful Goddamned country the world has ever seen."

"Which is a form of weakness," George said, "unless we aim to take over the world. I'm afraid this kind of backwards blackmail is something we're going to have to get used to."

Truman gave him another long stare. "Tell me the alternatives," he said to Marshall.

"Well, sir, first, we could announce publicly that we've had second thoughts about the proposals I made in my speech—that is, the formation, or certainly the composition, of this North Atlantic Treaty Organization. And at the same time we could privately convey to the Soviets that we're doing this on the condition that they reopen communications with West Berlin."

"In other words, surrender to their blackmail," Truman said.

"That is what it would amount to, yes," Marshall agreed. "Or, we could pull our people back out of Berlin."

"How?"

"We can fly them out. The Russians can't stop us from using the air, unless they fire on our planes, and then *they* would be the ones committing an act of war. They're not going to risk that."

"It would have to be a pretty massive airlift," George objected. "We couldn't abandon the West Berliners to the Communists."

"We have the capacity," Marshall said, "with some help from the British and the French. It'd be expensive, but it could be done."

"Go on," Truman invited.

"Or, third, we could use muscle. But there is no way the forces we have in Western Europe, even if you combined our boys with the British and the French—assuming *they'd* be interested in starting shooting all over again—could take on what the Russians have available, much less fight their way through to Berlin. In this context, muscle means atomic muscle, if we're going to achieve anything."

"Which'll cost us every friend we have in the world," George said.

"They have us across a barrel," Marshall agreed.

"Yes," the president said. His hands left their accustomed position, and his fingers drummed on the blotter for a few seconds. "There's a fourth alternative."

"Sir?" Marshall looked worried.

"That we call the Soviets' bluff."

"What bluff, Mr. President?" George asked. "They aren't *threatening* to close the autobahn. They have closed it."

"But as George has just said, Hayman, they can't close the skies. Not unless they're willing to be the ones to start shooting. We'll supply West Berlin by air."

"By air?" Marshall echoed.

"You said we had the capacity, with some help from our friends, to fly the entire population of West Berlin out of there. Doesn't that mean we have the capacity to fly enough food *in* to keep them going?"

"Well . . . have you any idea how much that would cost?"

"Would one week's airlift into Berlin—one *month's* airlift into Berlin—cost as much as one *day* of a shooting war with the Soviets?"

"Well . . . I suppose it wouldn't."

"But," George objected, "how long could you keep it up? It might turn out to be a matter of weeks, or even months."

"We'll keep it up, Hayman, just as long as the Soviets keep that autobahn closed. Like I said, we'll call those bastards' bluff. By God, we'll make it an event. *You* can do that. We're not going to be pushed, either into war, or into surrender. We'll *make* friends, not lose them. And Joe Stalin will get a bloody nose. Get started on that right away, George. I'll talk to Prime Minister Attlee on the phone, explain what we're going to do and why, just as soon as you can get him. And you give us maximum support in your papers, Hayman." He stood up to shake hands. "And we'll pray that the rest of the world doesn't explode until we get this one straightened out, eh? Especially Israel."

"Why, John." George Hayman sat in a deck chair on his upstairs sun porch, overlooking the beach and Long Island

Sound. "What a pleasant surprise! I didn't know they ever gave you the day off at that advertising agency of yours."

"I took this one." John Hayman sat beside his stepfather. "How's the news from Palestine? Or I should say Israel."

"They're holding. I've had no new reports from Judith, but her kibbutz got through that first attack. They're holding."

"Have they any chance at all? What are the odds? Twenty to one?"

"Disparity in numbers doesn't always mean that much. It never has in warfare, and I guess it means less now than ever before. It's the weapons, and the *will* of the people who handle them, that count in the long run. I think they'll make it." He grinned. "You know, if I thought your mother would stand for it, I'd go over there myself, for one last look."

"Um." John got up, hands thrust deep into the pockets of his jacket, as he strolled to the edge of the veranda.

"But I don't think you really have Israel on your mind," George said quietly. "Is it about your father coming to live over here?"

"No," John said. "I should be looking forward to that. But..." He came back to sit down again. "George, I'm in all kinds of trouble. I guess we all are, but I'm in the bull's-eye."

"You've found something on Gregory?" George asked, even more quietly.

John stared at him, incredulous.

"I wasn't ever supposed to tell you this," George said. "But it was I who suggested to Hoover that he use you. And I had Gregory principally in mind."

"But... my God. You always argued in his favor."

"Sure I did. I *wanted* him to be all right. Now I want him more than ever to be all right. And you passed him."

"I didn't, you know," John said. "I was never given the chance. That he came in with your say-so was enough for the FBI. Anyway, there's no point in recriminations. He was passed again, quite recently, when we started investigating *everybody*."

George was aware of a feeling as if he had been kicked in the stomach by a mule. But hadn't he *known*, for over a year, that such a kick was coming, even if he had refused to allow himself to believe it? He sat up. "And now you've found something." It was not a question.

"No. Not about Gregory, directly. George...Anna Ragosina is in Washington. Has been for more than two years, since the fall of 1945, masquerading as an embassy secretary, calling herself Yelena Gorchakova. Gorchakova. That was the name of one of her aides in the Pripet. A girl she executed for disobeying an order."

George frowned at him. "How can you be sure?"

John gave him the two photographs. "I don't know if you've ever met her."

George shook his head.

"Well, that's her," John said. "They arrived in a file a week ago."

"A *week?*"

John nodded. "Anna trained Gregory. And others. But if ever a man belongs to her, it's Gregory. She told me that, in the Pripet. And just the *fact* that she's here puts a different complexion on everything. Igor's death—everything. And she was probably here when Gregory *arrived*. She must have been waiting for him, must have been masterminding the whole Goddamned thing. George, do you think my father *knew?*"

George considered. "No," he said at last. "I have an idea your father knows very little about what actually goes on, because he doesn't *want* to. But what have you done with this information?"

"Well...I called Garrison. But it was the day the Berlin crisis broke, and he wasn't interested at that moment. And I didn't press the point. I wanted to think. Meanwhile I did a little investigating on my own, got the name she's using, and the address of her apartment—"

"Isn't it against the rules, to work on your own?"

"Sure. I suppose I've broken them all. As for telling you, that's treason. But George, it's impossible that Felicity is *not* involved. Sorry, but she's got to be in it up to her neck."

George gazed at him for several seconds, while the sick feeling spread. But he had known that, as well, deep down in his subconscious, for over a year.

"So I've sat on it, for a week," John said miserably, "trying to decide what to do. And getting nowhere at all."

"You think Felicity is a traitor?" George's brain was whirring, trying to think, to decide on a course of action. There had to be one. There had to be *something* he could do.

"I don't see how she can't be," John said. "Oh, sure, maybe she doesn't really understand what's going on, either, but that doesn't alter the fact."

George leaned back again. But John's words had given him an idea.

"What am I to do, George? What *am* I to do?"

"Play it straight," George said. "As of tomorrow."

"What do you mean?"

"You swore an oath, John. And we're in a serious situation. The whole damned world is in a serious situation, right now. If Anna Ragosina and Gregory are working against us down in Washington, God knows what damage they've already done. They must be stopped. Tomorrow morning you take these photographs to Garrison and Hoover, and tell them what you think."

"But . . . what about Felicity?"

"That gives me tonight to try to straighten her out," George said. "But John, stay by your telephone, just in case tomorrow won't wait."

Felicity was at Washington National Airport to meet him. "You have me worried stiff," she said. "What's the matter? Mother?"

"I told you on the telephone," he said. "Your mother's fine."

"Yet you had to fly down here, to see me?" She drove northwest along the Potomac, with the Pentagon on their left, the river gleaming in the evening sunlight on their right, the Jefferson Memorial rising amid the trees beyond. "Gregory will be home by now."

"I came to see you," George said. "Not Gregory."

Her head turned sharply, and she frowned. "I thought that was all over and done with, Dad. You said it was all over and done with."

"I wish it was," George said. "Felicity . . . is there somewhere we can park, and talk?"

"I've heard this is a famous place for lovers." But she wasn't smiling as she pulled off toward the riverside and found a space between two trees. She switched off the ignition, lit a cigarette with steady fingers, and stared across the river. "So?"

"Have you ever heard of a woman called Anna Ragosina?"

Felicity frowned. "Yes," she said thoughtfully. "She . . .

wasn't she the woman in John's memoirs? The sort of female Dracula who only enjoyed killing people?"

"She also happens to be the Russians' top woman spy. Did you know that?"

Felicity turned her head. "You mean she's real? I thought John had made her up. The archetypal villainess."

It was difficult to imagine she was lying. "She's very real," George said. "And she's here in Washington. Has been for more than two years. John recognized her in a photograph taken at the Russian Embassy."

"Anna Ragosina?" She was still no more than interested. "So?"

"She also happens to be Gregory Nej's spymaster. I suppose I should say spymistress."

"I don't know what that means." But for the first time a false note had crept into her voice. Her brain was suddenly whirring, he could tell.

"It means that she trained him. That he does what she tells him to do. The fact that they are both here in Washington almost certainly means that he is working for her."

Felicity opened her mouth, and closed it again; she could not prevent the rush of color to her cheeks. "Daddy! Gregory has defected. What it does mean is . . . my God, she must have been sent after him."

Now she *was* lying, using any words that came to mind, while she tried to think.

"His defection was all a part of it, Felicity. Anna Ragosina was here before Gregory arrived. You have to understand that."

"And you think that because she's here, Gregory must be a *spy?* Oh, Daddy . . ."

George took the cigarette from between her fingers and stubbed it out in the ashtray. She didn't protest or resist. Then he took her hands between his. She didn't resist or protest at that, either.

"Listen to me, my darling, darling girl," George said. "Fooling around with words, pretending things aren't what they are, isn't going to help anymore. Tomorrow the FBI will come to your apartment and arrest Gregory. They will also arrest you. I really have no idea what the charge against Gregory will be, but you stand a very good chance of being charged with treason. Do you understand that? Do you understand what that means, Felicity?"

She gazed at him. Her tongue came out and circled her lips, slowly. He could not imagine the turmoil her brain had to be in, the desire to trust him obviously jostling against the instructions she would have received from Gregory never to trust anyone but *him,* ever again.

"Now, Felicity," he said, speaking very slowly and carefully, "I don't know, and I don't want to know, how involved you have been over this last year. I cannot believe you ever intended to betray your country to the Soviets, but—"

"Betray my country?" she cried. "How can I betray a bunch of thugs who are out to dominate the world by force of arms?"

"Is *that* what he's been telling you? And you believed him?"

"It's true," she insisted. "All you have to do is look around you."

"That's all you have to do," he agreed. "But look a little wider afield than Gregory's reading matter. Look at what the Soviets are doing in Europe, and what they're trying to do all over the world. Look back a little at what happened to your own family. Look at what happened to Gregory's own mother. How does he explain *that* away?"

"Oh, really, Dad," she said. "Everyone knows she was murdered by Ivan Nej. Not even Gregory attempts to defend what he did. And Ivan Nej has been convicted of murder."

"Would it interest you to know that Ivan Nej has not only *not* been convicted of murder, but is back working for the NKVD? That it was he who was sent to Israel to kidnap Judith Petrov? That it is his bosses, who are also Gregory's bosses, who have locked poor Boris Petrov up in a lunatic asylum for no better reason than that he is Judith's husband?"

"Oh . . . that's all . . . Yankee propaganda," she shouted. But the certainty had left her voice.

"Felicity," he said, "listen to me. I think you've been taken for a ride from the beginning. But you have to wake up now, and you have to get out. You have to come back to New York with me, now, and you have to tell the FBI, tonight, that the moment you found out just what Gregory was up to, you pulled out. But you have to go to them, not wait for them to come to you."

"For God's sake," she said. "How can I possibly do that?"

"Because if you don't, you are going to be tried for treason. And if you are convicted, you will be sent to the electric chair. Do you understand that? You are going to *die.*" He was being deliberately brutal, to try to shock her into understanding her position, and all the while he felt the most dreadful awareness of déjà vu. He had tried to be brutal to poor Paul von Hassell, as well. But this was his own daughter.

She was staring at him with enormous, tear-filled eyes.

"So drive me back to the airport," he said, "and we'll catch the next flight. Don't worry about your things. We can get them later."

"I can't," she said. "I can't just walk out on him. He's there now, waiting for me. Waiting for his dinner."

"Felicity—"

"I *love* him," she cried.

"Do you really believe that he loves you?"

"Yes," she said. "Yes. He loves me. I know he does. And I . . ." Now the tears were streaming down her face. "Listen," she said. "You must let me go back and talk with him. I must talk with him. Then . . . then I'll come with you. I promise. I'll come to you at the airport in an hour. I promise."

"No way," he said. "I'll come with you now."

She shook her head. "I must talk with him alone."

"Felicity . . . this man is a trained NKVD officer. That means he's as cold-blooded as they come. He may genuinely love you, but that won't stop him from killing you if it's a choice between that and arrest. You've read John's memoirs. You know how Anna Ragosina treated her own people, when she thought it was necessary."

"Gregory isn't Anna Ragosina, Daddy. He should have killed me once before, when I first found out about him. But he didn't, because he loves me. And there is no way he is going to harm me now. That's why I'm not going to harm him, either. I'm going back to see him. To warn him. To give him a chance. I must."

"He won't be able to escape, you know."

"I *must* talk with him."

George hesitated. His misfortune was that he could see her point of view, understand her feelings too well. That had always been his misfortune, he supposed—an overdeveloped ability to see both sides of every question. And he knew her well enough to know that she could not be pushed too far. And Gregory loved her. George did believe that, for all his pretended skepticism; he had the evidence of his own eyes.

But it was his daughter's life at risk. And perhaps her sanity.

He sighed. "Okay," he said. "You can telephone him from the airport, ask him to meet us there. And you can talk with him. God knows how we'll explain *that* to the FBI, but we'll give it a try."

She hesitated, then nodded, and started the engine. "I'll always be grateful to you, Daddy, you know that, for giving us this chance."

"Let's hope you have something to be grateful for," he said.

They drove back to the airport in uncomfortable silence. At the entrance to the terminal, she pulled into a taxi space. "Don't you want the parking lot?" he asked.

"Let me call Gregory first," she said. "What's a parking ticket when there's so much else at stake?"

He shrugged, opened his door, got out, and watched in dismay as she suddenly gunned the engine and drove away. For a moment he stared after her, tremendously aware of how old he was, and how helpless.

But not *that* helpless.

He waved his arm to summon a taxi. "Follow—" He paused. He would still need muscle. And he knew her address. "Wait for me," he told the cabbie. "Just give me the time to make a phone call."

"Holy smoke!" Arthur Garrison studied the photograph. He had been as grumpily skeptical as usual, at being dragged away from his supper table, but suddenly he was totally interested. "Is that really her? Anna Ragosina?"

"It is," John said.

"And you've already made a preliminary investigation? That's not your job, you know."

"I had to be sure," John said. "Goddamn it, man, my sister is involved."

"Yeah," Garrison said. "You don't suppose she's a Russki spy too?"

"Of course not," John said. "But she's certainly living with one. That means she could be in some danger."

"Yeah," Garrison said. "But we're not going to have a chance like this again. Technically, the whole business should be handed over to the State Department, this Ragosina dame being an accredited member of the embassy staff, even if she is using a false name and masterminding a few spies. But I think we'll just go ahead and earn ourselves a rap on the knuckles, deliberately. Yes, sir. I aim to give this dame a bit of a grilling. So what I'm going to do is this, Johnnie my boy. I'm going to get me a warrant—I don't *have* to say she's got diplomatic immunity at this stage—and you and I are going to raid this Ragosina's apartment, and arrest her, and give her a going-over, *and* take her place apart—and then, maybe like lunchtime tomorrow, we'll believe her story that she's an embassy official, and hand her back with apologies and a demand for her expulsion." He grinned. "Hell, that's what the Russkis would do. Meanwhile, we don't touch your cousin until that's done. He won't know what's going on, so your sister won't be in any trouble until then."

John bit his lip. He didn't dare tell Garrison about George's visit to Arlington. "How long will it take you to get that warrant?"

Garrison shrugged. "We can pull strings. I'll have it by midnight, and we can be in Washington by two." Another grin. "We'll have to get the little lady out of bed. So you go home and grab yourself something to eat, and let me finish my meal, and I'll meet you at the airport at ten to twelve. Don't be late. And John, you'd better bring some hardware, just in case she's as tough as you say she is."

"I'll do that," John promised. "But I'm not going to meet you at the airport. I'll meet you outside Anna's apartment, in Washington."

"Now, you look here, son. I'm doing you a favor, letting you be in on this at all, when you're not even in the field. I'm only doing it because she's your pigeon. If you go and louse it up—"

"I'm not going to louse it up," John assured him. "But like you say, she's my pigeon. I intend to make sure she stays in the coop."

And to try to bail George and Felicity out of the mess they're in, he thought as he sped to the airport. If I can get there in time.

Felicity Hayman opened the apartment door, closed it softly behind herself, and leaned against it. She had determined not to think, on the drive back from the airport, not to consider anything about her situation at all, until she had got Gregory away from the apartment. But now her heart was pounding and she was aware of a drumming in her ears. It was all too unbelievably terrible to be true. Of course, Daddy, with his plans and his pat solutions, had been talking nothing but nonsense. But that the FBI should be onto them, that their snug little world should come crashing down—that was not nonsense.

"Is that you, Felicity?" Gregory, in his shirt sleeves, hurried through from the kitchen. "Where have you been? I've been terribly worried."

"With Daddy," she said. "And he's going to be here any moment, probably with a bunch of policemen. Grab your coat and let's get out of here!"

"George is coming here?" He looked past her, as if expecting to see him coming through the door.

Felicity ran into the living room, picked up his coat herself, and pushed him towards the door. "I left him at the airport, but he may be here any minute. He came down to talk to me."

Gregory was already at the stairs. "I do not understand," he protested. "What has happened?"

She ran at his side. "It's what's about to happen." They reached the street, and she pulled open the car door for him. "Get in."

"But . . ." He sat down, and she got behind the wheel, gunned the engine.

"Gregory . . . tomorrow, or maybe tonight, you are going to be arrested by the FBI."

"What?"

She turned into the traffic. "It's a fact. John has seen a photograph of some woman named Anna Ragosina here in Washington, and he knows her to be a high-ranking NKVD official. Daddy says she trained you. Do you know Anna Ragosina, Gregory?"

He hesitated, and she sighed.

"Well," she said. "The fact that she's been here for over two years makes them sure you're working for her."

She pulled down a side street, found a parking space, and switched off the engine. She couldn't think straight while driving.

Gregory was frowning. "But they haven't arrested me yet."

"John must have told Daddy first. Because of me, you see. I'm to be arrested too, on a charge of treason."

"My God!" He reached into his pocket for a cigarette, a habit he had picked up since coming to America.

She lit it for him. "Daddy says they could send me to the electric chair."

"Yes," he said. "They could." He inhaled, and glanced at her. "Your father told you this?"

She nodded.

"But . . . ?"

"Oh, he has a solution, naturally. He thought if I left with him tonight, went to the FBI and claimed I knew nothing about your being a spy until today and that I left you the moment I found out, they might let me off."

"Yes," Gregory said. "Yes. That is best. You must do that." He held her hands. "And Felicity, you must tell them everything they want to know, anything that will help them accept your story. After tomorrow it will not matter."

It was her turn to frown. "You mean you *want* me to go with Daddy?"

"You must."

"But . . . what about you? Don't you understand?—you're going to be arrested. You're a spy. I don't know if they'll send you to the chair, but they'll certainly send you to prison for the rest of your life."

He shook his head. "They won't even catch me, Felicity. By tomorrow I'll be in Mexico, or Canada, or somewhere, on my way home to Russia."

"But . . . how?"

"Anna will get me out," he explained. "I have to go to her anyway now, to warn her. But she will take care of everything. She'll have to get Bogolzhin out too, and warn some of our other operatives, but she will look after it all. She is a most remarkable woman. And *she's* in no danger, you see. She is embassy staff. All the FBI can do to her is demand her expulsion from the country. So you go to the airport and go home safely with your father, and to the FBI if he wants you to, and I will go to Anna and get her to arrange for me to leave the country. I only need a few hours. Believe me," he said, misinterpreting her expression. "It will be a simple matter. There are always contingency plans for this sort of accident."

Her fingers were tight on his. "But Gregory . . . if this Anna can smuggle you out of the country, then she can smuggle me out as well."

"You?"

"I don't want to leave you, Gregory. I couldn't live without you."

"But I will be returning to Russia. And there is no likelihood of my ever being allowed into the United States again."

"We'd be together."

"Felicity, you'd never ever see your family again. You'd go down in history as a traitor. Everyone in America would hate you."

"I'd be with you, Gregory," she said, very simply.

Anna Ragosina was a woman who liked routine. As soon as she got home from the Embassy in the evening, she bathed, wrapped herself in a dressing gown, and turned on the television while she prepared her supper. She had no social life at all, unless her regular meetings with Bogolzhin could be called social events; out of boredom, she had even tried attending one or two of the embassy cocktail parties, only to be more bored than ever. So television had become a very important part of her existence. She watched it every moment she was at home, and just about convinced herself that she was making an in-depth study of American culture.

Bogolzhin was in fact coming to see her tonight, but he would not arrive much before ten. That the embassy secretary living down this quiet street occasionally entertained a male friend was no doubt well known to many people, including the police. But she had decided it was not a risk. She made no attempt to hide the fact that she was a Russian, so what was more in character than that she should choose a Russian boyfriend? And Bogolzhin, in his capacity as field organizer, was not, so far as she knew, suspected of anything by the American police or the FBI. In fact, she rather wished he would be. She was thoroughly fed up with America, and utterly bored. And she had completed her mission. Yet she had been commanded to continue here, and maintain her network of information and observation, as well as her interference in the labor scene. To be expelled would be a blessing.

She placed the plate of frozen chicken pot pie—instant meals were another pleasure she had discovered in America—on the table in front of the sofa, picked up her cat, and settled back with a sigh of contentment. Tabasco was the first pet she had ever owned. She was a female, coldly unaffectionate, and a ruthless destroyer of everything that moved and happened to

be smaller than herself. Her character appealed to Anna. And
the constant companionship was a delight, however bored
Tabasco might appear about the whole thing. Undoubtedly,
Anna thought, living in this country had taught her a great deal
about the art of enjoying oneself.

But the best part about returning to Russia would mean an
end to play-acting, to constantly having to appear as less than
she was. In Russia she would again be Anna Ragosina, a name
and a face to be feared. Her power would again be visible,
instead of concealed.

The doorbell rang, and her head jerked, as she looked at
her watch. It certainly could not be Bogolzhin; she had made
it perfectly plain that she did not wish him ever to arrive until
she was actually ready for bed. She placed Tabasco on the
cushion, got up, and went into the bedroom for her pistol.
From time to time she received other callers. She was a good-
looking woman and it was known that she lived alone—her
female neighbors had long since given up trying to make friends
with her—but Anna had no intention of ever being caught
napping.

Pistol dangling at her side from the fingers of her right hand,
she returned to the living room, where the bell had jangled
again. She opened the peephole and saw Gregory Nej. Her first
reaction was one of extreme anger. Of all the crazy things,
coming here! Then she realized that something dramatic must
have happened, thrust the pistol into the deep pocket of her
dressing gown, opened the door, and looked past Gregory at
Felicity Hayman.

"Let us in, Anna," Gregory said. "It is very important."

Anna stepped back, and they came into the room, Felicity
giving her a curious stare.

"You," Anna said to Gregory, closing and chaining the
door. "You . . . *cretin*."

"Don't be angry, Anna," Gregory said. "Hear me out. There
is a crisis."

Anna gazed at him, then at the still-staring Felicity, who
could not take her eyes away. "Am I a freak or something?"
Anna demanded.

"I . . . I had no idea you were so beautiful," Felicity said.
"Gregory never—"

"So he has been discussing me with you," Anna said.

"I'd never heard of you before this evening," Felicity explained. "Well . . . I had *heard* of you, but—"

"What is happening?" Anna demanded. "Why is she here?"
But even as she spoke she knew what she would have to do.
A feeling almost of contentment spread through her system.

Gregory described their situation quickly and succinctly.
"So you see, Anna," he said, "it is not our fault that there is
a crisis. It is *your* fault, for being photographed. I knew it was
a risk, your being here at all."

"A million-to-one chance," Anna said, half to herself. She
was delighted by what had happened, despite her anger. "No,
a hundred-million-to-one chance." After all this time, John
Hayman had recognized her from an undoubtedly poor snap-
shot. How well he must remember her!

"So you'll understand that we must leave tonight," Gregory
was saying. "You must organize a route for us, either up to
Canada or down to Mexico. Unless there is a Russian ship in
harbor somewhere that we can board, or a flight back to Moscow."

Anna gazed at him. "You want me to get you—and her—
out of the country?"

"It is the only solution, if we are not to be taken. And
probably executed."

"I see what you mean." Anna reached into her pocket and
drew out the pistol.

"Now look here, Anna," Gregory began.

"I am not a fool," Anna said scornfully. "How was I to
know it was you at the door? Oh, sit down, both of you. Fix
yourself a drink. I will have to think."

"Well, don't take too long," Gregory said, going to the
cocktail cabinet. Felicity sat down beside the cat, who immediately jumped down to the floor.

"No," Anna said. "I will not take much time."

She went into her bedroom, opened the drawer, and took
out her silencer, to screw onto the muzzle of her pistol.

When she returned to the living room, Anna found herself
gazing at Felicity, who now stood beside Gregory, next to the
cocktail cabinet.

"You first, I think," she said, and levelled the pistol. Felicity
gave a gasp and turned away. The bullet, expelled from the
gun muzzle with not more than a gentle plop, struck her in the
shoulder and threw her against the wall. Anna clicked her

tongue in annoyance at having missed her target, and followed her with the pistol sight.

Gregory spun around at Felicity's cry and the unmistakable sound of a silenced pistol. He held a full martini pitcher in his hand, and he hurled it in the same instant. The movement distracted Anna, and her second shot went even wider, thudding into the plaster. She had turned to face him, but could not avoid the flying glass, which struck her a glancing blow on the jaw, and knocked her onto the sofa. Desperately she pushed herself up, but Gregory was upon her in a single leap, clear across the room, landing on her belly with a force that drove all the breath from her body, left her gasping and retching, while the pistol slipped from her temporarily nerveless fingers.

Dimly she became aware that Gregory had got off her, and had kicked the pistol across the room. Now he was bending over Felicity, who was sitting against the wall, whimpering like a sick dog, Anna thought contemptuously.

She stood up, and Gregory turned again. "Are you mad?" she asked.

"She is badly hurt," Gregory said. "There was no need for that."

"No need?" Anna demanded. "No need? Did I not warn you that I would have to destroy her one day? And you, if you persisted in this stupid affair. Now all you have done is cause her unnecessary pain." She went towards the pistol.

"No, Anna," Gregory said. "I will not let you."

"Silly boy," Anna said. "You had best pray I do *not* decide to terminate you as well."

She stooped to pick up the weapon and heard him behind her. She turned on her knees, the edge of her left hand scything for his legs in a blow that would leave him powerless, if it connected. But he had known what she would do, and side-stepped, at the same time kicking her in the backside so that she fell over, away from the pistol and onto the cat, who fled the room with an angry squawk. She remembered that she had taught this man everything he knew. But he had never been capable of the mental hardness necessary to kill someone, and certainly not with his bare hands.

"You *are* mad," she said, and rose to her feet. "Do you really suppose you can fight me?"

"Don't try me, Anna," he begged. "Don't try me."

Anna gazed at him, then sprang at him, steel-hard hands

whipping to and fro. To her utter amazement he waited for her, evaded her first blow, and caught her wrist. Her second blow landed with a crunching thud which she was sure would break a rib, but he hardly flinched, and caught that wrist as well. She jerked back, and kicked for his groin, teeth bared now, breath hissing, but she was hampered by her dressing gown, and he evaded her toes also, and threw her away from him. She staggered backwards, hit a chair and sat down hard, and then fell over, together with the chair. She pushed herself up, and saw that he had picked up the pistol.

"You are a fool, as well," she gasped. "If you kill me, the NKVD will get you, no matter where you go, where you hide." Her breathing returned to normal. "But you wouldn't kill me, anyway, Gregory Ivanovich. You haven't got the guts to kill anyone. Have you?"

She watched the indecision in his eyes, smiled as she pushed herself to her feet, and walked towards him. "Give me the pistol. I will settle with the woman. There is nothing to be alarmed about. Bogolzhin will be here in an hour, and we can dispose of her body. Then I will get you both out of the country. He will have to go too, you know."

She was within two feet of him, and the pistol was between them. She held out her hand. "Give me the gun, Gregory."

Anna was aware only of pain, and sickness. Although her brain returned to full alertness almost the moment she opened her eyes, it took her some seconds to realize that the pain arose from her head and her wrists and her shoulders, and not from her chest or her stomach. The poor young fool had not shot her, then.

She twisted her head to and fro, and dislodged Tabasco, who had been sitting on her hair, kneading her scalp. She realized that she was lying on the sofa. Gregory must have hit her on the head with the pistol—quite hard, she thought, judging by the pain, which had been aggravated by the cat's attentions, and by the lump, as well as the trickle of blood that had soaked into the cushion on which her cheek rested. And he had bound her wrists behind her back with her dressing-gown cord, then secured them to her ankles—tightly enough to cut off the circulation and to make movement almost impossible.

It was a pity, she thought, that he was now a case for execution on sight; she would very much have liked to have him in one of her cells at Lubianka, preferably number forty-seven, for just an hour—with that blond bitch beside him.

And that might still happen, she thought, as the rest of the room slowly swam into focus. He had of course gone, and taken the wounded Hayman woman with him; her blood formed a coagulating stain against the far wall. How long ago? She looked at the television screen. The program she had been watching had ended, but its successor was not more than fifteen minutes old, she estimated; she watched so much television she was an expert. Thus the pair of them were probably still close to Washington.

Going where? Since they were on the run from the FBI, he could hardly stage a real defection at this point, because that would mean surrendering the woman as a traitor. He still must be imagining he could reach Mexico or Canada—while carrying a badly wounded woman, as well. The poor fool, she thought again. And even assuming he could get out of the country, what then? Did he really suppose that because he was Michael Nej's nephew he could ever return to Russia, after disobeying orders, and assaulting her in the bargain?

She heard the latch of her door rattle, and twisted her head again. Bogolzhin? It was still early for him, but it couldn't be anyone else. Oh, thank God for Dimitri Igorovich, she thought. Sometimes she could almost love him.

"It is unlocked," she said. "Come in."

The door opened, and she stared at John Hayman. Behind him was a much older man she had never seen before, but she knew who he was because there were photographs of him in her file, both here in Washington and back in Moscow.

Desperately she pushed down with her feet, and managed to get herself a little way up the sofa, still staring at him, watching George Hayman closing the door and setting the chain.

John switched off the television. "Where are they?" he asked, standing above her. She realized that the dressing gown, lacking its cord, had fallen open when she had moved. But that was surely to her advantage; she could tell from his eyes.

"Good evening, John," she said calmly. "Do you know, it is almost a pleasure, seeing you again? I was becoming quite uncomfortable." She arranged her lips into a smile. "How long has it been? Four years?"

"Anna," John said, speaking very evenly. "I am looking for

my sister and Gregory Nej. We have been to their apartment, and they left there in a hell of a hurry. There must have been some kind of emergency rendezvous with you or your people. Now you give."

"The John Hayman I remember," Anna mused. "would at least have untied me before asking me questions."

"John!" George's voice was sharp; he had noticed the blood against the wall.

John touched it with his finger. "Not quite dry." He turned back to her. "Is one of them hurt? Is Felicity hurt?"

"You have no right to come breaking into my apartment," Anna said. "I am a Russian citizen, accredited as a stenographer at the embassy. You will cause an international incident."

John sat beside her on the sofa, looked into her face, and tried to stop himself from looking at her body. Once, he recalled, he had been very near to surrendering to her charms, and had, on occasion, regretted that he had not done so. To sleep with Anna Ragosina would surely be an unforgettable experience.

Like sleeping with a tigress.

But she was still one of the most beautiful women he had ever seen, and he belonged to an exceptionally handsome family himself. It was necessary to make himself hate her, as he had never hated anyone before. To his surprise, he did not find it at all difficult.

She was smiling at him. "You too are remembering," she said, "when we fought together. When it was you and I against an entire German army. Those others, they didn't count, John. It was you and I. Without us they would soon have been defeated. John, I will not report this break-in. I am too happy to see you again. I would like you to stay with me tonight. Send the old man away, and stay with me, and let us remember, together."

He did want to hurt her, very much, but it was at least partly sexual frustration, an understanding that she lay, bound and helpless and virtually naked before him, that he could do whatever he wished to that snow-white flesh—and that if he succumbed to his desire for a second he would be irrevocably lost.

But he had to convince her that he *would* hurt her.

He drove his fingers into her hair, and she winced as he lifted her head from the pillow. "Anna," he said. "I *do* re-

member. I remember everything that happened during those
years in the Pripet, everything you did to those you considered
your enemies, or those of your friends who did not obey you
absolutely. Anna, if you do not tell me what has happened to
my sister, I am going to hurt you worse than even you have
ever hurt anybody. Even you, Anna."

"You cannot frighten me, John," she said. "You are a gentleman. You will never harm me. If you will not stay the night,
then just *get out!*" She spat the last two words.

John hesitated, then he half-turned his head. "I imagine
there is a stove in the kitchen, George," he said. "Will you
turn it on, please? All the rings."

It was George's turn to hesitate, but only briefly. Then he
went into the kitchen.

"Come along," John said, and thrust one arm under her
shoulders and the other under her knees to lift her from the
sofa.

For the first time some of the confidence faded from her
eyes. "Are you mad?" she snarled.

"Just angry," he told her, and carried her into the kitchen.
The four burners on the electric stove were already glowing.
Anna gave a convulsive kick and a wriggle, but he would not
let her go.

"Now, Anna," he said. "I am going to sit you on that stove,
and hold you there, until you either tell me what I want to
know, or you cook. It's up to you."

"You . . . you bastard," she said, her teeth snapping as if she
would bite him. "You wouldn't dare. You wouldn't—"

"George," John said. "Do you think you could give me a
hand? I'd like you to gather the dressing gown to her waist,
please."

George stared at him in consternation, but he was standing
behind Anna, so she couldn't see his face. And John was
holding her so close to the stove, she could feel the heat scorch-
ing her flesh right through the material. Without it . . . She
gasped. "For God's sake," she shouted. "They hit me and left.
Can't you see the bruise? That's *my* blood on the pillow out
there."

George stood next to her and parted the dark hair. "That *is*
a recent blow," he said.

John dropped her to the floor. She gave a yelp of pain as
her head banged, and Tabasco, who had been hiding under the

table, gave another angry meaow and fled back to the living room.

"What happened to Felicity?" John stooped beside her.

"I shot her," Anna snapped. "I hit her in the shoulder. And then that young fool Gregory hit me. How should I know where they have gone? They just left."

George stooped as well. "Felicity—is she badly hurt?"

"She's bleeding," Anna said. "I hope she bleeds to death."

"How long ago?" John asked.

"Oh . . . half an hour."

"They won't have got far," John said. "We'll have an all-points bulletin out on them in five minutes." He gazed at his stepfather. "Or—?"

"We don't have much choice," George said, "if she's trying to bleed to death on top of everything else."

The doorbell rang, and all their heads jerked. But John saw Anna's mouth opening, and hastily grabbed her throat. "I think she's expecting someone," he said. "George, could you take a hold of this? I wouldn't worry about squeezing too hard."

George wrapped the fingers of both hands around the smooth flesh, and wondered just what thoughts were raging through the brain behind the blazing eyes beneath him. John went to the door, where the bell was ringing again.

"Anna?" someone asked. "Are you there, Anna?"

John drew his pistol, then opened the door. He waited for the man to step inside, jammed his pistol in his ribs, and realized that he knew who he was, from his photograph in the file. "Why, Dimitri Bogolzhin," he said. "I think this must be my lucky night."

Gregory Nej switched off the ignition and let the car coast to the side of the road. There was no possibility of going any further.

He should have surrendered in Washington itself. Instead he had driven aimlessly around and around in circles, listening to Felicity gasping in pain, knowing despite the bandage he had made from one of Anna's tablecloths, that she was losing too much blood, but knowing too that there was no way he could surrender her to American vengeance. Thus, eventually, he had taken this road leading northwest, and had, in fact, just passed a sign announcing that he was entering the town of

Frederick; already there were lighted houses to either side. Driving this way, he was at least making vaguely for Canada.

As if he had the slightest chance of being allowed across the Canadian border, even without a badly wounded woman beside him. So why not jettison her, throw her into a ditch and drive on, take his chances on his own? That was what all his training was shrieking at him to do. But if he was going to do that, why had he interfered with Anna's attempt to kill her? That way had lain safety.

That way, in fact, still lay safety. He could turn this car and drive back to Anna's apartment. She was undoubtedly very angry with him, but Anna had never let her anger obscure duty or common sense. Once there he would be looked after. Bogolzhin would have arrived by now; between them they could dispose of Felicity's body, and then Anna would see to their escape. It was the only sane course of action left open to him— assuming he sacrificed Felicity. That was what he had always known he would one day have to do. Thoughts like that had been perfectly simple, before he had fallen in love with her.

The realization came as something of a shock. It was not a thing he had ever admitted to himself, had ever supposed he *would* admit to himself. How could he have fallen in love with a thirty-four-year-old neurotic American who did not even have the sense to realize how well off she, and her country, were?

But he had. And he loved her with more than a young man's desire for a voluptuous and sexually aware woman. He loved her with a lifetime's pentup desire to love, and to be loved. His mother had had little time for him, and besides, his sister had always been her favorite. The only love he had ever tasted in his life before coming to America had been in the arms of Anna Ragosina, and that was not love. But Felicity . . . he looked down at her, huddled beneath the blanket, trying desperately not to upset him by moaning, body twisting with pain. She had given him everything she possessed. And in return— a bullet wound, and then the electric chair? That could never be.

"Felicity," he said. "My darling, listen to me. I am going to surrender."

Her head lifted. "You can't. Gregory—"

"Listen to me. There is no point in being foolish any longer. If you do not see a doctor immediately, you may die. And I cannot bear the thought of that, my darling."

She forced a smile, through tight-drawn lips. "If you take me to an American doctor, I am going to die, anyway."

"Not if you do as I say. Remember this. Your father's plan was quite valid. The moment you learned what I was really doing, you attempted to leave. But I stopped you, forced you to accompany me as a hostage. When you resisted, I shot you. *Remember that.*"

"Gregory," she said. "I can't—"

"You must."

"But . . . what will happen to you?"

He leaned down to kiss her on the nose. "They'll put me in prison. But only for a while."

She sighed, her strength, and therefore her will to resist, continuing to diminish. "I guess I'll be able to visit you every week."

He shook his head. "No, my darling. You must never see me again. You must never *wish* to see me again, at least publicly. But we will remember our time together, you and I."

He switched on the ignition again, and drove into Frederick. He realized that for the first time in too long he was quite happy and relaxed. Because for the first time in his life he was suddenly positive he was doing the right thing.

Chapter 13

J. EDGAR HOOVER GLOWERED ACROSS HIS DESK AT JOHN Hayman. "I ought to throw the whole Goddamned book at you," he said. "You are guilty of breaking just about every rule of the service. For Christ's sake, Garrison was on his way with a warrant. Why couldn't you wait? As for roping in old man Hayman—"

"We couldn't wait," John said quietly. "My sister was involved."

"Yeah?" Hoover asked. "You're just damned lucky things turned out the way they did."

"I gather Bogolzhin's talking," John said.

Hoover glanced at Garrison. "You could say that," he agreed. "He's singing like the sweetest canary in all the world. It's his only hope of saving his neck. But he's sure making one or two enemies—or he will, when the cases come to court. I wouldn't give a red cent for his chances of survival, even if he's acquitted. Some of the names on his list would take your breath away." He wagged his finger. "We'd have got him, you know, without your Dick Tracy act."

"You wouldn't, Mr. Hoover," John said, "and you know it. Garrison wasn't getting to Washington until two. Bogolzhin would have found Anna long before then, and they'd have been away. There's another thing. Our investigations seem to have been botched from the start. How come no report was ever made that Bogolzhin was visiting Anna, regularly, at her apartment?"

"Because we didn't know she was anything but a little typist, that's why. Sure, we thought maybe Bogolzhin was using her as a messenger between himself and the ambassador, but we weren't going to break it up. We were hoping for bigger things." Suddenly the angry face produced a smile. "And we got them, thanks to you. Considering the circumstances, I guess we won't pay too much attention to her squawks about invasion of privacy, and manhandling, and threats of bodily harm. She can tell old Joe all about them when she gets home."

"Were you really going to fry her in her own fat?" Garrison asked.

"You know," John admitted, "I think I might have. What I'd like to know is if we were in time."

Hoover shrugged. "Who knows? Bogolzhin says all these people he has listed gave information about the bomb. It really makes you sick to think people can betray their own country, like that."

"Maybe the idea of the bomb made *them* sick, in the first place," Garrison said quietly.

Both John and Hoover turned their heads in amazement; it was a totally un-Garrison-like statement.

"Well . . ." He flushed, and shrugged. "According to Bogolzhin, they sure weren't asking a fortune. And not all of them were even Commies."

"Yeah," Hoover said. "Well, we'll only know how much information actually got to Russia when they explode a device. *If* they explode a device. Hayman—"

"I'd like to know what is going to happen to Gregory Nej and my sister," John said.

"Hell, I'm not the judge, boy. Bogolzhin has testified that your sister passed him information supplied by Gregory Nej, and that she knew what she was doing. Gregory Nej has sworn that she *didn't* know what she was doing, that the moment she found out she tried to leave, to come to us, and that he shot her to stop her doing that, and then kidnapped her as a hostage, and only had a change of heart when he realized she was likely to die. And Miss Hayman isn't saying anything at all. So it all comes down to which story the jury believes. But my guess is that she'll be exonerated by Nej's testimony—if he sticks to it. But if he does stick to it, he's likely to find himself with a one-way ticket to the death chamber. He defected to us, and asked for political asylum. His citizenship papers were nearly through. Add to that attempted murder and kidnapping . . . he's got it coming."

"Yeah," John said thoughtfully, and got up. He dared not suggest that Gregory had actually done a rather splendid thing.

"Now you tell me," Hoover said. "Is she going to be all right?"

"You mean the bullet? Oh, she'll be all right. Physically. In time."

"Yeah. Well, it's a cruel world. Hayman, you landed on your feet this time, but you'd be a fool to think it's likely to happen again. And we'd be fools to chance it. I'm sorry, but there it is. You're fired."

John's head came up in surprise.

Hoover grinned at him. "You have another job. You're wanted by this new organization, the Central Intelligence Agency. Seems they're making up the rules as they go along, so it's difficult to break any. They think you're just the sort of character they're looking for."

"Thanks," John said. "Suppose I just want out?"

"Nobody gets out, from the service," Hoover said.

"Yeah," John said thoughtfully. "All right, Mr. Hoover. But after more than two years in *your* service, I think I deserve a bonus."

"You think so? Well, let me tell you—"

"It won't cost you a cent," John said. "I'd like to see Anna Ragosina one more time, before she's sent home."

Garrison walked beside him, through the crowded airport lounge, to the door of the private room, where there was a plainclothesman on duty. "What's with you and this dame, anyway?" he asked.

"I wish I knew," John said.

"Yeah? I read your memoirs, remember? I figure you and she had something going, in that swamp."

"Yeah," John said. "We had something going." The door was being opened. "You said we could be alone."

Garrison nodded. "Just remember, you can look, but you can't touch. She has diplomatic immunity."

"I'll remember," John said, and stepped inside.

Anna was seated in one of the two chairs in the room, reading an American magazine. Her cat was in its basket beside her chair. Both looked up as the door opened; the cat hissed, and Anna stood up. "If you lay a finger on me . . ." she said.

"You're not tied up now, Anna," John said, listening to the door closing behind him. "I imagine you could take me apart, if you wanted to. Does that animal bite?"

She gazed at him for several seconds, then suddenly smiled, sat down again, and crossed her knees. She was wearing a pink dress, silk stockings and high heels, and looked beautiful. "I imagine she'd like to bite *you*," she said. "But how nice of you to come to see me off." She opened her handbag, took out a packet of cigarettes, and offered him one. When he shook his head, she lit her own. "I wish I had known that you were a member of the secret police over here," she said. "It would have made life so much more interesting."

He sat in the other chair. "We don't really consider the FBI a secret police."

"I know," she said. "In America you are so *dishonest*. But I imagine you have scored quite a triumph. It is a pity that you have condemned your own sister to death. Mind you—" She blew smoke at him through pursed lips. "—Even in Russia, that would be considered true patriotism. Your future is assured."

"My sister isn't going to die, Anna," he said. "She is not even going to jail. I'm afraid Gregory let you down, there. I guess he let you down in a lot of ways; he actually seems to be a decent man, after all. He is even claiming that it was he who shot her, when she tried to escape."

"That is a lie," Anna said.

"Of course. But are *you* going to say so, Anna? Shooting people is a criminal offense, rather than a diplomatic one. We'd be able to arrest you after all, lock you up for attempted murder. Maybe for life."

Her eyes narrowed. "And Gregory?" she asked softly.

John shrugged.

"The fool," she commented. "The deluded young fool. But then, he was always a fool. I had occasion to tell him so, more than once."

"As Alexandra Gorchakova, the girl you left to freeze to death in the swamp, was a fool?"

She would not lower her eyes. "Of course. Any failure is

a fool. It is only the people like you and I, John, the successes, who matter in this world."

"And you count your mission a success?"

She gave him another appraising stare, then suddenly a low, throaty laugh. "I wondered why you had really come," she said. "Perhaps your FBI is smarter than I thought. But you do not need to try to trick me into telling you, John. Of course my mission has been a success. I am returning to a heroine's welcome. I have spent more than two years disrupting your industry, gathering your military and economic secrets. I have succeeded in everything I was sent here to do. You can tell your bosses that. And do you know what, John? I have even managed to enjoy myself. I count these years as the most successful of my career. But I will tell you something else— I was becoming bored. I was hoping someone would discover me, and have me sent home. That it should be you is perfect." She leaned across to squeeze his hand. "Because what I have achieved here is nothing compared to what I am *going* to achieve. I think it probable I will be the first woman commander of the NKVD, in a few years. Will you ever be the commander of the American secret police, John? We could have such fun together."

John realized that she was totally genuine in what she was saying, in her ambitions, and in her certainty that her ambitions would be fulfilled.

He got up. "I doubt that," he said. "I doubt that very much. So have a good flight." He turned to the door.

"John," she said softly. "Be a man, and admit that I have licked you, utterly and completely."

He hesitated, then shrugged. "I guess you did at that, Anna," he agreed.

"Only ten minutes, Mr. Nej," the guard said. "This is a treason case."

Michael Nej nodded, then stepped into the little room. It was empty but for Gregory, who was already seated behind the table, but there were glass panels on two sides, through which the guards were watching them.

"Presumably the room is wired for sound," Michael remarked.

"Presumably," Gregory agreed.

Michael sat opposite him, across the table. "Well, I will not be saying anything they should not hear. Have you been ill-treated?"

"I have been treated very well," Gregory said.

Michael studied him for some seconds, trying to decide whether that was true or not. But the boy certainly looked well-fed and clean, there were no visible bruises, and he sat without discomfort. "Then I wish, first of all," he said, "to tell you that I am proud of you. When I heard that you had defected, I hated you. I thought only of how your background had let you down. Now that I know the truth, I am proud of you. All Russia is proud of you."

Gregory made no comment.

"But it will not be so proud," Michael went on, "when it learns that you intend to confess to everything."

"I *have* confessed to everything," Gregory said.

"The case has not yet come to court," Michael reminded him. "Your lawyers can claim that your confessions were extracted from you by force. That you were beaten. They can do things like that over here, and get away with it."

"I had always thought you disapproved of our methods at home, Uncle Michael," Gregory commented.

"I wish things could be different," Michael agreed. "So many things. But then, I also wish for a perfect world. And there is no sign of that ever coming about. Right now I am concerned with saving your life, Gregory."

"Why?"

"For God's sake, you are my nephew. You are poor Tatiana's son. And I can tell you that your father is worried about you."

Gregory frowned at him. "My *father?* But . . . is he not in jail for Mother's murder?"

"Your father is commander of the NKVD in Tomsk," Michael said. "It has been a demotion, certainly. A recognition that he acted hastily. But Comrade Stalin has obviously decided that in these critical times he is too valuable to be dismissed altogether. And he will undoubtedly have the opportunity to rehabilitate himself."

"Rehabilitate himself? A cold-blooded murderer? And you condone it? *You*, Uncle Michael?"

Michael sighed. "I do not condone it. I recognize, perhaps, the necessity of what is being done. Gregory, listen to me. We are locked in a struggle now. I saw it coming, and I warned against it. But since it is here, and since we are loyal Russians and good Socialists, we *must* support our country and our Party, no matter what is involved. We may already be in the opening phases of a third world war. It is certain that we cannot weaken or deviate in any way. You were sent here to do a job. This job you have done, magnificently, until the very end. I have read Comrade Ragosina's report. You weakened at the very end . . ."

"You are talking about Ilona Hayman's daughter," Gregory said. "Your son John's sister."

"And you are my nephew—by blood. Besides, you are a Russian officer, while she is the daughter of an American capitalist."

"I had thought George Hayman was your friend."

"We are as much friends as two people espousing totally opposing ideologies can ever be. But nothing can alter the fact that when the final conflict begins, George Hayman and I will be on opposite sides, trying to kill each other, even if we are both too old actually to fire guns. And you must never forget that he and his family, however related to you they may be, are your enemies. Now, this absurd story that you are apparently telling, of how you seduced Felicity Hayman as a cover, and used her as a cover, and how when she learned the truth about you she attempted to flee, and you kidnapped her, and tried to execute her—everyone knows that is a bunch of lies."

"It is the truth," Gregory said.

"Listen to me. I have been informed that you have a defense, if you retract this statement and tell the truth: that you did defect to the United States, in good faith, and that you fell in love with this woman, who is an American socialist, and that she persuaded you that you had done the wrong thing in defecting, that she already had contacts with Anna Ragosina, and that it was she who introduced you to the Soviet network over here. I can tell you that Comrade Ragosina is prepared to submit written testimony to that effect in your support."

"I will not change my statement," Gregory said.

Michael stared at him through narrowed eyes. "Are you mad? Perhaps you do not understand the situation. Since you are not an American citizen, and since America and Russia are not actually at war, it is possible for your espionage to be treated as a political offense. But kidnapping, and transporting a person across a state line, carries the death penalty in this country. If you *forced* her to accompany you, that is a capital offense. Do you *want* to die?"

"I fell in love with her," Gregory said. "That part of what you have suggested is true. I did not mean to do so, but I did. She did not seduce me, I seduced her. But she also made me think. Everything that has happened has made me think. I believe our policies are wrong. I cannot understand how my father has not even been tried for my mother's death. I do not think the Americans ever mean to go to war with us, unless they are forced to do so in self-defense. I do not think their way of life is so very wrong. I think they have freedom, to do and think and say what they like. I think that is worth having. I do not think I can ever again be of any use, either to the NKVD or to the Soviet state. I very much regret what has happened here. But I will not change a single word of my statement."

Once again Michael studied him. Then he got up. "Gregory Ivanovich," he said, "you have too much of your mother in you, after all. But I will save you, even from yourself."

"George!" Michael Nej hurried across the hotel lobby, arms outstretched, only checking himself as he realized that George did not wish to be embraced. But he kept his smile in place. "Do you know, it has taken us so long to get together, I had almost formed the opinion that you have been avoiding me?"

George shook hands. "You could even have been right."

"My dear George." Michael ushered him to a table in the lounge, called a waiter, and ordered drinks. "I had so looked forward to coming to New York, to seeing Ilona and you again, and the family . . . Catherine was so looking forward to it, too. I really had not expected the cold shoulder."

"Quite a lot has happened since we last met," George said.

"Ah." Michael waited while the drinks were placed before them, and raised his glass. "To a happy future. You are thinking of poor Boris. Believe me, I have done what I could, and certainly I have secured for him the best of treatments. But he is far gone."

"Michael," George said, "you are a goddamned poor liar."

Michael stared at him.

"And Petrov is only the half of it," George went on. "What about this stranglehold you are trying to put on Berlin?"

"My dear George, that is entirely a technical matter—"

"Technical? It's been going on for weeks."

"Well," Michael said, "your people are not suffering. You are flying in all they need."

"And we're going to go on doing just that," George promised him. "And on top of all that, there's sending your nephew over here, not only to spy, but to seduce my daughter."

"I know," Michael said. "It is a tragedy. Will you believe that I did not know Gregory was sent over here to spy?"

"You sure as hell know now."

"Yes. It is sad. Very sad. Poor Felicity...how my heart bleeds for that girl. Is she going to be all right?"

"No," George said. "Felicity is never going to be all right."

"But I have been told she will recover from her bullet wound."

"Maybe."

"George," Michael said, "she is actually very lucky. You know as well as I that this 'confession' of Gregory's is a load of lies."

"It seems that everything to do with Gregory is a load of lies," George said. "Don't expect me to weep over Gregory, Michael. I brought him to this country. I took him into my home. I treated him like a son. And for what?"

"He is now risking his own neck to save that of your daughter."

"After endangering her neck in the first place? Like I said, don't expect me to weep."

Michael took a sip of vodka. "George...I cannot stand by and watch Gregory sent to the electric chair. And he is going to be convicted, as things stand."

"I would say so."

"And you do not care?"

"There is nothing I could do about it, even if I did care."

"George...I am very fond of Gregory. He is all that is left of Tattie. He is your nephew as well, George."

"Michael, there are certain things you just do not seem able to get straight. This isn't Russia. This is the United States of America. Over here, justice isn't at the whim of a few party members. Justice is justice. Gregory is a self-confessed spy. He has also confessed to attempted murder and to kidnapping. It is out of our hands now, and in the hands of the law. *Nobody* can interfere with that process."

Michael finished his drink. "You have but to tell me what you require."

"Michael . . ."

"Petrov's release? Is that what this is all about? All right. I will secure it for you."

George frowned at him. "You can *do* that?"

Michael shrugged. "I can probably convince Stalin it would be politic. Even for him to leave the country, emigrate to Israel. I can probably do that. If there is enough at stake."

"And you haven't felt enough is at stake up to now? What about Judith's peace of mind, for instance?"

Michael's face closed. "Judith has turned against us."

"And you think I'm still for you?"

"I am bargaining with you, George."

"And I've got nothing to bargain with, Michael. For God's sake, understand that. Maybe, if I *had* the power, I'd settle for Boris's freedom. But I just don't have that power. No one does."

"What about Truman?"

George slowly put down his glass.

Michael gazed at him. "Ask him what *he* wants, George. I know he cannot openly influence the courts, in America, but he has the ultimate power to commute a sentence. Ask him what *he* wants, George. I do not wish Gregory to die."

George helped Felicity down the steps of the hospital, a nurse on the other side. Ilona opened the door of the car for her. "Would you like to sit in the front, my dear?" she asked.

Felicity shook her head. "I'll sit in the back," she said.

Ilona looked at George, who gave a quick nod. Felicity was handed into the back seat. Ilona sat in the front, and half-turned to look over her shoulder. George drove over the bridge, slowly.

"Your old room is waiting for you," Ilona said brightly. "Everything is waiting for you. Brutus, and the dogs . . ." Her voice trailed away. Felicity was hugging herself, despite the warmth in the car.

"Does it still hurt?" Ilona asked.

Felicity looked at her.

"Dr. Patterson said the wound had healed perfectly," Ilona

said. "I suppose it will always twinge, though. There were three separate bones broken."

"Where is Gregory?" Felicity asked.

Ilona looked at George.

"He's in custody," George said.

"When is the trial?"

"Oh, that won't be for a long time yet. He's part of the whole thing. You do *know* that, Felicity? He was a member of a huge network of Soviet spies that infiltrated the United States over the past two years. And which did its damndest to bring us down."

"I was a part of it too," she said quietly.

"You want to forget that," George studied the road unwinding in front of them.

"I can never forget that," she said. "And we weren't trying to bring America down. We were trying to prevent her from committing a dreadful crime."

"But Felicity . . ." Ilona said, "you don't really believe any of the things those people told you? Not anymore?"

"Does anybody know what to believe, Mother?" Felicity asked.

Ilona looked at George again.

"We've been thinking," George said, "that perhaps the three of us might take a long trip, somewhere. You know what? I've a hankering to go back to Israel. Your mother has never been there, and neither have you. And I was only there at the beginning. I'd really like to see how they're getting on. Sure, I know they're still officially at war, but the shooting is all over. And they've survived, and are making quite a country, Judith tells me. It would be good to see them all again. And Ruth . . . you remember Ruth, Felicity? She's getting married again. Did you know that? To an Englishman named Nigel Brent. He went back and fought for them as a volunteer. Judith is very happy about it . . ." His voice trailed away as he looked in the rear-view mirror and watched Felicity staring out the window. He glanced at Ilona. "Felicity," he said, "what would *you* like to do, most?"

"Just to be left alone."

"Felicity . . ."

"Just leave me alone," she said. "To remember."

"You *can't* go through life reliving the past," Ilona said.

"What else have I got to do?" Felicity asked. "You tell me that, Mother. You tell me that."

And if I am left alone, she thought, I can hate. I can hate everybody. But principally Anna Ragosina. Not so much, she realized, for shooting her, but for ruining the dream. If ever a woman deserved to rot in hell, it was Anna Ragosina.

But what was the use in wishing for that? Because of them all, only Anna Ragosina had truly triumphed. As apparently she had always triumphed. As no doubt she always would triumph. Anna Ragosina.

Chapter 14

JOSEPH VISSARIONOVICH STALIN SURVEYED THE REPORT on his desk, and stroked his moustache. Almost, Anna thought, she expected him to purr, as Tabasco did on rare occasions.

"This is very good," Stalin murmured. "Oh, very good. It will be no more than a few months until we explode a bomb of our own. No one must learn of this, though. That is essential. When the bomb has been exploded, of course. . . ."

"It will be impossible for us to keep it a secret, Joseph," Beria explained. "It registers on seismographic equipment just like an earthquake."

"I will not wish it kept a secret," Stalin said. "I will wish the world to know that we possess an atomic weapon. I will wish the Americans to know, most of all."

Anna waited for the flood of congratulations that must surely now come. She had in fact been deeply hurt by the somewhat muted welcome she had received, the way she had been given a routine desk job for the past months—but of course they had been waiting for the proof of her success. Now the world was again at her feet. Her invitation into this office proved that: she had been here only once before, the day she had received the order to place Ivan Nej under arrest.

"Now we can take a fresh view of the international situation," Andrei Vyshinsky was saying, "of our gains and our losses. We will soon have the atomic bomb. That is an immense gain. But against this must be set the loss of almost our entire organization in the United States."

Their heads turned, to look at Anna Ragosina.

She shrugged. "It was inevitable, in my opinion. There was so much we had to do. But we did it all, comrades."

"We can never do it *all*, Comrade Ragosina," Molotov said. "In international relations, and therefore in our knowledge of what the other side is planning, and doing, there is no beginning, no end."

"I wish to know what is being done about Gregory Nej," Stalin said. "What is the news from Michael Nikolaievich?"

"Gregory has been condemned to death," Beria said. "So have several others, but they are Americans. Bogolzhin escaped by the skin of his teeth, by turning state's evidence."

"Bogolzhin," Anna said bitterly. "He is the foulest traitor that ever drew breath. If I could lay my hands on him—"

"We were talking about Gregory Nej," Stalin said mildly. "The boy did his best. I want him brought home. His knowledge of American procedures, of what it is like inside the Pentagon, of how the Americans *think*, will prove very valuable."

"Bring him home?" Anna inquired. "He has been condemned to death. And he has turned his back on Russia."

"Michael Nikolaievich has been conducting negotiations on our behalf. He has encountered endless difficulties. The Americans are really better negotiators than they appear. They keep telling him there is nothing they can do. But it appears that it *may* be possible to make a deal. Truman may be able to have the sentence commuted to life imprisonment, in exchange for certain concessions."

"What concessions?" Vyshinsky demanded.

"Well . . . they wish Boris Petrov released from the hospital, and allowed to leave the country." Stalin shrugged. "That is not very important, assuming he is in good health." He looked at Beria.

"Oh, he is in good health," Beria said. "He is as tough as old boots."

"They also wish a more positive attitude on our part towards those of our Jewish people who seek to emigrate to Israel." Again he shrugged. "Well, that is not too much of a problem either. We can allow one or two of the less important to go. The more Jews there are in Israel, the more sure we can be that the Arabs will keep trying to exterminate them." He stroked his moustache. "The Americans also wish a termination of the Berlin blockade."

Vyshinsky's head jerked. "In exchange for the life of one failed agent? That is a total absurdity."

"I entirely agree," Stalin said soothingly. "And we shall never concede it. But I think now is the time to take another careful look at the Berlin situation. The entire project has been a failure."

"With due respect, Joseph Vissarionovich—"

"It has been a failure," Stalin repeated. "There is no use in defending a failed project. We have not only lost friends over it, we have lost face. We have merely enabled the Americans and their allies to demonstrate the awesome power of their air forces, and the determination of their people. We may even have *helped* to reelect Truman by enabling him to demonstrate *his* determination to the American people. And we have not changed the American plans in any way. It has not merely been a failure, it has been a disaster."

"But to back down, merely because of Gregory Nej would be an absurdity," Vyshinsky objected.

"Of course. We shall never do that. But I am sure it is possible to convey privately to Truman that we *will* end the blockade. And if we make the other concessions, regarding Petrov and a few Jews, that should be sufficient to save Gregory Ivanovich's life. As I say, I would like to save his life, apart from practical considerations as to his value." He paused, thoughtfully. "I was really very fond of his mother."

"But why is any of this necessary?" Anna inquired. "Why should we concede *anything* to the Americans? You may save Gregory's life, but he will still be in prison, in America, for the rest of his life."

"That is a long time," Stalin pointed out. "Who can tell what deal we might be able to make regarding him over the next year or two? We know there are American agents in Russia. If we could nab one or two of them, and set up an exchange—who knows? In any event, Gregory Nej is not that important. The fact is, over this last year we have hurried too much." He gazed at Vyshinsky. "It has not worked. We have not stopped the Americans' plans to build up a Western European army, to pour money into Europe, and generally to stiffen their attitude all over the world. And what have we to

show for it that we would not have had by continuing in our
old quiet way? We have even lost because of it. I am positive
this business in Yugoslavia has been organized by the Americans. What do they call this new organization of theirs? The
CIA. Oh, yes. So, I think it is time for us to make a new
beginning with the West, once again offer them the hand of
friendship. We can do *that* without losing face, now that we
too have the bomb. And ending the Berlin blockade is the
surest way of showing them that we mean well."

"I still think it is unnecessary and dangerous," Anna said.
It was important, she knew, to remind these tired old men of
just how forceful and talented and decisive she was. "Berlin
is a test of will between the Americans and ourselves. In the
eyes of the world, if we end the blockade without having
achieved our aims, we will have surrendered. As for Gregory
Nej, he is a fool and very nearly a traitor. He assaulted me.
I very much doubt if he will ever be of any use to us again.
He *deserves* to be executed. If he returns here I will have a
good mind to do it myself."

They stared at her.

"He was *your* choice for the post, Comrade Ragosina,"
Beria said.

"Indeed he was," Stalin agreed. "And as I have studied the
reports, it has occurred to me that it is not his fault the organization was destroyed so suddenly and so completely. The
vital point seems to have been the recognition of you by John
Hayman. Something you were particularly warned to be careful
of, Comrade Ragosina."

"That was the purest chance, Joseph Vissarionovich," she
protested.

"I do not agree. It was not chance that you attended the
embassy cocktail party. That was carelessness."

"I had attended them before. How was I to know that the
FBI had stepped up its activities, was even infiltrating photo-
graphers into the embassy?" she demanded.

"I do not know *how* you should have known, Anna," Stalin
said mildly. "I only know that you *should* have known, and
that because of your carelessness, indeed your incompetence,
you have destroyed your own organization."

Anna frowned at him, aware that her heartbeat had quickened. "It had accomplished all it had been commanded to do,"
she said.

"As you have been reminded, Anna Pavlovna, there is never a case of everything being accomplished. Now we will have to build a new organization in America. Oh, we shall do so, but it will be a much harder task than the last time, with the Americans aware of our activities. I fear I am disappointed in you. I had high hopes of you. Who knows?—they may yet be realized, one day. But I think that for the moment you are still too young for an independent command." He looked at Beria. "Do you not think so, Lavrenti Pavlovich?"

"Oh, indeed, Joseph. I always thought so. I said so. I—"

"Yes," Stalin said, a trifle wearily. "Now I wish you to find a less responsible post for Comrade Ragosina, for a year or two, so that she can consider her mistakes, and decide how they might have been avoided. Have you such a post?"

Beria smiled.

"I got the atomic formulas for you," Anna shouted. "I. Nobody else."

"From your own reports, Anna, these American traitors were anxious to give the secrets away. To anyone. Had you not been there, they would have given them to somebody else. I do not think you can truly take any credit for that."

"Tomsk," Beria said.

Anna's head turned as if he had jerked a string attached to her ear.

"Tomsk is a good place for reflection," Beria said. "Do you not agree, Joseph Vissarionovich?"

"Oh, indeed. I understand Ivan Nikolaievich is doing very well in Tomsk."

"Ivan . . . Ivan Nej is in Tomsk?" Anna asked.

"And doing very well, as Comrade Stalin has said. He has had time to reflect, in Tomsk, to decide who are his friends and who are his enemies. You will go to Tomsk as his assistant."

Anna's face was pale. "You cannot," she said. "You cannot send me back to Ivan Nej!"

"Why not?" Beria inquired. "Oh, I know that you and he have had your little ups and downs. He once arrested you, and sent you to a labor camp. But then, my dear Anna, *you* arrested *him*, only a few years ago, and prepared him for interrogation. I am sure he would like to discuss your methods with you, perhaps show you where you went wrong. You will profit by your time in Tomsk, Comrade Ragosina. And besides," he added thoughtfully, "I did promise him, once, that you would be returned to his jurisdiction, at least for a while. He is going to be delighted."

"I thought," Harry Truman said, "since you've been in this thing from the beginning, Hayman, that you might like to see this."

George studied the paper, and raised his head. "Just about everything we could ask for."

"In time," Truman agreed. "None of that is for publication, of course. The deal is that the Soviets make the first move. But at least I am assured that Petrov's release is already under way, and that he will be in Israel within a month."

"I am very happy about that," George said. "Those two women have had the hardest of possible lives. Now, maybe . . . who knows?"

"Yes," the president agreed. "No one can say what's going to happen out there in the Mideast. But at least we're ahead on this one. All I have to do is commute the Nej boy's sentence to life imprisonment. I can't say I *want* to do that, in the case of such a thug. I guess you feel even more strongly about it than I do. But I guess it will be worth it."

"He did confess," George said, choosing his words very carefully. "And he exonerated my daughter. He can't be all bad. You do realize, sir, that Stalin wants him back, at some stage?"

"The thought had occurred to me."

"And I suspect that Nej won't want to go."

"Is that a fact? Well, that's a bridge he, and we, will cross when we come to it. I'm not letting old Joe pull any more wool over my eyes, Hayman. I'm well aware that all this talk of a new rapprochement, because he can now negotiate from strength, is just talk. He won't catch us napping again, Hayman. Not *this* administration. I can promise you that."

"But isn't he for once talking the absolute truth? *Isn't* he now negotiating from a position of equality? In fact, isn't Soviet Russia the real winner out of all this?" George asked. "They have the bomb. That's what they set out to do, and they've done it."

Truman gazed at him. "We always knew they'd do that eventually, Hayman. We can't stop them advancing. The secret we have to preserve is that of keeping one step ahead. You tell him, Dean. Remembering, Hayman, that everything said here is in the strictest confidence."

The Secretary of State leaned forward. "The Soviets have the atomic bomb, Hayman, but to us, it's already out of date," Acheson said. "Our people are working on a new weapon, a bomb so powerful one of it will equal a hundred, maybe a thousand, atomic bombs. It will be the most destructive weapon the entire universe will ever have known."

"But . . . good God!" George said. "Only a few months ago everyone was saying that atomic warfare would destroy the world. Now this . . ."

"The important thing," Truman said, "is having it first. That is the best means of making certain it won't ever be used in anger. Sure, I'm under no illusions. The Soviets will get that bomb as well, given time." His face relaxed into the semblance of a smile. "We just have to make sure that by the time they do, we have something better."

Sunday dinner at Cold Spring Harbor. George smiled down the length of the table at Ilona. If there was much cause for sadness, in the empty chair—Felicity preferred to take most of her meals in the privacy of her room, certainly on Sundays, when the entire family was assembled—there was much cause for happiness, as well, he thought, as he listened to the conversation.

"She's pregnant," Ilona was telling Beth and Natasha. "Who would have thought it, after . . . well, after everything Ruth's been through. I must say, I'm delighted."

"Is Prince Peter pleased?" Natasha asked.

"I doubt it. Nothing ever pleases Peter. He still thinks Ruth abandoned him—and the cause, of course. He still broods about ousting the Reds someday. He could have had so much, done so much with his life . . ." She sighed, and George knew she was thinking of Felicity, not unlike her uncle in the intensity of her personality, her ideals.

But Felicity was young enough, still, to recover, and even to find cause for hope, since Gregory was alive and might one day be released.

"But it's still advertising, isn't it, Uncle John?" Diana had changed the subject while he mused.

"Oh, yes," John agreed. "I'm afraid I'm in advertising for the rest of my life." He looked at George.

"How come we never actually see any of your ads?" George junior inquired.

"Because I'm a backroom boy," John said easily. "That's the story of my life, I guess. But actually, in this new job, I'll be *selling* advertising. That means I'll be away a lot, traveling. Sasha isn't too happy about it, but the money's good."

"How are things with your father?" George junior asked. "Mother was saying that now there's an official thaw on, he and his wife may come visit one day. I must say, I'd like to meet him."

"I'm sure he would like to meet you," John said.

And so they were all friends again, George thought, at least for the time being. But perhaps they could go on being friends, as long as people like Truman, and John, in his new job, always remembered that leopards *never* change their spots.

He tapped his glass with the back of his knife, and their faces turned towards him. "Today," he said. "I'd like to drink a toast." He raised his glass. "To Gregory Nej."

"To . . . *Gregory Nej?*" Ilona inquired.

"So he's on the other side," George said. "He was a courageous enemy. And a gallant one. And a chivalrous one. I'm as happy as I can be that the President has exercised clemency. Here's to Gregory." He smiled at them. "And damnation to his boss."